THE LAZARUS EFFECT

THE LAZARUS EFFECT

FRANK HERBERT AND BILL RANSOM

G. P. PUTNAM'S SONS
NEW YORK

Library of Congress Cataloging in Publication Data

Herbert, Frank.
The Lazarus effect.

I. Ransom, Bill.   II. Title.
PS3558.E63L3   1983   813'.54   82-23028
ISBN 0-399-12815-8

PRINTED IN THE UNITED STATES OF AMERICA

Second Impression

*For Brian, Bruce and Penny. For all the years they tiptoed while their
father was writing.*

Frank Herbert

*For all those healers who ease our suffering;
for people who feed people, then ask of them virtue;
for our friends—gratitude and affection.*

Bill Ransom

*The Histories assert that a binary system cannot support
life. But we found life here on Pandora. Except for the
kelp, it was antagonistic and deadly, but still it was life.
Ship's judgment is upon us now because we wiped out the
kelp and unbalanced this world. We few survivors are subject to the endless sea and the terrible vagaries of the two
suns. That we survive at all on our fragile Clone-rafts is as
much a curse as a victory. This is the time of madness.*

—Hali Ekel, the Journals

Duque smelled burning flesh and scorched hair. He sniffed,
sniffed again, and whined. His one good eye watered and pained
him when he tried to knuckle it open. His mother was out. *Out* was
a word he could say, like *hot* and *Ma*. He could not precisely
identify the location and shape of *out*. He knew vaguely that his
quarters were on a Clone-raft anchored off a black stone pinnacle,
all that remained of Pandora's land surface.

The burning smells were stronger now. They frightened him.
Duque wondered if he should say something. Mostly, he did not
talk; his nose got in the way. He could whistle through his nose,
though, and his mother understood. She would whistle back. Between them, they understood more than a hundred whistle-
words. Duque wriggled his forehead. This uncurled his thick,
knobby nose and he whistled—tentative at first to see whether she
was near.

"Ma? Where are you, Ma?"

He listened for the unmistakable *scuff-slap, scuff-slap* of her bare
feet on the soft slick deck of the raft.

Burning smells filled his nose and made him sneeze. He heard
the slaps of many feet out in the corridor, more feet than he had
ever before heard out there, but nothing he could identify as *Ma*.
There was shouting now, words Duque did not know. He sucked

7

in a deep breath and let go the loudest whistle he could muster. His thin ribs ached with it and the vibration made him dizzy.

No one responded. The hatch beside him remained closed. No one plucked him out of his twisted covers and held him close.

Despite the pain of the smoke, Duque peeled back his right eyelid with the two nubs on his right hand and saw that the room was dark except for a glow against the thin organics of the corridor wall. Dull orange light cast a frightening illumination over the deck. Acrid smoke hung like a cloud above him, tendrils of its oily blackness reaching downward toward his face. And now there were other sounds outside added to the shouting and the *slap-slap* of many feet. He heard big things dragging and bumping along his glowing wall. Terror held him curled into a silent lump under the covers of his bunk.

The burning smells contained a steamy, bitter flavor—not quite the sticky-sweet of the time when the stove scorched their wall. He remembered the charred melt of organics opening a new passage between their room and the next one along the corridor. He had poked his head through the burned opening and whistled at their neighbors. The smells now were not the same, though, and the glowing wall did not melt away.

A rumbling was added to the outside sounds. Like a pot boiling over on the stove, but his mother was not cooking. Besides, it was too loud for cooking, louder even than the other corridor noises. Now, there were screams nearby.

Duque kicked off his covers and gasped when his bare feet touched the deck.

Hot!

Abruptly, the deck pitched, first backward and then forward. The motion lurched him face-first through the bulkhead. The hot organics of the wall stretched and parted for him like a cooked noodle. He knew he was on the outer deck but stumbling feet kept him too busy covering his head and body with his arms. He could not spare a hand to open his good eye. The hot deck burned his knees and elbows. Duque caught his breath in the sudden onslaught of pain and wrenched out another shrill whistle. Somebody stumbled against him. Hands reached under his armpits and lifted him clear of the scorched bubbly that had been the deck. Some of it came loose with him and stuck to his bare skin. Duque knew who held him by the jasmine smell of her hair—Ellie, the neighbor woman with the short, stubby legs and beautiful voice.

8

"Duque," she said, "let's go find your ma."

He heard something wrong in her voice. It rasped low in a dry throat and cracked when she spoke.

"Ma," he said. He knuckled his eye open and saw a nightmare of movement and firelight.

Ellie shouldered them through the crowd, saw that he was looking around and slapped his hand away. "Look later," she said. "Right now you hang on to my neck. Hold tight."

After that one brief glimpse, there was no need to repeat the order. He clutched both arms around Ellie's neck. A small whimper escaped his throat. Ellie continued to push them through a crowd of people—voices all around saying words Duque did not understand. Movement against the others peeled away chunks of bubbly from his skin. It hurt.

That one look at *out* remained indelibly in Duque's memory. Fire had been coming out of the dark water! It coiled up out of the water accompanied by that thick, boiling sound and the air was so full of steam that people were shadow clumps against the hot red glow of flames. Screams and shouts still sounded all around, causing Duque to hold even tighter to Ellie's neck. Chunks of the fire had rocketed into the sky high above their island. Duque did not understand this but he heard the fire crash and sizzle through the body of the island into the sea beneath.

Why water burn? He knew the whistle-words but Ellie would not understand.

The raft tipped sharply under Ellie and sent her sprawling beneath the trampling feet with Duque atop her shielded from the burning deck. Ellie cursed and gasped. More people fell around them. Duque felt Ellie sinking into the melting organics of the deck. She struggled at first, thrashing like a fresh-caught muree that his mother had put into his hands once before she cooked it. Ellie's twisting slowed and she began moaning low in her throat. Duque, still clutching Ellie's neck, felt hot bubbly against his hands and jerked them away. Ellie screamed. Duque tried to push himself away from her but the press of bodies all around prevented his escape. He felt the hair at the nape of his neck standing up. A questing whistle broke from his nose but there was no response.

The deck tilted again and bodies rolled onto Duque. He felt hot flesh, some of it warm-wet. Ellie gasped once, very deep. The air changed. The people screaming, "Oh, no! Oh, no!" stopped screaming. Many people began coughing all around Duque. He coughed, too, choking on hot, thick dust. Someone nearby gasped: "I've got Vata. Help me. We must save her."

Duque sensed a stillness in Ellie. She wasn't moaning anymore. He could not feel the rise and fall of her breathing. Duque opened his mouth and spoke the two words he knew best:

"Ma. Hot, Ma. Ma."

Someone right beside him said: "Who's that?"

"Hot, Ma," Duque said.

Hands touched him and hauled him away from Ellie. A voice next to his ear said: "It's a child. He's alive."

"Bring him!" someone called between coughs. "We've got Vata."

Duque felt himself passed from hand to hand through an opening into a dimly lighted place. His one good eye saw through a thinner dust haze the glitter of tiny lights, shiny surfaces and handles. He wondered if this could be the *out* where Ma went but there was no sign of Ma, only many people crowded into a small space. Someone directly in front of him held a large naked infant. He knew about infants because Ma sometimes brought them from *out* and cared for them, cooing over them and letting Duque touch them and pet them. Infants were soft and nice. This infant looked larger than any Duque had ever seen but he knew she was only an infant—those fat features, that still face.

The air pressure changed, popping in Duque's ears. Something began to hum. Just when Duque was deciding to come out of his fears and join in this warm closeness of flesh, three gigantic explosions shook all of them, sending their enclosed space tumbling.

"Boom! Boom! Boom!" the explosions came one on top of the other.

People began extricating themselves from the tumble of flesh. A foot touched Duque's face and was withdrawn.

"Careful of the little ones," someone said.

Strong hands lifted Duque and helped him open his eye. A pale masculine face peered at him—a wide face with deeply set brown eyes. The man spoke. "I've got the other one. He's no beauty but he's alive."

"Here, give him to me," a woman said.

Duque found himself pressed close to the infant. A woman's arms held them both, flesh to flesh, warmth to warmth. A sense of reassurance swept through Duque but it was cut off immediately when the woman spoke. He understood her words! He did not know how he understood but the meanings were there unfolding as her voice rumbled against his cheek pressed to her breast.

"The whole island exploded," the woman said. "I saw it through the port."

"We're well below the surface now," a man said. "But we can't stay long with this many people breathing our air."

"We will pray to Rock," the woman said.

"And to Ship," a man said.

"To Rock and to Ship," they all agreed.

Duque heard all of this from a distance as more understanding flooded his awareness. It was happening because his flesh touched the flesh of the infant! He knew the infant's name now.

"Vata."

A beautiful name. The name brought with it a blossoming mindful of information, as though the knowledge had always been there, needing only Vata's name and her touch to spread it through his memory. Now, he was aware of *out*, all of it as known through human senses and kelp memories . . . because Vata carried kelp genes in her human flesh. He remembered the place of the kelp deep under the sea, the tendrils clinging to precious rock. He remembered the minuscule islands that no longer existed because the kelp was gone and the sea fury had been unleashed. Kelp memories and human memories revealed wondrous things happening to Pandora now that waves could roam freely around this planet, which was really a distorted ball of solid matter submerged in an endless skin of water.

Duque knew where he was, too: in a small submersible, which should have had a Lighter-Than-Air carrier attached to it.

Out was a place of marvels.

And all of this wondrous information had come to him directly from the mind of Vata because she had kelp genes, as did he. As did many of Pandora's surviving humans. Genes . . . he knew about those marvels, too, because Vata's mind was a magic storehouse of such things, telling him about history and the Clone Wars and the death of all the kelp. He sensed a direct link between Vata and himself, which endured even when he pulled away from physical contact with her. Duque experienced a great thankfulness for this and tried to express his gratitude but Vata refused to respond. He understood then that Vata wanted the deep sea-quiet of her kelp memories. She wanted only the wait-

11

ing. She did not want to deal with the things she had dumped onto him. She *had* dumped them, he realized, shedding these things like a painful skin. Duque felt a momentary pique at this realization but happiness returned immediately. He was the repository of such wonders!

Consciousness.

That's my department, he thought. *I must be aware for both of us. I am the storage system, the Ox Gate, which only Vata can open.*

There were giants in the earth in those days.
            —Genesis, The Christian Book of the Dead

22 Bunratti, 468.

Why do I keep this journal? This is a strange hobby for the Chief Justice and Chairman of the Committee on Vital Forms. Do I hope that a historian will someday weave rich elaborations out of my poor scribblings? I can just see someone like Iz Bushka stumbling onto my journal many years from now, his mind crammed full of the preconceptions that block acceptance of the truly new. Would Bushka destroy my journal because it conflicted with his own theories? I think this may have happened with other historians in our past. Why else would Ship have forced us to start over? I'm convinced that this is what Ship has done.

Oh, I believe in Ship. Let it be recorded here and now that Ward Keel believes in Ship. Ship is God and Ship brought us here to Pandora. This is our ultimate trial—sink or swim, in the most literal sense. Well . . . almost. We Islanders mostly float. It's the Mermen who swim.

What a perfect testing ground for humankind is this Pandora, and how aptly named. Not a shard of land left above its sea, which the kelp once subdued. Once a noble creature, intelligent, known to all creatures of this world as Avata, it is now simply kelp—thick, green and silent. Our ancestors destroyed Avata and we inherited a planetary sea.

Have we humans ever done that before? Have we killed off the thing that subdues the deadliness in our lives? Somehow, I suspect we have. Else, why would Ship leave those hybernation tanks to tantalize us in orbit just beyond our reach? Our Chaplain/Psychiatrist shares this suspicion. As she says, "There is nothing new under the suns."

I wonder why Ship's imprimatur always took the form of the eye within the pyramid?

13

I began this journal simply as an account of my own steward-ship on the Committee that determines which new life will be permitted to survive and perhaps breed. We mutants have a deep regard for the variations that the bioengineering of that brilliant madman, Jesus Lewis, set adrift in the human gene pool. From those incomplete records we still have, it's clear that *human* once had a much narrower definition. Mutant variations that we now accept without a passing glance were once cause for conster-nation, even death. As a Committeeman passing judgment on life, the question I always ask myself and try to answer with my poor understanding is: *Will this new life, this infant, help us all survive?* If there is the remotest chance that it will contribute to this thing we call human society I vote to let it live. And I have been rewarded time and again by that hidden genius in cruel form, that mind plus distorted body which enrich us all. I know I am correct in these decisions.

But my journal has developed a tendency to wander. I have decided that I am secretly a philosopher. I want to know not only what, but why.

In the long generations since that terrible night when the last of Pandora's true land-based islands exploded into molten lava, we have developed a peculiar social duality, which I am convinced could destroy us all. We Islanders, with our organic cities floating "willy-nilly" on the sea's surface, believe we have formed the per-fect society. We care for each other, for the inner other that the skin (whatever shape or shade) protects. Then what is it about us that insists on saying "us" and "them"? Is there a viciousness bur-ied in us? Will it explode us into violence against the excluded others?

Oh, Islanders exclude; this cannot be denied. Our jokes betray us. Anti-Mermen jokes. "Merms," we call them. Or "pretties." And they call us "Mutes." It's a grunt word no matter how you sound it.

We are jealous of Mermen. There it is. I have written it. Jealous. They have the freedom of all the land beneath the sea. Merman mechanization depends on a relatively uniform, traditional hu-man body. Few Islanders can compete under middle-class condi-tions, so they occupy the top of Merman genius or the depths of its slums. Even so, Islanders who migrate down under are con-fined to Islander communities . . . ghettos. Still the Islander idea of heaven is to pass for a pretty.

14

Mermen repel the sea to survive. Their living space benefits from a kind of stability underfoot. Historically, I must admit, humans show a preference for a firm surface underfoot, air to breathe freely (although theirs is depressingly damp) and solid *things* all around. They produce an occasional webbed foot or hand but that, too, was common all down the lineage of the species. Merman appearance is that of humans for as long as likenesses have been recorded; that much we can see for ourselves. Besides, *Clone Wars* happened. Our immediate ancestors wrote of this. Jesus Lewis did this to us. The visible evidence of *other* is inescapable.

But I was writing about Merman nature. It is their self-proclaimed mission to restore the kelp. But will the kelp be conscious? Kelp once more lives in the sea. I have seen the effects in my lifetime and expect we've just about seen the last of wavewalls. Exposed land will surely follow. Yet, how does that subtract from this nature that I see in the Mermen?

By bringing back the kelp, they seek to *control* the sea. That is the Merman nature: control.

Islanders float with the waves and the winds and the currents. Mermen would control these forces and control us.

Islanders bend with things that might otherwise overwhelm them. They are accustomed to change but grow tired of it. Mermen fight against certain kinds of change—and are growing tired of that.

Now, I come to my view of what Ship did with us. I think it is the nature of our universe that life may encounter a force that could overwhelm it if life cannot bend. Mermen would break before such a force. Islanders bend and drift. I think we may prove the better survivors.

15

We bear our original sin in our bodies and on our faces.
　　　　　　　—Simone Rocksack, Chaplain/Psychiatrist

　　　The cold *slap* of a sudden wave over the side snapped
Queets Twisp full awake. He yawned, unkinked his overlong
arms where they had tangled themselves in the tarp. He wiped the
spray from his face with his shirtsleeve. Not yet full sunrise, he
noted. The first thin feathers of dawn tickled the black belly of the
horizon. No thunderheads cluttered the sky and his two squawks,
their feathers preened and glistening, muttered contentedly on
their tethers. He rubbed the circulation back into his long arms
and felt in the bottom of the coracle for his tube of thick juice
concentrates and proteins.
　Blech.
　He made a wry face as he sucked down the last of the tube. The
concentrate was tasteless and odorless, but he balked at it just the
same.
　You'd think if they made it edible they could make it palatable, he
thought. *At least dockside we'll get some real food.* The rigors of setting and hauling fishing nets always built his appetite into a monumental thing that concentrates could support, but never satisfy.
　The gray ocean yawned away in all directions. Not a sign of
dashers or any other threat anywhere. The occasional splatter of a
sizable wave broke over the rim of the coracle but the organic
pump in the bilge could handle that. He turned and watched the
slow bulge of their net foam the surface behind them. It listed
slightly with its heavy load. Twisp's mouth watered at the prospect
of a thousand kilos of scilla—boiled scilla, fried scilla, baked scilla
with cream sauce and hot rolls . . .
　"Queets, are we there yet?" Brett's voice cracked in its adolescent way. Only the shock of his thick blonde hair stuck out from
under their tarp—a sharp contrast to Twisp's headful of ebony

16

fur. Brett Norton was tall for sixteen, and his pile of hair made him seem even taller. This first season of fishing had already begun to fill in some of his thin, bony structure.

Twisp sucked in a slow breath, partly to calm himself after being startled, partly to draw in patience.

"Not yet," he said. "Drift is right. We should overtake the Island just after sunrise. Eat something."

The boy grimaced and rummaged in his kit for his own meal. Twisp watched as the boy wiped the spout nearly clean, unstoppered it and sucked down great gulps of the untantalizing brown liquid.

"Yum."

Brett's gray eyes were shut tight and he shuddered.

Twisp smiled. *I should quit thinking of him as "the boy."* Sixteen years was more than boyhood, and a season at the nets had hardened his eyes and thickened his hands.

Twisp often wondered what had made Brett choose to be a fisherman. Brett was near enough to Merman body type that he could have gone down under and made a good life there.

He's self-conscious about his eyes, Twisp thought. *But that's something few people notice.*

Brett's gray eyes were large, but not grotesque. Those eyes could see well in almost total darkness, which turned out to be handy for round-the-clock fishing.

That's something the Mermen wouldn't let out of their hands, Twisp thought. *They're good at using people.*

A sudden lurch of the net caught both of them off-balance and they reached simultaneously for the rimline. Again, the lurch.

"Brett!" Twisp shouted, "Get us some slack while I haul in."

"But we can't haul in," the boy said, "we'd have to dump the catch . . ."

"There's a Merman in the net! A Merman will drown if we don't haul in." Twisp was already dragging in the heavy netlines hand-over-hand. The muscles of his long forearms nearly burst the skin with the effort. This was one of those times he was thankful he had a mutant's extra ability.

Brett ducked out of sight behind him to man their small electric scull. The netlines telegraphed a frantic twisting and jerking from below.

Merman for sure! Twisp thought, and strained even harder. He prayed he could get him up in time.

Or her, he thought. The first Merman he'd seen netbound was a woman. Beautiful. He shook off the memory of the crisscross lines, the net-burns in her perfect, pale . . . dead skin. He hauled harder.

Thirty meters of net to go, he thought. Sweat stung his eyes and small blades of pain seared his back.

"Queets!"

He looked from the net back to Brett and saw white-eyed terror. Twisp followed the boy's gaze. What he saw three or four hundred meters to starboard made him freeze. The squawks set up a fluttering outcry that told Twisp what his eyes were barely able to confirm.

"A hunt of dashers!"

He almost whispered it, almost let slip the netlines creasing his rock-hard palms.

"Help me here," Twisp shouted. He returned to the frantic tugging at the net. Out of the corner of one eye he saw the boy grab the port line, out of the other he watched the steady froth of the oncoming dashers.

A half-dozen of them at least, he thought. *Shit.*

"What'll they do?" Brett's voice cracked again.

Twisp knew that the boy had heard stories. Nothing could match the real thing. Hungry or not, dashers hunted. Their huge forepaws and saberlike canines killed for the sheer bloody love of it. These dashers wanted that Merman.

Too late, Twisp dove for the lasgun he kept wrapped in oiled cloth in the cuddy. Frantically, he scrabbled for the weapon, but the first of the dashers hit the net head-on and their momentum rocked the coracle. Two others fanned to the sides, closing on the flanks like a fist. Twisp felt the two hard hits as he came up with the lasgun. He saw the net go slack as slashing claws and fangs opened it wide. The rest of the hunt closed in, scavenging bits of meat and bone thrown clear of the frothy mess that had been a Merman. One dasher nipped another and, primed to kill, the rest turned on their wounded mate and tore him to bits. Fur and green gore splattered the side of the coracle.

No need wasting a lasgun charge on that mess! It was a bitter thought. Islanders had long ago given up the hope they might exterminate these terrible creatures.

Twisp shook himself alert, fumbled for his knife and cut the netlines.

18

"But why . . . ?"

He didn't answer Brett's protest, but toggled a switch under the scull housing. One of the dashers froze not a meter from their gunwale. It sank slowly, drifting back and forth, back and forth like a feather falling on a breezeless day. The others made passes at the coracle but retreated once they felt the edge of the stunshield on their noses. They settled for the stunned dasher, then thrashed their way out to sea.

Twisp rewrapped his lasgun and wedged it under his seat.

He switched off the shield then and stared at the ragged shards that had been their net.

"Why'd you cut loose the net?" Brett's voice was petulant, demanding. He sounded near tears.

Shock, Twisp thought. *And losing the catch.*

"They tore the net to get the . . . to get him," Twisp explained. "We'd have lost the catch anyway."

"We could've saved some of it," Brett muttered. "A third of it was right *here.*" Brett slapped the rimline at the stern, his eyes two gray threats against a harsh blue sky.

Twisp sighed, aware that adrenaline could arouse frustrations that needed release.

"You can't activate a stunshield with the lines over the side like that," he explained. "It's got to be all the way in or all the way out. With this cheap-ass model, anyway . . ." His fist slammed one of the thwarts.

I'm as shook as the kid, he thought. He took a deep breath, ran his fingers through the thick kinks of his black hair and calmed himself before activating the dasher-warning signal on his radio. That would locate them and reassure Vashon.

"They'd have turned on us next," he said. He flicked a finger against the material between thwarts. "This stuff is one thin membrane, two centimeters thick—what do you think our odds were?"

Brett lowered his eyes. He pursed his full lips, then stuck the lower lip out in a half-pout. His gaze looked away past a rising of Big Sun come to join its sister star already overhead. Below Big Sun, just ahead of the horizon, a large silhouette glowed orange in the water.

"Home," Twisp said quietly. "The city."

They were in one of the tight trade currents close to the surface. It would allow them to overtake the floating mass of humanity in an hour or two.

19

"Big fucking deal," Brett said. "We're broke."

Twisp smiled and leaned back to enjoy the suns.

"That's right," he said. "And we're alive."

The boy grunted and Twisp folded his meter-and-a-half arms behind his head. The elbows stuck out like two strange wings and cast a grotesque shadow on the water. He stared up across one of the elbows—caught as he sometimes was reflecting on the uniqueness of his mutant inheritance. These arms gangled in his way most of his life—he could touch his toes without bending over at all. But his arms hauled nets as though bred for it.

Maybe they were, he mused. *Who knows anymore?* Handy mostly for nets and for reach, they made sleeping uncomfortable. Women seemed to like their strength and their wrap-around quality, though. Compensation.

Maybe it's the illusion of security, he thought, and his smile widened. His own life was anything but secure. Nobody who went down to the sea was secure, and anybody who thought so was either a fool or dead.

"What will Maritime Court do to us?" Brett's voice was low, barely audible over the splashings of the waves and the continued ruffled mutterings of the two squawks.

Twisp continued to enjoy the drift and the warm sunlight on his face and arms. He gnawed his thin lips for a blink, then said, "Hard to say. Did you see a Merman marker?"

"No."

"Do you see one now?"

He listened to the faint rustle across the coracle and knew that the boy scanned the horizon. Twisp had picked the boy for those exceptional eyes. That, and his attitude.

"Not a sign," the boy said. "He must've been alone."

"That's not likely," Twisp said. "Mermen seldom travel alone. But it's a sure bet *somebody's* alone."

"Do we *have* to go to court?"

Twisp opened his eyes and saw the genuine fear in Brett's downturned mouth. The boy's wide eyes were impossible moons in his unstubbled face.

"Yep."

Brett plopped down on the thwart beside Twisp, rocking the little boat so hard that water lapped over the sides.

"What if we don't tell?" he asked. "How would they know?"

Twisp turned away from the boy. Brett had a lot to learn about the sea, and those who worked it. There were many laws, and most of them stayed unwritten. This would be a hard first lesson, but what could you expect of a kid fresh from the inside? Things like this didn't happen at Center. Life there was . . . nice. Scilla and muree were dinner to people living in the Island's inner circle, they weren't creatures with patterns and lives and a bright final flutter in the palm of the hand.

"Mermen keep track of everything," Twisp said flatly. "They know."

"But the dashers," Brett insisted, "maybe they got the other Merman, too. If there *was* another one."

"Dasher fur has hollow cells," Twisp said. "For insulation and flotation. They can't dive worth a damn."

Twisp leveled his black eyes at the kid and said, "What about his family waiting back home? Now shut up."

He knew the kid was hurt, but what the hell! If Brett was going to live on the sea he'd better learn the way of it. Nobody liked being surprised out here, or abandoned. Nobody liked being boat-bound with a motor-mouth, either. Besides, Twisp was beginning to feel the proximity and inevitable discomfort of the Maritime Court, and he thought he'd better start figuring out their case. Netting a Merman was serious business, even if it wasn't your fault.

The fearful can be the most dangerous when they gain power. They become demoniac when they see the unpredictable workings of all that life around them. Seeing the strengths as well as the weaknesses, they fasten only on the weaknesses.

—Shipquotes, the Histories

Except for the movements of the operators, and their occasional comments, it was quiet in Sonde Control this morning, a stillness insulated from the daylight topside beneath a hundred meters of water and the thick walls of this Merman complex. The subdued remoteness filled Iz Bushka with disquiet. He knew his senses were being assaulted by Merman strangeness, an environment alien to most Islanders, but the exact source of his unease escaped him.

Everything's so quiet, he thought.

All that weight of water over his head gave Bushka no special concern. He had overcome that fear while doing his compulsory service in the Islander subs. The attitude of superiority that he could detect in the Mermen around him, *that* was the source of his annoyance! Bushka glanced left to where his fellow observers stood slightly apart, keeping their distance from the lone Islander in this company.

GeLaar Gallow leaned close to the woman beside him, Kareen Ale, and asked: "Why is the launch delayed?"

Ale spoke in a softly modulated voice: "I heard someone say there was an order from the Chaplain/Psychiatrist—something about the blessing."

Gallow nodded and a lock of blonde hair dropped to his right eyebrow. He brushed it back with a casual movement. Gallow was quite the most beautiful human male Bushka had ever seen—a Greek god, if the histories were to be credited. As an Islander historian by avocation, Bushka believed the histories. Gallow's golden hair was long and softly waved. His dark blue eyes looked demandingly at everything they encountered. His even, white teeth flashed smiles that touched nothing but his mouth, as though he displayed the perfect teeth in that perfect face only for the benefit of onlookers. Some said he had been operated on to remove webs from fingers and toes but that could be a jealous lie.

Bushka studied Ale covertly. It was said that Mermen were petitioning Ale to mate with Gallow for the sake of beautiful off-spring. Ale's face was an exquisitely proportioned oval with full lips, widely spaced blue eyes. Her nose, slightly upturned, showed a smooth and straight ridgeline. Her skin—perfectly set off by her dark red hair—was a pinkish translucence that Bushka thought would require salves and ointments when her duties took her topside into the harsh presence of the suns.

Bushka looked past them at the giant console with its graphic operational keys and large screens. One screen showed brilliant light on the ocean surface far above them. Another screen revealed the undersea tube where the Lighter-Than-Air hydrogen sonde was being prepared for its upward drift and launch into Pandora's turbulent atmosphere. A thin forest of kelp wavered in the background.

On Bushka's right, a triple thickness of plazglas also revealed the LTA launch base with Mermen swimming around it. Some of the swimmers wore prestubes for oxygen, all encased in their tight-fitting dive suits. Others carried across their backs the organic airfish that Islander bioengineering had pioneered for sustained work undersea.

We can produce it, but we cannot have the freedom of the undersea in which to use it.

Bushka could see where the leechmouth of an airfish attached itself to a nearby Merman's carotid artery. He imagined the thousands of cilia pumping fresh oxygen into the worker's blood-stream. Occasionally, a worker equipped with an airfish vented carbon dioxide in a stream of drifting bubbles from the corner of his mouth.

How does it feel to float freely in the sea, dependent on the symbiotic relationship with an airfish? It was a thought full of Islander resentments. Islander bioengineering surpassed that of the Mermen, but everything Islander genius produced was gobbled up in the terrible need for valuable exchange.

23

As I would like to be gobbled up. But there's not much hope of that!

Bushka suppressed feelings of jealousy. He could see his reflection in the plaz. The Committee on Vital Forms had faced no trouble in accepting him as human. He obviously fell somewhere near the Merman-tip of the spectrum. Still, his heavyset body, his small stature, the large head with its stringy dark brown hair, thick brows, wide nose, wide mouth, square chin—none of this came near the standard Gallow represented.

Comparisons hurt. Bushka wondered what the tall, disdainful Merman was thinking. *Why that quizzical expression aimed at me?*

Gallow returned his attention to Ale, touching her bare shoulder, laughing at something she said.

A new flurry of activity could be seen at the LTA launch base, more lights within the tube that would guide the sonde on the start of its journey toward the surface.

The launch director at the control console said: "It'll be a few minutes yet."

Bushka sighed. This experience was not turning out the way he had expected . . . the way he had dreamed.

He sneered at himself. *Fantasy!*

When he had been notified that he would be the Islander observer at this launch into the realm of Ship, elation had filled him. His first trip into the core of Merman civilization! At last! And the fantasy: *Perhaps . . . just possibly, I will find the way to join Merman society, to abandon poverty and the grubby existence topside.*

Learning that Gallow would be his escort had fanned his hopes. GeLaar Gallow, director of the Merman Screen, one who could vote to accept an Islander into their society. But Gallow appeared to be avoiding him now. And there had never been any doubt of the man's disdain.

Only Ale had been warmly welcoming, but then she was a member of the Merman government, a diplomat and envoy to the Islanders. Bushka had been surprised to discover that she also was a medical doctor. Rumor had it that she had gone through the rigors of medical education as a gesture of rebellion against her family, with its long tradition of service in the diplomatic corps and elsewhere in the Merman government. The family obviously had won out. Ale was securely seated among the powerful—held, perhaps, greater power than any other member of her family. Both the Merman and Island worlds buzzed with the recent revelation that Ale was a major inheritor in the estates of the late Ryan

24

and Elina Wang. And Ale had been named guardian of the Wangs' only daughter, Scudi. Nobody had yet put a number on the size of the Wang estate, but the senior director of Merman Mercantile had probably been the wealthiest man on Pandora. Elina Wang, surviving her husband by less than a year, had not lived long enough to make serious changes in the Wang holdings. So there was Kareen Ale, beautiful and powerful and with the right words for any occasion.

"Delighted to have you with us, Islander Bushka."

How warm and inviting she had sounded.

She was just being polite . . . diplomatic.

Another burst of activity rippled through the workers at the console in Sonde Control. The screen showing the surface emitted a series of brilliant flickers and the view was replaced by the face of Simone Rocksack, the Chaplain/Psychiatrist. The background revealed that she spoke from her quarters at the center of Vashon far away on the surface.

"I greet you in the name of Ship."

A barely suppressed snort came from Gallow.

Bushka noted a shudder pass through the man's classic body at sight of the C/P. Bushka, accustomed to Islander variations, had never made note of Rocksack's appearance. Now, however, he saw her through Gallow's eyes. Rocksack's silvery hair flared in a wild mane from the top of her almost perfectly round head. Her albino eyes projected at the tips of small protuberances on her brows. Her mouth, barely visible under a flap of gray skin, was a small red slit abandoned without a chin. A sharp angle of flesh went directly back from beneath her mouth to her thick neck.

"Let us pray," the C/P said. "This prayer I offered just a few minutes ago in the presence of Vata. I repeat it now." She cleared her throat. "Ship, by whose omnipotence we were cast upon Pandora's endless waters, grant us forgiveness from Original Sin. Grant us . . ."

Bushka tuned her out. He had heard this prayer, in one version or another, many times. Doubtless his companions had heard it, too. The Mermen observers fidgeted at their stations and looked bored.

Original Sin!

Bushka's historical studies had made him a questioner of tradition. Mermen, he had discovered, thought Original Sin referred to the killing of Pandora's sentient kelp. It was their penance that they must rediscover the kelp in their own genes and fill the sea once more with submerged jungles of gigantic stems and fronds. Not sentient, this time, however. Merely kelp . . . and controlled by Mermen.

The fanatical WorShipers of Guemes Island, on the other hand, insisted that Original Sin came when humankind abandoned WorShip. Most Islanders, though, followed the C/P's lead: Original Sin was that line of bioengineering chosen by Jesus Lewis, the long-dead mastermind behind today's variations in the human norm. Lewis had created the Clones and "selected others re-formed to fit them for survival on Pandora."

Bushka shook his head as the C/P's voice droned on. *Who is surviving best on Pandora?* he asked himself. *Mermen. Normal humans.*

At least ten times as many Mermen as Islanders survived on Pandora. It was a simple function of available living space. Under the sea, cushioned from Pandora's vagaries, there was a far greater volume of living space than on Pandora's turbulent, dangerous surface.

"Into Ship's realm I commend you," the C/P said. "Let the blessing of Ship accompany this venture. Let Ship know that we mean no blasphemy by intruding ourselves into the heavens. Let this be a gesture that brings us closer to Ship."

The C/P's face vanished from the screen, replaced by a close-up of the launch tube's base. Telltales on the tube tipped left to a slow current.

At the console to Bushka's left, the launch director said: "Condition green."

From the prelaunch briefing, Bushka knew this meant they were ready to release the sonde. He glanced at another of the screens, a view transmitted down a communications cable from a gyro-stabilized platform on the surface. White froth whipped the tops of long swells up there. Bushka's practiced eye said it was a forty-klick wind, practically a calm on Pandora. The sonde would drift fast when it broached but it would climb fast, too, and the upper atmosphere, for a change, showed breaks in the clouds, with one of Pandora's two suns tipping the cloud edges a glowing silver.

The launch director leaned forward to study an instrument. "Forty seconds," he said.

Bushka moved forward, giving himself a better view of the instruments and the launch director. The man had been intro-

26

duced as Dark Panille—"'Shadow' to my friends." No overt rejection there; just a touch of the specialist's resentment that observers could be brought into his working space without his permission. Bushka's Mute-sensitive senses had detected immediately that Panille carried kelp genes, but was fortunate by Pandoran standards because he was not hairless. Panille wore his long black hair in a single braid—"a family style," he had said in answer to Bushka's question.

Panille displayed a countenance distinctly Merman-normal. The kelp telltale lay chiefly in his dark skin with its unmistakable undertone of green. He had a narrow, rather sharp-featured face with high planes on both his cheeks and his nose. Panille's large brown eyes looked out with a deep sense of intelligence beneath straight brows. The mouth was set in a straight line to match the brows and his lower lip was fuller than the upper. A deep crease rolled from beneath his lips to the cleft of a narrow, well-defined chin. Panille's body was compact, with the smooth muscles common to Mermen who lived much in the sea.

The name Panille had aroused a historian's interest in Bushka. Panille's ancestry had been instrumental in human survival during the Clone Wars and after the departure of Ship. It was a famous name in the Histories.

"Launch!" Panille said.

Bushka glanced out the plaz beside him. The launch tube climbed beyond his vision through green water with a backdrop of sparsely planted kelp—thick red-brown trunks with glistening highlights at odd intervals. The highlights wavered and blinked as though in agitation. Bushka turned his attention to the screens, expecting something spectacular. The display on which the others focused showed only the slow upward drift of the LTA within the tube. Brilliant lights in the tube wall marked the ascent. The wrinkled bag of the LTA expanded as it lifted, smoothing finally in an orange expanse of the fabric that contained the hydrogen.

"There!" Ale spoke in a sighing voice as the sonde cleared the top of the tube. It drifted slantwise in a sea current, followed by a camera mounted on a Merman sub.

"Test key monitors," Panille said.

A large screen at the center of the console shifted from a tracking view to a transmission from the sonde package trailing beneath the hydrogen bag. The screen showed a slanted green-tinged view of the sea bottom—thin plantations of kelp, a rocky outcrop. They dimmed away into murkiness as Bushka watched. A screen at the upper right of the console shifted to the surface platform's camera, a gyro-stabilized float. The camera swept to the left in a dizzying arc, then settled on an expanse of wind-frothed swells.

A pain in his chest told Bushka that he was holding his breath, waiting for the LTA to break the surface. He exhaled and took a deep breath. *There!* A bubble lifted on the ocean surface and did not break. Wind flattened the near side of the bag. It lifted free of the water, receding fast as the sonde package cleared. The surface camera tracked it—showing an orange blossom floating in a blue bowl of sky. The view zoomed in to the dangling package, from which water still dripped in wind-driven spray.

Bushka looked to the center screen, the transmission from the sonde. It showed the sea beneath the LTA, an oddly flattened scene with little sense of the heaving waves from which the LTA had recently emerged.

Is this all? Bushka wondered.

He felt let down. He rubbed his thick neck, feeling the nervous perspiration there. A surreptitious glance at the two Merman observers showed them chatting quietly, with only an occasional glance at the screens and the plaz porthole that revealed Mermen already cleaning up after the launch.

Frustration and jealousy warred for dominance in Bushka. He stared at the console where Panille was giving low-voiced orders to his operators. How rich these Mermen were! Bushka thought of the crude organic computers with which Islanders contended, the stench of the Islands, the crowding and the life-protecting watch that had to be kept on every tiny bit of energy. Islanders paupered themselves for a few radios, satellite navigation receivers and sonar. And just look at this Sonde Control! So casually rich. If Islanders could afford such riches, Bushka knew the possessions would be kept secret. Display of wealth set people apart in a society that depended ultimately on singleness of all efforts. Islanders believed tools were to be used. Ownership was acknowledged, but a tool left idle could be picked up for use by anyone . . . anytime.

"There's a willy-nilly," Gallow said.

Bushka bridled. He knew Mermen called Islands "willy-nillys." Islands drifted unguided, and this was the Merman way of sneering at such uncontrolled wandering.

"That's Vashon," Ale said.

Bushka nodded. There was no mistaking his home Island. The organic floating metropolis had a distinctive shape known to all of its inhabitants—Vashon, largest of all Pandora's Islands.

"Willy-nilly," Gallow repeated. "I should imagine they don't know where they are half the time."

"You're not being very polite to our guest, GeLaar," Ale said.

"The truth is often impolite," Gallow said. He directed an empty smile at Bushka. "I've noticed that Islanders have few goals, that they're not very concerned about 'getting there.'"

He's right, damn him, Bushka thought. The drifting pattern had seated itself deeply in the Islander psyche.

When Bushka did not respond, Ale spoke defensively: "Islanders are necessarily more weather-oriented, more tuned to the horizon. That should not be surprising." She glanced questioningly at Bushka. "All people are shaped by their surroundings. Isn't that true, Islander Bushka?"

"Islanders believe the *manner* of our passage is just as important as *where* we are," Bushka said. He knew his response sounded weak. He turned toward the screens. Two of them now showed transmissions from the sonde. One pointed backward to the stabilized camera platform on the surface. It showed the platform being withdrawn into the safety of the calm undersea. The other sonde view tracked the drift path. Full in this view lay the bulk of Vashon. Bushka swallowed as he stared at his home Island. He had never before seen this view of it.

A glance at the altitude repeater below the screen said the view was from eighty thousand meters. The amplified image almost filled the screen. Grid lines superimposed on the screen gave the Island's long dimension at nearly thirty klicks and slightly less than that across. Vashon was a gigantic oval drifter with irregular edges. Bushka identified the bay indentation where fishboats and subs docked. Only a few of the boats in Vashon's fleet could be seen in the protected waters.

"What's its population?" Gallow asked.

"About six hundred thousand, I believe," Ale said.

Bushka scowled, thinking of the crowded conditions this number represented, comparing it with the spaciousness of Merman habitats. Vashon squeezed more than two thousand people into every square klick . . . a space more correctly measured in cubic terms. Cubbies were stacked on cubbies high above the water and deep beneath it. And some of the smaller Islands were even more condensed, a crowding that had to be experienced to be believed. Space opened on them only when they began to run out of energy—dead space. Uninhabitable. Like people, organics rotted when they died. A dead Island was just a gigantic floating carcass. And this had happened many times.

"I could not tolerate such crowding," Gallow said. "I could only leave."

"It isn't all bad!" Bushka blurted. "We may live close but we help each other."

"I should certainly hope so!" Gallow snorted. He turned until he was facing Bushka. "What is your personal background, Bushka?"

Bushka stared at him, momentarily affronted. This was not an Islander question. Islanders *knew* the backgrounds of their friends and acquaintances, but the rules of privacy seldom permitted probing.

"Your working background," Gallow persisted.

Ale put a hand on Gallow's arm. "To an Islander, such questions are usually impolite," she said.

"It's all right," Bushka said. "When I got old enough, *Merman* Gallow, I was a wavewatcher."

"A sort of lookout to warn of wavewalls," Ale explained.

"I know the term," Gallow said. "And after that?"

"Well . . . I had good eyes and a good sense of distance, so I did my time as a driftwatch and later in the subs . . . then, as I showed navigational ability, they trained me as a timekeeper."

"Timekeeper, yes," Gallow said. "You're the ones who dead-reckon an Island's position. Not very accurate, I'm told."

"Accurate enough," Bushka said.

Gallow chuckled. "Is it true, Islander Bushka, that you people think we Mermen stole the kelp's soul?"

"GeLaar!" Ale snapped.

"No, let him answer," Gallow said. "I've been hearing recently about the fundamentalist beliefs of Islands such as Guemes."

"You're impossible, GeLaar!" Ale said.

"I have an insatiable curiosity," Gallow said. "What about it, Bushka?"

Bushka knew he had to answer but his voice was dismayingly loud when he responded. "Many Islanders believe Ship will return to forgive us."

"And when will that be?" Gallow asked.

"When we regain the Collective Consciousness!"

"Ahhhh, the old Transition Stories," Gallow sneered. "But do you believe this?"

"My hobby is history," Bushka said. "I believe something important happened to human consciousness during the Clone Wars."

"Hobby?" Gallow asked.

"Historian is not a fully accredited Islander job," Ale explained. "Superfluous."

"I see. Do go on, Bushka."

Bushka clenched his fists and fought down his anger. Gallow was more than self-important . . . he was truly important . . . vital to Bushka's hopes.

"I don't believe we stole the kelp's soul," Bushka said.

"Good for you!" Gallow really smiled this time.

"But I do believe," Bushka added, "that our ancestors, possibly with kelp assistance, glimpsed a different kind of consciousness . . . a momentary linkage between all of the minds alive at that time."

Gallow passed a hand across his mouth, an oddly furtive gesture. "The accounts appear to agree," he said. "But can they be trusted?"

"There's no doubt we have kelp genes in the human gene pool," Bushka said. He glanced across the control room at Panille, who was watching him intently.

"And who knows what may happen if we revive the kelp to consciousness, eh?" Gallow asked.

"Something like that," Bushka agreed.

"Why do you think Ship abandoned us here?"

"GeLaar, please!" Ale interrupted.

"Let him answer," Gallow said. "This Islander has an active mind. He may be someone we need."

Bushka tried to swallow in a suddenly dry throat. Was this all a test? Was Gallow actually screening him for entry into Merman society?

"I was hoping . . ." Again, Bushka tried to swallow. "I mean, as long as I'm down here anyway . . . I was hoping I might gain access to the material Mermen recovered from the old Redoubt. Perhaps the answer to your question . . ." He broke off.

An abrupt silence settled over the room.

Ale and Gallow exchanged an oddly veiled look.

"How interesting," Gallow said.

"I'm told," Bushka said, "that when you recovered the Redoubt's data base . . . I mean . . ." He coughed.

"Our historians work full-time," Gallow said. "After the Disaster, everything, including the material from the Redoubt, was subjected to exhaustive analysis."

"I would still like to see the material," Bushka said. He cursed himself silently. His voice sounded so plaintive.

"Tell me, Bushka," Gallow said, "what would be your response if this material revealed that Ship was an artifact made by human beings and not God at all?"

Bushka pursed his lips. "The Artifact Heresy? Hasn't that been . . ."

"You haven't answered my question," Gallow said.

"I would have to see the material and judge for myself," Bushka said. He held himself quite still. No Islander had ever been granted access to Redoubt data. But what Gallow hinted . . . explosive!

"I should be most interested to hear what an Islander historian has to say about the Redoubt accounts," Gallow said. He glanced at Ale. "Do you see any reason why we shouldn't grant his request, Kareen?"

She shrugged and turned away, an expression on her face that Bushka could not interpret. *Disgust?*

Gallow directed that measuring smile toward Bushka. "I quite understand that the Redoubt has mystical implications for Islanders. I hesitate to feed superstitions."

Mystical? Bushka thought. Land that once had protruded from the sea. A place built on a continent, a mass of exposed land that did not drift, the last place inundated in the Disaster. Mystical? Was Gallow merely toying with him?

"I'm a qualified historian," Bushka said.

"But you said hobby . . ." Gallow shook his head.

"Was everything recovered intact from the Redoubt?" Bushka ventured.

"It was sealed off," Ale said, turning once more to face Bushka. "Our ancestors put an air-bell on it before cutting through the plasteel."

"Everything was found just as it was left when they abandoned the place," Gallow said.

"Then it's true," Bushka breathed.

"But would you reinforce Islander superstitions?" Gallow insisted.

Bushka drew himself up stiffly. "I am a scientist. I would reinforce nothing but the truth."

"Why this sudden interest in the Redoubt?" Ale asked.

"Sudden?" Bushka stared at her in amazement. "We've always wanted to share in the Redoubt's data base. The people who left it there were our ancestors, too."

"In a manner of speaking," Gallow said.

Bushka felt the hot flush of blood in his cheeks. Most Mermen believed that only Clones and mutants had populated the drifting Islands. Did Gallow really accept that nonsense?

"Perhaps I should've said why the *renewed* interest?" Ale corrected herself.

"We've heard stories, you see, about the Guemes Movement," Gallow said.

Bushka nodded. WorShip was, indeed, on the increase among Islanders.

"There have been reports of unidentified things seen in the sky," Bushka said. "Some believe that Ship already has returned and is concealed from us in space."

"Do you believe this?" Gallow asked.

"It's possible," Bushka admitted. "All I really know for certain is that the C/P is kept busy examining people who claim to have seen visions."

Gallow chuckled. "Oh, my!"

Bushka once more felt frustration. They were toying with him! This was all a cruel Merman game! "What is so amusing?" he demanded.

"GeLaar, stop this!" Ale said.

Gallow held up an admonitory hand. "Kareen, look with care upon Islander Bushka. Could he not pass as one of us?"

Ale swept a swift glance across Bushka's face and returned her attention to Gallow. "What're you doing, GeLaar?"

Bushka inhaled deeply and held his breath.

Gallow studied Bushka a moment, then: "What would be your response, Bushka, if I were to offer you a place in Merman society?"

Bushka exhaled slowly, inhaled. "I . . . I would accept. Gratefully, of course."

"Of course," Gallow echoed. He smiled at Ale. "Then, since

Bushka will be one of us, there's no harm in telling him what amuses me."

"It's on your head, GeLaar," Ale said.

A movement at the Sonde Control console caught Bushka's attention. Panille was no longer looking at him, but the set of his shoulders told Bushka the man was listening intently. Ship save them! Was the Artifact Heresy true, after all? Was that the great Merman secret?

"These *visions* causing so much trouble for our beloved C/P," Gallow said. "They are Merman rockets, Bushka."

Bushka opened his mouth and closed it without speaking.

"Ship was not God, is not God," Gallow said. "The Redoubt records . . ."

"Are open to several interpretations," Ale said.

"Only to fools!" Gallow snapped. "We are sending up rockets, Bushka, because we are preparing to recover the hyb tanks from orbit. Ship was an artifact made by our ancestors. Other artifacts and *things* have been left in space for us to recover."

The matter-of-fact way Gallow said this made Bushka catch his breath. Stories about the mysterious hyb tanks permeated Islander society. What might be stored in those containers that orbited Pandora? Recovering those tanks, and really seeing what they contained, was worth anything—even destruction of the Ship-God belief that sustained so many people.

"You are shocked," Gallow said.

"I'm . . . I'm awed," Bushka replied.

"We were all raised on the Transition Stories." Gallow pointed upward. "Life awaits us up there."

Bushka nodded. "The tanks are supposed to contain countless life forms from . . . from Earth."

"Fish, animals, plants," Gallow said. "And even some humans." He grinned. "Normal humans." He waved a hand to encompass the occupants of Sonde Control. "Like us."

Bushka inhaled a trembling breath. Yes, the historical accounts said the hyb tanks held humans who had never been touched by the bioengineering machinations of Jesus Lewis. There would be people in those tanks who had gone to sleep in another star system, who had no idea of this nightmare world that awaited their awakening.

"And now you know," Gallow said.

Bushka cleared his throat. "We never suspected. I mean . . . the C/P has never said a word about . . ."

"The C/P does not know of this," Ale said. There was a warning note in her voice.

Bushka glanced at the plaz porthole with its view of the LTA tube.

"She knows about that, of course," Ale said.

"An innocuous thing," Gallow said.

"There has been no blessing of our rockets," Ale said.

Bushka continued to stare out the porthole. He had never counted himself a deeply religious person, but these Merman revelations left him profoundly disturbed. Ale obviously doubted Gallow's interpretation of the Redoubt material, but still . . . a blessing would be only common sense . . . just in case . . .

"What is your response, Merman Bushka?" Gallow asked.

Merman Bushka!

Bushka turned a wide-eyed stare on Gallow, who obviously awaited an answer to a question. A question. What had he asked? Bushka was a moment recovering the man's words.

"My response . . . yes. The Islanders . . . I mean, about these rockets. The Islanders . . . shouldn't they be told?"

"They?" Gallow laughed, a deep amusement that shook his beautiful body. "You see, Kareen? Already his former compatriots are 'they.'"

35

*The touch of the infant teaches birth, and our hands are
witness to the lesson.*

—Kerro Panille, the Histories

Vata did not experience true consciousness. She skirted the
shadow-edges of awareness. Memories flitted through her neu-
rons like tendrils from the kelp. Sometimes she dreamed kelp
dreams. These dreams often included a wondrous hatch of
hylighters—spore-filled gasbags that had died when the original
kelp died. Tears mixed with her nutrient bath as she dreamed
such things, tears for the fate of those huge sky-bound globes
tacking across the evening breezes of a million years. Her dream
hylighters clutched their ballast rocks in their two longest tentacles and Vata felt the comforting texture of rock hugged close.

Thoughts themselves were like hylighters to her, or silken
threads blowing in the dark of her mind. Sometimes she followed
awareness of Duque, who floated beside her, sensing events
within his thoughts. Time and again, she re-experienced through
him that terrible night when the gravitational wrenching of Pandora's two suns destroyed the last human foothold on the planet's
fragile land. Duque repeatedly let his thoughts plunge into that
experience. And Vata, linked to the fearful mutant like Mermen
diving partners on the same safety line, was forced to recreate
dreams that soothed and calmed Duque's terrors.

"Duque escaped," she muttered in his mind, "Duque was taken
away onto the sea where Hali Ekel tended his burns."

Duque would snuffle and whimper. Had Vata been conscious,
she would have heard with her own ears, because Vata and Duque
shared the same life support at the center of Vashon. Vata lay
mostly submerged in nutrient, a monstrous mound of pink and
blue flesh with definite human female characteristics. Enormous
breasts with gigantic pink nipples lifted from the dark nutrient

36

like twin mountains from a brown sea. Duque drifted beside her, a satellite, her familiar dangling in the endless mental vacuum.

For generations now, the two of them had been nurtured and reverenced in Vashon's central complex—home of the Chaplain/Psychiatrist and the Committee on Vital Forms. Merman and Islander guards kept watch on the pair under the command of the C/P. It was a ritualized observation, which, in time, eroded the awe that Pandorans learned early from the reactions of their parents.

"The two of them there like that. They'll always be there. They're our last link with Ship. As long as they live, Ship is with us. It's WorShip keeps them alive so long."

Although Duque occasionally knuckled an eye into glaring wakefulness and watched his guardians in the gloomy surroundings of the living pool that confined them, Vata's responses never lifted to consciousness. She breathed. Her great body, responding to the kelp half of her genetic inheritance, absorbed energy from the nutrient solution that washed against her skin. Analysis of the nutrient betrayed traces of human waste products, which were removed by the sucker mouths of blind scrubberfish. Occasionally, Vata would snort and an arm would lift in the nutrient like a leviathan rising from its depths before settling once more into the murk. Her hair continued to grow until it spread like kelp across the nutrient surface, tangling over the hairless skin of Duque and impeding the scrubberfish. The C/P would come into the chamber then and, with a reverence touched by a certain amount of cupidity, would clip Vata's locks. The strands were washed and separated to be blessed and sold in short lengths as indulgences. Even Mermen bought them. Sale of Vatahair had been the major source of C/P income for many generations.

Duque, more aware than any other human of his curious link with Vata, puzzled over the connection when Vata's intrusions left him with thinking time of his own. Sometimes he would speak of this to his guardians, but when Duque spoke there was always a flurry of activity, the summoning of the C/P, and a different kind of watchfulness from the security.

"She lives me," he said once, and this became a token label inscribed on the Vatahair containers.

In these speaking times, the C/P would try prepared questions, sometimes booming them at Duque, sometimes asking in a low and reverential voice.

"Do you speak for Vata, Duque?"

"I speak."

That was all they ever got from him on this question. Since it was known that Duque was one of the hundred or so original mutants who had been conceived with kelp intervention and thus bore kelp genes, they would sometimes ask him about the kelp that had once ruled Pandora's now-endless sea.

"Do you have memory of the kelp, Duque?"

"Avata," Duque corrected. "I am the rock."

Interminable arguments came out of this answer. "Avata" had been the kelp's name for itself. The reference to rock gave scholars and theologians room for speculation.

"He must mean that his consciousness exists at the bottom of the sea where the kelp lives."

"No! Remember how the kelp always clung to a rock, lifting its tendrils to the sunlight? And the hylighters used rock for ballast . . ."

"You're all wrong. He's Vata's grip on life. He's Vata's rock."

And there was always someone who would harken back to WorShip and the stories of that distant planet where someone calling himself Peter had given the same answer Duque had given.

Nothing was ever solved by such arguments, but the questioning continued whenever Duque showed signs of wakefulness.

"How is it that you and Vata do not die, Duque?"

"We wait."

"For what do you wait?"

"No answer."

This recurrent response precipitated several crises until the C/P of that time issued an order that Duque's answers could only be broadcast by permission of the C/P. This didn't stop the quiet whispering and the rumors, of course, but it relegated everything except the C/P's official version to the role of mystical heresy. It was a question no C/P had asked for two generations now. Current interest centered much more on the kelp that Mermen spread far and wide in Pandora's planetary sea. The kelp was thick and healthy, but showed no signs of acquiring consciousness.

As the great Islands drifted they were seldom out of sight of a horizon touched by the oily green flatness of a kelp bed. Everyone said it was a good thing. Kelp formed nurseries for fish and everyone could see there were more fish these days, though they weren't always easy to catch. You couldn't use a net amongst the kelp. Baited lines tangled in the huge fronds and were lost. Even the dumb muree had learned to retreat into kelp sanctuary at the approach of fishermen.

There was also the recurrent question of Ship, Ship who was God and who had left humankind on Pandora.

"Why did Ship abandon us here, Duque?"

All Duque would ever say was: "Ask Ship."

Many a C/P had engaged in much silent prayer over that one. But Ship did not answer them. At least, not with any voice that they could hear.

It was a vexing question. Would Ship return? Ship had left the hyb tanks in orbit around Pandora. It was a strange orbit, seeming to defy the gravitational index for such things. There were those among Pandora's Mermen and Islanders who said Vata waited for the hyb tanks to be brought down, that she would awaken when this occurred.

No one doubted there was some link between Duque and Vata, so why not a link between Vata and the dormant life waiting up there in the tanks?

"How are you linked to Vata?" a C/P asked.

"How are you linked to me?" Duque responded.

This was duly recorded in the Book of Duque and more arguments ensued. It was noted, however, that whenever such questions were asked, Vata stirred. Sometimes grossly and sometimes with only the faintest movement over her vast flesh.

"It's like the safety line we use between divers down under," an astute Merman observed. "You can always find your partner."

Vata's tendril-awareness stirred to the linkage with genetic memories of mountain climbers. They were climbing, she and Duque. This she showed him many times. Her memories, shared with Duque, showed a spectacular world of the vertical that Islanders could barely imagine and holos did not do justice. Only, she did not think of herself as one of the climbers, or even think of herself at all. There was only the line, and the climbing.

First, we had to develop a landless life-style; second, we preserved what technology and hardware we could salvage. Lewis left us with a team of bioengineers—both our curse and our most powerful legacy. We do not dare plunge our few precious children into a Stone Age.
                    —Hali Ekel, the Journals

Ward Keel looked down from the high bench and surveyed the two young petitioners in front of him. The male was a large Merman with the tattoo of a criminal on his brow, a wine-red "E" for "Expatriate." This Merman could never return to the rich land under the sea and he knew the Islanders accepted him only for his stabilizing genes. Those genes had not stabilized this time. The Merman probably knew what the judgment would be. He patted a damp cloth nervously over his exposed skin.

The woman petitioner, his mate, was small and slender with pale blonde hair and two slight indentations where she should have had eyes. She wore a long blue sari and when she walked Keel did not hear steps, only a rasping scrape. She swayed from side to side and hummed to herself.

Why does this one have to be the first case of the morning? Keel wondered. It was a perverse fate. *This morning of all mornings!*

"Our child deserves to live!" the Merman said. His voice boomed in the chambers. The Committee on Vital Forms often heard such loud protestation but this time Keel felt that the volume was directed at the woman, telling her that her mate fought for them both.

As Chief Justice of the Committee it was too often Keel's lot to perform that unsavory stroke of the pen, to speak directly the unutterable fears of the petitioners themselves. Many times it was otherwise and then this chamber echoed the laughter of life. But today, in this case, there would be no laughter. Keel sighed. The

40

Merman, even though a criminal by Merman ruling, made this matter politically sensitive. Mermen were jealous of the births that they called "normal," and they monitored every topside birth involving Merman parentage.

"We have studied your petition with great care," Keel said. He glanced left and right at his fellow Committee members. They sat impassively, attention elsewhere—on the great curve of bubbly ceiling, on the soft living deck, on the records stacked in front of them—everywhere but on the petitioners. The dirty work was being left to Ward Keel.

If they only knew, Keel thought. *A higher Committee on Vital Forms has today passed judgment on me . . . as it will pass judgment on them, eventually.* He felt a deep compassion for the petitioners in front of him but there was no denying the judgment.

"The Committee has determined that the subject"—*not "the child,"* he thought—"is merely a modified gastrula . . ."

"We want this child!" The man fisted the rail that separated him from the Committee's high bench. The security guardians at the rear of the chambers came to attention. The woman continued to hum and sway, not in time with the music that came from her lips.

Keel leafed through a stack of plaz records and pulled out a sheet thick with figures and graphs.

"The subject has been found to have a nuclear construction that harbors a reagent gene," he reported. "This construction insures that the cellular material will turn on itself, destroying its own cell walls . . ."

"Then let us have our child until that death," the man blurted. He swiped at his face with the damp cloth. "For the love of humanity, give us *that* much."

"Sir," Keel said, "for the love of humanity I cannot. We have determined that this construction is communicable should there be any major viral invasion of the subject . . ."

"Our *child!* Not a subject! Our *child!*"

"Enough!" Keel snapped. Security moved silently into the aisle behind the Merman. Keel tapped the bell beside him and all stirring in the chamber ceased. "We are sworn to protect human life, to perpetuate life forms that are not lethal deviants."

The Merman father stared upward, awed at the invocation of these terrible powers. Even his mate stopped her gentle swaying, but a faint hum still issued from her mouth.

Keel wanted to shout down at them, "I am dying, right here in

41

front of you. *I* am *dying*." But he bit back the impulse and decided that if he were going to give in to hysteria he'd do it in his own quarters.

Instead, he said, "We are empowered to carry out measures in the extreme to see that humankind survives this genetic mess we inherited from Jesus Lewis." He leaned back and steadied the shaking in his hands and voice. "We are in no way refreshed by a negative decision. Take your woman home. Care for her . . :"

"I want one . . ."

The bell rang again, cutting the man short.

Keel raised his voice: "Usher! See these people out. They will be given the usual priorities. Terminate the subject, retaining all materials as stated in Vital Form Orders, subparagraph B. Recess."

Keel arose and swept past the other Committee members without a glance at the rest of the chambers. The grunts and struggles of the heartsick Merman echoed and re-echoed down the corridors of Keel's anguished mind.

As soon as he was alone in his office, Keel unstoppered a small flask of boo and poured himself a stiff shot. He tossed it back, shuddered and caught his breath as the warm clear liquid eased into his bloodstream. He sat in the special chair at his desk then, eyes closed, and rested his long, thin neck against the molded supports that took the weight of his massive head.

He could not make a lethal decision as he had done this morning without recalling the moment when he, as an infant, had come before the Committee on Vital Forms. People said it was not possible for him to remember that scene, but he did remember it—not in bits and sketches, but in its entirety. His memory went back into the womb, through a calm birth into a gloomy delivery room and the glad awakening at his mother's breast. And he remembered the judgment of the Committee. They had been worried about the size of his head and the length of his thin neck. Would prosthetics compensate? He had understood the words, too. There was language in him from some genetic well and although he could not speak until growth caught up with what had been born in him, he knew those words.

"This infant is unique," that old Chief Justice had said, reading from the medical report. "His intestines must have periodic implantation of a remora to supply missing bile and enzyme factors."

The Chief Justice had looked down then, a giant behind that

enormous and remote bench, and his gaze had fixed on the naked infant in its mother's arms.

"Legs, thick and stubby. Feet deformed—one-joint toes, six toes, six fingers. Torso overlong, waist pinched in. Face rather small in that . . ." the Justice cleared his throat, "enormous head." The Justice had looked at Keel's mother then, noting the extremely wide pelvis. Obvious anatomical questions had lain unspoken in the man's mind.

"In spite of these difficulties, this subject is not a lethal deviant." The words issuing from the Justice's mouth had all been in the medical report. Keel, when he came to the Committee as a member, fished out his own report, reading it with a detached curiosity.

"Face rather small . . ." These were the very words in the report, just as he remembered them. "Eyes, one brown and one blue." Keel smiled at the memory. His eyes—"one brown and one blue"—could peek around from the nearly squared edges of his temples, allowing him to look almost straight back without turning his head. His lashes were long and drooping. When he relaxed, they fuzzed his view of the world. Time had put smile wrinkles at the corners of his wide, thick-lipped mouth. And his flat nose, nearly a handsbreadth wide, had grown until it stopped just short of his mouth. The whole face, he knew from comparisons, was oddly pinched together, top to bottom, as though put on his head as an afterthought. But those corner-placed eyes, they were the dominant feature—alert and wise.

They let me live because I looked alert, he thought.

This was a thing he, too, sought in the subjects brought before him. Brains. Intelligence. That was what humankind required to get them out of this mess. Brawn and dexterity, too, but these were useless without the intelligence to guide them.

Keel closed his eyes and sank his neck even deeper into the cushioned supports. The boo was having its desired effect. He never drank the stuff without thinking how strange it was that this should come from the deadly nerve runners that had terrified his ancestors in the pioneer days of Pandora when real land protruded above the sea.

"Worm hordes," the first observers had called them. The worm hordes attacked warm life and ate out every nerve cell, working their way to the succulent brain where they encysted their clutches of eggs. Even dashers feared them. Came the endless sea, though,

43

and nerve runners retreated to a subsea vector whose fermentation by-product was boo—sedative, narcotic, "happy juice."

He fondled the small glass and took another sip.

The door behind him opened and a familiar footstep entered—. familiar swish of garments, familiar smells. He didn't open his eyes, thinking what a singular mark of trust that was, even for an Islander.

Or an invitation, he thought.

The beginnings of a wry smile touched the corners of his mouth. He felt the tingling of the boo in his tongue and fingertips. Now in his toes.

Baring my neck for the axe?

There was always guilt after a negative decision. Always at least the unconscious desire for expiation. Well, it was all there in the Committee's orders, but he was not fool enough to retreat into that hoary old excuse: "I was just obeying orders."

"May I get you something, Justice?" The voice was that of his aide and sometimes-lover, Joy Marcoe.

"No, thank you," he murmured.

She touched his shoulder. "The Committee would like to reconvene in quarters at eleven hundred hours. Should I tell them you're too . . . ?"

"I'll be there." He kept his eyes closed and heard her start to leave. "Joy," he called, "have you ever thought how ironic it is that you, with your name, work for this Committee?"

She returned to his side and he felt her hand on his left arm. It was a trick of the boo that he felt the hand melt into his senses—more than a touch, she caressed a vital core of his being.

"Today is particularly hard," she said. "But you know how rare that is, anymore." She waited, he presumed, for his response. Then when none came: "I think Joy is a perfect name for this job. It reminds me of how much I want to make you happy."

He managed a weak smile and adjusted his head in the supports. He couldn't bring himself to tell her about his own medical reports—the final verdict. "You do bring me joy," he said. "Wake me at ten-forty-five."

She dimmed the light when she left.

The mobile device that supported his head began to irritate the base of his neck where it pressed into the chair's supports. He inserted a finger under the chair's cushions and adjusted one of the contraption's fastenings. Relief on his left side was transmitted to irritation on the right. He sighed and poured another short dash of boo.

When he lifted the slender glass, the dimmed overhead light shot blue-gray sparkles through the liquid. It looked cool, as refreshing as a supportive bath on a hot day when the double suns burned through the clouds.

What warmth the tiny glass contained! He marveled at the curve of his thin fingers around the stem. One fingernail peeled back where he had snagged it on his robe. Joy would clip and bind it when she returned, he knew. He did not doubt that she had noted it. This had happened often enough, though, that she knew it did not pain him.

His own reflection in the curvature of the glass caught his attention. The curve exaggerated the wide spacing of his eyes. The long lashes drooping almost to the bend of his cheeks receded into tiny points. He strained to focus on the glass so close in front of him. His nose was a giant thing. He brought the glass to his lips and the image fuzzed out, vanished.

Small wonder that Islanders avoid mirrors, he thought.

He had a fascination with his own reflection, though, and often caught himself staring at his features in shiny surfaces.

That such a distorted creature should be allowed to live! The long-ago judgment of that earlier Committee filled him with wonder. Did those Committee members know that he would think and hurt and love? He felt that the often-shapeless blobs that appeared before his Committee bore kinship to all humanity if only they showed evidence of thought, love and the terribly human capacity to be hurt.

From some dim passageway beyond his doors or, perhaps, from somewhere deep in his own mind, the soft tones of a fine set of water-drums nestled him into his cushions and drowsed him away.

Half-dreams flickered in and out of his consciousness, becoming presently a particularly soothing full-dream of Joy Marcoe and himself rolling backward on her bed. Her robe fell open to the smooth softness of aroused flesh and Keel felt the unmistakable stirrings of his body—the body in the chair and the body in the dream. He knew it was a dream of the memory of their first exploratory sharing. His hand slipped beneath her robe and pulled the softness of her against him, stroking her back. That had been the moment when he discovered the secret of Joy's bulky clothes, the clothes that could not hide an occasional firm trim line of hips or thighs, the small strong arms. Joy cradled a third breast under her left armpit. In the dream of the memory, she giggled nervously as his wandering hand found the tiny nipple hardening between his fingers.

Mr. Justice.

It was Joy's voice, but it was wrong.

That was not what she said.

"Mr. Justice."

A hand shook his left arm. He felt the chair and the prosthetics, a pain where his neck joined the massive head.

"Ward, it's wake-up. The Committee meets in fifteen minutes."

He blinked awake. Joy stood over him, smiling, her hand still on his arm.

"Nodded off," he said. He yawned behind his hand. "I was dreaming about you."

A distinctive flush darkened her cheeks. "Something nice, I hope."

He smiled. "How could a dream with you in it be anything but nice?"

The blush deepened and her gray eyes glittered.

"Flattery will get you anything, Mr. Justice." She patted his arm. "After Committee, you have a call to Kareen Ale. Her office said she would arrive here at thirteen-thirty. I told them you have a full appointment sheet through . . ."

"I'll see her," he said. He stood and steadied himself on the edge of his desk console. The boo always made him a little groggy at first recovery. Imagine the medics giving him their death sentence and then telling him to knock off the boo! *Avoid extremes, avoid anxiety.*

"Kareen Ale takes advantage of her position to presume on your good nature and waste your time," Joy said.

Keel didn't like the way Joy exaggerated the Merman ambassador's name: "ah-*lay*." True, it was a difficult name to carry through the cocktail parties of the diplomatic corps, but the woman had Keel's complete respect on the debating floor.

He was suddenly aware that Joy was leaving.

"Joy!" he called. "Allow me to cook for you in quarters tonight."

Her back straightened in the doorway and when she turned to face him she smiled. "I'd like that very much. What time?"

"Nineteen hundred?"

She nodded once, firmly, and left. It was just the economy of movement and grace that endeared her to him. She was less than half his age, but she carried a wisdom about her that age ignored. He tried to remember how long it had been since he'd taken a full-time lover.

Twelve years? No, thirteen.

Joy made the wait that much more right in his mind. Her body was supple and completely hairless—something that excited him in ways he'd thought he'd forgotten.

He sighed, and tried to get his mind set for the coming meeting with the Committee.

Old farts, he thought. One corner of his mouth twisted up in spite of himself. *But they're pretty interesting old farts.*

The five Committee members were among the most powerful people on Vashon. Only one person rivaled Keel, with his position as Chief Justice—Simone Rocksack, the Chaplain/Psychiatrist, who commanded great popular support and provided a check on the power of the Committee. Simone could move things by inference and innuendo; Keel could order them done and they were done.

Keel realized, with some curiosity, that as well as he knew the Committee members, he always had trouble remembering their faces. Well . . . faces were not all that important. It was what lay behind the face that mattered. He touched a finger to his nose, to his distended forehead, and as though it were a magic gesture his hand called up a clear image of those other faces, those four old justices.

There was Alon, the youngest of them at sixty-seven. Alon Matts, Vashon's leading bioengineer for nearly thirty years.

Theodore Carp was the cynic of the group and, so Keel thought, aptly named. Others referred to Carp as "Fish Man," a product of both his appearance and his bearing. Carp *looked* fishlike. A sickly-pale, nearly translucent skin covered the long narrow face and blunt-fingered hands. The cuffs of his robe came nearly to the tips of his fingers and his hands appeared quite finlike at first glance. His lips were full and wide, and they never smiled. He had never been considered seriously for Chief Justice.

Not a political enough animal, Keel thought. *No matter how bad things get, you've got to smile sometime.* He shook his head and chuckled to himself. Maybe that should be one of the Committee's

47

criteria for passing questionable subjects—the ability to smile, to laugh . . .

"Ward," a voice called, "I swear you'll daydream your life away."

He turned and saw the other two justices walking the hallway behind him. Had he passed them in the hatchway and not noticed? Possibly.

"Carolyn," he said, and nodded, "and Gwynn. Yes, with luck I'll daydream my life away. Are you refreshed after this morning's session?"

Carolyn Bluelove turned her eyeless face up to his and sighed. "A difficult morning," she said. "Clear-cut, of course, but difficult . . ."

"I don't see why you go through a hearing, Ward," Gwynn Erdsteppe said. "You just make yourself uncomfortable, it makes us *all* uncomfortable. We shouldn't have to whip ourselves over something like that. Can't we channel the drama outside the chambers?"

"They have their right to be heard, and the right to hear something as irreversible as our decision from those who make it," he said. "Otherwise, what might we become? The power over life and death is an awesome one, and it should have all the checks against it that we can muster. That's one decision that should never be easy."

"So what are we?" Gwynn persisted.

"Gods," Carolyn snapped. She put her hand on Keel's arm and said, "Walk these two dottering old gods to chambers, will you, Mr. Justice?"

"Delighted," he said. They scuff-scuffed down the hallway, their bare feet hardly more than sighs on the soft deck.

Ahead of them, a team of slurry workers painted nutrient on the walls. This team used broad brushes and laid on vivid strokes of deep blue, yellow and green. In a week all the color would be absorbed and the walls returned to their hungry, gray-brown hue.

Gwynn positioned herself behind Keel and Carolyn. Her lumbering pace hurried them on. Keel was distracted from Carolyn's small talk by the constant lurch of Gwynn's hulk behind them.

"Do either of my fellow justices know why we're meeting just now?" he asked. "It must be something disturbing because Joy didn't reveal it when she told me about the appointment."

"That Merman this morning, he's appealed to the Chaplain/Psychiatrist," Gwynn snorted. "Why won't they leave it be?"

"Curious," Carolyn said.

It struck Keel as very curious. He had sat the bench for a full five years before a case had been appealed to the Chaplain/Psychiatrist. But this year . . .

"The C/P's just a figurehead," Gwynn said. "Why do they waste their time and ours on—"

"And hers," Carolyn interrupted. "It's a lot of work, being the emissary to the gods."

Keel shuffled quietly between them while they reopened the ages-old debate. He tuned it out, as he'd learned to do years ago. People filled his life too much to leave any time for gods. Especially now—this day when the life burning inside him had become doubly precious.

Eight cases appealed by the C/P in this season alone, he thought. *And all eight involved Mermen.*

The realization made him extremely interested in the afternoon meeting with Kareen Ale, which was to follow this appeals hearing.

The three justices entered the hatchway to their smaller chambers. It was an informational room—small, well-lit, the walls lined with books, tapes, holos and other communications equipment. Matts and the Fish Man were already watching Simone Rocksack's introductory remarks on the large viewscreen. She would, of course, use the Vashon intercom. The C/P seldom left her quarters near the tank that sustained Vata and Duque. The four protrusions that made up most of the C/P's face bent and waved as she talked. Her two eye protuberances were particularly active.

Keel and the others seated themselves quietly. Keel raised the back of his chair to ease the strain on his neck and its support.

". . . and further, that they were not even allowed to view the child. Is that not somewhat harsh treatment from a Committee entrusted with the sensitive care of our life forms?"

Carp was quick to respond. "It was a gastrula, Simone, purely and simply a lump of cells with a hole in it. There was nothing to be gained by bringing the creature into public view . . ."

"The *creature's* parents hardly constitute a public viewing, Mr. Justice. And don't forget the association of *Creator* and *creature.* Lest you forget, sir, I am a Chaplain/*Psychiatrist.* While you may

49

have certain prejudices regarding my religious role, I assure you that my preparation as a psychiatrist is most thorough. When you denied that young couple the sight of their offspring, you denied them a good-bye, a closure, a finality that would help them grieve and get on with their lives. Now there will be counseling, tears and nightmares far beyond the normal scope of mourning."

Gwynn picked up at the C/P's first pause.

"This doesn't sound like an appeal for the life form in question. Since that is the express function of an appeal, I must ask your intentions here. Is it possible that you're simply trying to go on record as establishing a political platform out of the appeals process?"

The nodules on the C/P's face retracted as if struck, then slowly re-emerged at the ends of their long stalks.

A good psychiatrist has a face you can't read, Keel thought. *Simone certainly fills the bill.*

The C/P's voice came on again in its wet, slurpy fashion. "I defer to the decision of the Chief Justice in this matter."

Keel snapped fully awake. This was certainly an unlikely turn of argument—if it was argument. He cleared his throat and gave his full attention to the screen. Those four nodules seemed to hunt out the gaze of both his eyes and fix on his mouth at the same time. He cleared his throat again.

"Your Eminence," he said, "it is clear that we did not proceed with this case in the most sensitive fashion. I speak for the Committee when I voice my appreciation for your candid appraisal of the matter. Sometimes, in the anguish of our task, we lose sight of the difficulty imposed upon others. Your censure, for lack of a better word, is noted and will be acted on. However, Justice Erdsteppe's point is well made. You dilute the appeals process by bringing before us matters that do not, in fact, constitute an appeal on behalf of a condemned lethal deviant. Do you wish to proceed with such an appeal in this case?"

There was a pause from the viewscreen, then a barely audible sigh. "No, Mr. Justice, I do not. I have seen the reports and, in this case, I concur with your findings."

Keel heard the low grumbling from Carp and Gwynn beside him.

"Perhaps we should meet informally and discuss these matters," he said. "Would that be to your liking, Your Eminence?"

The head nodded slightly, and the voice slurped, "Yes. Yes,

that would be most helpful. I will make arrangements through our offices. Thank you for your time, Committee."

The screen went blank before Keel could respond. Amid the mutterings of his colleagues he found himself wondering, *What the devil is she up to?* He knew that it must deal with the Mermen somehow, and the itch between his shoulder blades told him it was more serious than this conversation suggested.

We'll find out how serious soon enough, he thought. *If it's bad, the appointment will be for me alone.*

Ward Keel had done a little psychiatric study himself and he was not one to waste a skill. He resolved to be particularly attentive to detail when he met later with Kareen Ale. The C/P's intrusion coincided with the Merman ambassador's appointment too well—surely more than coincidence.

Actually, I think I'll cancel the appointment, he thought, *and make a few calls. This meeting had best be on my time, on my turf.*

How cruel of Ship to leave everything we need circling out of reach above us while this terrible planet kills us off one by one. Six births last nightside, all mutant. Two survive.

—Hali Ekel, the Journals

Feeling the warmth of the suns through the open hatch, Iz Bushka rubbed the back of his neck and shook himself. It was as close as he could let his body get to a shudder in the presence of Gallow and the other men of this Merman submersible crew.

Pride made me accept Gallow's invitation, Bushka decided. *Pride and curiosity—food for the ego.* He thought it odd that someone, even someone as egocentric as Gallow, would want a "personal historian." Bushka felt the need for caution all around him.

The Merman sub they occupied was familiar enough. He had visited aboard Merman subs before when they docked at Vashon. They were strange craft, all of their equipment hard and unforgiving—dials and handles and glowing instruments. As a historian, Bushka knew these Merman craft were not much different from those constructed by Pandora's first colonists before the infamous Time of Madness that some called the "Night of Fire."

"Quite a bit different from your Islander subs, eh?" Gallow asked.

"Different, yes," Bushka said, "but similar enough that I could run it."

Gallow cocked an eyebrow, as if measuring Bushka for a different suit. "I was on one of your Islander subs once," Gallow said. "They stink."

Bushka had to admit the organics that formed and powered Islander submersibles did give off a certain odor reminiscent of sewage. It was the nutrient, of course.

Gallow sat at the sub's controls to one side and ahead of Bushka, holding the craft steady on the surface. The space around them

52

was larger than anything Bushka had seen in an Islander sub. But he had to avoid bumping into hard edges. Bushka had already collected bruises from hatch rims, seat arms and the handles of compartment doors.

The sea was producing a long swell today, gentle by Islander standards. Just a little wash and slap against the hull.

They had not been long into this "little excursion," as Gallow called it, before Bushka began to suspect that he was in actual danger—ultimate danger. He had the persistent feeling that these people would kill him if he didn't measure up. And it was left to him to find out what "measuring up" might mean.

Gallow was planning some kind of revolution against the Merman government, that much was clear from the idle chatter. "The Movement," he called it. Gallow and his "Green Dashers" and his Launch Base One. "All mine," he said. It was so explicit and unmistakable that Bushka felt the ages-old fear that crept up on those who'd dared record history while it happened all down the ages. It had a sweaty side.

Gallow and his men were revealed as conspirators who had talked too much in the presence of an ex-Islander.

Why did they do that?

It was not because they truly considered him one of their own—too much innuendo indicated otherwise. And they didn't know him well enough to trust him, even as Gallow's personal historian. Bushka was sure of that. The answer lay there, obvious to someone of Bushka's training—all of that historical precedent upon which to draw.

They did it to trap me.

The rest of it was just as obvious. If he were implicated in Gallow's scheme—whatever that turned out to be—then he would be Gallow's man forever because it would be the only place he could go. Gallow did indeed want a captive historian in his service, and maybe more. He wanted to go down in history on his own terms. He wanted to *be* history. Gallow had made it clear that he had researched Bushka—"the best Islander historian."

Young and lacking some practical experience, that was how Gallow rated him, Bushka realized. Something to be molded. And there was the terrifying attractiveness of that other appeal.

"*We* are the true humans," Gallow said.

And point by point, he had compared Bushka's appearance to the *norm*, concluding: "You're one of us. You're not a Mute."

One of us. There was power in that . . . particularly to an Islander, and particularly if Gallow's conspiracy succeeded.

But I'm a writer, Bushka reminded himself. *I'm not some romantic character in an adventure story.* History had taught him how dangerous it was for writers to mix themselves up with their characters—or historians with their subjects.

The sub took an erratic motion and Bushka knew someone must be undogging the exterior hatch.

Gallow asked, "Are you sure that you could run this sub?"

"Of course. The controls are obvious."

"Are they, really?"

"I watched you. Islander subs have some organic equivalents. And I do have a master's rating, Gallow."

"GeLaar, please," Gallow said. He unstrapped himself from the pilot's seat, stood up and moved aside. "We are companions, Iz. Companions use first names."

Bushka slid into the pilot's seat at Gallow's gesture and scanned the controls. He pointed to them one by one, calling out their functions to Gallow: "Trim, ballast, propulsion, forward-reverse and throttles, fuel mixture, hydrogen conversion control, humidity injector and atmospheric control—the meters and gauges are self-explanatory. More?"

"Very good, Iz," Gallow said. "You are even more of a jewel than I had hoped. Strap in. You are now our pilot."

Realizing he had been drawn even further into Gallow's conspiracy, Bushka obeyed. The flutter in his stomach increased noticeably.

Again, the sub moved erratically. Bushka flicked a switch and focused a sensor above the exterior hatch. The screen above him showed Tso Zent and behind him, the scarred face of Gulf Nakano. Those two were living examples of deceptive looks. Zent had been introduced as Gallow's primary strategist "and of course, my chief assassin."

Bushka had stared at the chief assassin, taken aback by the title. Zent was smooth-skinned and schoolboy-innocent in appearance, until you saw the hard antagonism in his small brown eyes. The wrinkle-free flesh had that soft deceptiveness of someone powerfully muscled by much swimming. An airfish scar puckered at his neck. Zent was one of those Mermen who preferred the fish to the air tanks—an interesting insight.

Then there was Nakano—a giant with hulking shoulders and

arms as thick as some human torsos, his face twisted and scarred by burns from a Merman rocket misfiring. Gallow had already told Bushka the story twice, and Bushka got the impression that he'd hear it again. Nakano allowed a few wispy beard hairs to grow from the tip of his scarred chin; otherwise he was hairless, the burn scars prominent on his scalp, neck and shoulders.

"I saved his life," Gallow had said, speaking in Nakano's presence as though the man were not there. "He will do anything for me."

But Bushka had found evidence of human warmth in Nakano —a hand outstretched to protect the new *companion* from falling. There was even a sense of humor.

"We measure sub experience by counting bruises," Nakano had said, smiling shyly. His voice was husky and a bit slurred.

There was certainly no warmth or humor in Zent.

"Writers are dangerous," he'd said when Gallow explained Bushka's function. "They speak out of turn."

"Writing history while it happens is always dangerous business," Gallow agreed. "But no one else will see what Iz writes until *we* are ready—that's an advantage."

It had been at this point that Bushka fully realized the peril of his position. They had been in the sub, seventy klicks from the Merman base, anchored on the fringes of a huge kelp bed. Both Gallow and Zent had that irritating habit of speaking about him as though he were not present.

Bushka glanced at Gallow, who stood, back to the pilot's couch, peering out one of the small plazglas ports at whatever it was that Zent and Nakano were making ready out there. The grace and beauty of Gallow had taken on a new dimension for Bushka, who had marked Gallow's deep fear of disfiguring accidents. Nakano was a living example of what Gallow feared most.

Another chanted notation went into Bushka's "true history," the one he elected to keep only in his mind in the ages-old Islander fashion. Much of Islander history was carried in memorized chants, rhythms that projected themselves naturally, phrase by phrase. Paper was fugitive on the Islands, subject to rot, and where could it be stored that the container itself would not eat it? Permanent records were confined to plazbooks and the memories of chanters. Plazbooks were only for the bureaucracy or the very rich. Anyone could memorize a chant.

"GeLaar fears the scars of Time," Bushka chanted to himself. "Time is Age and Age is Time. Not the death but the dying."

If only they knew, Bushka thought. He brought a notepad from his pocket and scribbled four innocuous lines on it for Gallow's official history—date, time, place, people.

Zent and Nakano entered the cabin without speaking. Sea water slopped all around them as they took up positions in seats beside Bushka. They began a run-through on the sub's sensory apparatus. Both men moved smoothly and silently, grotesque figures in green-striped, skin-tight dive suits. "Camouflage," had been Gallow's response to Bushka's unasked question when he first saw them.

Gallow watched with quiet approval until the check-list had been run, then said, "Get us under way, Iz. Course three hundred and twenty-five degrees. Hold us just beneath wave turbulence."

"Check."

Bushka complied, feeling the unused power in the craft as he gentled it into position. Energy conservation was second nature to an Islander and he trimmed out as much by instinct as by the instruments.

"Sweet," Gallow commented. He glanced at Zent. "Didn't I tell you?"

Zent didn't respond, but Nakano smiled at Bushka. "You'll have to teach me how you do that," he said. "So smooth."

"Sure."

Bushka concentrated on the controls, familiarizing himself with them, sensing the minute responses transmitted from water to control surface to his hands. The latent power in this Merman craft was tempting. Bushka could feel how it might respond at full thrust. It would gulp fuel, though, and the hydrogen engines would heat.

Bushka decided he preferred Islander subs. Organics were supple, living-warm. They were smaller, true, and vulnerable to the accidents of flesh, but there was something addictive about the interdependence, life depending on life. Islanders didn't go blundering about down under. An Islander sub could be thought of as just big valves and muscle tissue—essentially a squid without a brain, or guts. But it gave a pulsing ride, soothing and noiseless—none of this humming and clicking and metal throbbing, none of these hard vibrations in the teeth.

Gallow spoke from close to Bushka's ear: "Let's get more moisture in the air, Iz. You want us all to dry out?"

"Here." Nakano pointed at a dial and alphanumerical readout above Bushka's head on the sloping curve of the hull. A red "21" showed on the air-moisture repeater. "We like it above forty percent."

Bushka increased humidity in gentle increments, thinking that here was another Merman vulnerability. Unless they became acclimated to topside existence—in the diplomatic corps or some commercial enterprise—Mermen suffered from dry air; cracked skin, lung damage, bloody creases in exposed soft tissues.

Gallow touched Zent's shoulder. "Give us the mark on Guemes Island."

Zent scanned the navigation instruments while Bushka studied the man furtively. What was this? Why did they want to locate Guemes? It was one of the poorest Islands— barely big enough to support ten thousand souls just above the lip of malnutrition. Why was Gallow interested in it?

"Grid and vector five," Zent said. "Two eighty degrees, eight kilometers." He punched a button. "Mark." The navigation screen above them came alight with green lines: grid squares and a soft blob in one of them.

"Swing us around to two hundred and eighty degrees, Iz," Gallow said. "We're going fishing."

Fishing? Bushka wondered. Subs could be rigged for fishing but this one carried none of the usual equipment. He didn't like the way Zent chuckled at Gallow's comment.

"The Movement is about to make its mark on history," Gallow announced. "Observe and record, Iz."

The Movement, Bushka thought. Gallow always named it in capital letters and frequently with quotation marks, as though he saw it already printed in a plazbook. When Gallow spoke of "The Movement," Bushka could sense the resources behind it, with nameless supporters and political influence in powerful places.

Responding to Gallow's orders, Bushka kicked the dive planes out of their locks, checked the range detectors for obstructions, scanned the trim display and the forward screen. It had become almost automatic. The sub glided into an easy descent as it came around on course.

"Depth vector coming up," Zent said, smiling at Bushka.

Bushka noted the smile in the reflections of the screens and made a mental note. Zent must know it irritated a pilot to read his instruments aloud that way without being asked. Nobody likes being told what they already know.

Cabin air getting sticky, Bushka noted. His topside lungs found the high humidity stifling. He backed off the moisture content, wondering if they would object to thirty-five percent. He locked on course.

"On course," Zent said, still smiling.

"Zent, why don't you go play with yourself?" Bushka asked. He leveled the dive planes and locked them.

"I don't take orders from writers," Zent said.

"Now, boys," Gallow intervened, but there was amusement in his voice.

"Books lie," Zent muttered.

Nakano, wearing the hydrophone headset, lifted one earphone. "Lots of activity," he said. "I count more than thirty fishing boats."

"A hot spot," Gallow said.

"There's radio chatter from the Island, too," Nakano reported. "And music. That's one thing I'll miss—Islander music."

"Is it any good?" Zent asked.

"No lyrics, but you could dance to it," Nakano said.

Bushka shot a questioning look at Gallow.

What did Nakano mean, he would miss Islander music?

"Steady on course," Gallow said.

Zent took over Nakano's headphones and said, "GeLaar, you said Guemes Islanders were damned near floating morons. I thought they didn't have much radio."

"Guemes has lost almost half a kilometer in diameter since I started watching it last year," Gallow said. "Their bubbly's starving. They're so poor they can't afford to feed their Island."

"Why are we here?" Bushka asked. "If they only have low-grade radio and malnutrition, what good are they to The Movement?" Bushka experienced a bad feeling about all this. A *very* bad feeling. *Are they trying to set me up? Make the Islander a patsy for some of their dirty work?*

"A perfect first demonstration," Gallow said. "They're traditionalists, hard-core fanatics. I'll give 'em credit for one piece of good sense. When other Islands suggest it might be time to move down under, Guemes sends out delegations to stop it."

Was that Gallow's secret? Bushka wondered. Did he want all the Islanders to stay strictly topside?

"Traditionalists," Gallow repeated. "That means they wait for us to build land for them. They think we like them so much we'll make them the gift of a couple of continents. Keep toting that rock, slapping that mud! Plant that kelp!"

The three Mermen laughed and Bushka smiled in response. He didn't feel like smiling at all, but there was nothing else to do.

"Things would go much easier if Islanders would learn to live the way we do," Nakano said.

"All of them?" Zent asked.

Bushka noted a growing tension as Nakano failed to respond to Zent's question.

Presently, Gallow said, "Only the right ones, Gulf."

"Only the right ones," Nakano agreed, but there was no force in his voice.

"Damned religious troublemakers," Gallow blurted. "You've seen the missionaries from Guemes, Iz?"

"When our Islands have been on proximate drifts," Bushka said. "Any excuse for visiting is a good one, then. Mixing and visiting is a happy time."

"And we're always pulling your little boats out of the sea or giving you a tow," Zent said. "For that you want us to keep slopping mud!"

"Tso," Gallow said, patting Zent's shoulder, "Iz is one of us now."

"We can't get this foolishness under control any too soon for me," Zent said. "There's no reason for anyone to live anywhere but down under. We're already set up."

Bushka marked this comment but wondered at it. He felt Gallow's hatred of Guemes but the Mermen were saying that everyone should live down under.

Everyone living as rich as the Mermen? There was some sadness to that thought. *What would we lose of the old Islander ways?* He glanced up at Gallow. "Guemes, are we . . . ?"

"It was a mistake to elevate a Guemian to C/P," Gallow said. "Guemians never see things our way."

"Island on visual," Zent reported.

"Half speed," Gallow ordered.

Bushka complied. He felt the reduction in speed as an easing of the vibration against his spine.

"What's our vertical relationship?" Gallow asked.

"We're coming in about thirty meters below their keel," Zent said. "Shit! They don't even have outwatchers. Look, no small boats at all ahead of their drift."

"It's a wonder they're still in one piece," Nakano said. Bushka caught a wry edge to the statement that he didn't quite understand.

"Set us directly under their keel, Iz," Gallow said.

What are we doing here? Bushka wondered as he obeyed the order. The forward display screen showed the bulbous lower extremity of Guemes—a thick red-brown extrusion of bubbly with starved sections streaming from it. Yes, Guemes was in bad condition. They were starving essential parts of their Island. Bushka inhaled quick, shallow breaths of the thick moist air. The Merman sub was too close for simple observation. And this was not the way you approached an Island for a visit.

"Drop us down another fifty meters," Gallow ordered.

Bushka obeyed, using the descent propulsion system and automatically adjusting trim. He felt proud that the sub remained straight and level as it settled. The upward display, set wide-angle, showed the entire Island as a dark shadow against the surface light. A ring of small boats dappled its edges like beads in a necklace. Bushka estimated that Guemes was no more than six klicks in diameter at the waterline. He put the depth at three hundred meters. Long strips of organics floated dreamlike in the currents around the Island. Entire bulkheads of bubbly blackened the surrounding water with dead-rot. Thatchings of thin membranous material patched the holes.

Probably spinnarett webbing.

Bushka saw raw sewage pumping out of a valve off to his right, sure evidence that the Guemes nutrient plant had suffered a major breakdown.

"Can you imagine how that place smells?" Zent asked.

"Very nice on a hot day," Gallow said.

"Guemes needs help," Bushka offered.

"And they're going to get it," Zent said.

"Look at all the fish around them," Nakano said. "I'll bet the fishing's real good right now." He pointed at the upward display as a giant scrubberfish, almost two meters long, floated past the

60

external sensor. Half of the fish's whiskers had been nibbled away and the one visible eye socket was empty and white.

"It's so rotten around here that even the scrapfish are dying," Zent said.

"If the Island's this sick, you can bet the people are in sad shape," Nakano added.

Bushka felt his face get red, and pressed his lips shut tight.

"Those boats all around, maybe they're not fishing," Zent said. "Maybe they're living on their boats."

"This whole Island is a menace," Gallow said. "There must be all kinds of diseases up there. There's probably an epidemic in the whole system of organics."

"Who could live in shit and not be sick?" Zent asked.

Bushka nodded to himself. He thought he had figured out what Gallow was doing here.

He's brought the sub in close to confirm their desperate need for help.

"Why can't they see the obvious?" Nakano asked. He patted the hull beside him. "Our subs don't need nutrient slopped all over them. They don't rot or oxidize. They don't get sick or make us sick . . ."

Gallow, watching the upward display, tapped Bushka's shoulder. "Down another fifteen meters, Iz. We still have plenty of room under us."

Bushka complied and again it was that smooth, steady descent that brought an admiring look from Nakano.

"I don't see how Islanders can live under those conditions." Zent shook his head. "Sweating out weather, food, dashers, disease—any one of a hundred mistakes that would send the whole pack of them to the bottom."

"They've made that mistake, now, haven't they, Tso?" Gallow asked.

Nakano pointed at a corner of the upward display. "There's nothing but some kind of membrane where their driftwatch should be."

Bushka looked and saw a dark patch of spinnarett webbing where the large corneal bubble should have been, the observer tucked safely behind it watching for shallows, coordinating with the outwatchers. No driftwatch—Guemes probably had lost its course-correction system, too. They were in terrible condition! Guemes would probably do anything for the offer of help.

"The corneal bubble has died," Bushka told them. "They've patched it over with spinnarett webbing to keep watertight."

"How long do they think they can drift blind before scraping bottom someplace?" Nakano muttered. There was anger in his voice.

"They're probably up there praying like mad for Ship to come help them," Zent sneered.

"Or they're praying for us to stabilize the sea and bring back their precious continents," Gallow said. "And now that we're getting it whipped, they'll be crying about bottoming out on the land we've built. Well, let 'em pray. They can pray to us!" Gallow reached over Zent's shoulder and flipped a switch.

Bushka scanned the displays—up, down, forward, aft the sub's complement of tools sprang out of their hull sheaths all glittering and sharp—deadly.

So that's what Zent and Nakano had been doing out there topside! Iz realized. They'd been checking manipulators and mechanical arms. Bushka scanned them once more: trenchers, borers, tampers, cutters, a swing-boom and the forward heliarc welder on its articulated arm. They gleamed brightly in the wash of the exterior lights.

"What are you doing?" Bushka asked. He tried to swallow but his throat was too dry in spite of the humidity.

Zent snorted.

Bushka felt repelled by the look on Zent's face—a smile that touched only the corners of his mouth, no humor at all in those bottomless eyes.

Gallow gripped Bushka's shoulder with a powerful and painful pressure. "Take us up, Iz."

Bushka glanced left and right. Nakano was flexing his powerful hands and watching a sensor screen. Zent held a small needle burner with its muzzle carelessly pointed at Bushka's chest.

"Up," Gallow repeated, emphasizing the order with increased pressure on Bushka's shoulder.

"But we'll cut right through them," Bushka said. He felt his breath pumping against the back of his throat. The awareness of what Gallow intended almost gagged him. "They won't have a chance without their Island. The ones who don't drown right away will drift in their boats until they starve!"

"Without the Island's filtration system, chances are they'll die of thirst before they starve," Gallow said. "They'd die anyway, look at them. Up!"

Zent waved the needle burner casually and pressed his left phone tighter to his ear.

Bushka ignored the needle burner's threat. "Or dashers will get them!" he protested. "Or a storm!"

"Hold it," Zent said, leaning toward his left earphone while he pressed it harder. "I'm getting free sonics of some kind . . . a sweeping pulse from the membrane, I think . . ." Zent screamed and tore the earphone from his head. Blood trickled from his nostrils.

"Take it up, damn you!" Gallow shouted.

Nakano kicked the locks off the dive planes and reached across Bushka to blow the tanks. The sub's nose tipped upward.

Bushka reacted with a pilot's instincts. He fed power to the drivers and tried to bring them onto an even keel but the sub was suddenly a live thing, shooting upward toward the dark bottom of Guemes Island. In two blinks they were through the bottom membranes and into the Island's keel. The sub kicked and twisted as its exterior tools hacked and slashed under the direction of Nakano and Gallow. Zent still sat bent over, holding his ears with both hands. The needle burner lay useless in his lap.

Bushka pressed hard against his seatback while he watched in horror the terrible damage being done all around. Anything he did to the controls only added to the destruction. They were into the Island center now, where the high-status Islanders lived, where they kept their most sensitive equipment and organics, their most powerful people, their surgical and other medical facilities . . .

The cold-blooded slashing of blades and cutters continued—visible in every screen, felt in every lurch of the sub. It was eerie that there could be this much pain and not a single scream. Soft, living tissue was no match for the hard, sharp edges that the sub intruded into this nightmare scene. Every bump and twist of the sub wrought more destruction. The displays showed bits and pieces of humanity now—an arm, a severed head.

Bushka moaned, "They're people. They're *people*."

Everything he'd been taught about the sanctity of life filled him now with rebellion. Mermen shared the same beliefs! How could they kill an entire Island? Bushka realized that Gallow would kill

63

him at the first sign of resistance. A glance at Zent showed the man still looking stunned, but the bleeding had stopped and he had recovered the burner. Nakano worked like an automaton, shuttling power where necessary as cutters and torches continued their awful havoc in the collapsing Island. The sub had begun to twist on its own, turning end for end on a central pivot.

Gallow wedged himself into the corner beside Zent, his gaze fixed on the display screens, which showed Island tissue melting away from the heliarcs.

"There is no Ship!" Gallow exulted. "You see! Would Ship allow a mere mortal to do such a thing?" He turned emotion-glazed eyes on Bushka at the controls. "I told you! Ship's an artifact, a thing made by people like us. God! There is no God!"

Bushka tried to speak but his throat was too dry.

"Take us back down, Iz," Gallow ordered.

"What're you doing?" Bushka managed.

"I challenge Ship," Gallow said. "Has Ship responded?" A wild laugh issued from his throat. Only Zent joined it.

"Take us down, I said!" Gallow repeated.

Driven by fear, Bushka's pilot-conditioned muscles responded, shifting trim ballast, adjusting planes. And he thought: *If we get out fast, some of this Island may survive.* Gently, he maneuvered the sub downward through the wreckage left by its terrible ascent. Plazports and screens showed the water around them dim with blood, a dull gray in the harsh illumination from the sub's exterior lights.

"Hold us here," Gallow ordered.

Bushka ignored the command, his gaze intent on the exterior carnage— inert bodies and pieces of bodies glimpsed in the murk. Raw horror everywhere around him. A little girl's dancing frock with white lace ruffles in an ancient pattern floated past a port. Behind it could be seen strung out the remnants of someone's pantry, half a lover's portrait pasted against a remnant stone box: outline of a smile without eyes. Beyond the sub's hot lights, blood rolled and streamed, a cold gray fog reaching down the currents.

"I said hold us here!" Gallow shouted.

Bushka continued to gentle the sub downward. A well of tears brimmed against his eyelids.

Don't let me cry! he prayed. *Dammit! I can't break down in front of these . . . these . . .* No word in his memory could label what his companions had become. This realization burned its change in him. These three Mermen were now lethal deviants. They would have to be brought before the Committee. Judgment must be made.

Nakano reached across Bushka and adjusted the ballast controls to bring the sub's descent to a stop. His eyes looked a warning.

Bushka looked at Nakano through a swim of tears, then shifted his gaze to Zent. Zent still held his left ear, but he watched Bushka steadily, smiling that cold-liver smile. His lips moved silently: "Wait till I get you topside."

Gallow reached across Zent's head to the heliarc controls.

"Take us straight ahead," he ordered. He snapped a polarized shield in place and sighted down the twin snouts of the bow heliarc.

Bushka reached to his shoulder and brought his chest harness into place, snapping it closed at his side. He moved with purpose, which brought a questioning stare from Zent. Before Zent could react, Bushka kicked loose the dive planes, skewed the control surfaces to starboard and blew the rear ballast tanks while he opened the bow valves. The sub surged over onto its nose and corkscrewed toward the bottom, spinning faster and faster. Nakano was thrown to the left by the force of the spin. Zent lost his needle burner while trying to grab for a support. His body was thrown against Gallow. Both men lay pinned between hull and control panels. Only Bushka, strapped in at the center of the spin, could move with relative ease.

"You damn fool!" Gallow shouted. "You'll kill us!"

His right hand moving across the switches methodically, Bushka snapped off the cabin lights and all but the exterior bow light. Outside the glow of that one beacon, darkness closed in, surrounding them with a gray murk in which only a few shreds of torn humanity drifted and sank.

"You're not Ship!" Gallow screamed. "You hear me, Bushka? It's just you doing this!"

Bushka ignored him.

"You can't get out of this, Bushka," Gallow shouted. "You'll have to come up sometime and we'll be there."

He's asking if I mean to kill us all, Bushka thought.

"You're crazy, Bushka!" Gallow shouted.

Bushka stared straight ahead, looking for the first glimpse of bottom. At this speed, the sub would dig in and make Gallow's warning come true. Not even plasteel and plaz could withstand a twisting dive into the rocky bottom, not at this depth and this speed.

"You going to do it, Bushka?" That was Nakano, voice loud but level and more than a little admiration in the question.

For answer, Bushka eased the angle of dive but kept the hard spin, knowing his Island-trained equilibrium could better withstand the violent motion.

Nakano began to vomit, gagging and gasping as he tried to clear his throat in the heavy centrifugal pressure. The stench became a nauseating presence in the cabin.

Bushka keyed his console for display of the sub's gas displacement. Notations showed ballast was blown with CO_2. His gaze traced out the linked lines. Yes . . . exhausted cabin air was bled into the ballast system . . . conservation of energy.

Gallow had subsided into a low growling protest while he struggled to crawl out against the force of the spin. "Not Ship! Just another damn shit-eater. Gonna kill him. Never trust Islander."

Following the diagram in front of him, Bushka tapped out the valving sequence on the emergency controls. Immediately, an oxygen mask dropped in front of him from an overhead compartment. All other emergency oxygen remained securely in place. Bushka pressed the mask to his face with one hand while his other hand bled CO_2 from the ballast directly into the cabin.

Zent began gasping.

Gallow moaned: "Not Ship!"

Nakano's voice gurgled and rasped but the words were clear: "The air! He's . . . going . . . to . . . smother us!"

Justice does not happen by chance; indeed, something that subjective may never have happened at all.
                                        —Ward Keel, Journal

Maritime Court did not go at all as Queets Twisp had expected. Killing a Merman in the nets had never been an acceptable "accident" at sea, even when all the evidence said it was unavoidable. The emphasis was always on the deceased and the needs of the surviving Merman family. Mermen were always reminding you of all the Islanders they saved every year with their pickup crews and search teams.

Twisp walked the long mural-distorted hallway out of the Maritime offices scratching his head. Brett almost skipped along beside him, a wide grin on his face.

"See?" Brett said. "I knew we were worried for nothing. They said it wasn't a Merman in our net—no Mermen lost, nobody that wasn't accounted for. We didn't drown anybody at all!"

"Wipe that grin off your face!" Twisp said.

"But Queets . . ."

"Don't interrupt me!" he snapped. "I had my face down there in the net—I saw the blood. Red. Dasher blood's green. Now, didn't it seem to you that they got us out of court too fast?"

"It's a busy place and we're small-time. You said that yourself." Brett paused, then asked, "Did you really see blood?"

"Too much for a few beat-up fish."

The hallway let them out into the wide third-level perimeter concourse with its occasional viewports opening out onto the surging sea and the spume flying past. Weather had said there was a fifty-klick wind today with chance of rain. The sky hung gray, hiding the one sun that had headed downward into the horizon, the other already gone.

Rain?

67

Twisp thought Weather had made one of its infrequent errors. His fisherman's sense said the wind would have to increase before any rain came today. He expected sunshine before sunset.

"Maritime has other things to do than worry about every small-time . . ." Brett broke off as he saw the bitter expression on Twisp's face.

"I mean . . ."

"I know what you mean! We're really small-time now. Losing that catch cost me everything: depth gear, nets, new stunshield charges, food, the scull . . ."

Brett was almost breathless trying to keep up with the older man's longer, firmer strides. "But we can make another start if . . ."

"How?" Twisp asked with a toss of one long arm. "I can't afford to outfit us. You know what they'll advise me in Fisherman's Hall? Sell my boat and go back to the subs as a common crewman!"

The concourse widened into a long ramp. They walked down without speaking and out onto the wide second-level terrace with its heavily cultivated truck gardens. Mazelike access lanes crooked their way to the high railing overlooking the wider first level. As they emerged, gaps began to appear in the overcast and one of Pandora's suns made liars out of the meteorologists at Weather. It bathed the terrace in a welcome yellow light.

Brett pulled at Twisp's sleeve. "Queets, you wouldn't have to sell the boat if you got a loan and—"

"I've got loans up to here!" Twisp said, touching his neck. "I'd just cleared my accounts when I brought you on. I won't go through that again! The boat goes. That means I have to sell your contract."

Twisp sat on a mound of bubbly at the rail and looked out over the sea. The wind-speed was dropping fast, just as he'd expected. The surge at the rim of the Island was still high but the spume shot straight up now.

"Best fishing weather we've had in a long time," Brett said.

Twisp had to admit this was true.

"Why did Maritime let us off so easy?" Twisp muttered. "We had a Merman in the net. Even you know that, kid. Something funny's going on."

"But they let us off, that's the important thing. I thought you'd be happy about it."

"Grow up, kid." Twisp closed his eyes and leaned back against the rail. He felt the cool water breeze against his neck. The sun was hot on his head. *Too many problems,* he thought.

Brett stood directly in front of Twisp. "You keep telling me to grow up. It looks to me like you could do some growing up yourself. If you'd only get a loan and—"

"If you won't grow up, kid, then shut up."

"It couldn't have been a tripod fish in the net?" Brett persisted.

"No way! There's a different feel. That was a Merman and the dashers got him." Twisp swallowed. "Or her. Up to something, too, from the look of things." Without changing his position against the rail, Twisp listened to the kid shift from foot to foot.

"Is that why you're selling the boat?" Brett asked. "Because we accidentally killed a Merman who was where he wasn't supposed to be? You think the Mermen will be out to get you now?"

"I don't know what to think."

Twisp opened his eyes and looked up at Brett. The kid had narrowed his overly large eyes into a tight squint, his gaze steady on Twisp.

"The Merman observers at Maritime didn't object to the court's decision," Brett said.

"You're right," Twisp said. He jerked a thumb upward toward the Maritime offices. "They're usually ruthless in cases like this. I wonder what we saw . . . or almost saw."

Brett moved to one side and plopped himself onto the bubbly beside Twisp. They listened for a time to the *thlup-thlup-thlup* of waves against the Island's rim.

"I expected to be sent down under," Twisp said. "And you with me. That's what usually happens. You go to work for the dead Merman's family. And you don't always come back topside."

Brett grunted, then: "They'd have sent me, not you. Everybody knows about my eyes, how I can see when it's almost dark. The Mermen would want that."

"Don't give yourself airs, kid. Mermen are damned cautious about who they let into their gene pool. They call us Mutes, you know. And they don't mean something nice when they say it. We're mutants, kid, and when we go down under it's to fill a dead man's dive suit . . . nothing else."

"Maybe they didn't want this job filled," Brett said.

Twisp tapped a fist on the resilient organics of the rail. "Or they didn't want anybody from topside to know what that Merman's job was."

69

"That's crazy!"

Twisp did not respond. They sat quietly for a while as the lone sun dipped lower. Glancing over his shoulder, Twisp stared at the horizon. It bent away in the distance to a bank of black sky and water. Water everywhere.

"I can get us outfitted," Brett said.

Twisp was startled but remained silent, looking at the kid. Brett, too, was staring off at the horizon. Twisp noticed that the boy's skin had become fisherman-dark, not the sickly pale he had displayed when he first boarded the coracle. The kid looked leaner, too . . . and taller.

"Didn't you hear me?" Brett asked. "I said—"

"I heard you. For somebody who pissed and moaned most of the time he was out there fishing, you sound pretty anxious to get back on the water."

"I didn't moan about—"

"Just joking, kid." Twisp raised a hand to stop the objections. "Don't be so damned touchy."

His face flushed, Brett looked down at his boots.

Twisp asked, "How would you get this loan?"

"My parents would loan it to me and I'd loan it to you."

"Your parents have money?" Twisp studied the kid, aware that this revelation did not surprise him. In all the time they'd spent together, though, Brett had never talked about his parents and Twisp discreetly had never asked. Islander etiquette.

"They're close to Center," Brett said. "Next ring out from the lab and Committee."

Twisp whistled between his teeth. "What do your parents do that gets them quarters at Center?"

Brett's mouth turned up in a crooked grin. "Slurry. They made their fortune in shit."

Twisp laughed in sudden awareness. "Norton! Brett Norton! Your folks are *the* Nortons?"

"Norton," Brett corrected him. "They're a team and they bill themselves as one artist."

"Shitpainting," Twisp said. He chuckled.

"They were the first," Brett said. "And it's nutrient, not shit. It's processed slurry."

"So your folks dig shit," Twisp teased.

"Come on!" Brett objected. "I thought I got away from that when I left school. Grow up, Twisp!"

"All right, kid," he laughed, "I know what slurry is." He patted the bubbly beside him. "It's what we feed the Island."

"It's not that simple," Brett said. "I grew up with it, so I know. It's scraps from the fish processors, compost from the agraria, table scraps and . . . just about everything." He grinned. "Including shit. My mother was the first chemist to figure out how to color the nutrient like they do now without hurting the bubbly."

"Forgive an old fisherman," Twisp said. "We live with a lot of dead organics, like the membrane on the hull of my coracle. Islandside, we just pick up a bag of nutrient, mix it with a little water and spread it on our walls when they get a little gray."

"Don't you ever try the colored stuff and make a few of your own murals on your walls?" Brett asked.

"I leave that to the artists like your folks," Twisp said. "I didn't grow up with it the way you did. When I was a kid, we only had a bit of graffiti, no pictures. It was all pretty bland: brown on gray. We were told they couldn't introduce other colors because that interfered with absorption by the decks and walls and things. And you know, if our organics die . . ." He shrugged. "How'd your folks stumble onto this?"

"They didn't stumble! My mother was a chemist and my father had a flair for design. They went out with a wall-feeding crew one day and did a nutrient mural on the radar dome near the slurry-side rim. That was before I was born."

"Two big historical events," Twisp joked. "The first shit painting and the birth of Brett Norton." He shook his head in mock seriousness. "Permanent work, too, because no painting lasts more than about a week."

Brett spoke defensively. "They keep records. Holos and such. Some of their friends have worked up musical scores for the gallery and theater shows."

"How come you left all that?" Twisp asked. "Big money, important friends . . . ?"

"You never had some bigshot pat you on the head and say, 'Here's our new little painter.'"

"And you didn't want that?"

Brett turned his back on Twisp so fast that Twisp knew the kid was hiding something. "Haven't I worked out well enough for you?" Brett asked.

"You're a pretty good worker, kid. A little green, but that's part of the bargain on a new contract."

Brett didn't respond and Twisp saw that the kid was staring at the Maritime mural on the inner wall of the second level. It was a big and gaudy mural aglow in the hard light of the setting sun—everything washed a fine crimson.

"Is that one of their murals?" Twisp asked.

Brett nodded without turning.

Twisp took another look at the painting, thinking of how easy it was these days to walk past the decorated hallways, decks and bulkheads without even noticing the color. Some of the murals were sharply geometric, denying the rounded softness of Islander life. Famous murals, ones that kept Norton in constant, high-priced demand, were the great historical pieces barely applied before they began their steady absorption toward the flat gray of hungry walls. The Maritime mural was something new in a Norton wall—an abstraction, a study in crimson and the fluidity of motion. It glowed with an internal power in the low light of the sun, seeming to boil and seethe along its rim like an angry creature or a thunderstorm of blood.

The sun lay almost below the horizon, throwing the sea's surface into the little dusk. A fine line of double light skittered across the top of the painting, then the sun dipped below the horizon and they were left with the peculiar afterglow of sunset on Pandora.

"Brett, why didn't your parents buy your contract?" Twisp asked. "With your eyesight, it seems to me you'd have made a fine painter."

The dim silhouette in front of Twisp turned, a fuzzed outline against the lighter background of the mural.

"I never offered my contract for sale," Brett said.

Twisp looked away from Brett, oddly moved by the kid's response. It was as though they suddenly had become much closer friends. The unspoken revelations carried a kind of cement, which sealed all of their shared experiences out on the water . . . out there where each depended on the other for survival.

He doesn't want me to sell his contract, Twisp thought. He kicked himself for being so dense. It wasn't just the fishing. Brett could get plenty of fishing after his apprenticeship with Queets Twisp. The contract had increased in value simply because of that apprenticeship. Twisp sighed. No . . . the kid did not want to be separated from a friend.

"I still have credit at the Ace of Cups," Twisp said. "Let's go get some coffee and . . . whatever . . ."

Twisp waited, hearing the little shufflings of Brett's feet in the growing dark. The Island's rimlights began their nightly duty— homing beacons for the time between suns. The lights started with a blue-green phosphorescence of wave tops, bright because the night was warm, then grew even brighter as the organics ignited. Out of the corners of his eyes, Twisp saw Brett wipe his cheeks quickly as the lights came up.

"Hell, we're not breaking up a good team, yet," Twisp said. "Let's go get that coffee." He had never before invited the kid to share an evening at the Ace of Cups, although it was well-known as a fisherman's hangout. He stood and saw an encouraging lift to Brett's chin.

"I'd like that," Brett said.

They walked quietly down the gangway and along the passages with their bright blue phosphorescence to light the way. They entered the coffeehouse through the wool-lined arch and Twisp allowed Brett a moment to look around before pointing out the really fancy feature for which the Ace of Cups was known throughout the Islands—the rimside wall. From deck to ceiling, it was solid wool, a softly curling karakul of iridescent white.

"How do they feed it?" Brett whispered.

"There's a little passageway behind it that they use for storage. They roll the nutrient on from that side."

There were only a few other early drinkers and diners and these paid little attention to the newcomers. Brett ducked his head slightly into his shoulder blades, trying to see everything without appearing to look.

"Why did they choose wool?" Brett asked. He and Twisp threaded their way through the tables to the rimwall.

"Keeps out noise during storms," Twisp said. "We're pretty close to the rim."

They took chairs at a table against the wall—both table and chairs made of the same dried and stretched membrane as the coracles. Brett eased himself into a chair gingerly and Twisp remembered the kid's first time in the coracle.

"You don't like dead furniture," Twisp said.

Brett shrugged. "I'm just not used to it."

"Fishermen like it. It stays put and you don't have to feed it. What'll you have?"

Twisp waved a hand toward Gerard, the owner, who lifted head and shoulders from the raised well behind the bar, a questioning look on his enormous head. Tufts of black hair framed a smiling face.

"I hear they have real chocolate," Brett whispered.

"Gerard will slip a little boo in it if you ask."

"No . . . no thanks."

Twisp lifted two fingers with the palm of his other hand over them—the house signal for chocolate—then he winked once for a dash of boo in his own. Presently, Gerard signaled back that the order was ready. All of the regulars knew Gerard's problem—his legs fused into a single column with two toeless feet. The proprietor of the Ace of Cups was confined to a Merman-made motorized chair, a sure sign of affluence. Twisp rose and went to the bar to collect their drinks.

"Who's the kid?" Gerard asked as he slid two cups across the bar. "Boo's in the blue." He tapped the blue cup for emphasis.

"My new contract," Twisp said. "Brett Norton."

"Oh, yeah? From downcenter?"

Twisp nodded.

"His folks are the shitpainters."

"How come everybody except me knew that?" Twisp asked.

"'Cause you keep your head buried in a fish tote," Gerard said. His ridged forehead drew down and his green eyes twinkled in amusement.

"It's a mystery whatever brought him out to fish," Twisp said. "If I believed in luck, I'd say he was bad luck. But he's a damned nice kid."

"I heard about you losing your gear and your catch," Gerard said. "What're you going to do?" He nodded toward where Brett sat watching them. "His folks have money."

"So he says," Twisp said. He balanced the cups for his return to the table. "See you."

"Good fishing," Gerard said. It was an automatic response and he frowned when he realized he'd said it to a netless fisherman.

"We'll see," Twisp said and returned to the table. He noted that the action of the deck underfoot had picked up slightly. *Could be a storm coming.*

They sipped quietly at their chocolate and Twisp felt the boo settling his nerves. From somewhere in the quarters behind the counter someone played a flute and someone else tapped out a back-up on water drums.

"What were you two talking about?" Brett asked.

"You."

Brett's face flushed noticeably under the dim lights of the coffeehouse. "What . . . what were you saying?"

"Seems everybody but me knew about you being from downcenter. That's why you don't like dead furniture."

"I got used to the coracle," Brett said.

"Not everybody can afford organics . . . or wants them," Twisp said. "It costs a lot to feed good furniture. And organics don't make the best small boats because they can go wild when they get into a school of fish. The subs are specially designed to prevent that."

Brett's mouth began to twitch into a smile. "You know, when I first saw your boat and heard you call it a coracle, I thought 'coracle' meant 'carcass.'"

They both laughed, Twisp a little unsteadily from the boo.

Brett stared at him. "You're drunk."

Mimicking Brett's tone, Twisp said, "Kid, I am getting dowright inebriated. I may even have another boo."

"My folks do that after an art show," Brett said.

"And you didn't like it," Twisp said. "Well, kid, I am not your folks—neither one of 'em."

A hooter went off just outside the Ace of Cups hatchway. The wall pulsed with the blast of sound.

"Wavewall!" Brett shouted. "Can we save your boat?" Brett was already up and headed out of the coffeehouse in a press of pale-faced fishermen.

Twisp lurched to his feet and followed, motioning to Gerard not to dog the hatch. The deck outside already was awash from a few low breakers. The passage was filled with people lurching and splashing toward hatchways. Twisp shouted at Brett's retreating back far up the passage, "Kid! No time! Get inside!"

Brett didn't turn.

Twisp found an extruded safety line and worked himself along it out onto the rim. Lights glared out there, throwing high contrast onto scurrying people, contorted faces. People were shouting all around, calling out names. Brett was out on the fishboat slip tossing equipment into the coracle's cubby and lashing it

75

down. As Twisp came up to him, Brett lashed a long line to the coracle's bow cleat. The wind howled across them now and waves were breaking over the outer bubbly of the slip, filling the normally protected lagoon with frothing white water.

"We can sink it and haul it up later!" Brett shouted.

Twisp joined him, thinking that the kid had learned this lesson from listening to some of the old-timers. Sometimes it worked and certainly it was the only chance they had to save the coracle. All along the slip, other boats had been sunk, their lines dipping down sharply. Twisp found a store of ballast rocks near the slip and began passing the heavy load to Brett, who tossed them into the boat. The five-meter craft was almost awash. Brett jumped in and lashed a cover over the ballast.

"Open the valves and jump!" Twisp yelled.

Brett reached under the load. A strong jet of water pulsed up from the bottom. Twisp reached a long arm toward Brett just as the wavewall itself swept over the lagoon and crashed into the side of the sinking coracle. Brett's outstretched fingertips grazed Twisp's hand as the coracle went under. The line to the bow, passing across Twisp's right arm, played out in a wet hiss. Twisp grabbed it, burning his palms, yelling: "Brett! Kid!"

But the lagoon was a boil of white rage and two other fishermen grabbed him and forced him, soaked and still shouting, down the passage and through the hatch into the Ace of Cups. Gerard, in his motorized chair, dogged the hatch against the incoming sea behind them.

Twisp clawed at the resilient wool. "No! The kid's still out there!"

Someone forced a warm drink of almost pure boo against his lips. The liquid gushed into his mouth and he swallowed. The liquor washed through him in a soothing blankness. But it did not drive away the tingle of Brett's fingertips grazing his own.

"I almost had him," Twisp moaned.

*Space is mankind's natural habitat. A planet, after all, is
an object in space. I believe humans have a natural drive to
be mobile in space, their true habitat.*
>   —Raja Thomas, the Histories

The image caught on the small stretched sheet of organics
was that of a silvery tube flying through the sky. The tube had no
wings or any other visible means of support. Only that orange
glow from one end, pale fire against the silver and blue of Pandora's sky. The process that had caught the image was fugitive
and the colors already had begun to fade.

Ward Keel was held as much by the beauty of it as by its unique
implications. Images made this way were a much-loved art form
among Islanders, relying on the light-sensitivity of organisms that
could be made to adhere in a thin layer on the stretched organics.
Pictures on this preparation formed by exposure through a lens
were admired as much for their fleeting existence as for their
intrinsic beauty. This image, however, in spite of its exquisite play
of colors and composition, was deemed by its creator to possess
holy significance.

Was that not Ship or an artifact from Ship?

The man was reluctant to part with his creation, but Keel used
the power of his position to silence argument. He did this kindly
and without hurry, relying chiefly on delay—long and convoluted
sentences with many references to trust and the well-being of the
Islands, frequent pauses and silent noddings of his massive head.
Both of them were aware that the picture was fading and before
long would be a flat gray surface ready for renewal and the capture of another image. The man left finally, unhappy but resigned—a thin, spindly-legged fellow with too-short arms. An
artist, though, Keel had to admit.

It was early on a warm day and Keel sat a moment in his robes, enjoying the breeze that played through the vent system in his quarters. Joy had straightened some of the rumpled disarray around him before leaving, smoothing the covers on his couch and arranging his clothing across a translucent plaz slingchair. The matching table surface in front of him still bore the remains of the breakfast she had fixed for them—squawk eggs and muree. Keel pushed the plate and chopsticks aside and put the stretched sheet with its odd image flat on the table. He stared at it a moment longer, thinking. Presently, he nodded to himself and called the chief of Inner-Island Security.

"I'll send a couple of people down in two hours," the man said. "We'll get right on it."

"Two hours is not getting right on it," Keel said. "The image will be almost faded out by then."

The deeply lined face on the viewscreen frowned. The man started to speak, then thought better of it. He rubbed his fleshy nose with a thick finger and lifted his gaze. The chief appeared to be reviewing data from a source out of Keel's sight.

"Mr. Justice," he said, presently, "someone will meet you in a few minutes. Where will you be?"

"In my quarters. I presume you know where that is."

The chief flushed. "Of course, sir."

Keel switched off, regretting his sharpness with Security. They were irritating, but his reaction had come from thoughts aroused by that fading image. It was a disturbing thing. The artist who had captured the image of that object in the sky had not taken it to the C/P. Evidence of Ship's return, the man thought, but he had taken it to the Chief Justice.

What am I supposed to do about it? Keel wondered. *But I didn't call the C/P, either.*

Simone Rocksack would resent this, he knew. He would have to call her soon, but first . . . a few other matters.

The water drum at his door thrummed once, twice.

Security here already? he wondered.

Taking the fading image of the thing in the sky, Keel walked through the hatchway into his main room, sealing off the kitchen area as he passed. Some Islanders resented those who ate privately, those whose affluence removed them from the noisy, crowded press of the mess halls.

At the entrance to his quarters he touched the sense membrane and the responsive organics expanded, revealing Kareen Ale standing in the arched opening. She gave a nervous start as she saw him, then smiled.

"Ambassador Ale," he said, momentarily surprised at his own formality. They had been Kareen and Ward off the debate floor for several seasons now. Something about her nervous posture, though, said this was a formal visit.

"Forgive my coming to your quarters without warning," she said. "But we have something to discuss, Ward."

She glanced at the image in his hand and nodded, as though it confirmed something.

Keel stood aside for her to enter. He sealed the door against casual entry and watched Ale choose a seat and sink into it without invitation. As always, he was conscious of her beauty.

"I heard about that," Ale said, gesturing at the stretched sheet of organics in his hand.

He lifted the image and glanced at it. "You came topside because of this?"

She held her face motionless for an instant, then shrugged. "We monitor a number of topside activities," she said.

"I've often wondered about your spy system," he said. "I am beginning to distrust you, Kareen."

"What is making you attack me, Ward?"

"This is a rocket, is it not?" He waved the image at her. "A *Merman* rocket?"

Ale grimaced, but did not seem surprised that Keel had guessed.

"Ward, I would like to take you back down under with me. Let's call it an instructional visit."

She had not answered his question but her attitude was sufficient admission. Whatever was going on, the Mermen wanted the mass of Islanders and the religious community left out of it. Keel nodded. "You're after the hyb tanks! Why was the C/P not asked to bless this enterprise?"

"There were those among us . . ." She shrugged. "It's a political matter among the leading Mermen."

"You want another Merman monopoly," he accused.

She looked away from him without answering.

"How long would this instructional visit require?" he asked.

She stood. "Perhaps a week. Perhaps longer."

"What subject matter will be covered by this instructional visit?"

"The visit itself will have to answer that for you."

79

"So I'm to prepare myself for an indefinite visit down under whose purpose you will not reveal until I get there?"

"Please trust me, Ward."

"I trust you to be loyal to Merman interests," he said, "just as I'm loyal to the Islanders."

"I swear to you that you will come to no harm."

He allowed himself a grim smile. What an embarrassment it would be to the Mermen if he died down under! And it could happen. The medics had been indefinite about the near side of the death sentence they had passed on Chief Justice Ward Keel.

"Give me a few minutes to pack my kit and turn over my more urgent responsibilities to others," he said.

She relaxed. "Thank you, Ward. You will not regret this."

"Political secrets always interest me," he said. He reminded himself to take a fresh tablet for his journal. There would be things to record on this instructional visit, of that he was certain. Words on plaz and chants in his memory. This would be action, not speculative philosophy.

A planet-wide consciousness died with the kelp and with it went the beginnings of a collective human conscience. Was that why we killed the kelp?
—Kerro Panille's Collected Works

Shadow Panille's thickly braided black hair whipped behind him as he ran down the long corridor toward Current Control. Other Mermen dodged aside as he passed. They knew Panille's job. Word already had spread through the central complex— unspecified trouble with a major Island. Big trouble.

At the double hatch of Current Control, Panille did not pause to regain his breath. He undogged the outer hatch, ducked through and sealed the outer latch with one hand while spinning the dog for the inner hatch with his other hand. Definitely against Procedural Orders.

He was into the hubbub of Current Control then, a place of low illumination. Long banks of instruments and displays glowed and flashed against two walls. CC's activity and the displays told him immediately that his people were in the throes of a crisis. Eight screens had been tuned to remotes showing dark blotches of sea bottom strewn with torn bubbly and other Island debris. Surface monitors scanned decrepit scatterings of small boats, all of them overcrowded with survivors.

Panille took a moment trying to assess what he saw. The small craft bobbed amidst a wide, oily expanse of flotsam. The few Islander faces he saw showed dull shock and hopelessness. He could see many injured among the survivors. Those able to move attempted to staunch blood flowing from jagged slashes in flesh. Some of the injured twisted and writhed from the effects of high-temperature burns. All of the small craft drifted nearly awash. One had been piled with bodies and pieces of bodies. An older woman with gray hair and stubby arms was being restrained in a

81

long coracle, obviously to prevent her from throwing herself into the sea. There was no sound with the transmission but Panille could see that she was screaming.

"What happened?" Panille demanded. "An explosion?"

"It may have been their hydrogen plant, but we're not sure yet."

That was Lonson, Panille's daywatch number two, at the central console. Lonson spoke without turning.

Panille moved closer to the center of activity. "Which Island?"

"Guemes," Lonson said. "They're pretty far out, but we've alerted Rescue and the pickup teams in their area. And as you can see we've lifted scanners from the bottom."

"*Guemes*," Panille said, recalling the last watch report. Hours away even with the fastest rescue subs. "What time are we estimating for arrival of the first survivors?"

"Tomorrow morning at the earliest," Lonson said.

"Dammit! We need foils, not rescue subs!" Panille said. "Have you asked for them?"

"First thing. Dispatcher said they couldn't be spared. Space Control has priority." Lonson grimaced. "They *would* have!"

"Easy does it, Lonson. We'll be asked for a report, that's sure. Find out if the first rescue team on the scene can spare people to interrogate the survivors."

"You afraid Guemes may have bottomed out?" Lonson asked.

"No, it's got to be something else. Ship! What a mess!" Panille's straight mouth drew into a tight line. He rubbed at the cleft in his chin. "Any estimate yet on the number of survivors?"

A young woman at the computer-record center said, "It looks like fewer than a thousand."

"Their last census was a little over ten thousand," Lonson said.

Nine thousand dead?

Panille shook his head, contemplating the monumental task of collecting and disposing of that many bodies. The bodies would have to be removed. They contaminated Merman space. And when they floated, they could only encourage dashers and other predators to new heights of aggression. Panille shuddered. Few things were more upsetting to Mermen than going out for a sledge job and running into dead, bloated Islanders.

Lonson cleared his throat. "Our last survey says Guemes was poor and losing bubbly around its rimline."

"That couldn't account for this," Panille said. He scanned the location monitor for the coordinates of the tragedy and the approaching lines of rescue craft. "Much too deep for them to have bottomed out. It must've been an explosion."

Panille turned to his left and walked slowly down the line of displays, peering over the shoulders of his operators. As he paused and asked for special views, operators zoomed in or back.

"That Island didn't just fall apart," Panille said.

"It looks as though it was torn apart and burned," an operator said. "What in Ship's teeth happened out there?"

"The survivors will be able to tell us," Panille said.

The main access behind Panille hissed open and Kareen Ale slipped through. Panille scowled at her reflection in a dark screen. Of all the dirty turns of fate! They had to send Ale for his first report! There had been a time when . . . Well, that was past.

She came to a stop beside Panille and swept her gaze along the display. Panille saw the shock sweep over her features as the evidence on the screens registered.

Before she could speak, he said, "Our first estimates say we'll have at least nine thousand bodies to collect. And the current is setting them into one of our oldest and largest kelp plantations. It'll be hell itself getting them out of there."

"We had a sonde report from Space Control," she said.

Panille's lips shaped into a soundless *ahhh-hah!* Had she been notified as a member of the diplomatic corps or as a new director of Merman Mercantile? And did it make any difference?

"We've been unable to tune in any sonde reports," Lonson said, speaking from across the room.

"It's being withheld," Ale said.

"What does it show?" Panille asked.

"Guemes collapsed inward and sank."

"No explosion?" Panille was more startled by this than by the revelation that the sonde report was being withheld. Sonde reports could be suppressed for many reasons. But Islands as big as Guemes did not just collapse abruptly and sink!

"No explosion," Ale said. "Just some kind of disturbance near the Island center. Guemes broke up and most of it sank."

"It probably rotted apart," the operator in front of Panille said.

"No way," Panille said. He pointed to the screens showing the maimed survivors.

"Could a sub have done that?" Ale asked.

Panille remained silent, shocked by the import of her question.

"Well?" Ale insisted.

"It could have," Panille said. "But how could such an accident . . ."

"Don't pursue it," Ale said. "For now, forget that I asked."

There was no mistaking the command in her voice. The grim expression on Ale's face added a bitterness to the order. It sent a pulse of anger through Panille. What had that suppressed sonde view shown?

"When will we get the first survivors in here?" Ale asked.

"About daybreak tomorrow," Panille said. "But I've asked for the first rescue team to assign interrogators. We could have—"

"They are not to report on an open frequency," Ale said.

"But—"

"We will send out a foil," she said. She crossed to the communications desk and issued a low-voiced order, then returned to Panille. "Rescue subs are too slow. We must act with speed here."

"I didn't know we had the foils to spare."

"I am assigning new priorities," Ale said. She moved back one step and addressed the room at large. "Listen, everyone. This has happened at a very bad time. I have just brought the Chief Justice down under. We are engaged in very delicate negotiations. Rumors and premature reports could cause great trouble. What you see and hear in this room must be kept in this room. No stories outside."

Panille heard a few muttered grumblings. Everyone here knew Ale's power, but it said something about the urgency of the situation that she would give orders on his turf. Ale was a diplomat, skilled at cushioning the distasteful.

"There're already rumors," Panille said. "I heard talk in the corridors as I came over."

"And people saw you running," Ale said.

"I was told it was an emergency."

"Yes . . . no matter. But we must not feed the rumors."

"Wouldn't it be better to announce that there's been an Island tragedy and that we're bringing in survivors?" Panille asked.

Ale moved close to him and spoke in a low voice. "We're preparing an announcement, but the wording . . . delicate. This is a political nightmare . . . and coming at such a time. It must be handled properly."

Panille inhaled the sweet odor of the scented soap Ale used, touching off memories. He pushed such thoughts aside. She was right, of course.

"The C/P is from Guemes," Ale reminded him.

"Could Islanders have done this?" he asked.

"Possibly. There's widespread resentment of Guemes fanaticism. Still . . ."

"If a sub did that," Panille said, "it was one of ours. Islander subs don't carry the hardware to do that kind of damage. They're just fishermen."

"Never mind whose sub," she said. "Who would order such an atrocity? And who would carry it out?" Ale once more studied the screens, an expression of deep concern on her face.

She's convinced it was a sub, Panille thought. *That sonde report must've been dangerously revealing. One of our subs for sure!*

He began to sense the far-reaching political whiplash. *Guemes! Of all places!* Islanders and Mermen maintained an essential interdependency, which the Guemes tragedy could disrupt. Islander hydrogen, organically separated from seawater, was richer and purer . . . and the impending space shot increased the demand for the purest hydrogen.

Movement visible through the plaz port drew Panille's dazed and wandering attention. A full squad of Mermen swam by towing a hydrostatically balanced sledge. Their dive suits flexed like a second skin, showing the powerful muscles at work.

Dive suits, he thought.

Even *they* were a potential for trouble. Islanders made the best dive suits, but the market was controlled by Mermen. Islander complaints about price controls carried little weight.

Ale, seeing where he directed his attention, and apparently divining his thoughts, gestured toward the new kelp planting visible out the plaz port. "That's only part of the problem."

"What?"

"The kelp. Without Islander agreement, the kelp project will slow almost to a stop."

"Secrecy was wrong," Panille said. "Islanders should've been brought in on it from the first."

"But they weren't," Ale said. "And as we expose more land masses above the surface . . ." She shrugged.

"The danger that Islands will bottom out increases," Panille said. "I know. This is Current Control, remember?"

"I'm glad you understand the political dangers," she said. "I hope you impress this upon your people."

"I'll do what I can," he said, "but I think it's already out of hand."

Ale said something too low for Panille to hear. He bent even closer to her. "I didn't hear that."

"I said the more kelp the more fish. That benefits Islanders, too."

Oh, yes, Panille thought. The movements of political control made him increasingly cynical. It was too late to stop the kelp project absolutely, but it could be slowed and the Merman dream delayed for generations. Very bad politics, that. No . . . the benefits had to be there for all to see. Everything focused on the kelp and the hyb tanks. First recover the hyb tanks from orbit, and then deal with the dreamers. Panille saw the practicalities, recognizing that politics must deal in the practical while speaking mainly of dreams.

"We'll do the practical thing," he said, his voice almost a growl.

"I'm sure you will," Ale said.

"That's what Current Control is all about," he said. "I understand why you emphasize the kelp project to me. No kelp—no Current Control."

"Don't be bitter, Shadow."

It was the first time since entering Current Control that she had used his first name, but he rejected the implied intimacy.

"More than nine thousand people died out there," he said, his voice low. "If one of our subs did it . . ."

"Blame will have to be placed squarely," she said. "There can be no doubts, no questions . . ."

"No question that *Islanders* did it," he said.

"Don't play games with me, Shadow. We both know there are many Mermen who will look upon the destruction of Guemes as a benefit to all Pandora."

Panille glanced around Current Control, taking in the intent backs of his people, the way they concentrated on their work while appearing not to listen to this charged conversation. They heard, though. It dismayed him that even here would be some who agreed with the sentiment Ale had just exposed. What had been up to now just late-night scuttlebut, café chatter and idle stories took on a new dimension. He felt this realization as an unwanted maturation, like the death of a parent. Cruel reality no longer could be ignored. It startled him to recognize that he had entertained dream fancies about the essential good will underlying human interactions . . . until just moments ago. The awakening angered him.

"I'm going to find out personally who did that," he said.

"Let's pray it was a horrible accident," she said.

"You don't believe that and neither do I." He sent his gaze across the awful testimony of those flickering screens. "It was a big sub—one of our S-twenties or larger. Did it dive deep and escape under the scattering layer?"

"There's nothing definite in the sonde report."

"That's what it did, then."

"Shadow, don't make trouble for yourself," Ale said. "I'm speaking as a friend. Keep your suspicions to yourself . . . no rumor-spreading outside this room."

"This is going to be very bad for business," he said. "I understand your concern."

She stiffened and her voice took on a coldly clipped quality. "I must go and get ready to receive the survivors. I will discuss this with you later." She turned on one heel and left.

The hatch sealed with a soft hiss behind him and Panille was left with the memory-image of her angry back and the sweet scent of her body.

Of course she had to go, he thought. Ale was a medic and every available medic would be called up in this emergency. But she was more than a medic. *Politics! Why did every political crisis have the stink of merchants hovering around it?*

Consciousness is the Species-God's gift to the individual.
Conscience is the Individual-God's gift to the species. In
conscience you find the structure, the form of consciousness,
the beauty.

—Kerro Panille, "Translations from
the Avata," the Histories

"She dreams me," Duque said. His voice came strongly
from the shadows at the edge of the great organic tub that he
shared with Vata.

A watcher ran to summon the C/P.

Indeed, Vata had begun to dream. They were specific dreams,
part her own memories, part other memories she inherited from
the kelp. Avata memories. These latter included human memories acquired through the kelp's hylighter vector, and other human memories gained he knew not how . . . but there was death
and pain involved. There were even Ship memories, and these
were strangest of all. None of this had entered a human awareness in quite this way for generations.

Ship! Duque thought.

Ship moved through the void like a needle through wrinkled
fabric—in at one place, out far away, and all in a blink. Ship once
had created a paradise planet and planted humans on its surface,
demanding:

"You must decide how you will WorShip me!"

Ship had brought humans to Pandora, which was not a paradise, but a planet almost entirely seas, and those waters moved by
the unruly cycles of two suns. A physical impossibility, had Ship
not done it. All this Duque saw in the flashing jerks of Vata's
dreams.

"Why did Ship bring its humans to me?" Avata had asked.

Neither humans nor Ship answered. And now Ship was gone

but humans remained. And the new kelp, that was Avata, now had nothing but a toehold in the sea and its dreams filled Duque's awareness.

Vata dreamed endlessly.

Duque experienced her dreams as vision-plays reproduced upon his senses. He knew their source. What Vata did to him had its own peculiar flavor, always identifiable, never to be denied.

She dreamed a woman called Waela and another called Hali Ekel. The Hali dream disturbed Duque. He felt the reality of it as though his own flesh walked those paths and felt those pains. It was Ship moving *him* through time and other dimensions to watch a naked man nailed to a crosspiece. Duque knew it was Hali Ekel who saw this thing but he could not separate himself from her experience. Why did some of the spectators spit on him and some weep?

The naked man raised his head and called out: "Father forgive them."

Duque felt it as a curse. To forgive such a thing was worse than demanding revenge. To be forgiven such an act—that could only be more terrible than a curse.

The C/P arrived in the Vata room. Even her bulky robes and long strides couldn't disguise the fine curves of her slim hips and ample breasts. Her body was doubly distracting because she was C/P, and because she was imprisoned inside that Guemian face. She knelt above Duque and the room immediately went silent except for the gurgle of the life-support systems.

"Duque," the C/P said, "what occurs?"

"It is real," Duque said. His voice came out strained and troubled. "It happened."

"What happened, Duque?" she asked.

Duque sensed a voice far away, much farther away than the Hali Ekel dream. He felt Hali's distress, he felt the ancient flesh she wore for Ship's excursion to that hill of terrible crosses; he felt Hali's puzzlement.

Why were they doing this thing? Why did Ship want me to see this?

Duque felt both questions as his own. He had no answers.

The C/P repeated her demand: "What happened, Duque?"

The faraway voice was an insect buzzing in his ear. He wanted to slap it.

"Ship," he said.

A gasp arose from the watchers, but the C/P did not move.

"Is Ship returning?" the C/P asked.

The question enraged Duque. He wanted to concentrate on the Hali Ekel dream. If only they would leave him alone, he felt he might find answers to his questions.

The C/P raised her voice: "Is Ship returning, Duque? You must answer!"

"Ship is everywhere!" Duque shouted.

His shout extinguished the Hali Ekel dream completely.

Duque felt anguish. He had been so close! Just a few more seconds . . . the answers might have come.

Now, Vata dreamed a poet named Kerro Panille and the young Waela woman of that earlier dream. Her face merged with drifting kelp, but her flesh was hot against Panille's flesh and their orgasm shuddered through Duque, driving away all other sensations.

The C/P turned her protuberant red eyes toward the watchers. Her expression was stern.

"You must say nothing of this to anyone," she ordered.

They nodded agreement, but already some among them were speculating on who might share this revelation—just one trusted friend or lover. It was too great a thing to contain.

Ship was everywhere!

Was Ship in this very room in some mysterious way?

This thought had occurred to the C/P and she asked it of Duque, who lay half somnolent in postcoital relaxation.

"Everywhere is everywhere," Duque muttered.

The C/P could not question such logic. She peered fearfully around her into the shadows of the Vata room. The watchers copied her questioning examination of their surroundings. Remembering the utterance that had been repeated to her when she had been summoned, the C/P asked: "Who dreams you, Duque?"

"Vata!"

Vata stirred sluggishly and the murky nutrient rippled around her breasts.

The C/P bent close to one of Duque's bulbous ears and spoke so low that only the closest watchers heard and some of them did not hear it correctly.

"Does Vata waken?"

"Vata dreams me," Duque moaned.

"Does Vata dream of Ship?"

"Yesssss." He would tell them anything if only they would go away and leave him to these terrible and wonderful dreams.

"Does Ship send us a message?" the C/P asked.

"Go away!" Duque screamed.

The C/P rocked back on her heels. "Is that Ship's message?" Duque remained silent.

"Where would we go?" the C/P asked.

But Duque was caught up in Vata's birth-dream and the moaning voice of Waela, Vata's mother: "My child will sleep in the sea."

Duque repeated it.

The C/P groaned. Duque had never before been this specific.

"Duque, does Ship order us to go down under?" she demanded.

Duque remained silent. He was watching the shadow of Ship darken a bloody plain, hearing Ship's inescapable voice: "I travel the Ox Gate!"

The C/P repeated her question, her voice almost a moan. But the signs were clear. Duque had spoken his piece and would not respond further. Slowly, stiffly the C/P lifted herself to her feet. She felt old and tired, far beyond her thirty-five years. Her thoughts flowed in confusion. What was the meaning of this message? It would have to be considered with great care. The words had seemed so clear . . . yet, might there not be another explanation?

Are we Ship's child?

That was a weighty question.

Slowly, she cast her gaze across the awed watchers. "Remember my orders!"

They nodded, but within only a few hours, it was all over Vashon: Ship had returned. Vata was awakening. Ship had ordered them all to go down under.

By nightfall, sixteen other Islands had the message via radio, some in garbled form. The Mermen, having overheard some of the radio transmissions, had questioned their people among the Vata watchers and sent a sharp query to the C/P.

"Is it true that Ship has landed on Pandora near Vashon? What is this talk of Ship ordering the Islanders to migrate down under?"

There was more to the Merman query but C/P Rocksack, realizing that Vata security had been breached, invested herself in her most official dignity and answered just as sharply.

"All revelations concerning Vata require the most careful consideration and lengthy prayer by the Chaplain/Psychiatrist. When there is a need for you to know, you will be told."

It was quite the curtest response she had ever made to the Mermen, but the nature of Duque's words had upset her and the tone of the Merman message had been almost, but not quite, of a nature to bring down her official reprimand. The appended Merman observations she had found particularly insulting. Of course she knew there could be no swift and complete migration of Islanders down under! It was physically impossible, not to mention psychologically inadvisable. This, more than anything else, had told her that Duque's words required another interpretation. And once more she marveled at the wisdom of the ancestors in combining the functions of chaplain with those of psychiatrist.

They that go down to the sea in ships,
That do business in great waters;
These see the works of the Lord,
And his wonders in the deep.
                    —The Christian Book of the Dead

As he fell from the pier, the coracle's bowline whipping around his left ankle, Brett knew he was going under. He pumped in one quick breath before hitting the water. His hands clawed frantically for something to hold him up and he felt Twisp's hand rasp beneath his fingers but there was nothing to grip. The coracle, an anchor dragging him down, hit a submerged ledge of bubbly and upended, kicking him toward the center of the lagoon and, for a moment, he thought he was saved. He surfaced about ten meters from the pier and, over the howl of the hooters, he heard Twisp calling to him. The Island was receding fast and Brett realized the coracle's bowline had broken free of the dockside cable. He hauled in as much air as his lungs could grab and felt the line on his ankle pull him toward the Island. Doubling over underwater, he tried to free himself, but the line had tangled in a knot and his weight was enough to tug the coracle off the bubbly below the pier. He felt the line whip taut, dragging him down.

A warning rocket painted the water over him bloody orange. The surface appeared flat, the momentary calm ahead of a wavewall. Roiling water rolled him, the line on his ankle pulled steadily and he felt the pressure increase through his nose and across his chest.

I'm going to drown!

He opened his eyes wide, amazed suddenly at the clarity of his underwater vision—even better than his night vision. Dark blues and reds dominated his surroundings. The ache in his lungs increased. He held the breath tight, not wanting to let go of that last touch with life, not wanting that first gulp of water and the choking death behind it.

I always thought it would be a dasher.

The first trickle of bubbles squeezed past his lips. Panic began to pulse through him. A gush of urine warmed his crotch. He twisted his head, seeing the glow of the urine against him holding back the cold press of the sea.

I don't want to die!

His superb underwater vision followed the leak of bubbles upward, tracing them toward the distant surface, which was no longer a visible plane but only a hopeless memory.

In that instant, when he *knew* all hope was gone, a corner of his vision caught a dark flash, a flicker of shadow against shadow. He turned his head toward it and saw a woman swimming below him, her dive-suited flesh looking unclothed. She turned, something in her hand. Abruptly, the line of his ankle jerked once, then released.

Merman!

She rolled beneath him and he saw her eyes, open and white against a dark face. She slipped a knife into her leg sheath while she moved upward toward him.

The trickle of bubbles from his mouth became a stream, driving out of his mouth in a hot release. The woman grabbed him under an armpit and he saw clearly that she was young and supple, superbly muscled for swimming. She rolled over him. A white flash of oxygen despair began at the back of his head. Then she slammed her mouth against his and blew the sweet breath of life down his throat.

He savored it, exhaled, and again she blew a breath into him. He saw the airfish against her neck and knew she was giving him the half-used excess that her blood exuded into her lungs. It was a thing Islanders heard about, a Merman thing that he'd never expected to experience.

She backed off, dragging him by one arm. He exhaled slowly, and again she fed him air.

A Merman team had been working an undersea ridge, he saw, with kelp waving high beside it and lights glowing at the rocky top—small guide markers.

As panic receded, he saw that his rescuer wore a braided line around her waist with weights attached to it. The airfish trailing backward from her neck was pale and darkly veined, deep ridges along its length for the external gills. It was an ugly contrast to the young woman's smooth dark skin.

His lungs ceased aching, but his ears hurt. He shook his head, pulling at an ear with his free hand. She saw the movement and squeezed his arm hard to get his attention. She plugged her nose with her fingers and mimicked blowing hard. She pointed at his nose and nodded. He copied her and his right ear popped with a *snap*. An unpleasant fullness replaced the pain. He did it again and the left ear went.

When she gave him his next breath, she clung to him a bit longer, then smiled broadly when she broke away. A flooding sensation of happiness washed through Brett.

I'm alive! I'm alive!

He glanced past the airfish at the way her feet kicked so steadily, the strong flow of her muscles under the skin-tight suit. The light markers on the rocky ridge swept past.

Abruptly, she pulled back on his arm and stopped him beside a shiny metal tube about three meters long. He saw handgrips on it, a small steering rudder and jets. He recognized it from holos—a Merman horse. She guided his hand to one of the rear grips and gave him another breath. He saw her release a line at the nose of the device, then swing astraddle of it. She glanced backward and waved for him to do the same. He did so, locking his legs around the cold metal, both hands on the grips. She nodded and did something at the nose. Brett became conscious of a faint hum against his legs. A light glowed ahead of the woman and something snaky extruded from the horse. She turned and brought a breather mouthpiece against his lips. He saw that she also was wearing one and realized she was easing the double load the airfish had been forced to carry. The fish trailing from her neck and over his own shoulder appeared smaller, the gill ridges deeper and not as fat.

Brett gripped the mouthpiece in his teeth and pushed the lip cover hard against the flesh.

In by the mouth, out by the nose.

Every Islander had some sub schooling and parallel training with Merman rescue equipment.

Blow, inhale.

His lungs filled with rich, cool air.

He felt a lurch then and something bumped his left ankle. She rapped his knee and pulled him closer to her back, lifting his handgrips until they formed a brace against her buttocks. He had never seen a naked woman before and her dive suit left nothing for him to imagine. Unromantic as the situation was, he liked her body very much.

The horse surged upward, then dived, and her hair streamed backward, covering the head of the airfish and flickering against his cheeks.

He stared through a haze of her hair and over her right shoulder, feeling the water tumble around them. Far down the tunneling shadows of the sea past the smooth shoulder he saw a dazzling play of lights—uncounted lights—big ones, small ones, wide ones. Shapes began to grow visible: walls and towers, fine planes of platforms, dark passages and caves. The lights became plaz windows and he realized he was descending onto a Merman metropolis, one of the major centers. It had to be, with that much sprawl and that much light. The dance of illumination enthralled him, feeding through his mutated vision a rapture he had not known himself capable of feeling. A part of his awareness said this came from knowing he had survived overwhelming odds, but another part of him gloried in the new things his peculiar eyes could see.

Cross-currents began to turn and twist the horse. Brett had trouble holding his position; once he lost his leg grip. His rescuer felt this and reached back to guide one of his hand around her waist. Her feet came back and locked onto his. She crouched over her controls, guiding them toward a sprawling assemblage of blocks and domes.

His hands against her abdomen felt the smooth warmth there. His own clothing seemed suddenly ridiculous and he understood the Merman preference for dive suits and undersea nudity for the first time. They wore Islander-made dive suits for long, cold work, but their skin served them well for short spurts or warmer currents. Brett's pants chafed his thighs and cramped him, whipping in the currents of their passage.

They were much closer to the complex of buildings now and Brett began to have a new idea of the structures' sizes. The closest tower faded out of sight above them. He tried to trace it into the upper distances and realized that night had fallen topside.

We can't be very far down, he thought. *That tower could break the surface!*

But no one topside had reported such a structure.

Ship save us if an Island ever hit such a thing!

Lights from the buildings provided him with more than enough illumination, but he wondered how his rescuer was finding her way in what he knew to be deep darkness for ordinary human vision. He saw then that she was guided by fixed lights anchored to the bottom—lanes of red and green.

Even the darkest topside night had never kept him from moving around easily, but here the surface was just a faraway bruise. Brett drew a deep breath from the tube and settled himself closer to the young woman. She patted his hand on her stomach while jockeying the machine into a maze of steep-sided canyons. They rounded a corner and came onto a wide, well-lighted space between tall buildings. A dome structure loomed straight ahead with docking lips extruded from it. Many people swam in the bright illumination that glared all along the lips. Brett saw the on-off blink of a bank of hatchways opening and closing to pass the swimmers. His rescuer settled them onto a ramp with only a small sensation of grating. A Merman behind them took the horse by a rear handhold. The young woman motioned for Brett to take a deep breath. He obeyed. She gently pulled the breather from him, removed her airfish and caged it with others beside the hatch.

Through the hatch they went into a chamber where the water was quickly flushed out and replaced by air. Brett found himself standing in a dripping puddle facing the young woman, who shed water as though she and her translucent suit had been oiled.

"My name is Scudi Wang," she said. "What is yours?"

"Brett Norton," he said. He laughed self-consciously. "You . . . you saved my life." The statement sounded so ridiculously inadequate that he laughed again.

"It was my watch for search and rescue," she said. "We're always extra alert during a wavewall if we're near an Island."

He had never heard of such a thing but it sounded reasonable. Life was precious and his view of the world said everyone felt the same, even Mermen.

"You *are* wet," she said, looking him down and up. "Are there people who should know you are alive?"

Alive! The thought made his breathing quicken. *Alive!*

"Yes," he said. "Is it possible to get word topside?"

"We'll see to it after you're settled. There are formalities."

Brett noticed that she'd been staring at him much the same way he'd been intent on her. He guessed her age at close to his own—

97

fifteen or sixteen. She was small, small-breasted, her skin as dark as a topside tan. She stared at him calmly out of green eyes with golden flecks in them. Her pug nose gave her a gamin look—the look of wide-eyed corridor orphans back on Vashon. Her shoulders were sloping and muscular, the muscles of someone who kept in top shape. The airfish scar glowed at her neck, a livid pink against the dark wash of her wet black hair.

"You are the first Islander I've ever rescued," she said.

"I'm . . ." He shook his head, finding that he did not know how to thank her for such a thing. He finished lamely: "Where are we?"

"Home," she said with a shrug. "I live here." She dropped her ballast belt at the jerk of a knot and slung it over a shoulder. "Come with me. I'll get us both some dry clothes."

He slopped after her through a hatch, his pants dripping a trail of wetness. It was cold in the long passage where the hatchway left them, but he was not too cold to miss the pleasant bounce of Scudi Wang's body as she walked away from him. He hurried to catch up. The passage was disturbingly strange to an Islander—solid underfoot, solid walls lighted by long tubes of fluorescence. The walls glowed a silvery gray broken by sealed hatches with colored symbols on them—some green, some yellow, some blue.

Scudi Wang stopped at a blue-coded hatch, undogged it and led him into a large room with storage lockers lining the sides. Benches in four rows took up the middle. Another hatch led out the opposite side. She opened a storage locker and tossed him a blue towel, then bent to rummage through another locker where she found a shirt and pants, holding them up while she looked at Brett. "These'll probably fit. We can replace them later." She tossed the faded green pants onto the bench in front of him along with a matching pullover shirt. Both were a light material that Brett didn't recognize.

Brett dried his face and hair. He stood there indecisively, his clothes still dripping. Mermen paid little attention to nudity, he had been told, but he was not used to being unclothed . . . much less in the company of a beautiful young woman.

She removed her dive suit unselfconsciously, found a singlesuit of light blue in another locker and sat down to pull it over her body, drying herself with a towel. He stood up, looking down at her, unable to avoid staring.

How can I thank her? he wondered. *She seems so casual about saving my life*. Actually, she seemed casual about everything. He continued to stare at her and blushed when he felt the tightening erection beginning in his cold wet pants. Wasn't there a partition or something where he could get out of sight and dress? He glanced around the room. Nothing.

She saw him looking around and chewed her lower lip.

"I'm sorry," she said. "I forgot. They say Islanders are peculiarly modest. Is that true?"

His blush deepened. "Yes."

She pulled her singlesuit up and zipped it closed quickly. "I will turn around," she said. "When you have dressed, we will eat."

Scudi Wang's quarters were the same silvery gray as the passages, a space about four meters by five, everything squared corners and sharp edges alien to an Islander. Two cot-sized bedsettees extruded from the walls, both covered with blankets of bright red and yellow in swirling geometric patterns. A kitchen counter occupied one end of the room and a closet the other. A hatch beside the closet stood open to show a bath with a small immersion tub and shower. Everything was the same material as the walls, deck and ceiling. Brett ran a hand across one of the walls and felt the cold rigidity.

Scudi found a green cushion under one of the cots and tossed it onto the other cot. "Be comfortable," she said. She threw a switch on the wall beside the kitchen counter and odd music filled the room.

Brett sat down on the cot expecting it to be hard, but it gave way beneath him, surprisingly resilient. He leaned against the cushion. "What is that music?"

She turned from an open cupboard. "Whales. You have heard of them?"

He looked toward the ceiling. "They're on the hyb tank roster, I've heard. A giant earthside mammal that lives down under."

She nodded toward the small speaker grill above the switch. "Their song is most pleasant. I'll enjoy listening to them when we recover them from space."

Brett, listening to the grunts and whistles and thrills, felt their calming influence like a long fetch of waves in a late afternoon. He failed to focus immediately on what she had said. In spite of the whalesong, or perhaps because of it, there was a sense of deep quiet in the room that he had never before experienced.

"What do you do topside?" Scudi asked.

"I'm a fisherman."

"That's good," she said, busying herself at the counter. "It puts you on the waves. Waves and currents, that's how we generate our power."

"So I've heard," he said. "What do you do—besides rescues?"

"I mathematic the waves," she said. "That is my true work."

Mathematic the waves? He had no idea what that meant. It forced him to reflect on how little he knew about Merman life. Brett glanced around the room. The walls were hard but he was mistaken about the cold. They were warm, unlike the locker-room walls. Scudi, too, did not seem cold. As she had led him here along the solid passages, they had passed many people. Most had nodded greeting as they chattered with friends or workmates. Everyone moved quickly and surely and the passageways weren't full of people jostling shoulder-to-shoulder all the way. Except for workbelts, many had been naked. None of that outside bustle penetrated to this little room, though. He contrasted this to topside, where the organics tended to transmit even the smallest noises. Here, there was the luxury of noise and the luxury of quiet within a few meters of each other.

Scudi did something above her work area and the room's walls suddenly were brightly colored in flowing sweeps of yellow and green. Long strands of something like kelp undulated in a current—an abstraction. Brett was fascinated at how the color-motion on the walls accompanied the whalesong.

What do I say to her? he wondered. *Alone with a pretty girl in her room and I can't think of anything. Brilliant, Norton! You're a glittering conversationalist!*

He wondered how long he'd been with her. Topside, he kept good track of time by the light of the suns and the dark patches between. Down here, all light was similar. It was disorienting.

He looked at Scudi's back while she worked. She pressed a wall button and he heard her murmur something on a Merman transphone. Seeing the phone there impressed him with the technological gulf between Islanders and Mermen. Mermen had this device; Islanders were not offered it in the mercantile. He didn't doubt that some Islanders got them through the black market, but he didn't know how it would be of any use to them unless they dealt with Mermen all the time. Some Islanders did. Islander sub crews carried portable devices that picked up some transphone channels, but this was for the Mermen's convenience as well as Islanders'. Mermen were so damned snobbish about their riches!

There was a faint hiss of pneumatics at the counter where Scudi worked. She turned presently, balancing a tray carrying covered bowls and utensils. She placed the tray on the deck between the two cots and pulled up a cushion for her own back.

"I don't cook much myself," she said. "The central kitchen is faster, but I add my own spices. They are so bland at central!"

"Oh?" He watched her uncover the bowls, enjoying the smells.

"People already want to know of you," she said. "I have had several calls. I told them to wait. I'm hungry and tired. You, too?"

"I'm hungry," he agreed. He glanced around the room. Only these two cots. Did she expect him to sleep here . . . with her?

She pulled a bowl and spoon up to her lap. "My father taught me to cook," she said.

He picked up the bowl nearest him and took a spoon. This was not like Islander feeding ritual, he noticed. Scudi already was spooning broth into her mouth. Islanders fed guests first, then ate whatever the guests left for them. Brett had heard that this didn't always work well with Mermen—they often ate everything and left nothing for the host. Scudi licked a few drops of broth from the back of her hand.

Brett tasted a sip from his spoon.

Delicious!

"The air is dry enough for you?" Scudi asked.

He nodded, his mouth full of soup.

"My room is small but that makes it easier to keep the air the way I like it. And easier to keep clean. I work topside very often. Dry is comfort to me now and I don't feel comfortable with the humidity in passages and public places." She put the bowl to her lips and drained it.

Brett copied her, then asked, "What will happen to me? When will I go back topside?"

"We'll talk of this after food," she said. She brought up two more bowls and uncovered them, revealing bite-sized chunks of fish in a dark sauce. With the bowl she handed him a pair of carved bone chopsticks.

"After food," he agreed and took a bite of the sauced fish. It was peppery hot and brought tears to his eyes but he found the after-taste pleasant.

"It is our custom," Scudi said. "Food sets the body at ease. I can say, 'Brett Norton, you are safe here and well.' But I know down under is alien to you. And you have been in danger. You must speak to your body in the language it understands before sense returns to you. Food, rest—these are what your body speaks."

He liked the rational sense of her words and returned to the fish, enjoying it more with each bite. Scudi, he saw, was eating as much as he even though she was much smaller. He liked the delicate flick of her chopsticks into the bowl and at the edge of her mouth.

What a beautiful mouth, he thought. He remembered how she had given him that first breath of life.

She caught him staring and he quickly returned his attention to his bowl.

"The sea takes much energy, much heat," she said. "I wear a dive suit as little as possible. Hot shower, much hot food, a warm bed—these are always needed. Do you work the Islander subs topside, Brett?"

Her question caught him off guard. He'd begun to think that she had no curiosity about him.

Maybe I'm just some kind of obligation to her, he thought. *If you save someone, maybe you're stuck with them.*

"I'm a surface fisherman for a contractor named Twisp," he said. "He's the one I most want to get word to. He's a strange man, but the best in a boat that I've seen."

"Surface," she said. "That's much danger from dashers, isn't it? Have you seen dashers?"

He tried to swallow in a suddenly dry throat. "We carry squawks. They warn us, you know." He hoped that she wouldn't notice the dodge.

"We're afraid of your nets," she said. "Sometimes visibility is bad and they can't be seen. Mermen have been killed in them."

He nodded, remembering the thrashing and the blood and Twisp's stories of other Mermen deaths in the nets. Should he mention that to Scudi? Should he ask about the strange reaction of the Maritime Court? No . . . she might not understand. This would be a barrier between them.

Scudi sensed this, too. He could tell because she spoke too quickly. "Would you not prefer to work in your subs? I know they are soft-bellied, not like ours at all, but . . ."

"I think . . . I think I'd like to stay with Twisp unless he goes back to the subs. I'd sure like to know if he's all right."

"We will rest and when we wake, you will meet some of our people who can help. Mermen travel far. We pass along the word. You will hear of him and he of you . . . if that's your wish."

"My wish?" He stared at her, absorbing this. "You mean I could choose to . . . disappear?"

She shrugged her eyebrows, accenting the gamin look. "Where you want to be is where you should be. Who you want to be is the same, not so?"

"It can't be that simple."

"If you have not broken the law, there are possibilities down under. The Merman world is big. Wouldn't you like to stay here?" She coughed and he wondered if she had been about to say "stay here with me?" Scudi suddenly seemed much older, more worldly. Talk among the Islanders gave Brett the impression that Mermen had an extra sophistication, a sense of belonging anywhere they went, of knowing more than Islanders.

"Do you live alone?" he asked.

"Yes. This was my mother's place. And it's close to where my father lived."

"Don't Merman families live together?"

She scowled. "My parents . . . stubborn, both of them. They couldn't live together. I lived with my father for a long time, but . . . he died." She shook her head and he saw the memories pain her.

"I'm sorry," he said. "Where's your mother?"

"She is dead too." Scudi looked away from him. "My mother was net-bound less than a year ago." Scudi's throat moved with a convulsive swallow as she turned back to him. "It has been diffi-cult . . . there is a man, GeLaar Gallow, who became my mother's . . . lover. That was after . . ." She broke off and shook her head sharply.

"I'm sorry, Scudi," he said. "I didn't mean to bring back pain-ful—"

"But I want to talk about it! Down here, there is no one I can . . . I mean, my closest friends avoid the subject and I . . ." She rubbed her left cheek. "You are a new friend and you listen."

"Of course, but I don't see what . . ."

"After my father died, my mother signed over . . . You under-

103

stand, Brett, that my father was Ryan Wang, there was much wealth?"

Wang! he thought. *Merman Mercantile. His rescuer was a wealthy heiress!*

"I . . . I didn't . . ."

"It is all right. Gallow was to be my stepfather. My mother signed over to him control of much that my father left. Then she died."

"So there's nothing for you."

"What? Oh, you mean from my father. No, that is not my problem. Besides, Kareen Ale is my new guardian. My father left her . . . many things. They were friends."

"What . . . you said there's a problem."

"Everyone wants Kareen to marry Gallow and Gallow pursues this."

Brett noted that Scudi's lips tightened every time she spoke Gallow's name. "What is wrong with this Gallow?" he asked.

Scudi spoke in a low voice. "He frightens me."

"Why? What's he done?"

"I don't know. But he was on the crew when my father died . . . and when my mother died."

"Your mother . . . you said a net . . ."

"An Islander net. That is what they said."

He lowered his gaze, remembering his recent experience with a Merman in the net.

Seeing the look on his face, Scudi said: "I have no resentment toward you. I can see that you are sorry. My mother knew the danger of nets."

"You said Gallow was with your parents when they died. Do you . . ."

"I have never spoken of this to anyone before. I don't know why I say it to you, but you are sympathetic. And you . . . I mean . . ."

"I owe you."

"Oh, no! It is nothing like that. It's just . . . I like your face and the way you listen."

Brett lifted his gaze and met her staring at him. "Is there no one who can help you?" he asked. "You said Kareen Ale . . . everyone knows about her. Can't she—"

"I would never say these things to Kareen!"

Brett studied Scudi for a moment, seeing the shock and fear in her face. He already had a sense of the wildness in Merman life from the stories told among Islanders. Violence was no stranger down here, if the stories were to be believed. But what Scudi suggested . . .

"You wonder if Gallow had anything to do with the deaths of your parents," he said.

She nodded without speaking.

"Why do you suspect this?"

"He asked me to sign many papers but I pleaded ignorance and consulted Kareen. I don't think the papers he showed her were the same ones he brought to me. She has not said yet what I should do."

"Has he . . ." Brett cleared his throat. "What I mean is . . . you are . . . that is, sometimes Islanders marry young."

"There has been nothing like that, except he tells me to hurry and grow up. It is all a joke. He says he is tired of waiting for me."

"How old are you?"

"I will be sixteen next month. You?"

"I'll be seventeen in five months."

She looked at his net-calloused hands. "Your hands say you work hard, for an Islander." Immediately, she popped a hand over her mouth. Her eyes went wide.

Brett had heard Merman jokes about lazy Islanders sunning themselves while Mermen built a world under the sea. He scowled.

"I have a big mouth," Scudi said. "I find someone at last who can really be my friend and I offend him."

"Islanders aren't lazy," Brett said.

Scudi reached out impulsively and took his right hand in hers. "I have only to look at you and I know the stories are lies."

Brett pulled his hand away. He still felt hurt and bewildered. Scudi might say something soothing to smooth it over, but the truth had come out involuntarily.

I work hard, for an Islander!

Scudi got to her feet and busied herself removing the dishes and the remains of their meal. Everything went into a pneumatic slot at the kitchen wall and vanished with a click and a hiss.

Brett stared at the slot. The workers who took care of that probably were Islanders permanently hidden from view.

"Central kitchens and all this space," he said. "It's Mermen who have things easy."

She turned toward him, an intent expression on her face. "Is that what Islanders say?"

Brett felt his face grow hot.

"I don't like jokes that lie," Scudi said. "I don't think you do, either."

Brett swallowed past a sudden lump in his throat. Scudi was so direct! That was not the Islander way at all, but he found himself attracted by it.

"Queets never tells those jokes and I don't either," Brett said.

"This Queets, he is your father?"

Brett thought suddenly about his father and his mother—the butterfly life between intense bouts of painting. He thought about their downcenter apartment, the many things they owned and cared for—furniture, art work, even some Merman appliances. Queets, though, owned only what he could store in his boat. He owned what he truly needed—a kind of survival selectivity.

"You are ashamed of your father?" Scudi asked.

"Queets isn't my father. He's the fisherman who owns my contract—Queets Twisp."

"Oh, yes. You do not own many things, do you, Brett? I see you looking around my quarters and . . ." She shrugged.

"The clothes on my back were mine," Brett said. "When I sold my contract to Queets, he took me on for training and gave me what I need. There isn't room for useless stuff on a coracle."

"This Queets, he is a frugal man? Is he cruel to you?"

"Queets is a good man! And he's strong. He's stronger than anyone I've ever known. Queets has the longest arms you've ever seen, perfect for working the nets. They're almost as long as he is tall."

A barely perceptible shudder crossed Scudi's shoulders. "You like this Queets very much," she said.

Brett looked away from her. That unguarded shudder told it all. Islanders made Mermen shudder. He felt the pain of betrayal deep in his guts. "You Mermen are all the same," he said. "Mutants don't ask to be that way."

"I don't think of you as a mutant, Brett," she said. "Anyone can see that you're normalized."

"There!" Brett snapped, glaring at her. "What's normal? Oh, I've heard the talk: Islanders are having more 'normal' births these days . . . and there's always surgery. Twisp's long arms offend you? Well, he's no freak. He's the best fisherman on Pandora because he fits what he does."

"I see that I've learned many wrong things," Scudi said, her voice low. "Queets Twisp must be a good man because Brett Norton admires him." A wry smile touched her lips and was gone. "Have you learned no wrong things, Brett?"

"I'm . . . after what you did for me, I should not be talking to you this way."

"Wouldn't you save me if I were caught in your net? Wouldn't you . . ."

"I'd go in after you and damn the dashers!"

She grinned, an infectious expression that Brett found himself answering in kind.

"I know you would, Brett. I like you. I learn things about Islanders from you that I didn't know. You are different, but . . ."

His grin vanished. "My eyes are good eyes!" he snapped, thinking this was the difference she meant.

"Your eyes?" She stared at him. "They are beautiful eyes! In the water, I saw your eyes first. They are large eyes and . . . difficult to escape." She lowered her gaze. "I like your eyes."

"I . . . I thought . . ."

Again, she met his gaze. "I've never seen two Islanders exactly alike, but Mermen are never exactly alike, either."

"Everyone down under won't feel that way," he accused.

"Some will stare," she agreed. "It is not normal to be curious?"

"They'll call me Mute," he said.

"Most will not."

"Queets says words are just funny ripples in the air or printed squiggles."

Scudi laughed. "I would like to meet this Queets. He sounds like a wise man."

"Nothing much ever bothered him except losing his boat."

"Or losing you? Will that bother him?"

Brett sobered. "Can we get word to him?"

Scudi touched the transphone button and voiced his request over the grill in the wall. The response was too quiet for Brett to hear. She did it casually. He thought then that this marked the difference between them more firmly than his own overlarge eyes with their marvelous night vision.

Presently, Scudi said: "They will try to get word to Vashon." She stretched and yawned.

Even yawning, she was beautiful, he thought. He glanced around the room, noting the closeness of the two cots. "You lived here with just your mother?" he asked. Immediately, he saw the sad expression return to Scudi's face and he cursed himself. "I'm sorry, Scudi. I should not keep reminding you of her."

"It's all right, Brett. We are here and she is not. Life continues . . . and I do my mother's work." Again, that gamin grin twisted her mouth. "And you are my first roommate."

He scratched his throat, embarrassed, not knowing the moral rules between the sexes down under. What did it mean to be a roommate? Stalling for time, he asked: "What is this work of your mother's that you do?"

"I told you. I mathematic the waves."

"I don't know what that means."

"Where new waves or wave patterns are seen, I go. As my mother did and both her parents before her. It is a thing for which our family has a natural talent."

"But what do you do?"

"How the waves move, that tells us how the suns move and how Pandora responds to that movement."

"Oh? Just from looking at the waves, you . . . I mean, waves are gone just like that!" He snapped his fingers.

"We simulate the waves in a lab," she said. "You know about wavewalls, I'm sure," she said. "Some go completely around Pandora several times."

"And you can tell when they'll come?"

"Sometimes."

He thought about this. The extent of Merman knowledge suddenly daunted him.

"You know we warn the Islands when we can," she said.

He nodded.

"To mathematic the waves, I must translate them," she said. She patted her head absently, exaggerating her gamin appearance. "Translate is a better word than mathematic," she said. "And I teach what I do, of course."

Of course! he thought. *An heiress! A rescuer! And now an expert on waves!*

"Who do you teach?" he asked, wondering if he could learn this thing she did. How valuable that would be for the Islands!

"The kelp," she said. "I translate waves for the kelp."

He was shocked. Was she joking, making fun of Islander ignorance?

She saw the expression on his face because she went on, quickly: "The kelp learns. It can be taught to control currents and waves . . . when it returns to its former density, it will learn more. I teach it some of the things it must know to survive on Pandora."

"This is a joke, isn't it?" he asked.

"Joke?" She looked puzzled. "Don't you know the stories of the kelp as it was? It fed itself, it moved gases in and out of the water. The hylighters! Oh, I would love to see them! The kelp knew so many things, and it controlled the currents, the sea itself. All of this the kelp did once."

Brett gaped at her. He recalled schooltime stories about the sentient kelp, one creature alive as a single identity in all of its parts. But that was ancient history, from the time when men had lived on solid land above Pandora's sea.

"And it will do this again?" he whispered.

"It learns. We teach it how to make currents and to neutralize waves."

Brett thought about what this might mean to Island life—drifting on predictable currents in predictable depths. They could follow the weather, the fishing . . . An odd turn of thought put this out of his mind. He considered it almost unworthy, but who could know for certain what an alien intelligence might do?

Scudi, noting his expression, asked: "Are you well?"

He spoke almost mechanically. "If you can teach the kelp to control the waves, then it must know how to *make* waves. And currents. What's to prevent it from wiping us out?"

She was scornful. "The kelp is rational. It would not further the kelp to destroy us or the Islands. So it will not."

Again, she stifled a yawn and he recalled her comment that she had to go back to work soon.

The ideas she had put into his head whirled there, though, leaving him on edge, driving away all thought of sleep. Mermen did so many things! They knew so much!

The kelp will think for itself. He recalled hearing someone say that, a conversation at the quarters of his parents—important people talking about important matters.

But that could not happen without Vata, someone had said in response. *Vata is the key to the kelp.*

That had begun what he remembered as a sprightly and boo-inspired conversation, which, as usual, ran from speculative to paranoid and back.

"I'll turn out the light for your modesty," Scudi said. She giggled and touched the light down through dim to barely shadow. He watched her fumble her way to her bed.

It's dark to her, he thought. *For me she just turned down the glare.* He shifted on the edge of his bed.

"You have a girlfriend topside?" Scudi asked.

"No . . . not really."

"You have never shared a room with a girl?"

"On the Islands, you share everything with everyone. But to have a room, two people alone, that's for couples who are new to each other. For mating. It is very expensive."

"Oh, my," she said. In the shadow-play of his peculiar vision he watched her fingers dance nervously over the surface of her cot.

"Down under we share for mating, yes, but we also share rooms for other reasons. Work partners, schoolmates, good friends. I mean only for you to have one night of recovery. Tomorrow there will be others and questions and tours and much noise . . ." Still her hands moved in that nervous rhythm.

"I don't know how I can ever repay you for being so nice to me," he said.

"But it is our custom," she said. "If a Merman saves you, you can have what the Merman has until you . . . move on. If I bring life into this compound, I'm responsible for it."

"As though I were your child?"

"Something like." She sighed, and began undressing.

Brett found he could not invade her privacy and averted his eyes.

Maybe I should tell her, he thought. *It's not really fair to be able to see this way and not let her know.*

"I would prefer not to interfere with your life," he said.

He heard Scudi slip under her blankets. "You don't interfere," she said. "This is one of the most exciting things that has ever happened to me. You are my friend; I like you. Is that enough?"

Brett dropped his clothes and slipped under the covers, pulling them to his neck. Queets always said you couldn't figure a Merman. Friends?

"We are friends, not so?" she insisted.

He offered his hand across the space between the beds. Realizing that she couldn't see it, he picked up hers in his own. She pressed his fingers hard, her hand warm in his. Presently, she sighed and removed her hand gently.

"I must sleep," she said.

"Me, too."

Her hand lifted from the bed and found the switch on the wall. The whale sounds stopped.

Brett found the room exquisitely quiet, a stillness he had not imagined possible. He felt his ears relaxing, then, an alertness . . . suddenly listening for . . . what? He didn't know. Sleep was necessary, though. He had to sleep. His mind said: "Something is being done about informing your parents and Queets." He was alive and family and friends would be happy after their fears and sadness. Or so he hoped.

After several nervous minutes, he decided the lack of motion was preventing sleep. The discovery allowed him to relax more, breathe easier. He could remember with his body the gentle rocking motion topside and thought hard about that, tricking his mind into the belief that waves still lifted and fell beneath him.

"Brett?" Scudi's voice was little more than a whisper.

"Yes?"

"Of all the creatures in hyb, the ones I would like most are the birds, the little birds that sing."

"I've heard recordings from Ship," he said, his voice sleepy.

"The songs are as painfully beautiful as the whales. And they fly."

"We have pigeons and squawks," he said.

"The squawks are ducks and they do not sing," she said.

"But they whistle when they fly and it's fun to watch them."

Her blankets rustled as she turned away from him.

"Good night, friend," she whispered. "Sleep flat."

"Good night, friend," he answered. And there, at the edge of sleep, he imagined her beautiful smile.

Is this how love begins? he wondered. There was a tightness in his chest, which did not go away until he fell into a restless sleep.

The child Vata slipped into catatonia as the kelp and hylighters sickened. She has been comatose for more than three years now and, since she carries both kelp and human genes, it is hoped that she can be instrumental in restoring the kelp to sentience. Only the kelp can tame this terrible sea.

—Hali Ekel, the Journals

It was not so much that Ward Keel noticed the stillness as that he felt it all over his skin. Events had conspired to keep him topside throughout his long life, not that he had ever felt a keen desire to go down under.

Admit it, he told himself. *You were afraid because of all the stories— deprivation shock, pressure syndrome.*

Now, for the first time in his life there was no movement of deck under his bare feet, no nearby sounds of human activity and voices, no hiss of organic walls against organic ceilings—none of the omnipresent frictions to which Islanders adjusted as infants. It was so quiet his ears ached.

Beside him in the room where Kareen Ale had left him "to adjust for a few moments" stood a large plazglass wall revealing a rich undersea expanse of reds, blues and washed greens. The subtlety of unfamiliar shadings held him rapt for several minutes.

Ale had said: "I will be nearby. Call if you need me."

Mermen well knew the weaknesses of those who came down under. Awareness of all that water overhead created its own peculiar panic in some of the visitors and migrants. And being alone, even by choice, was not something Islanders tolerated well until they had adjusted to it . . . slowly. A lifetime of knowing that other human beings were just on the other side of those thin organic walls, almost always within the sound of a whispered call, built up blind spots. You did not hear certain things—the sounds of love-making, family quarrels and sorrows.

112

Not unless you were invited to hear them.

Was Ale softening him up by leaving him alone here? Keel wondered. Could she be watching through some secret Merman device? He felt certain that Ale, with her medical background and long association with Islanders, knew the problems of a first-timer.

Having watched Ale perform her diplomatic duties over the past few years, Keel knew she seldom did anything casually. She planned. He was sure she had a well-thought-out motive for leaving an Islander alone in these circumstances.

The silence pressed hard upon him.

A demanding thought filled his mind: *Think, Ward! That's what you're supposed to be so good at.* He found it alarming that the thought came to him in his dead mother's voice, touching his aural centers so sharply that he glanced around, almost fearful that he would see a ghostly shade shaking a finger of admonishment at him.

He breathed deeply once, twice, and felt the constriction of his chest ease slightly. Another breath and the edge of reason returned. Silence did not ache as much nor press as heavily.

During the descent by courier sub, Ale had asked him no questions and had supplied no answers. Reflecting on this, he found it odd. She was noted for hard questions to pave the way for her own arguments.

Was it possible that they simply wanted him down here and away from his seat on the Committee? he wondered. Taking him as an invited guest was, after all, less stressful and dangerous than outright kidnapping. It felt odd to think of himself as a commodity with some undetermined value. Comforting, though; it meant they would probably not employ violence against him.

Now, why did I think that? he wondered.

He stretched his arms and legs and crossed to the couch facing the undersea view. The couch felt softly supportive under him in spite of the fact that it was of some dead material. The stiffness of age made the soft seat especially welcome. He sensed the dying remora within him still fighting to survive. *Avoid anxiety,* the medics told him. That was most certainly a joke in his line of work. The remora still produced vital hormones, but he remembered the warning: "We can replace it, although the replacements won't last long. And their survival time will become shorter and shorter as new replacements are introduced. You are rejecting them, you see." His stomach growled. He was hungry and that he found to be a good sign. There was nothing to indicate a food preparation area in the room. No speakers or viewscreens. The ceiling sloped upward away from the couch to the view port, which appeared to be about six or seven meters high.

How extravagant! he thought. Only one person in all this space. A room this size could house a large Islander family. The air was a bit cooler than he liked but his body had adjusted. The dim light through the view port cast a green wash over the floor there. Bright phosphorescence from the ceiling dominated the illumination. The room was not far under the sea's surface. He knew this from the outside light level. Plenty of water over him, though: millions of kilos. The thought of all that weight pressing in on this space brought a touch of sweat to his upper lip. He ran a damp palm over the wall behind the couch—warm and firm. He breathed easier. This was Merman space. They didn't build anything fragile. The wall was plasteel. He had never before seen so much of it. The room struck him suddenly as a fortress. The walls were dry, testimony to a sophisticated ventilation system. Mermen topside tended to keep their quarters so humid he felt smothered by the air. Except for Ale . . . but she was like no other human he had ever met, Islander or Merman. The air in this room, he realized, had been adjusted for Islander comfort. That reassured him.

Keel patted the couch beside him and thought of Joy, how much she would like that surface. A hedonist, Joy. He tried to picture her resting on the couch. A desire for Joy's comforting presence filled him with sudden loneliness. Abruptly, he wondered about himself. He had been mostly a loner throughout his life, only the occasional liaison. Was the proximity of death working a fearful change on him? The thought disgusted him. Why should he inflict himself on Joy, saddle her with the sorrow of a permanent parting?

I am going to die soon.

He wondered briefly who the Committee would elect as Chief Justice to replace him. His own choice would be Carolyn, but the political choice would be Matts. He did not envy whoever they chose. It was a thankless job. There were things to do before he made his final exit, though. He stood and steadied himself against the couch. His neck ached, as usual. His legs felt rubbery and didn't want to support him at first. That was a new symptom. The

114

deck underfoot was hard plasteel and he was thankful that it, like the walls, was heated. He waited for strength to return, then, leaning against the wall, made his way toward the door at his left. There were two buttons beside the door. He pressed the lower one and heard a panel slide back behind the couch. He looked toward the sound and his heart shifted into triple-time.

The panel had concealed a mural. He stared at it. The thing was frighteningly realistic, almost photographic. It showed a surface construction site at least half-destroyed, flames everywhere and men wriggling in the tentacles of hylighters drifting overhead.

Hylighters died with the kelp, he thought. This was either an old painting or somebody's imaginative reconstruction of history. He suspected the former. The rich suns-set background, the intimate detail of hylighters—everything focused on one worker near the center who pointed a finger at the viewer. It was an accusing figure, dark-eyed and glaring.

I know that place, Keel thought. *How is it possible?* Familiarity was stronger than the flutterings of déjà vu. This was real seeing, a memory. The memory told him that somewhere in this room or nearby there was a red mandala.

How do I know this?

He examined the room carefully. Couch, plaz port, the mural, bare walls, an oval hatch-door. No mandala. He walked to the view port and touched it. Cool, the only cool surface in the room. How strange the fixed view port installation was—nothing like it at all on the Islands. Couldn't be. The flex of bubbly around the solid plaz would tear away the organics that sealed it and the heavy, solid material would turn into a thing of destruction during a storm. Driftwatchers, mutated cornea, were safer in rough weather even if they did require care and feeding.

The plaz was incredibly clear. Nothing in the feel of it suggested the extreme density and thickness. A small, heavily whiskered scrubberfish grazed the outside, cleaning the surface. Beyond the fish, a pair of Mermen came into view, jockeying a heavy sledge loaded with rocks and mud. They went past him out of sight beyond a slope to his right.

Out of curiosity, Keel fisted the plaz: *thump-thump.* The scrubberfish continued grazing, undisturbed. Anemone and ferns, grasses and sponges waved in the current beneath the fish. Dozens of other fish, a multicolored mixed school, cleaned the surface of kelp leaves beyond the immediate growth. Larger fish poked along the soft bottom mud, stirring up puffs of gray sediment. Keel had seen this sort of thing in holos but the reality was different. Some of the fish he recognized—creatures from the labs that had been brought for judgment by the Committee before being released in the sea.

A harlequin fish came up below the scrubber and nudged the plaz. Keel remembered the day the C/P had blessed the first harlequin fish before their release. It was almost like seeing an old friend.

Once more, Keel turned to his examination of the room and that elusive memory. Why did it feel so damned familiar? Memory said the missing mandala should be to the right of the mural. He walked to that wall and brushed a finger along it, looking for another panel switch. Nothing, but the wall moved slightly and he heard a clicking. He peered at it. It was not plasteel but some kind of light, composite material. A faint seam ran down the middle of the wall. He put a palm against the surface to the right of the seam and pushed. The panel slid back, revealing a passage, and immediately he smelled food.

He opened the panel wide and walked through. The passage made a sharp turn to the left and he saw lights. Kareen Ale stood there in a kitchen-dining area, her back to him. A rich smell of strong tea and fish broth assailed his nostrils. He drew a breath to speak but stopped as he saw the red mandala. The sight of it above Kareen's right shoulder brought a sigh from Keel. The mandala drew his consciousness into the shapes there, twisting him through circles and wedges toward the center. A single eye peered out from the center, out at the universe. It was unlidded, and rested atop a golden pyramid.

These can't be my memories, he thought. It was a terrifying experience. Ship memories flitted through his mind—someone walking down a long, curved passage, a violet-lighted agrarium fanned out to his left. He felt powerless before the stream of visions. Kelp waved to him from someplace under the sea and schools of fish his Committee had never approved swam past his eyes.

Ale turned and saw the enraptured expression on his face, the fixed intensity with which he stared at the mandala.

"Are you all right?" she asked.

Her voice shocked him out of the other-memories. He exhaled a trembling breath, inhaled.

"I'm . . . I'm hungry," he said. There was no thought of revealing the weird memories he had just experienced. How could she understand when he did not understand?

"Why don't you sit here?" she asked. She indicated a small table set for two at one end of the kitchen area beside a smaller plaz port. The table was low, Merman-style. His knees ached just thinking about sitting there.

"I've cooked for you myself," Ale said.

Noting his still bemused expression, she added: "That hatchway in the other room leads to a head with shower and washbasin. Beyond it you'll find office facilities if you require them. The exterior hatchways are out there as well."

He crowded his legs under the table and sat with his elbows on the surface in front of him, his hands supporting his head.

Was that a dream? he wondered.

The red mandala lay directly in front of him. He was almost afraid to focus on it.

"You're admiring the mandala," Ale said. She busied herself once more in the kitchen area.

He lifted his attention and let his gaze trace the ancient lines along their mysterious pathways. Nothing drew him inward this time. Slowly, bits of his own memories crept into his mind, images flashed behind his eyes and stuttered like a crippled larynx, then caught. Awareness reached back to one of his earliest history lessons, a holo being played in the center of a classroom. It had been a docudrama for young children. Islanders loved theatricals and this one had been fascinating. He could not remember the title, but he did recall that it dealt with the last days of Pandora's continents—they didn't look small at all in the holos—and the death of the kelp. That had been the first time Keel had heard the kelp called "Avata." Behind the holo figures playing out the drama in a command post there had been a wall . . . and that frightening mural from the outer room. Nearby, as the holo shifted its focus, there had been the red mandala, just as he saw it now. Keel did not want to think how long ago he had watched the drama—more than seventy years, anyway. He returned his attention to Ale.

"Is that the original mandala or a copy?" he asked.

"I'm told it's the original. It's very old, older than any settlement on Pandora. You seem taken by it."

117

"I've seen it and the mural out there before," he said. "These walls and the kitchen area are more recent, aren't they?"

"The space was remodeled for my convenience," she said. "I've always been drawn to these rooms. The mandala and mural are where they've always been. And they're cared for."

"Then I know where I am," he said. "Islander children learn history through holodramas and . . ."

"I know that one," she said. "Yes, this is part of the old Redoubt. Once it stood completely out of the sea, with some fine mountains behind it, I understand."

She brought food to the table on a tray and set out the bowls and chopsticks.

"Wasn't most of the Redoubt destroyed?" he asked. "The documentary holos were supposed to be reconstructions of a few from before . . ."

"Whole sections survived intact," she said. "Automatic latches closed and sealed off much of the Redoubt. We restored it very carefully."

"I'm impressed." He nodded, reassessing the probable importance of Kareen Ale. Mermen had remodeled a part of the old Redoubt for her convenience. She lived casually in a museum, apparently immune to the historical value of the objects and building surrounding her. He had never before met a Merman in a Merman environment, and he now recognized this blank spot in his experience as a weakness. Keel forced himself to relax. For a dying man, there were advantages to being here. He didn't have to decide life and death for new life. No pleading mothers and raging fathers would confront him with creatures who could not pass Committee. This was a world away from the Islands.

Ale sipped her tea. It smelled of mint and suddenly reignited Keel's hunger. He began to eat, Islander-style, setting aside equal portions for his host. The first taste of the fish broth convinced him that it was the richest and most delicately spiced broth he'd ever shared. Was this the general diet for Mermen? He cursed his lack of down-under experience. Keel noticed that Ale enjoyed her own helping of the steaming soup and felt insulted at first.

Another cultural thing, he realized. He marveled that a simple difference in table manners could need translation to avoid international disaster. Unanswered questions still buzzed in his head. Perhaps a more devious approach was indicated—a mixture of Merman directness with Islander obliqueness.

"It's pleasantly dry in these quarters," he said, "but you don't need a sponge. You don't oil your skin. I've often wondered how you get by in a topside environment?"

She dropped her gaze from his face and held her teacup to her lips with both hands.

Hiding, he thought.

"Ward, you are a very strange person," she said as she lowered the cup. "That is not the question I expected."

"What question did you expect?"

"I prefer to discuss my immunity from the need for a sponge. You see, we have quarters down under that are kept with a topside environment. I was raised in such quarters. I'm acclimated to Islander conditions. And I adapt very quickly to the humidity down under—when I have to."

"You were chosen as an infant for topside duty?" There was hesitation and shock in his voice.

"I was chosen then for my present position," she said. "A number of us were . . . set aside in the possibility that some of us would meet the mental and physical requirements."

Keel stared at her, astonished. He had never heard of such a cold dismissal of someone's entire life. Ale had not chosen her own life! And, unlike most Islanders, she had a body that in no way restricted her from any trade she chose. He remembered suddenly how she planned everything—a planned person who planned. Ale had been . . . distorted. She probably saw it as training, but training was just an acceptable distortion.

"But you do live a . . . a Merman life?" he asked. "You follow their customs, you swim and . . ."

"Look." She unfastened her tunic at the neck and dropped the top of it, turning her breasts away from him to expose the shoulders. Her back was as clear-skinned and pale as weathered bone. At the top of her shoulder blades the skin had been pinched into a short strip of ridge adjacent to the spine. There she carried the clear pucker-mark of an airfish, but in a peculiar place. He caught the meaning immediately.

"If that mark were on your neck, Islanders might be distracted when they met you, right?" It occurred to him that she would have undergone major arterial reshifting to carry this off—a complicated surgery.

"You have beautiful skin," he added, "it's a shame they marked it up that way at all."

"It was done when I was very young," she said. "I hardly think about it anymore. It's just a . . . convenience."

He resisted the urge to stroke her shoulder, her smooth strong back.

Careful, you old fool! he told himself.

She restored the top of her garment and when her gaze met his, he realized that he had been staring.

"You're very beautiful, Kareen," he said. "In the old holos, all humans look . . . something like you, but you're . . ." He shrugged, feeling the exceptional presence of his appliance against his neck and shoulders. "Forgive an old Mute," he added, "but I've always thought of you as the ideal."

She turned a puzzled frown on him. "I've never before heard an Islander call himself a . . . a Mute. Is that how you think of yourself?"

"Not really. But a lot of Islanders use the term. Joking, mostly, but sometimes a mother will use it to get a youngster's attention. Like: 'Mute, get your grubby little paws outa that frosting.' Or: 'You go for that deal, my man, and you're one dumb Mute.' Somehow, when it comes from one of us it's all right. When it comes from a Merman—it strikes deeper than I can describe. Isn't that what you call us among yourselves, 'Mutes'?"

"Boorish Mermen might, and . . . well, it's a rather common bit of slang in some company. Personally, I don't like the word. If a distinction has to be made, I prefer 'Clone,' or 'Lon,' as our ancestors did. Perhaps my quarters give me a penchant for antiquated words."

"So you've never referred to us as 'Mutes' yourself."

A rosy blush crept up her neck and over her face. He found it most attractive, but the response told him her answer.

She put a smooth, tanned hand over his wrinkled and liver-spotted fingers. "Ward, you must understand that one trained as a diplomat . . . I mean, in some company . . ."

"When on the Islands, do as the Islanders do."

She removed her hand. The back of his own cooled in disappointment. "Something like that," she said. She picked up her teacup and swirled the dregs. Keel saw the defensiveness in the gesture. Ale was somehow off-balance. He'd never seen her that way before, and he wasn't vain enough to attribute it to this exchange with her. Keel believed that the only thing that could bother Ale was something totally unplanned, something with no

120

body of knowledge behind it, no diplomatic precedent. Something out of her control.

"Ward," she said, "I think there is one point that you and I have always agreed on." She kept her attention on the teacup.

"We have?" He held his tone neutral, not giving her any help.

"Human has less to do with anatomy than with a state of mind," she said. "Intelligence, compassion . . . humor, the need to share . . ."

"And build hierarchies?" he asked.

"I guess that, too." She met his gaze. "Mermen are very vain about their bodies. We're proud that we've stayed close to the original norm."

"Is that why you showed me the scar on your back?"

"I wanted you to see that I'm not perfect."

"That you're deformed, like me?"

"You're not making this very easy for me, Ward."

"You, or yours, have the luxury of *choice* in their mutations. Genetics, of course, adds a particularly bitter edge to the whole thing. Your scar is not . . . 'like me,' but one of your freckles is. Your freckles have a much more pleasant quality to them than this." He tapped the neck support. "But I'm not complaining," he assured her, "just being pedantic. Now what is it that I'm not making easy for you?" Keel sat back, pleased for once about those tedious years behind the bench and some of the lessons those years had taught him.

She stared into his eyes, and he saw fear in her expression.

"There are Mermen fanatics who want to wipe every . . . *Mute* off the face of this planet."

The flat abruptness of her statement, the matter-of-fact tone caught him off guard. Lives were precious to Islanders *and* Mermen, this he'd witnessed for himself innumerable times during his many years. The idea of deliberate killing nauseated him, as it did most Pandorans. His own judgments against lethal deviants had brought him much isolation in his lifetime, but the law required that *someone* pass judgment on people, blobs and . . . things . . . He could never decree termination without suffering acute personal agony.

But to wipe out hundreds of hundreds of thousands . . . He returned Ale's stare, thinking about her recent behavior—the food cooked by her own hands, the sharing of these remarkable quarters. And, of course, the scar.

121

I'm on your side, she was trying to say. He felt the planning behind her actions, but there was more to it, he thought, than callous outlines and assignments. Otherwise, why had she been embarrassed? She was trying to win him over to some personal viewpoint. *What viewpoint?*

"Why?" he asked.

She drew in a deep breath. The simplicity of his response obviously surprised her.

"Ignorance," she said.

"And how does this ignorance manifest itself?"

Her nervous fingers *flip-flip-flipped* the corner of her napkin. Her eyes sought out a stain on the tabletop and fixed themselves there.

"I am a child before you," Keel said. "Explain this to me. 'Wipe every Mute off the face of this planet.' You know how I feel about the preservation of human life."

"As *I* feel, Ward. Believe me, please."

"Then explain it to this child and we can get started defeating it: Why would someone wish death to so many of us just because we're . . . extranormal?" He had never been quite so conscious of his smear of a nose, the eyes set so wide on his temples that his ears picked up the fine liquid *click-click* of every blink.

"It's political," she said. "There's power in appealing to base responses. And there are problems over the kelp situation."

"What kelp situation?" His voice sounded toneless in his own ears, far away and . . . yes, afraid. *Wipe every Mute off the face of this planet.*

"Do you feel up to a tour?" she asked. She glanced at the plaz beside them.

Ward looked out at the undersea view. "Out there?"

"No," she said, "not out there. There's been a wavewall topside and we've got all our crews reclaiming some ground we've lost."

His eyes strained to focus forward on her mouth. Somehow, he didn't believe anyone's mouth could be so casual about a wavewall.

"The Islands?" He swallowed. "How bad was the damage?"

"Minimal, Ward. To our knowledge, no fatalities. Wavewalls may very well be a thing of the past."

"I don't understand."

"This wavewall was smaller than many of the winter storms you survive every year. We've built a series of networks of exposed land. Land above the sea. Someday, they will be islands . . . real islands fixed to the planet, not drifting willy-nilly. And some of them, I think, will be continents."

Land, he thought, and his stomach lurched. *Land means shallows.* An Island could bottom out in shallow water. An ultimate disaster, in the vernacular of historians, but she was talking about voluntarily increasing the risk of an Islander's worst fear.

"How much exposed land?" he asked, trying to maintain a level tone.

"Not very much, but it's a beginning."

"But it would take forever to . . ."

"A long time, Ward, but not forever. We've been at it for generations. And lately we've had some help. It's getting done in our lifetime, doesn't that excite you?"

"What does this have to do with the kelp?" He felt the need to resist her obvious attempts to mesmerize him.

"The kelp is the key," she said, "just as people—Islanders *and* Mermen—have said all along. With the kelp and a few well-placed artificial barriers, we can control the sea currents. All of them."

Control, he thought. *That's the Merman way of it.* He doubted they could control the seas, but if they could manipulate currents, they could manipulate Island movement.

How much control? he wondered.

"We're in a two-sun system," he said. "The gravitational distortions guarantee wavewalls, earthquakes . . ."

"Not when the kelp was in its prime, Ward. And now there's enough of it to make a difference. You'll see. And currents should begin an aggrading action now—dropping sediment—rather than degrading."

Degrading, he thought. He looked at Ale's beauty. Did she even know the meaning of the word? A technical understanding, an engineering approach was not enough.

Mistaking the reason of his silence, Ale plunged on.

"We have records of everything. From the first. We can play the whole reconstruction of this planet from the beginning—the death of the kelp, everything."

Not everything, he thought. He looked once more at the wondrous garden beyond the plaz. Growth there was so lush that the bottom could only be glimpsed in a few places. He could see no rock. As a child, he had given up watching drift because all he ever saw was rock . . . and silt. When it was clear enough or shallow enough to see at all. Seeing the bottom from an Island had a way of running an icy hand down your back.

"How close are these 'artificial barriers' to the surface?" he asked.

She cleared her throat, avoiding his eyes.

"Along this section," she said, "surflines are beginning to show. I expect watchers on Vashon already have seen them. That wave-wall drifted them pretty close to . . ."

"Vashon draws a hundred meters at Center," he protested. "Two-thirds of the population live below the waterline—almost half a million lives! How can you speak so casually about endangering that many . . . ?"

"Ward!" A chill edged her voice. "We are aware of the dangers to your Islands and we've taken that into account. We're not murderers. We are on the verge of complete restoration of the kelp and the development of land masses—two monumental projects that we've pursued for generations."

"Projects whose dangers you did not share with nor reveal to the Islanders. Are we to be sacrificed to your—"

"No one is to be sacrificed!"

"Except by your friends who want to wipe out every Mute on Pandora! Is this how they intend to do it? Wreck us on your barrier walls and your continents?"

"We knew you wouldn't understand," she said. "But you must realize that the Islands have reached their limits and people haven't. I agree that we should have brought Islanders into the planning picture much earlier, but"—she shrugged—"we didn't. And now we are. It's my job to tell you what we must do together to see that there is no disaster. It's my job to gain your cooperation in—"

"In the mass annihilation of Islanders!"

"No, Ward, dammit! In the mass *rescue* of Islanders . . . *and* Mermen. We must walk on the surface once more, all of us."

He heard the sincerity in her tone but distrusted it. She was a diplomat, trained to lie convincingly. And the enormity of what she proposed . . .

Ale waved a hand toward the exterior garden. "Kelp is flourishing, as you can see. But it's just a plant; it is not sentient, as it was before our ancestors wiped it out. The kelp you see there was, of course, reconstructed from the genes carried by certain humans in the—"

124

"Don't try to explain genetics to the Chief Justice," Ward growled, "we know about your 'dumbkelp.'"

She blushed, and he wondered at the emotional display. It was something he had never before seen in Ale. A liability in a diplomat, no doubt. How had she concealed it before . . . or was this situation simply too much for normal repression? He decided to watch the emotional signal and read it for her true feelings.

"Calling it 'dumbkelp' like the schoolchildren is hardly accurate," she said.

"You're trying to divert me," he accused. "How close is Vashon to one of your surflines right now?"

"In a few minutes I will take you out and show you," she said. "But you must understand what we're—"

"No. I must not understand—by which you mean *accept*—such peril for so many of my people. So many *people,* period. You talk of control. Do you have any idea of the energy in an Island's movement? The long, slow job of maneuvering something that big? Your word, this control of which you seem so proud, does not take in the kinetic energy of—"

"But it does, Ward. I didn't bring you down here for a tea party. Or an argument." She stood. "I hope you have your legs under you because we've a lot of walking to do."

He stood at that, slowly, and tried to unkink his knees. His left foot tingled in the first stages of waking. Was it possible, all that she said? He could not escape the in-built fear all Islanders felt at the idea of a crashing death on solid bottom. A white horizon could only mean death—a wavewall or some tidal exposure of the planet's rocky surface. Nothing could change that.

How do Mermen make love?
Same way every time.

—Islander joke

The two coracles, one towing the other, bobbed along on the open sea. Nothing shared the horizon with them except gray waves, long deep rollers with intermittent white lines of spume at the crests. Vashon was long gone below the horizon astern and Twisp, holding his course by the steady wind and the fisherman's instinct for shifts in light, had settled into a patient, watchful wait, giving only rare glances to his radio and RDF. He had been all night assembling the gear to hunt for Brett—raising the coracles, repairing the wavewall damage, loading supplies and gear.

Around him now was a Pandoran late morning. Only Little Sun was in the sky, a bright spot on a thin cloud cover—ideal navigation weather. Driftwatch had given him a fix on Vashon's position at the time of the wavewall and he knew that by midafternoon he should be near enough to start search-quartering the seas.

If you made it this far, kid, I'll find you.

The futility of his gesture did not escape Twisp. There was nearly a day's delay, not to mention the ever-prowling hunts of dashers. And there was this odd current in the sea, sending a long silvery line down the sweep of waves. It flowed in his direction, for which Twisp was thankful. He could mark the swiftness of it by the doppler on his radio, which he kept tuned to Vashon's emergency band. He hoped to hear a report of Brett's recovery.

It was possible that Mermen had found Brett. Twisp kept looking for Merman signs—a flag float for a work party, one of their swift skimmers, the oily surge of a hardbelly sub surfacing from the depths.

Nothing intruded on his small circle of horizon.

Getting away from Vashon had been a marvel of secret scurrying, all the time expecting Security to stop him. But Islanders

126

helped each other, even if one of them insisted on being a fool. Gerard had packed him a rich supply of food gifts from friends and from the pantry at the Ace of Cups. Security had been informed of Brett's loss overboard. Gerard's private grapevine said the kid's parents had set up a cry for "someone to do something." They had not come to Twisp, though. Strange, that. Official channels only. Twisp suspected Security knew all about his preparations for a search and deliberately kept hands off—partly out of resentment over the Norton family pressures, partly . . . well, partly because Islanders helped each other. People knew he had to do this thing.

The docks had been a madhouse of repair when Twisp went down to see whether he could recover his boat. Despite the hard work going on all around, fishermen made time to help him. Brett had been the only person lost with this wavewall and they all knew what Twisp had to attempt.

All through the night people had come with gear, sonar, a spare coracle, a new motor, eelcell batteries, every gift saying: "We know. We sympathize. I'd be doing the same thing if I were you."

At the end, ready to set off, Twisp had waited impatiently for Gerard to appear. Gerard had said for him to wait. The big man had come down in his motorized chair, his single fused leg sticking out like a blunted lance to clear the way. His twin daughters ran skipping behind him, and behind them came five Ace of Cups regulars wheeling carts with the food stores.

"Got you enough for about twenty-five or thirty days," Gerard had said, humming to a stop beside the waiting boats. "I know you, Twisp. You won't give up."

An embarrassed silence had fallen over the fishermen waiting on the docks to see Twisp off. Gerard had spoken what was in all of their minds. How long could the kid survive out there?

While friends loaded the tow-coracle, Gerard said: "Word's out to the Mermen. They'll contact us if they learn anything. Hard telling what it'll cost you."

Twisp had stared at his coracles, at the friends who gave him precious gear and even more precious physical help. The debt was great. And if he came back . . . well, he was going to come back—and with the kid. The debt would be a bitch, though. And only a few hours ago he had been considering abandonment of the independent fisherman's life, going back to the subs. Well . . . that was the way it went.

Gerard's twin girls had come up to Twisp then, begging for him to swing them. The coracles were almost ready and a strange reluctance had come over everyone . . . including Twisp. He extended his arms to let each of the girls grip a forearm tight, then he turned, fast, faster, swinging the children wide while the spectators stood back from his long-armed circle. The girls shrieked when their toes pointed at the horizon. He stumbled to a stop, dizzy and sweating. Both girls sat hard on the pier, their eyes not quite caught up with the end of the whirl.

"You come back, you hear?" Gerard had said. "My girls won't forgive any of us if you don't."

Twisp thought about that oddly silent departure as he held his course with the wind on his cheek and an eye to the light and the swift hiss of the current under his craft. The old axiom of the fishing fleets nurtured him in his loneliness: *Your best friend is hope.*

He could feel the tow coracle tug his boat at the crests. The carrier hum of his radio provided a faint background to the *slap-slap* of cross-chop against the hull. He glanced back at the tow. Only the static-charge antenna protruded from the lashed cover. The tow rode low in the water. The new motor hummed reassuringly near his feet. Its eelcell batteries had not started to change color, but he kept an eye on them. Unless the antenna picked up a lightning strike, they'd need feeding before nightfall.

Gray convolutions of clouds folded downward ahead of him. Sometime soon it was going to rain. He unrolled the clear membrane another fisherman had given him and stretched it over the open cockpit of his coracle, leaving a sag-pocket to collect drinking water. The course beeper went off as he finished the final lashings. He corrected for slightly more than five degrees deviation, then hunkered under the shelter, sensing the imminent rain, cursing the way this would limit visibility. But he had to keep dry.

I never really get miserable if I'm dry.

He felt miserable, though. Was there even the faintest hope he could find the kid? Or was this one of those futile gestures that had to be made for one's own mental well-being?

Or is it that I have nothing else to live for . . . ?

He put that one out of his mind as beyond debate. To give himself physical activity, something to drive out his doubts, he rigged a handline with a warning bell from the starboard thwart, baited it with a bit of bright streamer that glittered in the water.

128

He payed it out carefully and tested the warning bell with a short tug on the line. The tinkling reassured him.

All I'd need, he thought. *Drag a dead fish along and call in the dashers.* Even though dashers preferred warm-blooded meat, they'd go for anything that moved when they were hungry.

A lot like humans.

Settling back with the tiller under his right armpit, Twisp tried to relax. Still nothing on the radio's emergency band. He reached down and switched to the regular broadcast, coming in on the middle of a music program.

Another gift, a nav-sounder, with its bottom-finding sonar and its store of position memories, rested between his legs. He flipped it on for a position check, worked out the doppler distance figure from the radio and nodded to himself.

Close enough.

Vashon was drifting at a fairly steady seven klicks per hour back there. His coracle was doing a reliable twelve. Pretty fast for trolling with a handline.

The radio interrupted its music program for a commentary on Chief Justice Keel. No word yet from the Committee, but observers were saying that his unprecedented fact-finding trip down under could have "deep significance to Vashon and all other Islands."

What significance? Twisp wondered.

Keel was an important man, but Twisp had trouble extending that importance beyond Vashon. Occasional grumbles over a decision swept through the Island communities, but there had been few real disturbances since Keel's elevation, and that was some time back. Sure sign that he was a wise man.

The C/P had been asked to comment on Keel's mission, however, and this aroused Twisp's curiosity. What did the old Shipside religion have to do with the Chief Justice's trip? Twisp had always paid only cursory attention to both politics and religion. They were good for an occasional jawing session at the Ace of Cups, but Twisp had always found himself unable to understand what drove people to passionate arguments over "Ship's real purpose."

Who the hell knew what Ship's real purpose had been? There might not have been a purpose!

It was possible, though, that the old religion was gaining new strength among Islanders. It was certainly an unspoken issue between Mermen and Islanders. There was enough polarization already between topside and down under—diplomats arguing about the "functional abilities" characteristic of Pandora's split population. Islanders claimed eminence in agriculture, textiles and meteorology. Mermen always bragged they had the bodies best adapted for going back to the land.

Stupid argument! Twisp always noticed that a group of people— Islander or Merman—got less intelligent with every member added. *If humans can master that one, they've got it made,* he thought.

Twisp sensed something big was afoot. He felt well away from it out in the open sea. No Ship here. No C/P. No religious fanatics— just one seasoned agnostic.

Was Ship God? Who the hell cared now? Ship had abandoned them for sure and nothing else of Ship really mattered.

A long, sweeping roller lifted the coracle easily to almost twice the height of the prevailing seas. He glanced around from the brief vantage and saw something large bobbing on the water far ahead. Whatever it was, it lay in the silvery channel of the odd current, which was adding to his forward speed. He kept his attention ahead until he picked up the unknown thing much closer, realizing then that it was several things clumped together. A few minutes later he recognized the objects in the clump.

Dashers!

The squawks lay quiet, though. He glanced at them as he put a hand on the field switch, ready to repel the hunt when they attacked. None of the dashers moved.

That's strange, he thought. *Never seen dashers sit still before.*

He lifted his head, raising the catchment sag of his cockpit cover, and peered ahead. As the coracle neared the clump, Twisp counted seven adults and a tighter cluster of young dashers in the center of the group. They rode the waves together like a dark chunk of bubbly.

Dead, he realized. *A whole hunt of dashers and all of them dead. What killed them?*

Twisp eased back the throttle, but still kept a hand on the field switch . . . just in case. They were dead, though, not pretending as a ruse to lure him close. The dashers had locked themselves into a protective circle. Each adult linked a rear leg to the adult on either side. They formed a circle with forepaws and fangs facing out, the young inside.

Twisp set a course around them, staring in at the dashers. How long had they been dead? He was tempted to stop and skin at least one. Dasher skins always brought a good price. But it would take precious time and the hides would rob him of space.

They'd stink, too.

He circled a bit closer. Up close now he could see how dashers had adapted so quickly to water. Hollow hairs—millions of trapped air cells that became an efficient flotation system when sea covered all of Pandora's land. Legend said dashers once had feared the water, that the hollow hairs insulated them then against cold nights and oven-hot days among the desert rocks. Because of those hollow hairs, dasher hides made beautiful blankets—light and warm. Again, he was tempted to skin some of them. They were all in pretty good shape. Have to jettison part of his survival cargo if he did, though. What could he spare?

One of the dashers displayed a great hood that floated out from its ugly, leather-skinned head like a black mantle. Experts said this was a throwback characteristic. Most dashers had shed the hood in the sea, becoming sleek killing machines with saber fangs and those knife-sharp claws, almost fifteen centimeters long on the bigger animals.

Lifting a corner of his cockpit cover, he poked at the hooded dasher with a boathook, lifting it far enough to see that the underside had been burned. A deep, crisp line from brisket to belly. The limpness of the beast told him it couldn't have been dead more than a few hours. A half-day, at the most. He withdrew the boathook and refastened the cockpit cover.

Burned? he wondered. What had surprised and killed this entire hunt—from below?

Swinging the tiller, he resumed his course down the silvery channel of current, checking by compass and the relative signal from Vashon. The radio was still playing popular music. Soon, the mysterious clump of dashers lay below the horizon astern.

The clouds had lifted slightly and still there was no rain. He gauged his course by the bright spot on the clouds, the uncertain compass and the ripple of steady wind across the transparent cover above him. The wind drove spray runnels in parallel lines, giving him a good reading on relative direction.

His thoughts turned back to the dashers. He was convinced that Mermen had killed them from beneath, but how? A Merman

131

sub crew, maybe. If this were an example of a Merman weapon, Islands were virtually defenseless.

Now, why would I think Mermen would attack us?

Mermen and Islanders might be polarized, but war was ancient history, known only through records saved from the Clone Wars. And Mermen were known to go to great trouble to save Islander lives.

But the whole planet was a hiding place if you lived down under. And Mermen did want Vata, that was true. Always coming up with petitions demanding that she be moved to "safer and more comfortable quarters down under."

"Vata is the key to kelp consciousness," the Mermen said. They said it so often it had become a cliché, but the C/P seemed to agree. Twisp had never believed everything the C/P said, but this was something he kept to himself.

In Twisp's opinion, it was a power struggle. Vata, living on and on like that with her companion, Duque, beside her, was the nearest thing Pandora had to a living saint. You could start almost any story you wanted about why she lay there without responding.

"She is waiting for the return of Ship," some said.

But Twisp had a tech friend who was called in occasionally by the C/P to examine and maintain the nutrient tank in which Vata and Duque lived. The tech laughed at this story.

"She's not doing anything but living," the tech said. "And I'll bet she has no idea she's even doing that!"

"But she does have kelp genes?" Twisp had asked.

"Sure. We've run tests when the religious mumbo-jumbos and the Mermen observers have their backs turned. A few cells is all it takes, you know. The C/P would be livid. Vata has kelp genes, I'll swear to that."

"So the Mermen could be right about her?"

"Who the fuck knows?" The tech grinned. "Lots of us have 'em. Everybody's different, though. Maybe she *did* get the right batch. Or, for all we really know, Jesus Lewis *was* Satan, like the C/P says. And Pandora's Satan's pet project."

The tech's revelations did little to change Twisp's basic opinions.

It's all politics. And politics is all property.

Lately everything came down to license fees, forms and supporting the right political group. If you had someone on the inside helping you, things went well—your property didn't cost

you so much. Otherwise, forget it. Resentments, jealousy, envy
. . . these were the things really running Pandora. And fear. He'd
seen plenty of fear in the faces of Mermen confronted by the
more severely changed Islanders. People even Twisp sometimes
thought of as Mutes. Fear bordering on horror, disgust, loathing.
It was all emotions and he knew politics was at the bottom of it,
too—"Dear Ship," the horrified Mermen were saying with their
unmasked faces, "don't let me or anybody I love own a body like
that!"

The beeper interrupted Twisp's black thoughts. Sonar said his
depth here was a little under one hundred meters. He glanced
around at the open sea. The silvery current-channel had been
joined by tributaries on both sides. He could feel the current
churn beneath his coracle. Bits of flotsam shared the water
around him now—kelp tendrils mostly, some short lengths of
floating bone. Those would have to be from squawks. Wouldn't
float otherwise.

A hundred meters, he thought. Pretty shallow. Vashon drew just
about that much at Center. Mermen preferred building where it
remained shallow most of the time, he recalled. Was this a Merman area? He looked around for signs: dive floats, the surface
boiling with a sub's backwash or a foil coming up from the depths.
There was only the sea and the folding current that swept him
along in its steady grip. Lots of kelp shreds in this current. Could
be an area where Mermen were replanting the stuff. Twisp had
found himself taking the Merman side on that project in many a
bar argument. More kelp meant more cover and feed for fish.
Nursery areas. More fish meant more food for the Islands and for
Mermen. In more predictable locations.

His depth finder said the bottom was holding steady at ninety
meters. Mermen had reason to prefer shallows. Better for the
kelp. Easier to trade topside, as long as Islands had plenty of
clearance. And there were all those stories that the Mermen were
trying to reclaim land on the surface. There might be a Merman
outpost or trading station nearby and they could give him word
on whether they had rescued the kid. Besides, the little he knew
about Mermen made him that much more fascinated by them,
and the prospect of contact excited him for its own sake.

Twisp began to build a fantasy—a dream-truth that Mermen
had saved Brett. He scooped a handful of the kelp and found
himself daydreaming that Brett had been rescued by a beautiful

young Merman girl and was falling in love somewhere down under.

Damn! I've got to stop that, he thought. The dream collapsed. Bits of it kept coming back to him, though, and he had to repress them sharply.

Hope was one thing, he thought. Fantasy was quite another thing . . . and dangerous.

*This may be the better age for the Faith, but this is certainly
not an age of Faith.*
—Flannery O'Connor, from her letters, Shiprecords

Those who watched Vata that day said her hair was alive,
that it clutched her head and shoulders. As Vata's agitation grew
her shudders became a steadily progressing convulsion. Her thick
spread of hair snaked itself around her and curled her gently into
a fetal ball.

The convulsions tapered off and ceased in two minutes, twelve
seconds. Four minutes and twenty-four seconds after that, the
tendrils of her hair became hair again. A thick spread of it fanned
out behind her. She stayed in that position, tight and rigid,
through three full shifts of watchers.

The C/P was not the first to equate the agitation in the tank with
the sinking of Guemes, nor was she the last. She was, however, the
only one who wasn't surprised.

Not now! she thought, as though she could ever have found a
convenient time for thousands of people to die. That was why she
needed Gallow. This was something she could live with if it were
done, but it was not something that she could do. None of that
diminished the horrors she was forced to imagine as Vata lay
writhing in her tank.

And scooped up like that by her hair! This thought raised every thin
stalk on the back of the C/P's shoulders and neck.

At Vata's first abrupt stirrings, Duque had stiffened, flinched,
then slipped quickly and deeply into shock. His only coherent
utterance was a high-pitched, quickly blurted, "Ma!"

Those med-techs among the watchers, Islander and Merman
alike, vaulted the rim of the pool.

"What's wrong with him?" a young clerk asked. She was chinless
and hook-nosed, but not at all unpretty. The C/P noticed her wide
green eyes and the white eyelashes that flickered as she spoke.

Rocksack pointed at the telltales above the monitor center across the pool. "Fast, high heartbeat, agitation, shallow breathing, steadily dropping blood pressure—shock. Nothing touched him and they've ruled out stroke or internal bleeding." The C/P cleared her throat. "Psychogenic shock," she said. "Something scared him almost to death."

Forceful rejection of the past is the coward's way of removing inconvenient knowledge.

—the Histories

The weather around Twisp had shifted from scattered showers to a warm wind with clear skies directly overhead. Little Sun was wending its way toward the horizon. Twisp checked the rain water he had recovered—almost four liters. He removed the cockpit cover, rolled it forward and lashed it in place where it could be snatched back quickly if the weather changed once more.

He thought only briefly of the daydream he had entertained about Brett and a beautiful Merman woman. What nonsense! Mermen wanted *normal* children. Brett would only find disappointment down under. One look at his big eyes and parents would steer their daughters away from him. Islander births might be stabilizing, more births in the pattern of Gerard's girls, more near-normals like Brett every season, but that changed nothing in basic attitudes. Mermen were Mermen and Islanders were Islanders. Islanders were catching up, though: fewer lethal deviants and longer life spans.

The warning beeper on Twisp's depth finder sounded once, and again. He glanced at it and reset the lower limit. The sea had been shallowing here for some time. Only seventy-five meters now. Fifty meters and he could start trying to see bottom. One of his dockside gifts had been a small driftwatcher, organic and delicately beautiful. It held corneal material at one end that would focus at his demand. At the other end, a mouthlike aperture fitted itself over his eyes. The thing could only exist immersed most of the time in nutrient, and it grew inexorably, eventually becoming too large for a small boat. Custom dictated that it then be passed along to a larger boat. Twisp ran a hand absently along the smooth organic tube of the thing, feeling its automatic response.

He sighed. What could he hope to find on the bottom even if it did get shallow enough? He removed his hand from the little driftwatcher and lifted his attention to his surroundings.

The air felt warm, almost balmy and quite moist after the rains. The seas were calmer. Only that shifting, boiling current stretched ahead of him and for more than a kilometer on both sides. Odd. He had never seen a current quite like it, but then Pandora was always turning up new things. The one constant was the weather: It changed and it changed fast. He looked east at the cloud bank there, noting how far toward the horizon Little Sun had moved. Big Sun would come up soon—more light, more visibility. He glanced back at the strip of rich blue along the horizon. Yes, it was clearing. The dark bank of clouds east of him receded faster than his motor and the current chased it. Sunlight tapped his cheeks, his arms. He settled back beside the tiller, feeling the warmth like an old friend. It was as though Pandora had smiled upon his venture. He knew he was very close to where the wavewall had struck Vashon, and now visibility opened up. He moved his gaze around the horizon, seeking a black speck that was not the sea.

I'm here, kid.

His gaze, sweeping left, glimpsed a distinct line of froth. The sight of it prickled the hairs on his neck and sent a chill down his spine. He sat stiffly upright, staring.

A white line on the sea!

Wavewall? No . . . it wasn't growing larger or receding. Just off to the left of his course and dead ahead a white line of foam grew more distinct as he approached. Sonar read fifty meters. He slipped the little driftwatcher from its container and fixed it to the coracle's side with the corneal end underwater. Fitting his forehead to the mouth aperture, he stared downward.

When his eyes adjusted, the view took a moment shaping itself into something identifiable. It was not the rolling contour of the deeps, which he had seen from the subs. It was not the jagged, surreal landscape of the danger areas. This bottom climbed high, almost to the surface. Twisp tore his gaze away from the driftwatcher and looked at the sonar reading: twenty meters!

He returned his attention to the bottom. It was so shallow he could see delicate, sinewy steps—curving terraces covered with kelp fronds. Rock buttresses and walls guarded the outer edges of the terraces. It all looked artificial . . . manmade.

A core of the Merman kelp project! he thought.

He had seen many segments of the project, but this was vastly different and, he suspected, much larger. Merman engineers experimented with the kelp, he knew that. Supposedly some of the beds would live and grow even on land—if there ever was such a thing. Now Twisp found himself much closer to believing—if this bed was an example. Mermen were doing all that they claimed they'd do. He'd seen the fine latticework strung for kilometers undersea, a structure where the kelp could climb and secure itself. Undersea walls of rock sheltered other plantations. Islanders had complained about the latticework supports, arguing that they were nets to entangle the fishing subs. Twisp had doubted this argument, remembering all the stories of net-bound Mermen. Islander complaints had not stopped the project.

He gave up studying the bottom and looked at the foam line again. The silvery current that carried him curved off to starboard, sweeping close to that disquieting line. He guessed the intersection to be about five klicks off. A distant, recurrent roar accompanied the surfline.

Could it be waves foaming across one of the latticeworks? he wondered.

Both coracles bobbed heavily in a cross-chop, the towed craft pulling at its line and making his job at the tiller a tough one.

Surf! he thought. *I'm actually seeing surf.*

Islanders had reports of this phenomenon, few of them reliable. It occurred to him that they were unreliable only because the incidents were so infrequent. The great Island of Everett, almost as large as Vashon, had reported a surf sighting just before crashing bottom in a swing-surge of Pandora's sea that left it suddenly awash in a mysterious shallows. Everett had been lost without survivors, bottomed out, thirty years back.

The course beeper sounded.

Twisp boxed up the driftwatcher, kicked off the warning switch and pulled the tiller hard into his belly. Now he was cutting across the great curve of current that still drifted him toward the foaming white line. The current took on a new character. It rolled and twisted along the surface, dispersing waves in its track. There was a determination about it, a feeling of purpose, as though it were a live thing remorselessly savaging anything in its way. Twisp only wanted out of it. He had never felt such a force. He notched the

139

motor up another hundred revs. At this point a burnout seemed worth the risk—he had to shake this current.

The coracles twisted at the rim of the surge, forcing him to fight the tiller. Then, suddenly, he was through and onto open waves. The white line of surf still lay too close but now he felt he could beat it. He cranked the motor up another notch, pushing full speed. The silver line of current grew thinner and thinner as he left it behind him. It swept in a great curve around the surfline and disappeared.

What if the kid was caught in that? Twisp wondered. *Brett could be anywhere.*

He crouched over his instruments, read the doppler on Vashon's range signal, and prepared to make a sun-sight to report the location of this danger. A red telltale blinked on his radio—another Island's signal. He rotated and homed in on it, identified it as little Eagle Island, off to the northeast. It was almost at range limit, too far away to ask for distance and a cross-check. His depth finder had nothing in its memory circuits to match the stretch of bottom under him. Dead reckoning, the sun-sight and Vashon's doppler, however, told him the swift current had taken him at least ten klicks to the west of his intended course. The current had moved him rapidly, but the diversion meant he saved no time reaching the coordinates where the wavewall had struck Vashon.

Twisp coded in the bearings and location, keyed the automatic transmitter and activated it. The signal went out for anyone listening: "Dangerous shallows in this location!"

Presently, he scanned the water around him, squinting and shading his eyes. No sign of Mermen—not a buoy, no flag, nothing. That terrifying current had become nothing more than a silver thread glinting along the surface. He took a course reading and prepared for another hour or more of careful dead reckoning. In a moment, he knew, he would be back into that watchful waiting from which anything unusual could bring him instantly alert.

A noisy boiling hissing and clatter came from astern, an eruption of sound that drowned out the quiet pulsing of his motor and the slap of waves against his hull.

Twisp whirled and was just in time to see a Merman sub leap nose-first out of the water and fall back onto its side. The hard metal glittered gold and green. He had a brief glimpse of exterior tools on the sub, all in active mode, whirling and twisting like spastic limbs. The sub splashed down not a hundred meters away, sending up a great wave that swept under the coracles and carried Twisp high. He fought for steerage as he watched the sub roll, then right itself.

Without thinking about it, Twisp swung his tiller into his gut, turning to go to the rescue. No sub did that sort of thing. The crew could be beaten half to death—particularly inside one of those all-metal Merman wonders. This crew was in trouble.

As he came around, the sub's hatch popped open. A man wearing only green utility pants clambered out onto the hull. The conning tower already was awash, the sub nosing back under the surface. A wave swept the man from his perch. He started swimming blindly, great thrashing strokes that took him at an angle across Twisp's course. The sub vanished behind him with a great slurping air bubble.

Twisp changed course to intercept the swimmer. Cupping his great hands around his mouth, Twisp shouted: "This way! Over here!"

The swimmer did not change course.

Twisp swung wide and pulled up alongside the man, cut the motor and extended a hand.

Now in the coracle's shadow, the swimmer twisted his head upward and gave Twisp a frightened look, seeing the extended hand.

"Come aboard," Twisp said. It was a traditional Islander greeting, matter-of-fact. Not even an implied question, such as "What in Ship's name are you doing out here?"

The swimmer took Twisp's hand and Twisp pulled him aboard, nearly swamping the coracle as the man clumsily tried to grasp a thwart. Twisp pulled him to the center and returned to the tiller.

The man stood there a moment, looking all around, dripping a damp pool into the bilges. His bare chest and face were pale, but not as pale as most Mermen's.

Is this a Merman who lives a lot topside? Twisp wondered. *And what the hell happened to him?*

The swimmer looked older than Brett but younger than Twisp. His green utility pants were dark with seawater.

Twisp glanced to where the sub had been. Only a slow roiling of the water showed where it had gone down.

"Trouble?" Twisp asked. Again, it was the Islander way—a

laconic overture that said: "What help do you need that I can give?"

The man sat down and lay back against the coracle's deck cover. He drew in several deep, shuddering breaths.

Recovering from shock, Twisp thought, studying him. The man was small and heavyset, with a large head.

An Islander? Twisp wondered. He put it as a question, hoping directness would shock the man back to normal.

The man remained silent, but he scowled.

That was a reaction, anyway. Twisp took his time examining this strange figure from the sea: dark brown hair lay dripping against a wide forehead. Brown eyes returned Twisp's gaze from beneath thick brows. The man had a wide nose, wide mouth and square chin. His shoulders were broad, with powerful upper arms thinning to rather delicate forearms and slender hands. The hands appeared soft but the fingertips were calloused and shiny. Twisp had seen such fingertips on people who spent a lot of time at keyboard controls.

Hooking a thumb back to where the sub had gone down, Twisp asked: "You care to tell me what that was all about?"

"I was escaping." The voice was a thin tenor.

"The sub's hatch was still open when it went under," Twisp said. That was just a comment and could be taken as such if the man desired.

"The rest of the sub was secured," the man said. "Only the engine compartment will flood."

"That was a Merman sub," Twisp said; another comment.

The man pushed himself away from the deck cover. "We'd better get out of here," he said.

"We're staying while I look for a friend," Twisp said. "He was lost overboard in that last wavewall." He cleared his throat. "You care to tell me your name?"

"Iz Bushka."

Twisp felt that he had heard that name before, but could not make the connection. And now as he looked at Bushka there was a sensation that Twisp had seen this face before—in a Vashon passage, perhaps . . . somewhere.

"Do I know you?" Twisp asked.

"What's your name?" Bushka asked.

"Twisp. Queets Twisp."

"Don't think we're acquainted," Bushka said. He sent another fearful gaze across the water around the coracles.

"You haven't said what you were escaping from," Twisp said. Another comment.

"From people who . . . we'd all be better off if they were dead. Damn! I should've killed them but I couldn't bring myself to do it!"

Twisp remained silent in shock. Did all Mermen speak so casually of killing? He found his voice: "But you sent them down under with a flooded engine room!"

"And unconscious, too! But they're Mermen. They'll get out when they recover. Come on! Let's get out of here."

"Perhaps you didn't hear me, Iz. I'm looking for a friend who went overboard from Vashon."

"If your friend's alive, he's safe down under. You're the only thing on the surface for at least twenty klicks. Believe it. I was looking. I came up because I saw you."

Twisp glanced back at the distant white line of the surf. "That's on the surface."

"The barrier? Yeh, but there's nothing else. No Merman base, nothing."

Twisp considered for a moment—the way Bushka said "Merman." *Fear? Loathing?*

"I know where there's a Search and Rescue base," Bushka said. "We could be there by daybreak tomorrow. If your friend's alive . . ." He left it there.

Talks a bit like an Islander, acts a lot like a Merman, Twisp thought. *Damn! Where have I seen him?*

Twisp glanced at the distant surfline. "You called that a barrier."

"Mermen are going to have land on the surface. That's part of it."

Twisp let this sink in, not believing it or disbelieving it. Fascinating, if true, but there were other muree to fry at that moment.

"So you scuttled a sub and you're escaping from people who would be better dead."

Twisp did not believe half of this Bushka's story. The hospitality of the sea said you had to listen. Nothing said you had to agree.

Bushka sent an agitated gaze over their surroundings. Second

143

sun was up but in this season it made a quick sweep and the half-night would be on them soon. Twisp was hungry and irritated.

"Do you have a towel and some blankets?" Bushka asked. "I'm freezing my ass off!"

Abruptly contrite because he had failed to provide for the man's comfort, Twisp said: "Towel and blankets are rolled up in the cuddy behind you."

As Bushka turned and found the roll, Twisp added: "You saw me so you came up hoping I'd save you."

Bushka looked out from beneath the towel with which he was drying his hair. "If I'd left them under CO_2 any longer it would've killed them. I couldn't do it."

"Are you going to tell me who they are?"

"People who'd kill us while eating lunch and not miss a bite!"

Something in the way Bushka said this set Twisp's stomach trembling. Bushka believed what he said.

"I don't suppose you have an RDC," Bushka said. He spoke with more than a little snobbishness.

Twisp kept his temper and uncovered the instrument near his feet. His relative drift compensator was one of his proudest possessions. The compass arrow in its top was pointing now far off their course.

Bushka approached and looked down at the RDC. "A Merman compass is more accurate," he said, "but this will do."

"Not more accurate between Islands," Twisp corrected him. "Islands drift and there's no fixed point of reference."

Bushka knelt beside the RDC and worked its settings with a sureness that told Twisp this was not the first time the man had used such an instrument. The red arrow atop the housing swung to a new setting.

"That should get us there," Bushka said. He shook his head. "Sometimes I wonder how we found any place without Merman instruments."

We? Twisp wondered.

"I think you're an Islander," Twisp accused, barely holding in his anger. "We're a pretty backward lot, aren't we!"

Bushka stood and returned to his position near the opening of the cuddy.

"Better work a bit more with that towel," Twisp said. "You missed behind your ears!"

144

Bushka ignored him and sat down with his back against the cuddy.

Twisp fed more power to his motor and swung around on the course indicated by the RDC arrow. *Might as well go to this Rescue Base! Damn that Bushka!* Was he one of those down-under Islanders who had become more Merman than the Mermen?

"You going to tell me what happened on that sub?" Twisp asked. "I'm through playing and I want to know what I'm into."

With a sullen expression, Bushka settled himself into his former position against the deck. Presently, he began describing his trip with Gallow. When he got to the part about Guemes Island, Twisp stopped him.

"You were at the controls?"

"I swear to you I didn't know what he was doing."

"Go on. What happened next?"

Bushka picked up his story after the sinking of the Island. Twisp stared at him with a hard expression throughout the recital. Once, Twisp felt under the tiller housing behind him for the lasgun he stored there—a real Merman lasgun that had cost him half a boatload of muree. The cold touch of the weapon settled his mind somewhat. He couldn't help asking himself, *What if this Bushka's lying?*

When Bushka finished, Twisp thought a moment, then: "You strapped the crew into their seats, including this Gallow, and sent them to the bottom. How do you know you didn't kill them?"

"They were tied loose enough to get free once they came around."

"I think I'd have . . ." Twisp shook his head sharply. "You know, don't you, that it's your word against theirs and you were at the controls?"

Bushka buried his face in the blanket around his knees. His shoulders shook and it was a few blinks before Twisp realized the man was sobbing.

For Twisp, this was the ultimate intimacy between two men. He had no more doubts that the story was true.

Bushka lifted a tear-streaked face to Twisp at the tiller. "You don't know all of it. You don't know what a perfect fool I was. Fool and tool!"

It all came out, then—the bookish Islander who wanted to be a

145

Merman, the way Gallow had fastened on this dream, luring the innocent Islander into a compromising position.

"Why didn't you take the sub back to this Rescue Base?" Twisp asked.

"It's too far. Besides, how do I know who's with them and who's against? It's a secret organization, even from most Mermen. I saw you and . . . I just had to get away from them, out of that sub."

Hysterical kid! Twisp thought. He said, "The Mermen won't care a lot for your scuttling their sub."

A short, bitter laugh shook Bushka. "Mermen don't lose anything! They're the greatest scavengers of all time. If it goes to the bottom, it's theirs."

Twisp nodded. "Interesting story, Iz. Now I'll tell you what happened. The part about Guemes, I believe that and I—"

"It's true!"

"I'd like to disbelieve you, but I don't. I also think you got sucked into it by this Gallow. But I don't think you're all as innocent as you let on."

"I swear to you, I didn't know what he intended!"

"Okay, Iz. I believe you. I believe you saw me on the sub's scanner. You came up intending to be rescued by me."

Bushka scowled.

Twisp nodded. "You swam at an angle away from me so I'd be sure to go after you instead of making a try for the sub. You wanted to pass yourself off as Merman, have me take you to this base, and you were going to use your knowledge of the Guemes destruction to insure that Mermen really made good on keeping you down under. You were going to trade that for—"

"I wasn't! I swear."

"Don't swear," Twisp said. "Ship's listening."

Bushka started to speak, thought better of it and remained silent. A religious bluff usually worked with Islanders, even if they claimed nonbelief.

Twisp said: "What did you do topside? What Island?"

"Eagle. I was a . . . historian and pump-control tech."

"You've been to Vashon?"

"A couple of times."

"That's probably where I saw you. I seldom forget a face. Historian, eh? Inside a lot. That accounts for your pale complexion."

"Have you any idea," Bushka asked, "of the historical records the Mermen have preserved? The Mermen themselves don't even know everything they have. Or the value of it."

"So this Gallow saw you as valuable to record his doings?"

"That's what he said."

"Making history's a little different from writing it. I guess you found that out."

"Ship knows I did!"

"Uh huh. Bushka, for now, we're stuck with each other. I'm not going to throw you overboard. But your story doesn't make me comfortable, you understand? If there's a base where you say there's one . . . well, we'll see."

"There's a base," Bushka said. "With a tower sticking out of the water so far you can see it for fifty klicks."

"Sure there is," Twisp said. "Meanwhile, you stay over there by the cuddy and I'll stay here at the tiller. Don't try to leave your position. Got that?"

Bushka put his face back into the blanket without answering. By the rocking of his body and the shaking sobs, it was obvious to Twisp that he'd heard.

What's so tough about making love to a Mute?
Finding the right orifice.

—Merman joke

Following Ale at a pace painful for his old and weak legs, Ward Keel stepped through a hatchway marked by a red circle. He found himself in a roomful of noisy activity. There were many viewscreens, every one attended by a tech, at least a dozen console desks with Merman-style control switches and graphics. Alphanumerical indicators flashed wherever he looked. He counted ten very large viewscreens showing underwater and topside vistas. It all had been crowded into a space only a bit larger than Ale's quarters.

But it's not cramped, he thought.

Somewhat like Islanders, these Mermen had become skillful at using limited areas, although Keel noted that what they thought small an Islander would see as spacious.

Ale moved him around the desks and screens for introductions. Each worker glanced up when introduced, nodded curtly and returned to work. From the looks they shot Ale, Keel could tell that his presence in this room was particularly distressing to several of the Mermen.

She stopped him at a slightly larger desk set on a low dais to command the entire room. Ale had called the young man at this desk "Shadow" but introduced him as Dark Panille. Keel recognized the surname—a descendant of the pioneer poet and historian, no doubt. Panille's large eyes stared out with demanding focus over high cheekbones. His mouth moved only minimally from its straight line when he acknowledged the introduction.

"What is this place?" Keel asked.

"Current Control," Ale said. "You'll learn details momentarily. They are involved in an emergency right now. We must not inter-

148

fere. You see those orange lights flashing over there? Emergency calls for Search and Rescue teams who are on standby duty."

"Search and Rescue?" Keel asked. "Are some of your people in trouble?"

"No," she replied with a tight set to her jaw, "your people."

Keel clamped his mouth shut. His gaze skittered across the room at the intense faces studying each viewscreen, at the cacophony of typing set up by the blur of two dozen technicians' hands at their keyboards. It was all very confusing. Was this the beginning of that threat Ale had mentioned? Keel found it difficult to remain silent . . . but she had said "Search and Rescue." This was a time to watch carefully and record.

Immediately after the medics had passed their death sentence on him, Keel had begun to feel that he was living in a vacuum that desperately needed filling. He felt that even his long service on the Committee on Vital Forms had been emptied. It was not enough to have been Chief Justice. There must be something more . . . a thing to mark his end with style, showing the love he had for his fellows. He wanted to send a message down the long corridors that said: "This is how much I cared." Perhaps there was a key to his need in this room.

Ale whispered in his ear. "Shadow—his friends call him that, a more pleasant name than 'Dark'—he's our ablest coordinator. He has a very high success rate recovering Islander castaways."

Was she hoping to impress him with her benign concern for Islander lives? Keel spoke in a low voice, his tone dry: "I didn't know it was this formalized."

"You thought we left it to chance?" she asked. Keel noted the slight snort of disgust. "We always watch out for Islanders in a storm or during a wavewall."

Keel felt an emotional pang at this revelation. His pride had been touched.

"Why haven't you made it known that you do this for us?" he asked.

"You think Islander pride would abide such a close watch?" Ale asked. "You forget, Ward, that I live much topside. You already believe we're plotting against you. What would your people make of this set-up?" She gestured at the banks of controls, the viewscreens, the subdued clicking of printers.

"You think Islanders are paranoid," Keel said. He was forced to admit to himself that this room's purpose had hurt his pride.

Vashon Security would not like the idea of such Merman surveillance, either. And their fears might be correct. Keel reminded himself that he was only seeing what he was shown.

A large screen over to the right displayed a massive section of Island hull.

"That looks like Vashon," he said. "I recognize the driftwatch spacing."

Ale touched Panille's shoulder and Keel wondered at the proprietary air of her movement. Panille glanced up from the keys.

"An interruption?" she asked.

"Make it short."

"Could you put Justice Keel's fears to rest? He has recognized his Island there." She nodded toward the viewscreen on the right. "Give him its position relative to the nearest barrier wall."

Panille turned to his console and tapped out a code, twisted a dial and read the alphanumerics on a thin dark strip at the top of his board. The smaller screen above the readout shifted from a repeat of the hull view to a surrounding seascape. A square at the lower right of the screen flashed "V-200."

"Visibility two hundred meters," Ale said. "Pretty good."

"Vashon's about four kilometers out from submerged barrier HA-nine, moving parallel the wall," Panille said. "In about an hour we'll begin to take it farther out. The wavewall had it within two-kilometer range. We had to do some shuffling, but nothing to worry about. It was never out of control."

Keel had to suppress a gasp at these figures. He fought down anger at the younger man's presumption and managed to ask, "What do you mean, 'Nothing to worry about'?"

Panille said, "We have had it under control—"

"Young man, diverting a mass like Vashon"—Keel shook his head—"we're lucky to adjust basic positioning when we contact another Island. Getting out of the way of danger in a mere two kilometers is not possible."

The corners of Panille's mouth came up in a tight smile—the kind of know-it-all smile that Keel really hated. He saw it on many adolescents, sophomoric youths thinking that older people were just too slow.

"You Islanders don't have the kelp working for you," Panille said. "We do. That's why we're here and we haven't time for your Islander paranoia."

"Shadow!" Ale's voice carried a cautionary note.

"Sorry." Panille bent to his controls. "But the kelp gives us a control that has kept Vashon out of real danger through this area for the past few years. Other Islands, too."

What an astonishing claim! Keel thought. He noted from the edge of his vision how carefully Ale watched every move Panille made. The young man nodded at something on his readouts.

"Watch this," he said. "Landro!" An older woman across the room glanced back and nodded. Panille called out a series of letters and numbers to her. She tapped them into her console, paused, hit a key, paused. Panille bent to his own board. A flurry of movement erupted from his fingers across the keys.

"Watch Shadow's screen," Ale said.

The screen showed a long stretch of waving kelp, thick and deep. The V-200 still blinked in the corner square. From it, Keel estimated he was looking at kelp more than a hundred meters tall. As he watched, a side channel opened through the kelp, the thick strands bending aside and locking onto their neighbors. The channel appeared to be at least thirty meters wide.

"Kelp controls the currents by opening appropriate channels," Ale said. "You're seeing one of the kelp's most primitive feeding behaviors. It captures nutrient-rich colder currents this way."

Keel spoke in a hushed whisper. "How do you make it respond?"

"Low-frequency signals," she said. "We haven't perfected it yet, but we're close. This is rather crude if we believe the historical records. We expect the kelp to add a visual display to its vocabulary at the next stage of development."

"Are you trying to tell me you're *talking* to it?"

"In a crude way. The way a mother talks to an infant, that kind of thing. We can't call it sentient yet, it doesn't make independent decisions."

Keel began to understand Panille's know-it-all look. How many generations had Islanders been on the sea without even coming close to such a development? What else did Islanders lack that Mermen had perfected?

"Because it's crude we allow plenty of margin for error," Ale said.

"Four kilometers . . . that's safe?" Keel asked.

"Two kilometers," Panille said. "That's an acceptable distance now."

"The kelp responds to a series of signal clusters," Ale said.

Why this sudden candor with Vashon's highest Islander official? Keel wondered.

"As you can see," Ale said, "we're training the kelp as we use it." She took his arm and stared at the widening channel through the kelp.

Keel saw Panille glance at Ale's intimate grip and caught a brief hardening of the young man's mouth.

Jealous? Keel wondered. The thought flickered like a candle in a breezy room. Perhaps a way to put Panille off-balance. Keel patted Ale's hand.

"You see why I brought you in here?" Ale asked.

Keel tried to clear his throat, finding it painfully restricted. Islanders would have to learn about this development, of course. He began to see Ale's problem—the Merman problem. They had made a mistake in not sharing this development earlier. Or had they?

"We have other things to see," Ale said. "I think the gymnasium next because it's closest. That's where we're training our astronauts."

Keel had been turning slightly as she spoke, scanning the curve of screens across the room. His mind was only partly focused on Ale's words and he heard them almost as an afterthought. He lurched and stumbled into her, only her strong grip on his arm kept him steady.

"I know you're going after the hyb tanks," he said.

"Ship would not have left them in orbit if it was not intended for us to have them, Ward."

"So that's why you're building your barriers and recovering solid ground above the sea."

"We can launch rockets from down here but that's not the best way," she said. "We need a solid base above the sea."

"What will you do with the contents of the tanks?"

"If the records are correct, and we've no reason to doubt them, then the riches of life in those tanks will put us back on a human path—a human way."

"What's a human way?" he asked.

"Why, it's . . . Ward, the life forms in those tanks can . . ."

"I've studied the records. What do you expect to gain on Pandora from, say, a rhesus monkey? Or a python? How will a mongoose benefit us?"

"Ward . . . there are cows, pigs, chickens . . ."

"And whales, how can they help us? Can they live compatibly with the kelp? You've pointed out the importance of the kelp . . ."

"We won't know until we try it, will we?"

"As Chief Justice on the Committee on Vital Forms, and that is who you're addressing now, Kareen Ale, I must remind you that I have considered such questions before."

"Ship and our ancestors brought—"

"Why this sudden religious streak, Kareen? Ship and our ancestors brought chaos to Pandora. They did not consider the consequences of their actions. Look at me, Kareen! I am one of those consequences. Clones . . . mutants . . . I ask you, was it not Ship's purpose to teach us a hard lesson?"

"What lesson?"

"That there are some changes that can destroy us. You speak so glibly of a human way of life! Have you defined what it is to be human?"

"Ward . . . we're both human."

"Like me, Kareen. That's how we judge. Human is 'like me.' In our guts, we say: It's human if it's 'like me.'"

"Is that how you judge on the Committee?" Her tone was scornful, or hurt.

"Indeed, it is. But I paint the likeness with a very broad brush. How broad is your brush? For that matter, this scornful young man seated here, could he look at me and say, 'like me'?"

Panille did not look up but his neck turned red and he bent intently over his console.

"Shadow and his people save Islander lives," she remarked.

"Indeed," Keel said, "and I'm grateful. However, I would like to know whether he believes he is saving fellow humans or an interesting lower life form?

"We live in different environments, Kareen. Those different environments require different customs. That's all. But I've begun to ask myself why we Islanders allow ourselves to be manipulated by *your* standards of beauty. Could you, for example, consider me as a mate?" He put up a hand to stop her reply and noticed that Panille was doing his best to ignore their conversation. "I don't seriously propose it," Keel said. "Think about everything involved in it. Think how sad it is that I have to bring it up."

Choosing her words carefully, spacing them with definite pauses, Ale said, "You are the most difficult . . . human being . . . I have ever met."

"Is that why you brought me here? If you can convince me, you can convince anyone?"

"I don't think of Islanders as Mutes," she said. "You are humans whose lives are important and whose value to us all should be obvious."

"But you said yourself that there are Mermen who don't agree," he said.

"Most Mermen don't know the particular problems Islanders face. You must admit, Ward, that much of your work force is ineffective . . . through no fault of your own, of course."

How subtle, he thought. *Almost euphemistic.*

"Then what is our 'obvious value'?"

"Ward, each of us has approached a common problem—survival on this planet—in somewhat different ways. Down here, we compost for methane and to gain soil for the time when we'll have to plant the land."

"Diverting energy from the life cycle?"

"Delaying," she insisted. "Land is far more stable when plants hold it down. We'll need fertile soil."

"Methane," he muttered. He forgot what point he was going to make in the wake of the new illumination dawning on him. "You want our hydrogen facilities!"

Her eyes went wide at the quickness of his mind.

"We need the hydrogen to get into space," she said.

"And we need it for cooking, heating and driving our few engines," he countered.

"You have methane, too."

"Not enough."

"We separate hydrogen electronically and—"

"Not very efficient," he said. He tried to keep the pride out of his voice, but it leaked through all the same.

"You use those beautiful separation membranes and the high pressure of deep water," she said.

"Score one for organics."

"But organics are not the best way to build a whole technology," she said. "Look how it's bogged you down. Your technology should support and protect you, help you to progress."

"That was argued out generations ago," he said. "Islanders know what you think about organics."

"That argument is not over," she insisted. "And with the hyb tanks . . ."

154

"You're coming to us, now," he said, "because we have a way with tissues." He allowed himself a tight smile. "And I note that you also come to us for the most delicate surgery."

"We understand that organics once represented the most convenient way for you to survive topside," she said. "But times are changing and we—"

"You are changing them," he challenged. He backed off at the frustration visible in her clenched jaw, noting the flash of something bright in her blue eyes. "Times are always changing," he said, his voice softer. "The question remains: How do we best adapt to change?"

"It requires all of your energies just to maintain yourselves and your organics," she snapped, not softening. "Islands starve sometimes. But we do not starve. And within a generation we will walk beneath open sky on dry land!"

Keel shrugged. The shrug irritated the prosthetic supports for his large head. He could feel his neck muscles growing tired, snaking their whips of pain up the back of his neck, crowning his scalp.

"What do you think of that old argument in light of this change?" she asked. It was voiced as a challenge.

"You are creating sea barriers, new surflines that can sink Islands," he said. "You do this to further a Merman way of life. An Islander would be foolish not to ask whether you're doing this to sink the Islands and drown us Mutes."

"Ward." She shook her head before continuing. "Ward, the end of Island life as you know it will come in our lifetime. That's not necessarily bad."

Not in my lifetime, he thought.

"Don't you understand that?" she demanded.

"You want me to facilitate your kind of change," he said. "That makes me the Judas goat. You know about Judas, Kareen? And goats?"

A shadow of unmistakable impatience crossed her face. "I'm trying to impress on you how soon Islanders must change. That is a fact and it must be dealt with, distasteful or not."

"You're also trying to get our hydrogen facilities," he said.

"I'm trying to keep you above our Merman political squabbles," she said.

"Somehow, Kareen, I don't have confidence in you. I suspect that you don't have the approval of your own people."

"I've had enough of this," Panille interrupted. "I warned you, Kareen, that an Islander—"

"Let me handle this," she said, and quieted him with a lift of her hand. "If it's a mistake, it's my mistake." To Keel, she said, "Can you find confidence in retrieving the hyb tanks or settling the land? Can you see the value in restoring the kelp to consciousness?"

It's an act, he thought. *She's playing to me. Or to Shadow.*

"To what end and by what means?" he asked, stalling for more time.

"To what end? We'll finally have some real stability. All of us. It's something that'll pull all of us together."

She seems so cool, so smooth, he thought. *But something's not quite right.*

"What're your priorities?" he asked. "The kelp, the land or the hyb tanks?"

"My people want the hyb tanks."

"Who are your people?"

She looked at Panille, who said, "A majority, that's who her people are. That's how we operate down under."

Keel looked down at him. "And what are your priorities, Shadow?"

"Personally?" His eyes left the screen reluctantly. "The kelp. Without it this planet's an endless struggle for survival." He gestured to the screens, which, Keel reminded himself, somehow had Islander lives balancing on them. "You saw what it can do," Panille said. "Right now it's keeping Vashon in deep water. That's handy. It's survival."

"You think that's a sure thing?"

"I do. We have everything that was recovered from the old Redoubt after the inundation. We've a good idea what's in the hyb tanks. They can wait."

Keel looked at Ale. "Sure, things worry me. I know what's supposed to be in those tanks. What do your records say?"

"We have every reason to believe the hyb tanks contain earthside plant and animal life, everything Ship considered necessary for colonization. And there may be as many as thirty thousand human beings—all preserved indefinitely."

Keel snorted at the phrase "every reason to believe." *They don't know after all,* he thought. *This is a blind shot.* He looked up at the

156

ceiling, thinking of those bits of plasteel and plaz and all that flesh swinging in a wide loop around Pandora, year after year.

"There could be anything up there," Keel said. "Anything." He knew it was fear speaking. He looked accusingly at Ale. "You claim to represent a majority of Mermen, yet I sense a furtiveness in your activities."

"There are political sensitivities—" She broke off. "Ward, our space project will continue whether I'm successful with you or not."

"Successful? With me?" There seemed to be no end to her manipulative schemes.

Ale exhaled, more of a hiss than a sigh. "If I fail, Ward, the chances for the Islanders look bad. We want to start a civilization, not a war. Don't you understand? We're offering the Islanders land for colonization."

"Ahhhh, the bait!" he said.

Keel thought about the impact such an offer might have on Islanders. Many would leap at it—the poor Islanders, such as those of Guemes, the little drifters living from sea to mouth. Vashon might be another matter. But Merman riches were being exposed in this offer. Many Islanders harbored deep feelings of jealousy over those riches. It would worsen. The complexity of what Ale proposed began to lay itself out in his mind—a problem to solve.

"I need information," he said. "How close are you to going into space?"

"Shadow," Ale said.

Panille punched keys on his console. The screen in front of him displayed a pair of images with a dividing line down the middle. On the left was an underwater view of a tower, its dimensions not clear to Keel until he realized that the tiny shapes around it were not fish, but Mermen workers. The view on the right showed the tower protruding from the sea and, with the proportions clear from the left screen, Keel realized that the thing must lift fifty meters above the surface.

"There will be one space launch today or tomorrow, depending on the weather," Ale said. "A test, our first manned shot. It won't be long after that when we go up after the hyb tanks."

"Why has no Island reported that thing?" Keel asked.

"We steer you away from it," Panille said with a shrug.

157

Keel shook his aching head.

"This explains the sightings you've heard of, the Islander claims that Ship is returning," Ale said.

"How amusing for you!" Keel blurted. "The simple Islanders with their primitive superstitions." He glared at her. "You know some of my people are claiming your rockets as a sign the world is ending. If you'd only brought the C/P into this . . ."

"It was a bad decision," she said. "We admit it. That's why you're here. What do we do about it?"

Keel scratched his head. His neck ached abominably against the prosthetic braces. He sensed things between the lines here . . . Panille coming in on cue. Ale saying mostly what she had planned to say. Keel was an old political in-fighter, though, aware that he could not tip his hand too soon. Ale wanted him to learn things— things she had planned for him to learn. It was the concealed lesson that he was after.

"How do we make Islanders comfortable with the truth?" Keel countered.

"We don't have time for Islander philosophizing," she said.

Keel bristled. "That's just another way of calling us lazy. Just staying alive occupies most of us full-time. You think we're not busy because we're not building rockets. We're the ones who don't have time. We don't have time for pretty phrases and planning—"

"Stop it!" she snapped. "If the two of us can't get along, how can we expect better of our people?"

Keel turned his head to look at her with one eye and then with the other. He suppressed a smile. Two things amused him. She had a point, and she could lose her composure. He lifted both hands and rubbed at his neck.

Ale was instantly solicitous, aware of Keel's problem from their many encounters on the debate floor. "You're tired," she said. "Would you like to rest and have a cup of coffee or something more solid?"

"A good cup of Vashon's best would suit me," he said. He tugged at the prosthetic on his right. "And this damned thing off my neck for a while. You wouldn't happen to have a chairdog, would you?"

"Organics are rare down under," she said. "I'm afraid we can't provide Islander comforts for everything."

"I just wanted a massage," he said. "Mermen are missing a bet by not having a few chairdogs."

"I'm sure we can find you a massage," Kareen said.

"We don't have the high incidence of health problems that you have topside," Panille interrupted. Again, his eyes were on the screen filled with numbers and he spoke almost out of another consciousness. Still, Keel couldn't let the remark pass.

"Young man," he said, "I suspect you are brilliant in your work. Don't let the confidence of that accomplishment spill over into other areas. You have a great deal yet to learn."

Turning to lean on Ale's arm, he allowed himself to be assisted out into the passageway, feeling the stares that followed them. He was glad to get out of that room. Something about it wriggled chills up and down his spine.

"Have I convinced you?" Ale asked. He shuffled along beside her, his legs aching, his head filled with bits of information that he knew would soon inflict themselves upon his people.

"You have convinced me that Mermen will do this thing," he said. "You have the wealth, the organization, the determination." He lurched and caught himself. "I'm not used to decks that don't roll," he explained. "Living on land is hard for an old-timer."

"Everyone can't go onto the land at once," she said. "Only the most needy at first. We think other Islands will have to be moored offshore . . . or rafts may be built for such nearby moorage. They'll be temporary living quarters until the agricultural system is well along."

Keel thought about this a moment, then: "You have been thinking this out for a long time."

"We have."

"Organizing Islanders' lives for them and—"

"Trying to figure out how to save the lot of you!"

"Oh?" He laughed. "By putting us on bedroom rafts near shore?"

"They'd be ideal," she said. He could see a genuine excitement in her eyes. "As the need for them vanished, we could let them die off and use them for fertilizers."

"Our Islands, too, no doubt—fertilizer."

"That's about all they'll be good for when we have enough open land."

Keel could not keep the bitterness out of his voice. "You do not understand, Kareen. I can see that. An Island is not a dead piece of . . . of land. It's alive! It is our mother. It supports us because

159

we give it loving care. You are condemning our mother to a bag of fertilizer."

She stared at him a moment, then: "You seem to think Islanders are the only ones giving up a way of life. Those of us who go back to the surface—"

"Will still have access to the deeps," he said. "You are not cutting the umbilical cord. We would suffer more in the transition. You seem willing to ignore this."

"I'm not ignoring it, dammit! That's why you're here."

Time to end the sparring, he thought. *Time to show her that I don't really trust her or believe her.*

"You're hiding things from me," he said. "I've studied you for a long time, Kareen. There's something boiling in you, something big and important. You're trying to control what I learn, feeding me selected information to gain my cooperation. You—"

"Ward, I—"

"Don't interrupt. The quickest way to gain my cooperation is to open up, share everything with me. I will help if that's what should be done. I will not help, I will resist, if I feel you are concealing anything from me."

She stopped them at a dogged hatch and stared at it without focusing.

"You know me, Kareen," he prompted. "I say what I mean. I will fight you. I will leave . . . unless you restrain me . . . and I will campaign against—"

"All right!" She glared up at him. "Restrain you? I wouldn't dare consider it. Others might, but I would not. You want me to share? Very well. The bad trouble has already started, Ward. Guemes Island is under the waves."

He blinked, as if blinking would clear away the force of what she'd said.

An entire Island, under the waves!

"So," he growled, "your precious current controls didn't work. You've driven an Island onto—"

"No." She shook her head for emphasis. "No! No! Someone has done it deliberately. It had nothing to do with Current Control. It was a cruel, vicious act of destruction."

"Who?" He spoke the word in a low, shocked voice.

"We don't know yet. But there are thousands of casualties and we're still picking up survivors." She turned and undogged the hatch. Keel saw the first signs of age in her slow movements.

She's still holding something back, he thought as he followed her into her quarters.

160

*Humans spend their lives in mazes. If they escape and can-
not find another maze, they create one. What is this passion
for testing?*
—"Questions from the Avata," the Histories

Duque began to curse, rolling in the nutrient bath and
pounding his fists against the organic sides until great blue stains
appeared along the edge.

The guardians summoned the C/P.

It was late and Simone Rocksack had been preparing for bed.
At the summons, Simone pulled her favorite robe over her head
and let it drop over the firm curves of her breasts and hips. The
robe in its purple dignity erased all but the slightest traces of
womanliness from her bearing. She hurried down the passage
from her quarters, pulling at her robe to restore some of its
daytime crispness. She entered the gloomy space where Vata and
Duque existed. Her anxiety was obvious in every moment. Kneel-
ing above Duque, she said: "I am here, Duque. It is the Chaplain/
Psychiatrist. How can I help you?"

"Help me?" Duque screamed. "You wart on the rump of a
pregnant sow! You can't even help yourself!"

Shocked, the C/P put a hand over the flap covering her mouth.
She knew what a sow was, of course—one of the creatures of Ship,
a female swine. This she remembered well.

A pregnant sow?

Simone Rocksack's slender fingers couldn't help pressing
against the smooth flatness of her abdomen.

"The only swine are in the hyb tanks," she said. She concentrated on keeping her voice loud enough for Duque to hear.

"So you think!"

"Why are you cursing?" the C/P asked. She tried to keep a
proper reverence in her tone.

"Vata's dreaming me into terrible things," Duque moaned. "Her hair . . . it's all over the ocean and she's breaking me into little pieces."

The C/P stared at Duque. Most of his form was a blurred hulk under the nutrient. His lips sought the surface like a bloated carp. He seemed to be all in one piece.

"I don't understand," she said. "You appear intact."

"Haven't I told you she dreams me?" Duque moaned. "Dreams hurt if you can't get out. I'll drown down there. Every little piece of me will drown."

"You're not drowning, Duque," the C/P assured.

"Not here, baboon. In the sea!"

Baboon, she thought. That was another creature from Ship. Why was Duque recalling the creatures of Ship? Were they at last coming down? But how could he know? She lifted her gaze to the fearful watchers around the rim of the organic tank. Could one of them . . . ? No, it was impossible.

His voice suddenly clear and extremely articulate, Duque proclaimed, "She won't listen. They're talking and she won't listen."

"Who won't listen, Duque? Who are 'they'?"

"Her hair! Haven't you heard a thing I've said?" He pounded a fist weakly against the tank side below the C/P. She stroked her abdomen again, absently.

"Are the creatures from Ship to be brought down to Pandora?" Rocksack asked.

"Take them where you want," Duque said. "Just don't let her dream me back into the sea."

"Does Vata wish to return to the sea?"

"She's dreaming me, I tell you. She's dreaming me away."

"Are Vata's dreams reality?"

Duque refused to answer. He merely groaned and twisted at the edge of the tank.

Rocksack sighed. She stared across the tank at the mounded bulk of Vata, quiescent . . . breathing. Vata's long hair moved like seaweed in the currents of Duque's disturbance. How could Vata's hair be in the ocean and here on Vashon simultaneously? Perhaps in dreams. Was this another miracle of Ship? Vata's hair was almost long enough to be cut once more, it had been over a year. Was all of that hair that had been cut from Vata . . . was all of it somehow still attached to Vata? Nothing was impossible in the realm of miracles.

But how could Vata's hair speak?

There was no mistaking what Duque had said. Vata's hair spoke and Vata would not listen. Why would Vata not listen? Was it too soon to return to the sea? Was this a warning that Vata would lead them all back into the sea?

Again, Rocksack sighed. The Chaplain/Psychiatrist's job could be troublesome. Terrible demands were made upon her. Word of this would be out by morning. There was no way to silence the guardians. Rumors, distorted stories. Some interpretation would have to be made, something firm and supportive. Something good enough to silence dangerous speculations.

She stood, grimacing at a pain in her right knee. Looking at the awed faces around the tank's rim, she said, "The next lot of Vata's hair will not go to the faithful. Every clipping must be cast into the sea as an offering."

Below her, Duque groaned, then quite clearly he shouted, "Bitch! Bitch! Bitch!"

Rocksack placed this reference immediately, having been prepared by Duque's previous mutterings. Bitch was the female of the canine family. Great things were in store for Pandora, the C/P realized. Vata was dreaming Duque into wondrous experiences and Duque was calling forth the creatures of Ship.

Looking once more at the awed guardians, Rocksack explained this carefully. She was pleased by the way heads nodded agreement.

All Pandorans will be free when the first hylighter breaks the sea's surface.
            —Sign over a Merman kelp project

Five water-drum tones sounded a musical call, pulling Brett up . . . up . . . lifting him out of a dream in which he reached for Scudi Wang but never quite touched her. Always, he fell back into the depths as he had sunk when the wavewall swept him off Vashon.

Brett opened his eyes and recognized Scudi's room. There were no lights, but his light-gathering eyes discerned her hand across the short distance between their beds. The hand reached out from the covers and groped sleepily up the wall toward the light switch.

"It's a little higher and to the right," he said.

"You can see?" There was puzzlement in her voice. Her hand stopped its groping and found the switch. Brilliance washed the room. He sucked a deep breath, let it out slowly and rubbed his eyes. The light hurt him all the way out to the temples.

Scudi sat upright on her bed, the blankets pulled loosely around her breasts. "You can see in the dark?" she persisted.

He nodded. "Sometimes it's handy."

"Then modesty is not as strict with you as I thought." She slipped from the covers and dressed in a singlesuit striped vertically in yellow and green. Brett tried not to watch her dress, but his eyes no longer would obey.

"I check instruments in a half-hour," she said. "Then I ride outpost."

"What should I do about . . . you know, checking in?"

"I have reported. I should be finished in a few hours. Don't go wandering; you could get lost."

"I need a guide?"

"A friend," she said. Again, that quick smile. "If hunger strikes, there is food." She pointed toward the alcove end of her quarters. "When I get back, you will report in. Or they may send someone for you."

He glanced around the room, feeling that it would shrink without Scudi here and with nothing to do.

"You did not sleep well?" Scudi asked.

"Nightmares," he said. "I'm not used to sleeping still. Everything's so . . . dead, so quiet."

Her smile was a white blur in her dark face. "I have to go. Sooner out, sooner back."

When the hatch clicked shut behind her, the stillness of the little room boomed in Brett's ears. He looked at the bed where Scudi had slept.

I'm alone.

He knew that sleep was impossible. His attention wouldn't leave the slight impression left by Scudi's body on the other bed. Such a small room, why did it feel bigger when she was in it?

His heartbeat was fast, suddenly, and as it got faster he found a constriction of his chest whenever he tried to take a deep breath.

He swung his legs off the bed, pulled on his clothes and started to pace. His gaze moved erratically around the room—sink and water taps, the cupboards with conchlike whorls in the corners, the hatch to the head . . . everything was costly metal but plain and rigid in design. The water taps were shiny silver dolphins. He felt them and touched the wall behind them. The two metals had entirely different textures.

The room had no ports or skylights, nothing to show the exterior world. The walls with their kelplike undulations were breached only by the two hatches. He felt that he had an unlimited amount of energy and nowhere to use it.

He folded the beds back into their couch positions and paced the room. Something boiled in him. His chest became tighter and a swarm of wriggling black shapes intruded on his vision. There was nothing around him, he thought, but water. A loud ringing swelled in his ears.

Abruptly, Brett jerked open the outside hatch and lurched into the passageway. He only knew that he needed air. He fell to one knee there, gagging.

Two Mermen stopped beside him. One of them gripped his shoulder.

A man said, "Islander." His voice betrayed only curiosity.

"Easy does it," another man said. "You're safe."

"Air!" Brett gasped. Something heavy was standing on his chest, and his heart still raced inside his straining chest.

The man gripping his shoulder said: "There's plenty of air, son. Take a deep breath. Lean back against me and take a deep breath."

Brett felt the tension clawing at his belly lift a bony finger, then another. A new, commanding voice behind him demanded: "Who left this Mute alone here?" There was a scuffling sound, then a shout: "Medic! Here!"

Brett tried to take a fast, deep breath but couldn't. He heard a whistling in his constricted throat.

"Relax. Breathe slow and deep."

"Get him to a port," the commanding voice said. "Get him somewhere he can see outside. That usually works."

Hands straightened Brett and lifted him with arms under his shoulders. His fingertips and lips conveyed the buzz and tingle of electric shock. A blurred face bent close to him, inquiring, "Have you ever been down under before?"

Brett's lips shaped a silent "No." He was not sure he could walk.

"Don't be afraid," the blur said. "This occasionally happens your first time alone. You'll be all right."

Brett grew aware that people were hurrying him along a pale orange passageway. A hand patted his shoulder. The tingling receded, and the black shapes floating across his vision began to shrink. The people carrying him stopped and eased him to the deck on his back, then propped him upright. His head was clearing, and Brett looked up at a string of lights. The light cover directly overhead had blobs of dust and bugs inside. A head blotted out his view and Brett had an impression of a man about Twisp's age with a backlighted halo of dark hair.

"You feeling better?" the man asked.

Brett tried to speak in a dry mouth, then managed to croak, "I feel stupid."

In the sudden laughter all around him, Brett ducked his head and looked out a wide port into the sea. It was a horizontal view of low-lying kelp with many fish grazing between its leaves. This was a perspective of undersea life far different from the driftwatch views topside.

The older man patted his shoulder and said, "That's all right, son. Everyone feels stupid some time or other. It's better than *being* stupid, eh?"

Twisp would have said that, Brett thought. He grinned up at the long-haired Merman. "Thanks."

"Best thing for you to do, young man," the Merman said, "is to go back to a quiet room. Try being alone again."

The thought pumped Brett's pulse rate back up. He imagined himself alone once more in that little room with those metal walls *and all that water* . . .

"Who brought you in here?" the man asked.

Brett hesitated. "I don't want to cause any trouble."

"You won't," the medic reassured him. "We can get the person who picked you up freed from regular duty to make your entry into life here a little easier."

"Scudi . . . Scudi Wang picked me up."

"Oh! There are people waiting for you nearby. Scudi will be able to guide you. Lex," he spoke to a man out of Brett's line of vision, "call down to Scudi at the lab." The medic returned his attention to Brett. "There's no hurry, but you do have to get used to being alone."

A voice behind Brett said, "She's on her way."

"Lots of Islanders have a rough time of it down under at first. I'd say every one, in some way or other. Some recover all at once, a few brood for weeks. You look like you're getting over it."

Someone on the other side of Brett lifted Brett's chin and pressed a container of water to his lips. The water felt cold and tasted faintly of salt.

Brett saw Scudi rushing down the long passage, her small face twisted with worry. The Merman helped Brett to his feet, gripped his shoulder, then hurried toward Scudi. "Your friend's had a stress flash." The man hurried past Scudi, speaking back at her. "Put him through the solo drill before he learns to like the panic, though."

She waved her thanks, then helped Brett manage the walk back to her room.

"I should've stayed," Scudi said. "You were my first, and you seemed to be doing so well . . ."

"I thought I was, too," he said, "so don't feel bad. Who was that medic?"

"Shadow Panille. I work with his department in Search and Rescue—Current Control."

"I thought he was a medic, they said—"

"He is. Everyone in S and R holds that rating." Scudi took his arm. "Are you all right now?"

He blushed. "It was stupid of me. I just felt I had to get some air, and when I got out into the passage . . ."

"It's my fault," she insisted. "I forgot about stress flash and they're always telling us about it. I felt . . . well, like you'd *always* been here. I didn't think of you as a newcomer."

"The air in the passage felt so thick," Brett said. "Almost like water."

"Is it all right now?"

"Yes." He inhaled a deep breath. "Kind of . . . wet, though."

"It gets heavy enough to do your laundry in sometimes. Some Islanders have to carry dry bottles while they're adjusting. If you feel well now, we can report in. Some people are waiting for you." She shrugged at his inquiring look. "You have to be processed, of course."

He stared at her, reassured by her presence but still nursing an abrupt hollow feeling. Islanders heard many stories of the way Mermen regulated everything in their lives—reports for this, tests for that. He started to ask her about this processing but was interrupted as a large group of Mermen clattered past carrying equipment—tanks, hoses, stretchers.

Scudi called after them, "What is it?"

"They're bringing in the accident survivors," one of them hollered.

Ceiling speakers came alive then: "Situation Orange! Situation Orange! All emergency personnel to your stations. This is not a drill. This is not a drill. Keep docking areas clear. Keep passageways clear. Essential duty stations only for regular personnel. Essential duty stations only. All others report to alternate stations. Medical emergencies only in the passages or trauma shed vicinity. Situation Orange. This is not a drill . . ."

More Mermen dashed past them. One shouted back, "Clear the passageways!"

"What is it?" Scudi called after him.

"That Island that sank off Mistral Barrier. They're bringing in the survivors."

Brett yelled, "Was it Vashon?"

They ran on without answering.

Scudi pulled at his arm. "Hurry." She directed him down a side

168

passage and pulled up a large hatchway, which slid aside at her touch. "I'll have to leave you here and report to my station."

Brett followed her through a double-hatchway into a café. Booths with low-set tables lined the walls. More low tables were scattered throughout the room. Plasteel pillars in rows defined aisleways. Each pillar was set up as a serving-station. A booth in the corner held two people bent toward each other across the table. Scudi hurried Brett toward this booth. As they approached the figure on the right became clear. Brett missed a step. Every Islander knew that face—that craggy head with its elongated neck and its bracework: *Ward Keel!*

Scudi stopped at the booth, her hand gripping Brett's. Her attention was on Keel's companion. Brett recognized the red-haired woman. He'd glimpsed her on Vashon. Until he'd met Scudi, he'd considered Kareen Ale the most beautiful woman alive. Scudi's low-voiced introduction was not necessary.

"There were supposed to be registration and processing personnel here," Ale said, "but they've gone to their stations."

Brett swallowed hard and looked at Keel. "Mr. Justice, they said a whole Island's been sunk."

"It was Guemes," Keel said, his voice cold.

Ale looked at Keel. "Ward, I suggest that you and young Norton go to my quarters. Don't stay long in the passages and stay inside until you hear from me."

"I must go, Brett," Scudi said. "I'll come for you when this is over."

Ale touched Scudi's arm and they hurried away.

Slowly, painfully, Keel eased himself from the booth. He stood, letting his legs adjust to the new position.

Brett listened to the people rushing through the passage outside the hatchway.

Laboriously, Keel began shuffling toward the exit hatch.

"Come along, Brett."

As they stepped into the aisle leading toward the exit, a hatch behind them hissed open, gushing the rich smells of garlic fried in olive oil and spices he couldn't name. A man's voice called out: "You two! No one in the passages!"

Brett whirled. A heavyset man with dark gray hair stood in the open hatchway to the kitchen. His rather flat features were set in a scowl, which changed into a forced smile as he looked past Brett and recognized Keel.

169

"Sorry, Mr. Justice," the man said. "Didn't recognize you at first. But you still shouldn't be in the passages."

"We were instructed to vacate this place and meet the ambassador at her quarters," Keel said.

The man stepped aside and gestured toward the kitchen. "Through here. You can occupy Ryan Wang's old quarters. Kareen Ale will be notified."

Keel touched Brett's shoulder. "This is closer," he said.

The man led them into a large, low-ceilinged room flooded with soft light. Brett could not find the light source; it seemed to wash the room equally in gentle tones. Thick, pale blue carpeting caressed Brett's bare feet. The only furnishings appeared to be plump cushions in browns, burnt red and dark blue, but Brett, knowing how Mermen swung things out of walls, suspected other furniture might be concealed behind the hangings.

"You will be comfortable here," the man said.

"Who do I have the pleasure of thanking for this hospitality?" Keel asked.

"I am Finn Lonfinn," the man said. "I was one of Wang's servants and now have the task of caring for his quarters. And your young friend is . . . ?"

"Brett Norton," Brett answered. "I was on my way to registration and processing when the alarm sounded."

Brett studied the room. He had never seen a place quite like it. In some respects, it was vaguely Islander—soft cushions, all the metal covered by woven hangings, many recognizably of topside manufacture. But the deck did not move. Only the faint sigh of air pulsing through vents.

"Do you have friends on Guemes?" Lonfinn asked.

"The C/P is from Guemes," Keel reminded him.

Lonfinn's eyebrows lifted and he turned his attention to Brett. Brett felt required to give a reply. "I don't think I know anyone from Guemes. We haven't been in proximate drift since I was born."

Lonfinn focused once more on Keel. "I asked about friends, not about the C/P."

In the man's tone, Brett heard the hard slam of a hatch between Merman and Islander. The word *mutant* lay in the air between them. Simone Rocksack was a Mute, possibly a friend of Mute Ward Keel . . . probably not. Who could be friendly with someone

170

who looked like that? The C/P could not be a normal object of friendship. Brett felt suddenly threatened.

Keel had realized with an abrupt shock that Lonfinn's assumptions of obvious Merman superiority were barbed. This attitude was a common one among less-traveled Mermen, but Keel felt himself filled with disquiet at an abrupt inner awakening.

I was ready to accept his judgment! Part of me has assumed all along that Mermen are naturally better.

An unconscious thing, borne for years, it had unfolded in Keel like an evil flower, showing a part of himself he had never suspected. The realization filled Keel with anger. Lonfinn had been asking: "Do you have any little friends on Guemes? How sad that some of your less fortunate playmates have been killed or maimed. But maiming and death are such an integral part of your lives."

"You say you were a servant," Keel said. "Are you telling me these quarters are no longer occupied?"

"They belong rightfully to Scudi Wang, I believe," Lonfinn said. "She says she doesn't care to live here. I presume they'll be leased before long and the income credited to Scudi."

Brett gave the man a startled look and glanced once more around these spacious quarters—everything so rich.

Still in shock at his inner revelation, Keel shuffled to a pile of blue cushions and eased himself onto them, stretching his aching legs in front of him.

"Lucky Guemes was a small Island," Lonfinn said.

"Lucky?" The word was jerked from Brett.

Lonfinn shrugged. "I mean, how much more terrible if it had been one of the bigger Islands . . . even Vashon."

"We know what you mean," Keel said. He sighed. "I'm aware that Mermen call Guemes 'The Ghetto.'"

"It . . . doesn't mean anything, really," Lonfinn said. There was an undertone of anger in his voice as he realized he had been put on the defensive.

"What it means is that the larger Islands have been called upon to help Guemes from time to time—basic foods and medical supplies," Keel pressed him.

"Not much trade with Guemes," Lonfinn admitted.

Brett looked from one man to the other, detecting the subterranean argument boiling. There were things behind those words

171

but Brett suspected that it would take more experience with Mermen before he understood just what those things were. He sensed only the fact of argument, the barely concealed anger. Some Islanders, Brett knew, made slanted references to Guemes as "Ship's Lifeboat." There was often laughter in the label, but Brett had understood it to mean that Guemes held a large number of WorShipers—very religious, fundamentalist people. It was no surprise that the C/P was a native of Guemes. Somehow, it was right for Islanders to joke about Guemes, but it rankled him to hear Lonfinn's intrusions.

Lonfinn strode across the room and tested the controls on a hatch. He turned. "The head's through this hatch and guest bedrooms are down the hallway here in case you wish to rest." He returned and looked down at Keel. "I imagine that thing around your neck becomes tiresome."

Keel rubbed his neck. "It does indeed. But I know we all must put up with tiresome things in our world."

Lonfinn scowled. "I wonder why a Merman has never been C/P?"

Brett spoke up, recalling Twisp's comment on this very question. He repeated it: "Maybe Mermen have too many other things to do and aren't interested."

"Not interested?" Lonfinn looked at Brett as though seeing him for the first time. "Young man, I don't think you're qualified to discuss political matters."

"I think the boy was really asking a question," Keel offered, smiling at Brett.

"Questions should be asked directly," Lonfinn muttered.

"And answered directly," Keel persisted. He looked at Brett. "This matter has always been in dispute among 'the faithful' and their political lobby. Most of Ship's faithful topside think it would be a disaster to turn over the C/P's power to a Merman. They have so much power over other aspects of our otherwise dreary lives."

Lonfinn smiled without humor. "A difficult political subject for a young man to understand," he said.

Brett gritted his teeth at the patronizing attitude.

Lonfinn crossed to the wall behind Keel, touched a depression there and a panel slid away. It revealed a huge port that looked out on an undersea courtyard with transparent ceiling and a watery center where clusters of small fishes flashed and turned among delicate, richly colored plants.

"I must be going," Lonfinn said. "Enjoy yourselves. This"—he indicated the area he had just exposed—"should keep you from feeling too enclosed. I find it restful myself." He turned to Brett, paused and said, "I'll see that the necessary forms and papers are sent for you to sign. No sense wasting time."

With that, Lonfinn departed, leaving by the same hatch they had entered.

Brett looked at Keel. "Have you filled out these papers? What are they?"

"The papers fulfill the Merman need to feel they have every-thing pinned down. Your name, your age, circumstances of your arrival down under, your work experience, any talents you might have, whether you desire to stay . . ." Keel hesitated, cleared his throat. ". . . your parentage, their occupations and mutations. The severity of your own mutation."

Brett continued to regard the Chief Justice silently.

"And in answer to your other question," Keel continued, "no, they have not required this of me. I'm sure they have a long dossier on me giving all the important details . . . and many unimportant tidbits, too."

Brett had fastened onto one thing in Keel's statement. "They may ask me to stay down under?"

"They may require you to work off the cost of your rescue. A lot of Islanders have settled down under, something I mean to look into before going topside. Life here can be very attractive, I know." He ran his fingers through the soft nap of carpet as if for emphasis.

Brett looked at the ceiling, wondering how it would be to live most of his life here away from the suns. Of course, people from down under did go topside lots of times, but still . . .

"The best disaster-recovery team is composed mostly of ex-Islanders," Keel said. "So says Kareen Ale."

"I've heard the Mermen always want you to pay your own way," Brett said. "But it shouldn't take long to work off the cost of my . . ." He suddenly thought of Scudi. How could he ever repay Scudi? There was no coin for that.

"Mermen have a great many ways of attracting desirable and acceptable Islanders," Keel said. "You appear to be someone they'd be interested in having aboard. However, that should not be your chief concern of the moment. By any chance, do you have medical training?"

173

"Just first aid and resuscitation through school."

Keel drew in a deep breath and expelled it quickly. "Not enough, I'm afraid. Guemes went down quite a while ago. I'm sure the survivors they're just now bringing in will require more expert attention."

Brett tried to swallow in a tight throat.

Guemes, a whole Island sunk.

"I could carry a stretcher," he said.

Keel smiled sadly. "I'm sure you could. But I'm also sure you wouldn't be able to find the right place to take it. Either one of us would just be in the way. At the moment, we're just what they think of us—two Islander misfits who might do more harm than good. We'll just have to wait."

We seldom get rid of an evil merely by understanding its causes.

—C. G. Jung, Shiprecords

"There's a curse in the Histories," Bushka said, "old as humans. It says, 'May you live in interesting times.' I guess we got it."

For some time now, as the coracles cruised through the half-night of Pandora's open sea, Bushka had been telling Twisp what he'd learned from Gallow and from members of Gallow's crew. Twisp could not see Bushka. Only the thin red light of the RDC's arrow glowed in the coracle. All else was darkness—not even stars overhead. A damp cloud cover had swept over them shortly after nightfall.

"There'll be more open land than you can possibly imagine," Bushka continued. "As much land as you see water around you now. So they say."

"It's all bad for the Islands," Twisp said. "And those rockets you say they're launching . . ."

"Oh, they're well-prepared," Bushka said. His voice came out of the darkness with a smug sound that Twisp did not like. "Everything's ready for bringing down the hyb tanks. Warehouses full of equipment."

"It's hard for me to imagine land," Twisp admitted. "Where will they lift it out of the sea first?"

"The place that the settlers here called 'Colony.' On the maps, it's a slightly curved rectangle. The curve is being widened and lengthened into an oval with a lagoon at its center. It was a complete city before the Clone Wars, walled in with plasteel, so it makes a good place to start. Sometime this year they'll pump it out and the first city will be exposed to the sky."

"Waves will wipe it out," Twisp said.

"No," Bushka countered. "They've been five generations preparing for this. They've thought of everything—the politics, economics, the kelp . . ." He broke off as one of the squawks uttered a sleepy bleat.

Both men froze, listening expectantly. Was there a night-roaming hunt of dashers nearby? The squawks remained quiet.

"Bad dream," Bushka muttered.

"So Guemes Island with its religious fanatics stood in the way of this land-colonization project, is that it?" Twisp asked. "Them and their 'stick-to-the-Islands-where-Ship-left-us' attitude?"

Bushka did not respond.

Twisp thought about the things the man had revealed. A lifetime of fisherman's isolation clouded Twisp's imagination. He felt provincial, incapable of understanding matters of world-wide politics and economics. He knew what worked, and that seemed simple enough. All he knew was that he distrusted this grand scheme, which Bushka seemed half-enamored of in spite of the experience with Gallow.

"There's no place in this plan for Islanders," Twisp noted.

"No, no place for mutants. They're to be excluded," Bushka said. His voice was almost too low to hear.

"And who's to say what a mutant is?" Twisp demanded.

Bushka remained silent for a long time. Finally, he said, "The Islands are obsolete, that much I can't argue with. In spite of everything else, Gallow's right about that."

Twisp stared into the darkness where Bushka sat. There was a spot just to the left that felt a little darker than the rest. That's where Twisp aimed his attention. An image of Merman life came to him—their habitation, places Bushka had described. *Home,* he thought. *What kind of person calls this home?* Everything sounded regular and nearly identical, like some insect hive. It gave him the creeps.

"This place you're guiding us to," Twisp asked, "what is it? Why is it safe for us to go there?"

"The Green Dashers are a small organization," Bushka said. "Launch Base One is huge—by the numbers alone our odds are better there than anyplace else in decent range."

This is hopeless, Twisp thought. If Mermen had not found Brett already, what else could he do? The sea was too big and it had been a fool's errand trying to fix on the place where the wavewall hit Vashon.

176

"It'll be dawn soon," Bushka said. "We should be there shortly after dawn."

Twisp heard the spat-spattering of rain on the tarp. He checked his eelcells with the handlight and found that they were turning a noticeable gray. Right on cue there was a tremendous deafening lightning thunder flash behind them. In the aftershock stillness, he heard Bushka holler, "What the fuck was *that?*"

Twisp flashed the handlight in that direction. Bushka had gone under the tarp head-first and somehow got himself turned around. He clutched the edges of the tarp, steadying himself, and in the glow from the handlight, his wide eyes punctuated his bleached face.

"We just charged our batteries," Twisp said. "We might take one more of those if it comes around. Then I'll bring in the antenna."

"Holy shit," Bushka snorted, "fishermen are crazier than I thought. It's a wonder any of you come back."

"We manage," Twisp said. "Tell me, how did you become an expert on Mermen so fast?"

Bushka emerged from the tarp. "As a historian, I already knew a great deal about them before going down under. And then . . . you learn fast when it's necessary for survival." There was the sound of chest-puffing behind his words.

Survival, Twisp thought. He extinguished the handlight and wished that he could see Bushka's face without having to flash the light on him. The man was not a total coward; that seemed evident. He had crewed in the subs, like many other Islanders putting in their service time. Obviously knew how to navigate. But then, most Islanders learned that in school. With all that, Bushka was driven to seek a life down under. According to him, it was because the Mermen had better historical records, some they had never even examined themselves.

Bushka was like some of the Guemes fanatics, Twisp realized. *Driven.* A seeker after hidden knowledge. Bushka wanted his facts from the source and he didn't care how he got there. A dangerous man.

Twisp renewed his alertness, sensitive to any shift in Bushka's position. The coracle would transmit such movement . . . should Bushka try to take him.

177

"You'd better believe it's happening," Bushka said. "There'll be no place for Islands pretty soon."

"Radio says Ward Keel's gone down under on some fact-finding mission," Twisp said. "You suppose he knew about it all along?"

A foot scraped the deck as Bushka shifted his weight. "According to Gallow, they did it without word topside."

Silence settled between them for a time. Twisp kept his attention on the guiding arrow, a red glowing pointer. How could some of the things Bushka said be believed? The barrier above the sea was real, though. And there was no doubt Bushka had run-for-it fever—something truly big and ugly chased him.

For his part, Bushka lay prisoned in his own thoughts. *I should've had the guts to kill them.* But the thing Gallow represented was bigger than Gallow. No mistaking that. To a historian, it was a familiar pattern. Ship's surviving records reported a plenitude of violence, leaders who tried to solve human problems by mass killing. Until the madness of Guemes, Bushka had thought such things distantly unreal. Now, he *knew* the madness, a thing with teeth and shadows.

Pale dawn lightened the wavetops and revealed Twisp working over a small cooking burner on the seat beside him. Bushka wondered whether, in the growing clarity of daylight, Twisp might not rather foreclose on the loan of the kid's shirt and pants.

Seeing Bushka's attention on him, Twisp asked, "Coffee?"

"Thanks." Then: "How could I have been that blind and ignorant?"

Twisp stared at Bushka silently for a while, then asked, simply, "Going along with them, or letting them go?"

Bushka coughed and cleared his throat. His mouth felt full of lint as soon as he swallowed the hot coffee.

I'm still afraid, he thought. He looked up at Twisp, cooling his coffee at the tiller. "I've never been that afraid," he said.

Twisp nodded. The signs of fear on Bushka were easily read. Fear and ignorance drifted the same currents. There would be anger soon, when the fear receded. For now, though, Bushka's mind was chewing on itself.

"Pride, that's what made me do it," Bushka said. "I wanted Gallow's story, history in the making, political ferment—a powerful movement among the Mermen. One of their best took a liking to me. He knew I'd work hard. He knew how grateful I'd be . . ."

"What if this Gallow and his crew are dead?" Twisp asked. "You

178

scuttled their sub and only you are left to say what happened at Guemes."

"I tell you, I made sure they could escape!"

Twisp suppressed a grim smile. The anger was beginning to surface.

Bushka studied Twisp's face in the gray light. The fisherman was dark in the way of many Islanders who worked out in the weather. Vagrant breezes whipped Twisp's shaggy brown hair across his eyes. A two days' growth of beard shadowed his jaws and caught an occasional strand of hair. Everything in the man's manner—the steady movement of his eyes, the set of his mouth—spoke to Bushka of strength and resolution. Bushka envied the untroubled clarity in Twisp's gaze. Bushka was sure that no mirror would ever again return such clarity to his own eyes—not after the Guemes massacre. Bushka could see his own death in that butchery.

How could anybody believe I didn't know what was happening until it happened? How can I believe it?

"They tricked me good," Bushka said. "And oh, was I ready! I was all ready to trick myself."

"Most people know what it's like to be tricked," Twisp agreed. His voice was flat and almost devoid of emotion. It kept Bushka talking.

"I won't sleep for the rest of my life," Bushka muttered.

Twisp looked away at the surging sea around them. He didn't like the note of self-pity in Bushka's tone.

"What about the survivors of Guemes?" He spoke flatly. "What about their dreams?"

Bushka stared at Twisp in the growing light. A good man trying to save a partner's life. Bushka scrunched his eyes tightly closed but the images of Guemes imprinted themselves on his eyelids.

His eyes snapped open.

Twisp was staring intently off to the right ahead of them.

"Where's this Launch Base we're supposed to see at dawn?"

"It'll show before long."

Bushka stared at the lowering sky ahead of them. And when the Launch Base did show . . . what then? The question tightened a band around his chest. Would the Mermen believe? Even if they did believe, would they act on that belief in a way to protect Islanders?

179

Never trust a great man's love.

Keel looked down from the observation platform onto a
nightmare scene of controlled pandemonium—rescue sleds wallowed into a small docking basin, coming through hatches lining
the far wall of the courtyard below him. This was no nightmare,
Keel reminded himself. Triage teams moved among the human
shapes that littered the deck. Trauma teams conducted emergency surgery on the scene while other survivors were carried or
carted off. The dead, and Keel had never imagined that much
death, were stacked like the meat they were against the wall to his
left. A long, oval port above the hatches gave a sea view of the
arriving rescue sledges queued up and waiting their turns at the
hatches. Trauma teams serviced these, too, as best they could.

Behind Keel, Brett uttered a sharp gasp as the shreds of someone's lower jaw tumbled to the deck from a body bag in transit to
the mounting pile of similar bags against the wall. Scudi, standing
beside Brett, shook with silent sobs.

Keel felt numb. He began to understand why Kareen Ale had
sent Scudi to fetch him and Brett. Ale had not really grasped the
enormity of this tragedy. Seeing it, she had wanted Islander wit-
nesses to the fact that Mermen were doing everything physically
possible for the survivors.

And she'll bring up the dirty work of the dead, he thought.

Keel glimpsed Ale's red hair among the medics working over
the few survivors scattered across the courtyard. From the piles of
dead, it was obvious that survivors were not even meeting the
odds of pure chance. They were a tiny minority.

Scudi moved up beside him, her attention fixed on the deck
below them. "So many," she whispered.

"How did it happen?" Brett demanded, speaking from beside
Keel's left elbow.

Keel nodded. Yes, that was the real question. He did not want to conjecture on the matter, he wanted to be certain.

"So many," Scudi repeated, louder this time.

"The last census put Guemes at ten thousand souls," Keel said. This statement surprised him even as it escaped his mouth. *Souls.* The teachings of Ship *did* come to the surface in a crisis.

Keel knew he should assert himself, use the power of his position to demand answers. He owed it to the others if not to himself. The C/P would be after him the minute he returned, for one thing. Rocksack still had family on Guemes, of this Keel was certain. She would be angry, terribly angry in spite of her training, and she would be a force to reckon with.

If I return.

Keel felt sickened by the sight on the deck below him. He noted Scudi swiping at her tears. Her eyes were red and swollen. Yes, she had been helping down there, right in the middle of it, during the worst pressures.

"No need for you to stay here with me, Scudi," Keel said. "If they need you down—"

"I've been relieved of duty," she said. She shuddered, but her gaze remained on the receiving area.

Keel, too, could not take his attention from that scene of carnage. The receiving area had been cordoned off into sections by color-coded ropes. Emergency medical teams worked throughout the area, bending over pale flesh, moving patients onto litters for transfer.

A squad of Mermen entered from beneath the platform where Keel stood with Brett and Scudi. The Mermen began sorting through the sacks of bodies, opening them to attempt identification. Some of the bags contained only shreds and pieces of flesh and bone. The identification teams moved in a businesslike fashion, but where their jaws were visible, Keel detected clenched muscles. All of them appeared pale, even for Mermen. Several of the workers took pictures of faces and identifying marks. Others made notes on a portable trans-slate. Keel recognized the device. Ale had tried to interest his Committee in this system, but he had seen it as another way to keep the Islands in economic bondage. *"Everything you write on the transmitter-slate is sorted and stored in the computer,"* Ale had said.

Some things are best not recorded, he thought.

A man cleared his throat behind Keel. Keel turned to find

Lonfinn and another Merman standing there. Lonfinn carried a plaz box under his left arm.

"Mr. Justice," Lonfinn said. "This is Miller Hastings of Registration."

In contrast to the dark, heavyset Lonfinn, Hastings was a tall, dark-haired man with a thick lower jaw and unwavering blue eyes. Both men wore crisp Merman suits of plain gray cloth—the kind of smoothly pressed and well-tended clothing Keel had come to identify with the worst Merman officiousness.

Hastings had turned his attention to Brett standing a few steps to one side. "We were told we would find a Brett Norton up here," Hastings said. "There are a few formalities . . . for yourself, too, I'm afraid, Mr. Justice."

Scudi moved behind Keel and took Brett's hand, an action that Keel's wide peripheral vision took in with some surprise. She was clearly frightened.

Hastings focused on Keel's mouth. "Our job, Mr. Justice, is to help you adjust to this tragic—"

"Shit!" Keel said.

Brett wondered whether he had heard correctly. The look of surprise on Hastings' face made it apparent that the Chief Justice and Chairman of the Committee on Vital Forms had, indeed, said "Shit." Brett looked at the Chief Justice's face. Keel had positioned himself with one eye on the two Mermen and the other eye still looking down on that bloody deck below them. It was a split of attention that appeared to disconcert the two Mermen. Brett found it natural; everyone knew that some Islanders could do this.

Hastings made another try: "We know this is difficult, Mr. Justice, but we are prepared for such matters and have developed procedures, which—"

"Have the decency to leave before I lose my temper," Keel said. His voice betrayed no sign of a quaver.

Hastings glanced at the plaz box under Lonfinn's arm, then at Brett.

"Hostility is an expected reaction," Hastings said. "But the sooner we overcome that barrier, the sooner—"

"I say it plain," Keel said, "leave us. We have nothing to say to you."

The Mermen exchanged glances. The looks on their faces told Brett that this pair had no intention of leaving.

182

"The young man should speak for himself," Hastings said. His tone was even and cordial. "What do you say, Brett Norton? Just a few formalities."

Brett swallowed. Scudi's hand in his felt slick with perspiration. Her fingers were tense sticks clenched between his own. What was Keel doing? More important, perhaps: Could Keel get away with it? Keel was an Islander and a powerful one, someone to admire. This was not the Island, however. Brett squared his shoulders in sudden decision. "Stuff your formalities," he said. "Any decent person would come another time."

Hastings let out a long breath slowly, almost a sigh. His face darkened and he started to speak but Keel cut him short.

"What the young man is saying," Keel said, "is that it's pretty insensitive of you to come here with your formalities while your cousins stack the bodies of our cousins against that wall down there."

The silence between the two groups became stiff. Brett could find no particular familial feeling toward the mangled dead being brought in from the depths, but he decided that the Mermen didn't need to know this.

Them and us.

But there was still Scudi's hand in his. Brett felt that the only Merman he could trust might be Scudi . . . and perhaps that medic in the passageway, Shadow Panille. Panille had clear eyes and . . . *he cared.*

"We didn't kill those people," Hastings said. "Please note, Mr. Justice, that we have gotten right down to the dirty work of bringing them in, identifying the dead, helping the survivors—"

"How noble of you," Keel said. "I was wondering how long it would take to get down to this. You haven't mentioned your fee, of course."

Both Mermen looked grim but they did not appear particularly flustered.

"Someone has to pay," Hastings said. "No one topside has the facilities to—"

"So you pick up the dead," Keel said. "And their families topside pay for your trouble. With a tidy profit for certain contractors, too."

"Nobody expects to work for nothing," Hastings said.

Keel rolled one eye toward Brett, then back. "And when you

rescue a live fisherman, you find a way to accommodate him, keeping a close account of the expenses, naturally."

"I don't want anything for my part," Scudi said. Her eyes flashed anger at both Keel and Hastings.

"I respect that, Scudi," Keel said. "I wasn't indicting you. But your fellow Mermen here have a different viewpoint. Brett has no fishing gear to seize, no nets or sonar or beaten-up boat. How will he pay for his life? Ten years of chopping onions in a Merman kitchen?"

Hastings said, "Really, Mr. Justice, I don't understand your reluctance to make matters easier."

"I was lured here under false pretenses," Keel said. "I haven't been out of sight of my . . . hosts . . . long enough to spit." He pointed to the view port across from them. "Look there!" He lowered his pointing finger to indicate the deck below. "Those bodies are shredded, burned, cut to pieces. Guemes was assaulted! I think a reconstruction will show that it was assaulted from below by a hardshell sub."

For the first time, Hastings appeared as though he might lose control. His eyes squinted and his brows drew down over his beak of a nose. His jaw clenched and he hissed between his teeth: "See here! I'm only doing what Merman law requires me to do. In my judgment—"

"Oh, please," Keel interrupted, "judgment is my job and I'm experienced in it. To me, you look like a pair of leeches. I don't like leeches. Please leave us."

"Since you are who you are," Hastings said, "I will accept that for the moment. This boy, however—"

"Has me here to look out for his interests," Keel said. "This is not the time nor the place for your services."

Lonfinn stepped to one side, casually blocking the exit passage from the observation platform.

"The boy will answer for himself," Hastings said.

"The Justice asked you to leave," Brett said.

Scudi squeezed Brett's hand and said, "Please. I will be responsible for them. Ambassador Ale sent me personally to bring them here. Your presence is disruptive."

Hastings looked her in the eyes as though he wanted to say, "Big talk for a little girl," but he swallowed it. His right index finger indicated the plaz box under Lonfinn's arm, then dropped. "Very well," he said. "We were trying to smooth out the red tape but the situation is difficult." He shot a quick glance at the congested deck below them. "However, I am required to escort you back to Ryan Wang's quarters. It may have been a mistake to bring you here."

"I find it agreeable to leave," Keel said. "I've seen enough." His voice was once more smooth and diplomatic.

Brett heard the double meaning in Keel's statement and thought, *That old spinnarett has a web or two left in him.*

The thought stayed with Brett as they returned to Wang's spacious quarters. It had been wise to follow the Chief Justice's lead. Even Scudi had fallen in with Keel. She had kept her hand in Brett's most of the way back to her father's quarters, in spite of disapproving little glances from Hastings and Lonfinn. Her hand in his conveyed a feeling of closeness that Brett enjoyed.

Once inside the plush room of colored cushions, Keel said, "Thank you, gentlemen. I'm sure we can contact you if you're needed."

"You'll hear from us," Hastings said before he sealed the hatch behind him.

Keel crossed to the hatch and pressed the switch but nothing happened. The hatch stayed sealed. He glanced at Scudi.

"Those men worked for my father," she said. "I don't like them." She slipped her hand from Brett's and crossed to a dark red cushion where she sat with her chin on her knees and her arms clasped around her legs. The yellow-and-green stripes along her singlesuit curved as she curved.

"Brett," Keel said, "I will speak openly, because one of us may be able to get back topside to warn the other Islands. My suspicions are being confirmed at every turn. I believe our Island way of life is about to be drowned in a shallow sea."

Scudi lifted her chin and stared up at him with dismay. Brett could not find his voice.

Keel looked down at Scudi, thinking how her pose reminded him of a many-legged mollusc that rolled up into a tight ball when disturbed.

"The popular teaching," Keel said, "is that Island life is just temporary until we get back to the land."

"But Guemes . . ." Brett said. He could not get further.

"Yes, Guemes," Keel said.

"No!" Scudi blurted. "Mermen *couldn't* have done that! We protect the Islands!"

185

"I believe you, Scudi," Keel said. His neck pained him but he lifted his great head the way he did when passing judgment in his own court. "Things are happening that the people are not aware of . . . the people topside and the people down under."

Scudi asked Keel, "You really think Mermen did this?"

"We must reserve judgment until all the evidence is gathered," he said. "Nevertheless, it seems the most likely possibility."

Scudi shook her head. Brett saw sorrow and rejection there.

"Mermen wouldn't do such a thing," she whispered.

"It's not the Merman government," Keel said. "Principles of government sometimes take one course while people take another—a political double standard. And perhaps neither really controls events."

What's he saying? Brett wondered.

Keel continued: "Mermen and Islanders both have tolerated only the loosest kind of government. I am Chief Justice of a most powerful arm of that government—the one that says whether the newborn of our Islands will live or die. It pleases some to call me Chairman and others to call me Chief Justice. I do not feel that I dispense justice."

"I can't believe anyone would just eliminate the Islands," Scudi said.

"Someone certainly eliminated Guemes," Keel said. One sad eye drifted toward Brett, the other remained focused on Scudi. "It should be investigated, don't you think?"

"Yes." She nodded against her knees.

"It would be good to have inside help," Keel said. "On the other hand, I would not want to endanger anyone who helped me."

"What do you need?" Scudi asked.

"Information," he said. "Recent news recordings for the Merman audience. A survey of Merman jobs would help—which categories still have openings, which are filled to overflowing. I need to know what's really happening down here. And we'll need comparable statistics on the Islander population that's living down under."

"I don't understand," Scudi said.

"I'm told you mathematic the waves," Keel said, looking at Brett. "I want to mathematic Merman society. I cannot assume that I'm dealing with traditional Merman politics. I suspect that even Mermen don't realize they're no longer in the grip of their traditional politics. News is a clue to fluctuations. Jobs, too. They might be a clue to permanent changes and the intent behind those changes."

"My father had a comconsole in his den," Scudi said. "I'm sure I could get some of this through it . . . but I'm not sure I understand how you . . . mathematic it."

"Judges are sensitized to the assimilation of data," Keel said. "I pride myself on being a good judge. Get me this material, if you can."

Brett suggested, "Maybe we should see other Islanders living down under."

Keel smiled. "Don't trust the paperwork already, huh? We'll save that for later. It could be dangerous right now." *Good instincts,* he noted.

Scudi pressed her palms to her temples and closed her eyes. "My people don't kill," she said. "We aren't like that."

Keel stared down at the girl, thinking suddenly how similar at the core were Mermen and Islanders.

The sea.

He had never before thought of the sea in quite this way. How must their ancestors have adapted to it? The sea was always there—interminable. It was a thing unending, a source of life and a threat of death. To Scudi and her people, the sea was a silent pressure, whose sounds were always muted by the depths, whose currents moved in great sweeps along the bottom and through the shadows up to light. For the Merman, the world was muted and remote, yet pressing. To an Islander, the sea was noisy and immediate in its demands. It required adjustments in balance and consciousness.

The result was a quickness about Islanders which Mermen found charming. *Colorful!* Mermen, in contrast, were often studied and careful, measuring out their decisions as though they shaped precious jewels.

Keel glanced from Scudi to Brett and back to Scudi. Brett was taken by her, that much was clear. Was it the infatuation of differences? Was he some exotic mammal to her, or a man? Keel hoped something deeper than adolescent sexual attraction had been ignited there. He did not think himself so crass as to believe that Islander-Merman differences would be solved in the sexual thrashings of the bedroom. But the human race was still alive in these two and he could feel it moving them. The thought was reassuring.

"My father cared for both Islanders and Mermen," Scudi said. "His money made the Search and Rescue system a system."

"Show me his den," Keel said. "I would like to use his com-console."

She stood and crossed to a passage hatch on the far side of the atrium. "This way."

Keel motioned for Brett to stay behind while he followed Scudi. Perhaps if the young woman were away from the distractions of Brett's presence she might think more clearly—less defensive, more objective.

When Keel and Scudi had gone, Brett turned to the locked hatch. He and Keel and Scudi had been sealed away from whatever the exterior Merman world might reveal. Ale had wanted them to see that world, but others objected. Brett felt this the complete answer to his present isolation.

What would Queets do? he wondered.

Brett felt it unlikely that Queets would stand vacant-eyed in the middle of a strange room and stare stupidly at a locked hatch. Brett crossed to the hatch and ran a finger around the heavy metal molding that framed the exit.

Should've asked Scudi about communications systems and the ways they move freight, he thought. He could remember nothing of the passageways except their sparse population—sparse by crowded Islander standards.

"What are you thinking?"

Scudi's voice from close behind him startled him. Brett hadn't heard her approach over the soft carpet.

"Do you have a map of this place?" he asked.

"Somewhere," she said. "I'll have to look."

"Thanks."

Brett continued to stare at the locked hatch. How had they locked it? He thought of Island quarters, where the simplest slash of a knife would let you through the soft organics separating most rooms. Only the laboratories, Security's quarters and Vata's chamber could be said to have substantial resistance to entry—but that was as much a function of the guards as of the thickness of the walls.

Scudi returned with a thin stack of overlays, on which thick and thin lines with coded symbols indicated the layout of this Merman complex. She put it into Brett's hands as though giving away something of herself. For no reason he could explain, Brett found her gesture poignant.

"Here we are," she said, pointing to a cluster of squares and rectangles marked "RW."

He studied the overlays. This was not the free-flowing, action-dictated environment of an Island, where the idiosyncracies of organic growth directed the kind of changes that flaunted individuality. Islands were personalized, customized, carved, painted and dyed—shaped to the synergistic needs of support systems and those the systems supported. The schematic in Brett's hands reeked of uniformity—identical rows of cubicles, long straight passages, tubing and channels and access tunnels that ran as straight as a sun's rays through dust. He found it difficult to follow such uniformity, but forced his mind to it.

Scudi said: "I asked the Justice if a volcano might have destroyed Guemes."

Brett raised his attention from the schematic. "What did he say?"

"There were too many people shredded and not burned." She pressed the palms of her hands against her eyelids. "Who could do . . . *that?*"

"Keel's right about one thing," Brett said, "we need to find out *who* as soon as possible."

He returned his attention to the stack of colloids and its mysterious mazes. All at once he was awash with the simplicity of it. It was clear to him that Mermen must find it impossible to travel any Island, where sheer memory guided most people. He set about memorizing the schematics, with their lift shafts and transport tubes. He closed his eyes and confidently read the map that displayed itself behind his eyelids. Scudi paced the room behind him. Brett opened his eyes.

"Could we escape from here?" he asked, nodding toward the locked hatch.

"I can get us through the hatch," she said. "Where would you go?"

"Topside."

She looked at the hatch, her head shaking a slow "no" from side to side. "When we open the hatch, they will know. An electronic signal."

"What would those men do if we left here together?"

189

"Bring us back," she said. "Or try. The odds favor them. Nothing moves down under without someone knowing. My father had an efficient organization. That's why he hired men like those." She nodded at the hatch. "My father directed a very large business—a food business. He had much trade with Islanders . . ."

Her eyes shifted away from his, then back. She indicated the walls and ceiling. "This was his building, the whole thing. As high as the docking tower, all of it." She defined an area on the schematics with a finger. "This."

Brett drew slightly away from her. She had defined an area as large as some of the smaller Islands. Her father had *owned* it. He knew that by Merman law she probably inherited it. She was no simple worker in the seas, an apprentice physicist who mathematicked the waves.

Scudi saw the look of withdrawal in his eyes and touched his arm. "I live my own life," she said, "as my mother did. My father and I hardly knew each other."

"Didn't know each other?" Brett felt shocked. He knew himself to be estranged from his own parents, but he had certainly *known* them.

"Until shortly before he died, he lived at the Nest—a city about ten kilometers away," Scudi said. "In all that time I never saw him." She took a deep breath. "Before he died, my father came to our room one night and spoke to my mother. I don't know what they said but she was furious after he left."

Brett thought about what she had said. Her father had owned and controlled enormous wealth—much of Merman society. Topside, such matters as Ryan Wang controlled were the property of families or associations, never of one person. Community was law.

"He controlled much of your Islands' food production," she continued. A flush bloomed across her cheeks. "A lot of it he accomplished through bribery. I know because I listened, and sometimes when he was gone I used his comconsole."

"What is this place, the Nest?" Brett asked.

"It is a city that has a high Islander population. It was the site of the first settlement after the Clone Wars. You know of this?"

"Yes," he said. "One way or another, we all came from there."

Ward Keel, standing in the shadows of the open passage from Ryan Wang's den, had been listening to this exchange for several minutes. He shuddered, wondering whether he should interrupt

190

and demand some answers of this young woman. The anguish in her voice held Keel in place.

"Did those Islanders in the Nest work for your father?" Keel asked.

She didn't turn away from Brett to answer. "Some of them. But no Islander has any high position on anything. They are controlled by a government agency. I think Ambassador Ale is in charge of it."

"It seems to me that an Islander should head an agency that deals with Islanders," Brett said.

"She and my father were to be married," Scudi said. "A political matter between the two families . . . a lot of Merman history that isn't important now."

"Your father and the ambassador—that would have linked the powers of the government and the food supply under one blanket," Brett said. The insight came so quickly that it startled him.

"That's all ancient history," Scudi said. "She'll probably marry GeLaar Gallow now." Her words came out with an underlying misery that held Brett speechless. He could see the dark confusion in her eyes, the frustration of being a piece in some unruled game.

In the shadows of the passage, Ward Keel nodded to himself. He had shuffled back from Wang's den with a feeling of helpless anger. It was all there for the discerning eye—the shifts of control, the quiet and remorseless accumulation of power in a few hands, an increase in local identity. A term from the Histories kept rattling in his memory: *Nationalization.* Why did it give him such a feeling of loss?

The land is being restored.
The good life is coming.
This is why Ship gave Pandora to us.
To us—to Mermen—not to Islanders.

Keel's throat pained him when he tried to swallow. The kelp project lay at the base of it all, and that had gone too far to be lost or slowed. It was being taken over, instead. Justifications for the project could not be denied. The late Ryan Wang's comconsole was full of those justifications: Without the kelp the suns would continue to fatigue the crust of Pandora, constant earthquakes

191

and volcanics would ravage them as they had all those generations back.

Lava built up undersea plateaus along fault lines. Mermen were taking advantage of this for their project. The last wavewall had been a consequence of a volcanic upheaval, not the gravitational swings that inflicted themselves on Pandora's seas.

Brett was speaking: "I would like to see the Nest and the Islanders there. Maybe that's where we should go."

Out of the mouths of babes, Keel thought.

Scudi shook her head in negation. "They would find us there easily. Security there is not like here—there are badges, papers . . ."

"Then we should run topside," Brett said. "The Justice is right. He wants us to tell the Islanders what's happening down here."

"And what *is* happening?" she asked.

Keel stepped out of the shadows, speaking as he moved: "Pandora is being changed—physically, politically, socially. That's what's happening. The old life will not be possible, topside or down under. I think Scudi's father had a dream of great things, the transformation of Pandora, but someone else has taken it over and is making it a nightmare."

Keel stopped, facing the two young people. They stared back at him, aghast.

Can they feel it? Keel wondered.

Runaway greed was working to seize control of this new Pandora.

Scudi jabbed a finger at the schematic, which Brett still held. "The Launch Base and Outpost Twenty-two," she said. "Here! They are near Vashon's current drift. The Island will be at least a full day past this point by now but . . ."

"What're you suggesting?" Keel asked.

"I think I can get us to Outpost Twenty-two," she said. "I've worked there. From the outpost, I could compute Vashon's exact position."

Keel looked at the chart in Brett's hands. A surge of homesickness surged through the Justice. To be in his own quarters . . . Joy near at hand to care for him. He was going to die soon . . . how much better to die in familiar surroundings. As quickly as it came, the feeling was suppressed. Escape? He did not have the energy, the swiftness. He could only hold these young people back. But he saw the eagerness in Scudi and the way Brett picked up on it. They might just do it. The Islands had to be told what was happening.

"Here is what we will do," Keel said. "And this is the message you will carry."

Perseverance furthers.

—I Ching, Shiprecords

A flock of wild squawks came flying past the coracles, their wings whistling in the dull gray light of morning. Twisp turned his head to follow the birds' path. They landed about fifty meters ahead of him.

Bushka had sat up at the sudden sound, fear obvious in his face.

"Just squawks," Twisp said.

"Oh." Bushka subsided with his back against the cuddy.

"If we feed 'em, they'll follow us," Twisp said. "I've never seen 'em this far from an Island."

"We're near the base," Bushka said.

As they approached the swimming flock, Twisp tipped some of his garbage over the side. The birds came scrambling for the handout. The smaller ones churned their legs so fast they skipped across the water.

It was the birds' eyes that interested him, he decided. There was living presence in those eyes you never saw in the eyes of sea creatures. Squawk eyes looked back at you with something of the human world in them.

Bushka moved up and sat on the cuddy top to watch the birds and the horizon ahead of them. *Where is that damned Launch Base?* The motions of the birds kept attracting his attention. Twisp had said the squawks acted out of an ancient instinct. Probably true. Instinct! How long did it take to extinguish instinct? Or develop it? Which way were humans going? How strongly were they driven by such inner forces? Historian questions thronged his mind.

"That dull-looking squawk is a female," Bushka said, pointing to the wild flock. "I wonder why the males are so much more colorful?"

194

"Has to be some survival in it," Twisp said. He looked at the flock swimming beside the coracle, their eyes alert for another handout. "That's a female, all right." A scowl settled over his face. "One thing you can say for that hen squawk: she'll never ask a surgeon to make her *normal!*"

Bushka heard the bitterness and sensed the old familiar Islander story. It was getting to be ever more common these days: A lover had surgery to appear Merman-normal, then pressured the partner to do the same. A lot of angry fights resulted.

"Sounds like you got burned," Bushka said.

"I was crisped and charred," Twisp said. "Have to admit it was fun at first . . ." He hesitated, then: ". . . but I hoped it would be more than fun, something more permanent." He shook his head.

Bushka yawned and stretched. The wild flock took his movement as a threat and scattered in a flurry of splashes and loud cries.

Twisp stared toward the wild birds, but his eyes were not focused on them. "Her name's Rebeccah," he said. "She really liked my arms around her. Never complained about how long they were until—" He broke off in sudden embarrassment.

"She chose surgical correction?" Bushka prompted.

"Yeah." Twisp swallowed. *Now what set me talking about Rebeccah to this stranger? Am I that lonesome?* She had liked to feed the squawks at rimside every evening. He had enjoyed those evenings more than he could tell, and remembered details in a flood that he shut off as soon as it started.

Bushka was staring at his own hands. "She dumped you after the surgery?"

"Dumped me? Naw." Twisp sighed. "That would've been easy. I know I'd always feel like some kind of freak around her afterwards. No Mute can afford to feel that way, ever. It's why a lot of us more obvious types shy away from the Mermen. It's the stares and the way we think of ourselves then—our own eyes looking back from the mirror."

"Where is she now?" Bushka asked.

"Vashon," Twisp said. "Someplace close to Center, I'd guess. That's one thing good looks can get you on Vashon. I'd bet big money she's down there where the rich and powerful live. Her job was preparing people psychologically for surgical correction—she was sort of a living model of how life would be if they went through everything right."

"She made the choice, and it worked for her."

"If you talk about something like that long enough it becomes an obsession. She used to say: 'Changing some bodies is easy. A good surgeon knows just where to work. Minds are a little tougher.' I think she didn't really listen to herself."

Bushka looked at Twisp's long arms, a sudden insight flooding his mind.

Twisp saw the direction of Bushka's gaze and nodded. "That's right," he said. "She wanted me to get my arms fixed. She didn't understand, not even with all of her psychological crap behind her. I wasn't afraid of the knife or any of that eelshit. It was that my body would be a lie, and I can't stand liars."

This is no ordinary fisherman, Bushka thought.

"I finally figured it out about her," Twisp said. "A little too much boo and she started with this pitch for all of us to be 'as normal as possible.' Like you, Bushka."

"I don't feel that way."

"'Cause you don't have to. You're all ready to join the Mermen on their open land, on their terms."

Bushka found no words to answer. He had always been proud of his Merman-normal appearance. He could pass without surgery.

Twisp pounded his fist against the rim of the coracle. It startled the caged squawks, who sat up and fluffed their feathers in frustration.

"She wanted kids . . . with me," Twisp said. "Can you imagine that? Think of the surprises you'd find in the nursery when all these corrected, lying Mutes started bedding each other. And what about the kids growing up to find out that they're Mutes while their parents appear to be norms? Not for me!" His voice was husky. "No way."

Twisp fell silent, lost in his own memories.

Bushka listened to the *slep-slep* of waves against the coracle's sides, the faint rustling of the squawks preening and stretching in their cage. He wondered how many love affairs drowned on Twisp's style of principles.

"Damn that Jesus Lewis!" Twisp muttered.

Bushka nodded to himself. *Yes, that was where the problem had started. Or, at least, where it was precipitated.* The question remained for the historian: What made Jesus Lewis? Bushka looked at Twisp's arms—muscular, well-developed, tan and over half a length too long. The Island mating pool was still a genetic lottery, thanks to Jesus Lewis and his bioengineering experiments.

Twisp was still angry. "Mermen will never understand what growing up an Islander is like! Someone around you is always frail or dying . . . someone close. My little sister was such a nice kid . . ." Twisp shook his head.

"We don't say 'mutation' much except when we're being technical," Bushka prompted. "And deformity is a dirty word. 'Mistakes,' that's what we call them."

"You know what, Bushka? I deliberately avoid people with long arms. There are only a few of us in this generation." He raised his arm. "Are these a mistake? Does that make *me* a mistake?"

Bushka didn't answer.

"Damn!" Twisp said. "My apprentice, Brett, he's sensitive about the size of his eyes. Shit, you can't tell anything just by looking at him, but you can't tell him that. Ship! Can he ever see in the dark! Is that a mistake?"

"It's a lottery," Bushka said.

Twisp grimaced. "I don't envy the Committee's job. You have any idea of the grotesques and the dangerous forms they have to judge? How can they do it? And how can they guess at the mental mistakes? Those don't usually show up until later."

"But we have good times, too," Bushka protested. "Mermen think our cloth is the best. You know the price we get for Islander weaving down under. And our music, our painting . . . all of our art."

"Sure," Twisp sneered. "I've heard Mermen pawing over our stuff. 'How bright! Such fun. Oh! Isn't this pretty? Islanders are so full of fun.'"

"We are," Bushka muttered.

Twisp merely looked at him for a long time. Bushka wondered if he had committed some unforgivable blunder.

Suddenly, Twisp smiled. "You're right. Damn! No Merman knows how to have a good time the way we do. It's either grief and despair or dancing and singing all night because somebody got married, or born, or got a new set of drums, or hauled in a big catch. Mermen don't celebrate much, I hear. You ever see Mermen celebrating?"

"Never," Bushka admitted. And he remembered Nakano of Gallow's crew talking about Merman life.

"Work, get a mate, have a couple of kids, work some more and die,"

Nakano had said. *"Fun is a coffee break or hauling a sledge to some new outpost."*

Was that why Nakano had joined Gallow's movement? Precious little fun or excitement down under. Rescue an Islander. Work at building a barrier. Bushka did not think of life down under as grim for people like Nakano. Just drab. They hadn't the lure of an intellectual goal, nor even the nearness of grief to make them snatch at joy. But topside, there you found dazzle and color and a great deal of laughter.

"If we go back to the open land, it'll be different," Bushka said.

"What do you mean, 'if'? Just a few minutes ago you were saying it was inevitable."

"There are Mermen who want only an undersea empire. If they—"

Bushka broke off as Twisp suddenly pointed ahead and blurted, "Ship's balls! What is *that?*"

Bushka turned and saw, almost directly ahead of them, a gray tower with a lace of white surf at its base. It was like a thick stem to the great flower of sky, a blue flower edged in pink. The storm that had been skirting them for the past few hours framed the scene in a halo of black cloud. The tower, almost the same drab shade as the clouds, climbed up like a great fist out of the depths.

Twisp stared in awe. It wasn't visible for fifty klicks, as Bushka had first stated, but it was impressive. *Ship!* He'd not expected it to be so big.

Beyond the gray press of sea and sky, the clouds began to open. The interrupted horizon became two bright flowers and neither man could take his gaze off the launch tower. It was the center of a giant stormcloud whirlpool.

"That's the Launch Base," Bushka said. "That's the heart of the Merman space program. Every political faction they have will be represented there."

"You'd never mistake it for something floating on the surface," Twisp said. "No movement at all."

"It clears high water by twenty-five meters," Bushka said. "Mermen brag about it. They've only sent up unmanned shots. But things are moving fast. That's why Gallow and his people are acting now. The Mermen expect a manned shot into space soon."

"And they control the currents with the kelp?" Twisp asked. "How?"

"I don't really know. I've seen where they do it but I don't understand it."

Twisp looked from the tower to Bushka and back to the tower. The foaming collar of surf around its base had expanded as the coracles drew closer, opening up a wider view. Twisp estimated their distance from the base at more than five kilometers, and even from that distance he saw that the surf reached left and right of the tower for several hundred meters on either side. More human activity could be seen there. One of the big Merman foils stood off in the calmer water beyond the surf with smaller craft shuttling back and forth to the tower. A Lighter-Than-Air hovered nearby, either for observation or use as a sky-crane. The coracles were close enough now to make out Mermen on the breakwater that fanned out from the base near the tower.

The hydrofoil with its hydrogen ramjets sticking out like big egg sacks astern drew Twisp's attention. He had seen them only at a distance and in holos before this. The thing was at least fifty meters long, riding there easily on its flotation hull with the planing foils hidden underwater. A wide hatch stood open in its side with much Merman activity around the opening—bulky objects being lowered on an extruded crane.

Bushka sat with one arm resting on the cuddy top, his other arm hanging loosely at his side. His head was turned away from Twisp, attention fixed on the Launch Base and its commanding tower. There was no sign yet that the Mermen had taken notice of the approaching coracles, but Twisp knew they had been seen and their course plotted. Bushka's reason for bringing them to this particular place seemed clear, if you believed his story about Gallow. There was little chance that Gallow's people would be the only ones at this base. And there would be Merman attention on every detail of this operation. All factions would hear Bushka's story. Would they believe it?

"Have you thought about how they're going to receive you and your story?" Twisp asked.

"I don't think my chances are very good no matter where I turn up," Bushka answered. "But better here than anywhere else." He brought his gaze around to meet Twisp's questioning stare. "I think I'm a dead man any way you look at it. But people have got to know."

"Very commendable," Twisp said. He cut the motor and pulled

199

the tiller into his stomach, holding it there until the two boats circled slowly around each other. Time to apprise Bushka of the facts as Twisp saw them after a night's reflection.

"What're you doing?" Bushka demanded.

Twisp stretched both arms across the tiller and stared at Bushka. "I came out here to find my apprentice. Kinda stupid of me, I know. I tell you true I didn't believe there was such a thing as that base, but I thought there would be something, and I came with you because what you said about help from the Mermen made sense."

"Of course it does! Somebody probably picked him up already and—"

"But you're in trouble, Bushka. Deep shit. And I'm in it, too, just by being with you. I wouldn't feel right about just dumping you or handing you over to them." He nodded toward the tower. "Especially if your story about this Gallow happens to be true."

"If?"

"Where's the proof?"

Bushka tried to swallow. Mermen already would be bringing in the Guemes dead and the survivors. He knew this. There was no turning back. Someone at the Launch Base already had these coracles and their occupants on a screen. Somebody would be sent to investigate or to warn them off.

"What do I do?" Bushka asked.

"You sank a whole fucking island," Twisp growled. "And you're just now asking yourself that?"

Bushka merely lifted his shoulders and let them fall in a futile shrug.

"Guemes must've had small boats out, some in sight of the Island," Twisp said. "There'll be survivors and they'll have their story to tell. Some of them may have seen your sub. You any idea what they'll be reporting?"

Bushka cringed under the weight of accusation in Twisp's voice.

"You were the pilot," Twisp said. "They'll put you through more than this. You did it and they'll get every detail out of you before you talk to anybody outside of Merman Security. If you ever get outside their Security."

Bushka lowered his chin to his knees. He felt that he might vomit. With a terrible sense of wonder, he heard coming from his

200

own mouth a groan that pulsed in a rising pitch: *nnnnnh nnnnnnh nnnnnnh.*

There's nowhere I can run, Bushka thought. *Nowhere, nowhere.*

Twisp was still speaking to him but Bushka, lost in his own misery, no longer understood the words. Words could not reach into this place where his consciousness lay. Words were ghosts, things that would haunt him. He no longer felt that he could tolerate such haunting.

The thrum of the coracle's little motor being switched on brought Bushka's attention back from its hiding place. He did not dare look up to see where Twisp might be taking them. All of the *wheres* were bad. It was just a matter of time until someone somewhere killed him. His mind floated on a sea while his muscles pulled him into a tighter and tighter ball so that he might fit into that sea without touching anything there. Voices cried to him, high-pitched screeches. His mind exposed glimpses of a universe fouled by carnage—the shredded Island and its broken shards of flesh. Dry heaves shook his body. He sensed movement in the coracle, but only vaguely. Something inside of him had to come out. Hands touched his shoulders and lifted him, laying him over the thwart. A voice said: "Puke over the side. You'll choke to death in the bilge." The hands went away, but the voice left one last comment: "Dumb fuck!"

The acid in Bushka's mouth was bitterly demanding, stringy. He tried to speak but every sound felt like sandpaper bobbing in his larynx. He vomited over the side, the smell strong in his nostrils. Presently, he dropped a hand into the passing sea and splashed cold salt water over his face. Only then could he sit up and look at Twisp. Bushka felt emptied of everything, all emotion drained.

"Where can I go?" he asked. "What can I tell them?"

"You tell 'em the truth," Twisp said. "Dammit. I never heard of anybody as dumb as you, but I do believe you're a dumb fuck, and I don't think you're a killer."

"Thanks," Bushka managed.

"What you did," Twisp said, "you've marked yourself. No Mute will ever get the stares you'll get. You know what? I don't envy you one bit."

Twisp nodded toward the tower ahead. "Here comes someone to get us. One of their little cargo boats. Ship! I'm done for! I know it."

201

At any given moment of history it is the function of associations of devoted individuals to undertake tasks which clearsighted people perceive to be necessary, but which nobody else is willing to perform.
    —A. Huxley, *The Doors of Perception*, Shiprecords

After seeing Scudi expose the master control panel for her father's quarters, find the hatch controls and trace out the exit hatch circuiting, Brett was ready to believe his new friend a genius. She quickly argued against this when he praised her.

"Most of us learn how to do this very young." She giggled. "If your parents try to lock you in . . ."

"Why would they lock you in?"

"Punishment," she said, "if we—" She broke off, threw a circuit breaker and closed the panel cover. "Quick, someone is coming." She leaned close to Brett's ear. "I have set the emergency hatch on manual and the same with the main hatch. Emergency is the little hatch in the middle of the big one."

"Where do we go when we get out?"

"Remember the plan. We have to leave here before they guess what I've done." Scudi took his hand and hurried Brett out of the service room, down a passage and into the entry lounge.

Hastings and Lonfinn were already there and involved in a heated conversation with Keel.

The Chief Justice raised his voice as Brett and Scudi entered the room: "And furthermore, if you try to blame Islanders for the Guemes massacre, I shall demand an immediate committee of investigation, a committee you will not control!"

Keel rubbed his eyelids with both hands. The eye looking directly at Hastings focused a hard glare on him. Keel found he enjoyed the small shudder that the man could not hide.

"Mr. Justice," Hastings said, "you are not helping yourself or

202

those youngsters." He glanced briefly at Brett and Scudi, who had stopped just inside the room.

Keel studied Hastings for a moment, thinking how abruptly the mood had turned ugly. Two hatchetmen! He passed a glance across Hastings and Lonfinn, noting that they blocked the way to the exit hatch.

"I was always told there were no dangerous insects down under," Keel said.

Hastings scowled but his partner did not change expression. "This is not a joking matter!" Hastings said. "Ambassador Ale has asked us to—"

"Let her tell me herself!"

When Hastings did not respond, Keel said: "She lured me down here under false pretenses. She saw to it that I didn't bring any of my own staff. Her stated reason, even as sketchy as that was, does not wash. I have to conclude that I am a prisoner. Do you deny that?" Again, he sent a cold gaze across the two men standing between him and the hatch.

Hastings sighed. "You are being protected for your own good. You are an important Islander; there has been a crisis—"

"Protected from whom?"

Keel watched Hastings deciding what to say, choosing and discarding alternatives. Several times Hastings started to speak and thought better of it.

Keel rubbed the back of his neck where the prosthetic support already had begun to chafe his neck raw after his brief rest.

"Are you protecting me from whoever destroyed Guemes?" he prompted.

The two Mermen exchanged an unreadable glance. Hastings looked back at Keel. "I would like to be more candid with you, but I can't."

"I already know the structure of what's happening," Keel said. "Very powerful political forces are on a collision course among the Mermen."

"And topside!" Hastings snapped.

"Oh, yes. The two wild cards—my Committee and the Faith. Wiping out Guemes was a blow at the Faith. But liquidating me would not deter the Committee; they would simply replace me. It's more effective to keep me incommunicado. Or, if I were liquidated, Islanders would be distracted enough while selecting a new Chief Justice that Mermen could take advantage of the confusion. I no longer think I can stay down here. I am returning topside."

Hastings and his companion stiffened.

"I am afraid that is impossible just now," Hastings said.

Keel smiled. "Carolyn Bluelove will be the next Chief Justice," he said. "You won't have any better luck with her than you have with me."

Impasse, Keel thought.

A loaded silence fell over the room while Hastings and Lonfinn studied him. Keel could see Hastings composing new arguments and discarding them. He needed the Chief Justice's cooperation for something—blind cooperation. He needed agreement without revealing the thing to which Keel must agree. Did Hastings think an old political infighter could not see through this dilemma?

Where they stood just inside the room, Scudi and Brett had listened carefully to this argument. Scudi now leaned close to Brett's ear and whispered. "The guest head is that hatch over to the right. Go in there now and open the sealed switch plate by the hatch. Throw a glass of water into the switch. That will short out all the lights in this section. I will unlock the emergency hatch. Can you find it in the dark?"

He nodded.

"We can be out before they even know we're running," she whispered.

"The passageway lights will shine in through the emergency hatch when you open it."

"We have to be quick," she said. "They will try to use the main controls. It will be a blink before they realize they'll have to use the manual system."

He nodded again.

"Follow me and run fast," she said.

Where he stood confronting Keel, Hastings had decided to expose part of his knowledge.

"Justice Keel, you are wrong about the next Chief Justice," he said. "It'll be Simone Rocksack."

"GeLaar Gallow's choice?" Keel asked, working from the knowledge he had gained at the late Ryan Wang's comconsole.

Hastings blinked in surprise.

"If so, he's in for another surprise," Keel said. "C/Ps are notoriously incorruptible."

"Your history's slipping," Hastings said. "Without the first Pandoran C/P, Morgan Oakes, Jesus Lewis would've been just another lab technician."

A solemn expression settled over Keel's face. Petitioners before him on the high bench had seen this look and trembled but Hastings only stared at him, waiting.

"You work for Gallow," Keel said. "Of course you want total political and economic control of Pandora and you're going to work through the Faith. Did the C/P know you were going to destroy her family on Guemes to do it?"

"You're wrong! It's not like that!"

"Then how is it?" Keel asked.

"Please, Mr. Justice! You—"

"Someone has latched on to a basic truth," Keel said. "Control the food supply, control the people."

"We're running out of time for argument," Hastings said.

"When we actually run out, will I then become one of the Guemes casualties?" Keel asked.

"The future of Pandora is at stake," Hastings said. "Right-thinking people will steer a safe course through these hard times."

"And for this, you will kill anyone who opposes you," Keel said.

"We did not destroy Guemes!" Hastings said, spacing out his words in a low, cold voice.

"Then how do you know that whoever did it will not turn on you?" Keel demanded.

"Who are *you* to talk about killing?" Hastings asked. "How many thousands have you destroyed under the authority of your Committee? *Hundreds* of thousands? You've been at it a long time, Mr. Justice."

Keel was momentarily stunned by this attack. "But the Committee—"

"Does what you tell it to do! The almighty Ward Keel points his finger and death follows. Everybody knows that! What's life to someone like you? How can I expect a mind that alien to understand our Merman dilemma?"

Keel was at a loss how to meet this attack. The accusation stung him. Reverence for life guided his every decision. Lethal deviants had to be weeded out of the gene pool!

As Keel stood silently, wondering what might happen next, Brett stepped toward the hatch to the head. Lonfinn moved to stand between the hatch and the exit. Brett ignored the man and went into the head, closing the hatch behind him.

Brett studied the small room for a moment. The switch plate was a gasketed cover beside the hatch. It had two exposed sealing screws. Brett found the tool Scudi had told him about in the drawer under the sink: a fingernail file. He removed the cover, revealing a paired junction, shiny green and blue conducting plastics. The n and p circuits lay exposed to his view beneath the shielded depressions that changed polarity and activated the switch.

Glass of water, Scudi had said.

There was a glass beside the sink. He filled it and, putting one hand on the hatch dog, flung the water at the exposed switch. A blue-green spark flashed up the wall and all the lights went out. In the same moment he opened the hatch and slipped out into darkness. Hastings was shouting, "Get Keel! Hold him!"

Brett slipped to his right along the wall and bumped into Scudi at the hatch. She touched his face, then pulled his shoulder close. Abruptly, the little hatch opened and she was through it, rolling to one side. Brett dove through behind her and Scudi dogged the little hatch. Leaping to her feet, she darted off down the passage. Brett scrambled up and followed.

It was the first time in his life that Brett had run more than a hundred meters at one stretch. Scudi was far ahead of him, darting into a side passage. Brett skidded around the corner behind her just in time to see her feet disappear through a tiny round hatch low to the deck. She practically pulled him in behind her as he knelt at the opening. The hatch swung closed and she sealed it in darkness. Brett was panting from the exertion. Sweat stung his eyes.

"Where are we?" he whispered.

"Service passage for the pneumatic system. Hold on to my waistband and stay close. We have to crawl through the first part."

Brett gripped her waistband and found himself almost dragged along a low, narrow passage where his shoulders brushed the sides and he frequently bumped his head against the ceiling. It was very dim even for him in here, and he was sure she was operating in total darkness. The passage turned left, then right, then sloped upward for a time. Scudi stopped and reached back. She gripped his hand, taking it forward and placing it on a ladder that disappeared somewhere above them.

"Ladder," she whispered. "Follow me up."

He didn't remind her that he could see. "Where're we going?" he asked.

"All the way up. Don't slip. It's twenty-one levels with only three ledges to take breaks."

"What's up there?"

"The docking bay for my father's cargo foils."

"Scudi, are you sure you want to do this?"

Her voice came to him small and tightly controlled. "I won't believe anything without proof, but they're holding the Justice and they'd have stopped us. That's wrong, and it's Ale's doing. The Islands should know at least that much."

"Right."

She pulled away from him, the slither of her clothing and their breathing were the only sounds.

Brett followed her, his hands occasionally touching Scudi's feet on the rungs. The climb felt long to Brett, and he knew it must seem interminable to Scudi, operating in total darkness. He regretted that he had not started counting the rungs, that would help keep his mind off the ever-growing drop to the deck below. It was stomach-tightening for him to think about it, and when he did his hands didn't want to move from rung to rung. He couldn't see to the bottom or the top, just Scudi's trim form working ahead of him. Once, he stopped and looked behind him. Several diameters of pipes were faintly visible to him. One was hot to the touch. There was cold condensation on another. It felt slick when he ran his fingers over it.

Algae, he thought. He was thankful for something familiar. There was no such structure or rigidity on an Island. Organic conduits grew where they were guided to grow, but guidance had its limits.

At the first ledge, Scudi put an arm around his waist and helped him to a place against another ladder. She waited a blink while he caught his breath, then:

"We have to hurry. They may guess where we've gone."

"Can they know where we are?"

"There are no sensors here, and they won't know I have a key to the service passages."

"How did you get it?"

"From my father's desk. I found it while showing the Justice the den."

"Why would your father have had such a key?"

"Probably for the same reason we're using it. Emergency escape."

She patted his chest gently and turned away. With a sigh, she started on the next stage of their climb.

Again, Brett followed.

He pressed faster and faster, but she was always farther up, widening the distance between them. Then there was the second ledge and Brett drew himself onto it, panting. Scudi guided him to the next ladder. When he could control his breathing, he asked, "How do you move so fast?"

"I run the passageways and work out in the gym," she said. "Those of us who will go back to the open land must be prepared for the demands to be made on our bodies. It will be different from the sea."

He knew it was an inadequate response, but all he could manage was, "Oh."

"Are you rested enough for the last stage?" she asked.

"Lead on."

This time, he stayed with her enough that his hand met her foot from time to time. He knew she was setting a slower pace because of him and this pained him. Still, he was glad for the reserves it might give him. There was still that yawning void below, a place made even more frightening by its drop into a dim void. When he felt the final rung and another ledge, he wrapped an arm around the ladder's vertical supports and drew in deep, gasping breaths.

Scudi's hand touched his head. "You all right?"

"Just . . . catching my breath."

She put a hand underneath his right arm. "Come up. I will help. It is safer up here. There is a railing."

With Scudi's hand lifting, Brett crawled over the lip of the ledge. He saw the rail and caught a good grip on it, pulling himself the last few millimeters and then stretching out on the hard metal grate. Scudi rested a hand on his back and, when she felt his breathing smooth out, drew away.

"Let's review the plan," she said.

She sat with her back against a metal wall.

"Go ahead," he said. He drew himself up beside her, smelling the sweet freshness of her breath, feeling the brush of her hair against his cheek.

"The hatch is directly behind me. It's a double hatch. The docking bay is kept under enough pressure to hold a working level on the water. We'll open in an alcove off the docking bay. If no one is there, we will just go out and walk normally toward one of the foils. You are my charge and I am showing you around."

"What if someone sees us coming out of the hatch?"

"We laugh and giggle. We're young lovers on a rendezvous. We may get a lecture. If so, we should at least appear to be sorry."

Brett looked at the smooth profile of Scudi's face.

Clever. Close enough to the truth that he wished it were so.

"Where can we hide in this docking bay?" he asked.

"We won't hide. We will go to one of the foils, one where the operating crew is not aboard. We will escape topside in the foil."

"Can you really operate a foil?"

"Of course. I go topside often in the lab foil." She was all seriousness. "Do you understand what we're going to do?"

"Lead the way," he said.

Scudi slid away from him. There was the slightest sound of metal grating against metal. A small hatch swung wide, letting in dim light. It was bright enough to Brett that he was forced to squint. Scudi slipped out and reached back a hand for him. Brett followed, wriggling through the tight opening. He found himself in a low, rectangular space with gray metal walls. Light came in from a port at the far end. Scudi dogged the hatch behind them, then opened the far hatch. As she had promised, they emerged into a narrow alcove.

"Now," she whispered, taking his hand. "I am showing you the landing bay and the foils."

She led Brett out onto a narrow platform with a railing and stairs down to a deck about three meters below them. Brett stopped and resisted Scudi's attempts to drag him farther. They were under a transparent dome that stretched away from him for several hundred meters.

Plaz, he thought. *Has to be. Nothing else could take that pressure.* The docking bays were located inside this gigantic inverted cup that held out the sea. A plaz umbrella! He looked up at the surface, no more than fifty meters away, a milky silver region with the doubled shafts of light indicating that both suns stood above the horizon.

Scudi tugged at his arm.

Brett looked down to the deck—a giant metal grate with piers stretching out the far side toward the descending lip of the facility's plaz cover. As he watched, a submerged foil cruised under the far lip and lifted into the bay with a cascade of water off its hull. The foil slid into an empty bay, its engines a painful growl in his ears even at this low speed. With the newcomer, Brett counted six of the huge boats lined up in a row. Mermen worked busily around them on the piers, securing the lines of the new arrival, wheeling cargo on carts to and from the open hatches in the line of craft.

"They're so big," Brett said, craning his neck at the prow of the foil directly ahead of them. Someone was working up there, dreamily scraping a dry skin of green kelp off the extruded fenders.

"Come along," she said, her voice slightly louder than conversation required, "I'll take you aboard one of them. Kareen wants you to see it all."

This, Brett realized, was for the benefit of a Merman who had stopped below them and was watching them with a questioning tilt to his head. As Scudi spoke, he smiled and strode away.

Brett allowed her to lead him down the stairs.

"Food transport uses only the seventy-meter cargo model," she said. "In spite of their size, they'll do at least eighty knots. Somewhat slower in heavy seas. I'm told they can top a hundred knots with a light load."

Her hand in his, Scudi guided Brett down the line of foils, weaving in and out of the passing workers and stepping aside for loaded carts. At the end, they met six white-uniformed workers wheeling a covered cart toward them along the pier.

"Repair crew," Scudi explained. She spoke to the first man in the group. "Something wrong with this one?"

"Just a little trouble with the thrust reverser, Miss Wang." All six stopped while the leader spoke to Scudi. They all looked very much alike in their white coveralls. Brett saw no name tags.

"Can I take our guest aboard to show him around? I'm familiar with this one," she said. Brett thought he detected a note of false petulance in her voice.

"I'm sure you are," the crewman said. "But be careful. They've just finished refueling it for the test run. You'll have to be out in about an hour. The next shift will be loading it then."

"Oh, good," Scudi said, dragging Brett around the repair cart. "We'll have it all to ourselves and I can show you everything." She called back over her shoulder. "Thanks!"

The crewman waved and helped his men trundle their cart down the pier.

Midway down the hull, Scudi led the way up a narrow gangplank. Brett followed her into a passage lighted by overhead tubes. She motioned for him to wait while she peered back out the open hatch. Presently, she pressed a switch beside the hatch. A low hum sounded and the gangplank slid in. The hatch sealed behind it with a soft hiss.

"Quick!" she said. She turned and once more they were running. Scudi led him up a series of gangways and along a wide corridor, emerging finally into a plaz-windowed control room high above the prow.

"Take the other seat."

She slid into one of the two command couches that faced a bank of instruments. "I'll show you how to run one of these things. It's really simple."

Brett watched her, seeing the way she became another person as she touched the controls. Every movement was quick and sure. "Now this one," she said, hitting a yellow button.

A low thrumming could be felt through the deck under their feet. Several Mermen working on the pier below them turned and looked at the foil.

Scudi moved her hand up to a red button labeled "Emergency release—docking lines." She touched the button and immediately drew a lever at her left all the way back. The foil slid smoothly out of its dock. Mermen below them began to run and wave at the foil.

Before they cleared the dock Scudi began pumping ballast aboard. The foil slipped under the water, banking sharply to the left. Scudi lifted a stick from the deck beside her. Brett saw that it was socketed into the deck and wondered what it controlled. Her left hand moved the lever on the other side of her, throwing it full forward. The foil dove toward the lip of the inverted plaz cup. Brett looked up as they passed under the lip, watching the lighted edge pass away astern.

Once on the other side, Scudi began blowing ballast as she lifted the bow toward the surface. Brett swiveled around and saw the docking bay recede behind them. There was no pursuit yet.

Brett was stunned at the size of the boat. *Seventy meters. That's ten coracles long!*

"Watch what I'm doing," Scudi ordered. "You might have to run one of these things."

Brett turned back to take in the levers, buttons, gauges and switches.

"Hydrogen ramjets for both underwater and surface," she said. "Fuel conservation system reduces our speed underwater. Here's the governor." She indicated a clip-locked toggle between them. "Dangerous to exceed governed speed but it can be done in an emergency."

She moved the stick in her right hand, swinging it to starboard and pulling back on it slightly. "This steers us," she said. "Pull back to lift, down to dive."

Brett nodded.

"These . . ." She indicated a bank of instruments across the top of the board. "You read the labels: topside fuel flow, ballast— slower than on a sub. Ignition. Air supply for down under. Always remember to switch it off topside. If the cockpit is breached, we're automatically ejected. Manual ejection is by that red lever at the center."

Brett responded with a series of grunts or "Got it." He was thankful that all the switches and instruments carried clear labels.

Scudi pointed overhead where a black hood framed a large, gridded screen. "Charts are projected there. That's something Islanders have been trying to get for a long time."

"Why can't we have it?" Brett knew the system she had indicated. Fishermen grouched about it often. *Steeran*, the Mermen called it. A navigation system that worked by reading Merman fixed underwater transmission stations.

"Too complicated and too costly for upkeep. You just don't have the support facilities."

He had heard that story before. Islanders didn't believe it, but Scudi obviously did.

"Topside," she announced.

The foil broke the surface in a long wave trough that crested under them. Water cascaded off the plaz all around.

Brett clapped his hands over his eyes. The stabbing blast of light made his eyeballs feel like two hot coals in his head. He ducked his face down onto his knees with a loud moan.

"Is something wrong?" Scudi asked. She did not look at him but busied herself dropping the foils from their hull slots and increasing speed.

"It's my eyes," he said. He blinked them open, adjusting slowly. Tears washed over his cheeks. "It's getting better."

"Good," she said. "You should watch what I do. It's best to put the foil up on the step parallel to the waves, then quarter into them as you bring it up to speed. I'll get the course in a blink after we're at cruise. Look back and see if there's any pursuit."

Brett turned and stared back along their wake, aware suddenly of how fast they already were moving. The big foil throbbed and bounced under them, then suddenly the ride smoothed and there was only the high whine of the hydrogen rams and the jumping jostle of the foils bridging the waves.

"Eighty-five knots," Scudi said. "Are they after us yet?"

"I don't see anything." Brett wiped at his eyes. The pain was almost gone.

"I don't see anything on the instruments," she said. "They must know it's hopeless. Every other foil in the bay has at least some cargo aboard. We have none and full fuel tanks."

Brett returned his attention to the front, blinking away the pain as his eyes reacted to the sunlight off the waves.

"The RDF is over to your right, that green panel," she said. "See if you can raise Vashon's signal."

Brett turned to the radio direction finder. He saw at once it was a more sophisticated model than the one on which Twisp had trained him, but the dials were labeled and the frequency arc was immediately identifiable. He had the signal in a moment. The familiar voice of Vashon's transmission to its fishing fleet crackled from the overhead speakers.

"It's a good fishing day, everyone, and big cargoes expected. Muree are running strong in quadrant nineteen." Brett turned down the volume.

"What is quadrant nineteen?" Scudi asked.

"It's a grid position relative to Vashon."

"But the Island moves as it drifts!"

"So do the muree, and that's all that's important."

Brett twisted the dials, homed on the signal and read the coordinates. "There's your course," he said, pointing to the dial above the RDF. "Is that sun-relative or compass?"

"Compass."

"Doppler distance reads five hundred and ninety klicks. That's a long way!"

"Seven plus hours," she said. "We can run ten hours without stopping to recharge fuel. We can regenerate our own hydrogen from seawater during daylight hours, but we'll be sitting squawks if they come after us or try to block us from some station up ahead."

"They could do that?"

"I'm sure they'll try. There are four outposts along our course."

"We would need more fuel," he said.

"And they'll be looking for us from down under."

"What about one of the smaller Islands?"

"I saw the latest plot on the current board yesterday. Vashon's closest by more than five hundred klicks."

"Why can't I get on the emergency frequency and tell Vashon what we know. We should report in anyway," he added.

"What do we know?" she asked, adjusting the throttle. The foil lurched slightly and tipped, climbing one of the periodic high waves.

"We know they're holding the Chief Justice against his will. We know there are a lot of dead Islanders."

"What about his suspicions?"

"They're *his* suspicions," Brett said, "but don't you think he deserves a hearing?"

"If he's right, have you thought about what may happen if the Islands try to force his return?"

Brett felt a lump in his throat. "Would they kill him?"

"Somewhere, there seem to be people who kill," she said. "Guemes proves that."

"Ambassador Ale?"

"It occurs to me, Brett, that Hastings and Lonfinn may be watching her to see that she does not do something dangerous to them. My father was very rich. He warned me often that this created danger for everyone around him."

"I could just call in and tell Vashon I'm safe and returning," he said. He shook his head. "No. To those that listen in—"

"And they *are* listening," she added.

"It would be the same thing as just spilling the story right now," he said. "What'll we do?"

"We will go to the Launch Base," she said. "Not to Outpost Twenty-two."

"But you told Justice Keel—"

"And if they force him to talk, they will look for us in the wrong place."

"Why the Launch Base?" he asked.

"No single group controls that," she said. "That's a part of all of our dreams—get the hyb tanks down from where Ship left them in orbit."

"It's still a Merman project."

"It is *all* Merman. We will say our piece there. Everyone will hear it. Then all will know what a few people may be doing."

Brett stared straight ahead. He knew he should feel elation at their escape. He was in the biggest vessel he had ever seen, rocketing along the wavetops at more than eighty knots, faster than he had ever gone before. But unknowns crowded in on him. Keel did not trust the Mermen. And Scudi was Merman. Was she being honest? Had he heard her real reasons for wanting him to avoid the radio? He looked at Scudi. For what other reason could she help him escape?

"I've been thinking," Scudi said. "If no word has reached them, your family will be sick with worry about you. And your friend, Twisp. Call Vashon. We'll make do. Maybe my suspicions are foolish."

He saw her throat pulse with a swallow and he remembered her tears over the heaped bodies of the Islanders.

"No," he said, "we should go to your Launch Base."

Again, Brett concentrated on the sea ahead of them. The two suns lifted heat-shimmers off the water. When he had been much younger, seeing the Island rim for the first time, the heat shimmers had created images for him. Long-whiskered sea dragons coiled above the ocean surface, giant muree and fat scrubberfish. The shimmer play now was nothing but heat reflected off water. He felt the warmth on his face and arms. He thought of Twisp leaning back against the coracle's tiller, eyes closed, soaking up the heat through his hairy chest.

"Where is this base?" he asked.

She reached up and turned a small dial below the overhead screen. Beside the dial, an alphanumerical keyboard glowed with its own internal lights. She typed HF-i, then LB-1. The screen flashed 141.2, then overprinted a spray of lines with a common focal point. A bright green spot danced at the wide outer arc of the lines. Scudi pointed at the spot.

"That's us." She pointed to the base of the spray. "We go here on course one forty-one point two." She pointed to a dial with a red arrow on the console in front of them. The arrow indicated 141.2.

"That's all there is to it?"

215

"All?" Scudi smiled. "There are hundreds of transmitter stations all around Pandora, a whole manufacturing and servicing complex—all to insure that we get from here to there."

Brett looked up at the screen. The spray of lines had pivoted until the bright green dot lay centered on course. The 141.2 still glowed in the lower left corner of the screen.

"If we require a course change, it will sound a klaxon and show the new numbers," she said. "Steeran homing on LB-one."

Brett looked out across the water beside them, seeing the spray kicked up by the foils, thinking how valuable such a system would be to Vashon's fishing fleet. The sun burned hot on him through the plaz, but the air felt good. Rich topside air blew in the vents. Scudi Wang was at his side and suddenly Pandora didn't seem to be the adversary that he'd always imagined. Even if it was a deadly place, it had its measure of beauty.

One measure of humanity lies in the lengths taken to right the wrongs perpetrated against others. Recognition of wrongdoing is the first crucial step.
                    —Raja Thomas, the Journals

Shadow Panille covered the dead Mute. He washed his hands in the alcohol basin beside the litter. The rest of the room bustled with the *clink* of steel instruments against trays. Low-voiced, one-word commands and grunts came from several busy groups of doctors and med-techs. Panille looked back over his shoulder at the long row of litters strung down the center of the room, each one surrounded by medics. Splashes and blotches of blood stained gray gowns and the eyes above the antiseptic masks looked more tired, more hopeless every hour. Of all the survivors brought in by the pickup teams, only two had escaped physical harm. Panille reminded himself that there were other kinds of harm. What the experience had done to their minds . . . he hesitated to think of them as survivors.

The Mute behind Panille had died under the knife for lack of replacement blood. The medical facility had been unprepared for bleeders on such a tremendous scale. He heard Kareen Ale snap off her gloves behind him.

"Thanks for the assist," she said. "Too bad he didn't make it. This was a close one."

Panille watched one of the teams lift a litter and carry it toward the recovery area. At least a few would make it. And one of his men had said they were herding together the few fishing boats that had escaped and fled the drift. Panille rubbed his eyes and was immediately sorry. They burned from the touch of alcohol and started streaming tears.

Ale took him by the shoulder and led him to the sink beside the hatchway. It had a tall, curved spout that he could get his head under.

217

"Let the water run over the eyes," she said. "Blinking helps the rinse."

"Thanks."

She handed him a towel. "Relax," she said, "that's the last of them."

"How long have we been at it?"

"Twenty-six hours."

"How many made it?"

"Not counting those in shock, we have ninety still breathing in recovery. Several hundred with only minor injuries. I don't know. Fewer than a thousand, anyway, and six still under the knife here. Do you believe what this one told us?"

"About the sub? It's hard to write it off to hallucinations or delirium, considering the circumstances."

"He was clear-headed when they brought him in. Did you see what he managed to do with his legs? It's too bad he didn't make it; he tried harder than most people."

"Both legs severed below the knees and he managed to stop the bleeding himself," Panille said. "I don't know, Kareen. I guess I don't want to believe him. But I do."

"What about the part about the sub rolling upside-down before its dive?" Ale asked. "Couldn't that mean somebody just lost control of the machine? Surely no Merman would do something like that deliberately."

"That patient"—Panille waved towards the litter behind them—"claimed that a Merman sub deliberately sank their Island. He said he saw the whole thing, the sub came directly up through their center and—"

"It was an Islander sub," she insisted. "Must've been."

"But he *said* . . ."

Kareen inhaled deeply and sighed. "He was mistaken, my dear," she said. "And to avoid serious trouble, we'll have to prove it."

They both stepped aside as two attendants carried the litter with the dead Mute out the hatchway, bound for the mortuary. Kareen began to recite what Panille knew would become the Merman line: "He was a Mute. Mutes don't have all of their faculties, even under the best of circumstances."

"You've been spending too much time with Gallow," Panille said.

"But look at what we had to work with here," she said. Her voice bordered on a whisper. Panille didn't like it, nor did he like the turn of conversation. Frustration and fatigue brought out a side of Kareen Ale that he had not known existed. "Missing parts, extra parts, misplaced parts." She gestured with a whimsical wave of her hand. "What their medical people do for an anatomy class boggles the mind. No, Shadow, it *must* have been an Islander sub. Some interior score they were settling. What could any of us gain by such an act? Nothing. I say we should have a drink. Just have a drink and forget it. How about it?"

"What he described was not an Islander sub," Panille insisted. "What he described was a kelp sub, with cutters and welders."

Kareen pulled him aside, as a mother might take a troublesome child aside during WorShip. "Shadow! You're not making sense. *If* Mermen sank that Island, then why go to all the trouble to man the pickup teams? Why not just let them go? No, we worked hard here to save what we could. Not that it mattered."

"What do you mean, 'Not that it mattered'?"

"You saw them, their condition. The best of them were starving. Leather on bone. They looked like furniture."

"Then we should feed them," Panille said. "Ryan Wang didn't develop the largest food distribution in history just to let people starve."

"Feeding them's a lot easier than hauling them in dead," she said.

"These are *people!*" Panille snapped.

Ale's quick eyes flicked from Panille, around the room to the surgical and trauma teams, then back. Her lips were trembling, and he saw with surprise that she was only barely under control.

"That patient may have been a Mute, but he was no fool," Panille insisted. "He reported what he observed, and he did it clearly."

"I don't want to believe him," Ale said.

"But you do." Panille put an arm around her shoulders.

Ale trembled at his touch. "We must talk," she said. "Would you go back to my quarters with me?"

They rode the tubes, Ale's head lolling on his shoulder. She snored a little, caught herself and settled closer against him. He liked the feeling of her warmth soaking into him. When their car started into a curve he held her shoulder a little tighter to keep the movement from waking her, giving himself time to think.

219

Kareen wanted to talk. Did she want to persuade? How would she argue? With her body?

Panille decided this thought was unworthy of him. He rejected it.

Twenty-six hours in surgery, he thought. Soon Ale would face the difficult politics that the surgery represented. He had noticed the deepening circles of sleepless nights settling under Ale's beautiful eyes. Panille was glad for one aspect of the surgery—it brought out the doctor in Ale, a part of her personality that had become more ghostlike during her brief association with Ryan Wang. Though she'd been alert and awake during the whole frustrating business with the Guemes Islanders, Ale had fallen asleep almost before the transport hatch closed on them. As the Islanders died under the knife one by one, he had watched her blue eyes darken over her mask.

"They're so frail," she had said. "So poor!"

The replacement blood had run out in two hours. Plasma and oxygen were gone in sixteen. Surgical supervisors suggested sterilizing sea water and using that for plasma, but Ale refused.

"Stick with what we know," she said. "This is not the time for experimentation."

In her sleep, Ale's hand reached around Panille's waist and pulled him closer. Her hair smelled of antiseptics and perspiration, but he found the mixture comforting because it was her. He liked the brush of her hair against his bare neck. The hours of sweat in his own hair made him glad he'd kept it braided. He ached for a shower even more than he ached for a bed. Panille caught himself dozing off just as they jerked to a stop. The panel above their heads flashed the message: *Organization and Distribution.*

"Kareen," he said, "we're here."

She sighed and squeezed his waist tighter. He pressed the *hold* button on the panel with his free hand.

"Kareen?"

Another sigh. "I heard you, Shadow. I'm *so* tired."

"We've arrived," he said. "You'll be more comfortable inside."

She looked up at him but didn't move away. Her eyes were red and puffy from lack of sleep but she managed a smile. "I just got acquainted with you," she said. "I thought I knew you, but now I'm not letting you out of my sight."

220

He placed a finger against her lips. "I'll just take you to your quarters. We can talk later."

"What makes this mysterious Shadow Panille tick?" she asked in a whisper. Then she kissed him. It was a brief kiss, but warm and powerful. "You don't mind, do you?" she asked.

"What about Gallow?"

"Well," she said, "the sooner we get out of here the sooner life goes on."

They uncurled themselves from each other. He liked the way the warm spots lingered and tingled on his skin. Ale stepped out of the hatch onto the docking bay and reached back a slender hand to pull him through.

"You're beautiful," he said, and her strong grip pulled him right up to her, then she hugged him close. Again, he put down his doubts about her.

"You have a way with words," she said.

"Runs in my family."

"You could've been a surgeon," she said. "You have good hands. I'd like to spend more time studying your hands."

"I'd like that," he murmured against her hair. "I've always wanted to know you better. You know that."

"I have to warn you, I snore."

"I noticed," he said. They held each other and swayed on the docking bay. "You drool, too," he said.

"Don't be crude." She pinched him in the ribs. "Ladies don't drool."

"What's this wet spot on my shoulder?"

"How embarrassing," she said. Then she took his hand and guided him up the walkway toward her building. She glanced back at him and said, "Nobody lives long enough for dilly-dallying. Let's get to it."

Panille realized right then that the pace of his life had just turned itself up a full notch. Tired as he had been, he sparked with the measure of energy that she injected into the air around them. There was a new bounce to her step that he hadn't noticed in surgery. Her body moved smoothly, quickly across the black-tiled foyer and he matched her step-for-step. When they walked into the ambassadorial quarters they were still holding hands.

221

Pattern is his who can see beyond shape:
Life is his who can tell beyond words.

—Lao Tzu, Shiprecords

Both suns stood high in the dark sky, raising heat shimmers off the water. Brett's sensitive eyes, shielded by dark glasses Scudi had found in the foil's lockers, scanned the sea. The foil cut through the waves with an ease that thrilled him. He marveled at how quickly his senses had adapted to speed. A feeling of freedom, of escape soothed him. Pursuit could not move this fast. Danger could only lie ahead, where heat shimmers distorted the horizon. Or, as Twisp called it, "the Future."

When Brett had been quite young, standing with his mother at Vashon's edge for the first time, the heat-dazzled air had been inhabited by coils of long-whiskered dragons. Today's sun felt new on his arms and face, glistening through the canopy onto the instruments. The suns ignited golden glints in Scudi's black hair. There were no dragons.

Scudi bent intently over the controls, watching the sea, the dials, the guidance screen above her head. Her mouth was set in a grim line, which softened only when she looked at Brett.

A wide stretch of kelp drew a dark shadow on the water off to his right. Scudi steered them into the lee of the kelp, finding smoother water there. Brett stared out at an ovoid green mat within the kelp. At the very center of the oval, this particular green was a vivid reflector of the sunlight. The green darkened away from the center until the kelp patch became yellowed and brown at the edges.

Seeing where he was looking, Scudi said, "The outer edges die off, curl under and fortify the rest of the patch."

They rode without speaking for a time.

Abruptly, Scudi shocked him by shutting down the foil's engines. The big craft dropped off the step with a rocking lurch.

222

Brett looked wildly at Scudi, but she appeared calm.

"You start us," Scudi said.

"What?"

"Start us up." Her voice was calmly insistent. "What if I were injured?"

Brett sank into his seat and looked down at the control panel. Below the screen near the center of the cockpit lay four switches and a sticker labeled "Starting Procedure."

He read the instructions and depressed the switch marked "Ignition." The hot hiss of the hydrogen ram came from the rear of the foil.

Scudi smiled.

As the instructions told him, Brett glanced up at the guidance screen. A miniature line-drawing of a foil appeared around a green dot on the screen. A red line speared outward from the green dot. He touched the button marked *forward* and pushed the throttle gently ahead, gripping the wheel tightly with his free hand. He could feel sweat under his palms. The craft began to lift, tipping on the flank of a wave.

"Right down the trough," Scudi reminded him.

He turned the wheel slightly and pushed the throttle farther ahead. The foil came out of the water with a gentle gliding motion and he gave it more throttle. They came up on the step and he saw the speed-distance counter flicker, then settle on "72." The green dot tracked on the red line.

"Very good," Scudi said. "I'll take it now. Just remember to follow the instructions."

Scudi increased speed. Cabin air felt cooler as vents exchanged topside air from a clear and sunny day.

Brett scanned as much of the horizon as he could see from the cabin, a thing he had learned from Twisp, almost unconsciously. It was his landscape, the view he had known since infancy—open ocean with long rollers broken here and there by patches of kelp, silvery current intersections and wind-foamed crests. There was a rhythm to it that satisfied him. All the divergent variety became one thing inside him, as everything was one in the sea. The suns came up separately but met before they sank below the horizon. Waves crossed each other and told him of things beyond his view. It was all one. He tried to say something of this to Scudi.

"The suns do that because of their ellipses," she said. "I know

223

about the waves. Everything that touches them tells us something of itself."

"Ellipses?" he asked.

"My mother said the suns met at midday when she was young."

Brett found this interesting but he felt that Scudi had missed his point. Or she didn't want to discuss it. "You must've learned a lot from your mother."

"She was very smart except for men," Scudi said. "At least, that's what she used to say."

"When she was mad at your father?"

"Yes. Or different men at the outposts."

"What are these outposts?"

"Places where we are few, where we work hard and have our different ways. When I come into the city, or even the launch site, I'm aware that I am different. I speak different. I have been warned about it."

"Warned?" Brett felt undertones of some dark savagery among the Mermen.

"My mother said if I took outpost-talk into the city I couldn't blend. People would look at me as an outsider—a dangerous perspective."

"Dangerous?" he asked. "To see things differently?"

"Sometimes." Scudi glanced at him. "You must blend in. You could pass, but I know you for an Islander by the sound of your talk."

Scudi was trying to warn him, he thought.

Or teach me.

He noted that her accent was different out here than it had been back in her quarters. It wasn't her choice of words so much as the way she said them. There was a sparseness about her now. She was even more direct.

Brett looked out at the ocean speeding past. He thought about this Merman unity, this Merman society that measured danger in an accent. Like the waves, which met at odd angles, currents in Merman society were refracting off each other. "Interference," the physicists called it; he knew that much.

The ease with which Scudi kept the big foil skipping the wave-tops told Brett something of her past. She had only to glance at the guidance screen and out at the ocean to become one with all of it. She avoided the thick stretches of wild kelp and kept them securely on course toward this mysterious Launch Base.

"There's more wild kelp lately," he said. "No Mermen attending it."

"Pandora belonged to the kelp once," she said. "Now kelp grows and spreads at the top of an exponential curve. Do you know what that means?"

"The more kelp there is the faster it spreads and the faster it grows," he said.

"It is more like an explosion at this point," she said, "or like the moment of crystallization in a saturated solution. Add one tiny crystal and the whole thing precipitates out one massive crystal. That's what the kelp will do next. Right now it is learning to care for itself."

Brett shook his head. "I know what the history says. Still . . . sentient *plants?*"

She shrugged off his incredulity like a shawl. "If the C/P is right—if they've all been right—Vata is the key to the kelp. She is the crystal that will precipitate its consciousness. Or its soul."

"Vata," he whispered, a childlike awe in his voice. He was not one for WorShip, but he respected any human being who had outlived so many generations. No Merman had ever done that. Did Scudi believe in that Chaplain/Psychiatrist stuff?

He asked her.

Scudi shrugged. "I only know what I can arrange in my mind. I have seen the kelp learn. It *is* sentient, but very low-grade. There is no magic in sentiency except life and time. Vata has kelp genes, that is a fact."

"Twisp says last time it took the kelp a quarter of a billion years to come awake. How will we ever know . . ."

"We've helped. The rest is up to it."

"What does Vata have to do with it?"

"I don't really know. I suspect she's some kind of catalyst. The last natural link with the kelp's ancestor. Shadow says Vata's really in a coma. She went into the coma when the kelp died. Shock, maybe."

"What about Duque? Or any number of us—Mermen in-cluded—who have kelp genes? Why aren't we the catalysts you talk about?"

"No one human has all kelp genes—such a being would be kelp, not human," she said. "Each one may have wholly different combinations."

"Duque says Vata dreams him."

225

"Some of our more religious types say Vata dreams us all," Scudi said. She sniffed. "The fact that you and I were prisoners and escaped, that was no dream." She shot him a warm glance. "We are a good team."

Brett blushed and nodded.

"How close are we to Launch Base?" he asked.

"Before nightfall," she said.

Brett thought about the coming encounter. Launch Base would be an important place, many people. Among those people might be the ones who had deliberately destroyed Guemes. His Islander accent could mean danger. He turned to Scudi and tried to speak of this casually. He didn't want to argue with her or scare her. But it became immediately apparent that Scudi had been thinking along the same lines.

"In the red locker beside the main hatch," she said. "Dive suits and kitpacks. We'll be in colder water at the Launch Base."

"Hypothermia kills," he said. He had seen the two words in bright yellow on the red locker, reminding him of his earliest survival lessons. Island children were taught the dangers of the cold water as soon as they could talk. Apparently Mermen taught the same lesson, although Twisp claimed that Mermen had greater tolerance for cold.

"See if you can find suits to fit us," she said. "If we have to go over the side . . ." She left the sentence unfinished, knowing it was unnecessary to continue.

The sight of the pile of gray dive suits inside the locker brought a smile to Brett's face. The organic suits, of Islander design and manufacture, represented one of the few advancements they held over the Mermen. He selected a "small" and a "medium" and tore open the packages to activate them. He picked up two of the orange kitpacks with the suits and stowed them under the command couch seats in the cabin.

"What are those kitpacks for?" he asked.

"They're survival kits," she said. "Inflatable raft, knife, lines, pain pills. There are even repellent grenades for dashers."

"Have you ever had to use grenades?"

"No. But my mother did once. One of her team did not get away."

Brett shuddered. Dashers seldom came near Islands anymore, but fishermen had been lost and there were stories of children taken by sneak attacks at an Island's rim. Suddenly, the wide

226

ocean around their speeding foil lost some of its warm softness, its protective familiarity. Brett shook his head to clear it. He and Twisp had lived out here on a tiny coracle. For the love of Ship! A foil could not be as vulnerable as a flimsy coracle. But they had no squawks on the foil and if they had to take to the water in dive suits . . . Could their own senses warn them in time? Dashers were blindingly fast.

The two suns had moved perceptibly closer to each other, nearing their sunset meeting. Brett stared ahead, looking for the first sign of their goal. He knew this fear of dashers was foolishness, something they'd laugh about someday . . .

Something bobbing on the water ahead commanded his whole attention.

"What's that?" he asked, pointing at a spot far ahead and slightly to starboard.

"I think it's a boat," Scudi said.

"No," he mused, "whatever it is, it's two things."

"Two boats?"

The foil's speed was bringing the objects closer at an astonishing rate. His voice was barely audible: "Two coracles."

"One is towing the other," Scudi said. She veered the foil toward them.

Brett stood and leaned against the control console, squinting out at the coracles. He waved a hand at Scudi, palm down: "Slow down!" She throttled back and he gripped the console to keep his balance as the hull dropped into the water with a surge of the bow wave.

"It's Queets!" Brett shouted, pointing at the man at the tiller. "Ship's teeth, it's Queets!"

Scudi shut down one ram and maneuvered the foil upwind of the coracles. Brett fumbled at the dogs to the canopy and swung it back, leaning out to shout at the boats only fifty meters downwind. "Twisp! Queets!"

Twisp stood and shielded his eyes with a hand, the long arm held awkwardly against his side.

"Kid!"

Brett tossed him a traditional greeting of fishermen at sea: "Do you have a full load?"

Twisp stood at the tiller, rocking the coracle from side to side, and clapped his hands high over his head. "You made it!" he hollered. "You made it!"

Brett pulled back into the cockpit. "Scudi, take us alongside."

"So that's Queets Twisp," she said. She restarted the ram and eased them gently ahead. She rounded the coracles in a wide curve and came alongside the lead boat, opening the access hatch as the coracles drew near.

Twisp grabbed a foil brace and in less than a minute he was inside the cockpit, his long arms wrapped around Brett. His huge hands pummeled Brett's back.

"I knew I'd find you!" Twisp held Brett at a long arm's length and gestured wide to take in the foil, Scudi, his clothes and dark glasses. "What's all this?"

"A very long story," Brett said. "We're heading for a Merman Launch Base. Have you heard anything . . . ?"

Twisp dropped his arms and sobered. "We've been there," he said. "At least, near enough as makes no difference." He turned, indicating the other man in the coracle. "That bit of flotsam is Iz Bushka. I tried to take him to Launch Base on a piece of very heavy business."

"Tried?" Scudi asked. "What happened?"

"Who's this little pearl?" Twisp asked, extending a hand. "I'm Queets Twisp."

"Scudi Wang," she and Brett said at once. They laughed.

Twisp stared at her, startled. Was this the beautiful young Merman rescuer he had visualized in his daydreams? No! That was foolishness.

"Well, Scudi Wang," Twisp said, "they wouldn't listen to us at the Launch Base—wouldn't let us into the base at all." Twisp pursed his lips. "Towed us away with a foil bigger than this one. Told us to stay away. We took their advice." He glanced around him. "So what're you doing here, anyway? Where's the crew?"

"We're the crew," Brett said.

Brett explained why they were heading for the base, what had happened to them, the Chief Justice and the political scene down under. Bushka stepped into the cabin as Brett was finishing. Brett's recital had a marked effect on Bushka, who grew pale and breathed in shallow gasps.

"They're ahead of us," Bushka muttered, "I know they are."

He stared at Scudi. "Wang," he said. "You're Ryan Wang's daughter."

Brett, edging toward a temper flare-up, asked Twisp, "What's wrong with him?"

"Something on his conscience," Twisp said. He, too, looked at Scudi. "Is that right? Are you Ryan Wang's daughter?"

"Yes."

"I told you!" Bushka wailed.

"Oh, shut up!" Twisp snapped. "Ryan Wang's dead and I'm tired of listening to your crap." He turned to Brett and Scudi. "The kid says you saved his life. Is that right?"

"Yes." She spoke with one of her small shrugs. Her eyes stared into the console's instruments.

"Anything else we should know?"

"I . . . don't think so," she said.

Twisp caught Brett's eye and decided to get all the bad news out. He hooked a thumb toward Bushka. "This bit of dasher bait here," he said, "piloted the sub that sank Guemes. He claims he didn't know what they had in mind until the sub chewed into the bottom of the Island. Says he was tricked by the Merman commander, a guy named Gallow."

"Gallow," Scudi whispered.

"You know him?" Brett asked.

"I've seen him many times. With my father and Kareen Ale, often—"

"I told you!" Bushka interrupted. He prodded Twisp's ribs. Twisp grabbed Bushka's wrist, twisted it back suddenly, then flung it aside.

"And I told you to stow it," Twisp said. Brett and Scudi both turned to face Bushka.

He stepped back instinctively.

"Why are you looking at me like that?" Bushka asked. "Twisp can tell you the whole story—I couldn't stop them—" He broke off when they continued to stare at him silently.

"They don't trust you," Twisp said, "and neither do I. But if Scudi delivered you all packaged and safe to Launch Base, that might be just what this Gallow would want. If he's a manipulator, he'll have people crawling all over a political scene like that. You might just disappear, Bushka." Twisp rubbed the back of his neck and spoke low. "We have to do this one right the first time. We'll have no way of regrouping."

"Brett and I could take the coracles and get back to Vashon," Twisp said.

"No," Brett insisted. "Scudi and I stay together."

"I should go to the base alone," Scudi said. "When they see me

229

alone, they'll know you and I have separated and others will listen to our story."

"No!" Brett repeated. He tightened his grip on her shoulders. "We're a team. We stick together."

Twisp glared at Brett, then his expression and his bearing softened. "So that's the way it is?"

"That's the way it is," Brett said. He kept his arm firmly around Scudi's shoulders. "I know you could order me to go with you. I'm still your apprentice. But I wouldn't obey."

Twisp spoke in a mild voice. "Then I better not be giving any orders." He grinned to take the sting from his words.

"So what do we do?" Brett asked.

Bushka startled them when he spoke. "Let me take the foil and go to Launch Base alone. I could—"

"You could spread the word to your friends and tell them where to pick up a couple of slow-moving coracles," Twisp said.

Bushka paled even further. "I tell you, I'm *not*—"

"You're an unknown right now," Twisp said. "That's what you are. If your story's true, you're dumber than you look. Whatever, we can't afford to trust you—not with our lives."

"Then let me go back in the coracles," Bushka said.

"They'd just tow you away again. Farther this time." Twisp turned to Brett and Scudi. "You two are determined to stick together?"

Brett nodded; so did Scudi.

"Then Bushka and I go in the coracles," Twisp said. "We're better off split up, I'm sure of that, but we don't want to get out of touch again. We'll turn on our locator transmitter. You know the frequency, kid?"

"Yes, but—"

"There must be a portable RDF on this monster," Twisp said. He glanced around the cockpit.

"There are small portable direction finders in all emergency kitpacks," Scudi said. Her toe nudged a pack under the seat.

Twisp bent and looked at the small orange kit. He straightened. "You keep them handy, eh?"

"When we think it necessary," she said.

"Then I suggest we follow in the coracles," Twisp said. "If you have to take to the water, you'll be able to find us. Or vice versa."

"If they're alive," Bushka muttered.

Twisp studied Brett for a moment. Was the kid man enough to

230

make the decision? Brett could not be shamed in front of the young woman. Scudi and Brett were, indeed, a team. One that had a bond he couldn't match. It was the kid's decision, and in Twisp's mind it was making Brett a man.

Brett's arm stroked Scudi's shoulder. "We've already shown that we work well together. We got this far. What we're going to do may be dangerous, but you always said, Twisp, that life gives you no guarantees."

Twisp grinned. *Going to do* . . . The kid had made his decision and the young woman agreed. That was that.

"All right, partner," Twisp said. "No shilly-shally and no regrets." He turned to Bushka. "Got that, Bushka? We're the back-up."

"How long can you hang around?" Brett asked.

"Count on at least twenty days, if you need that much."

"In twenty days there might not be any Islands to save," Brett said. "We'd better move faster than that."

Twisp took two of the kitpacks for the coracles, and loaded a grumbling Bushka back aboard.

Scudi slipped an arm around Brett's waist and hugged him. "We should get into those dive suits now," she said. "We may not get time later."

She pulled hers out from under her couch and draped it across the back of the seat. Brett did the same. Undressing was easy for him this time, and he thought maybe it was seeing all of those Mermen swimming around their base, most of them with only weightbelts full of tools around their waists. Maybe it was the ride out from the foil bay with his shirt open. It gave Brett a feeling of security in the integrity of his own skin. Besides, Scudi didn't react one way or another. He liked that. And he liked the fact that this time she didn't comment on his modesty. He was beginning to get a feel for the matter-of-fact Merman nudity. But he was only beginning. When Scudi slipped out of her shirt, skinning it over her head, he followed every bounce her firm breasts took and knew it would be very hard to keep from staring. He wanted to look at her forever. She kicked her deck shoes off in two easy flicks of her feet and dropped her pants behind her couch. She had a very small patch of black hair—wispy, silky and inviting.

He noted suddenly that she was standing with her head cocked to one side. She moved gently, not telling him to quit staring but letting him know that she knew what he was doing.

"You have a very beautiful body," he said. "I don't mean to stare."

"Yours, too, is nice," she said. She placed her hand in the middle of his chest, pressed her palm against him. "I just wanted to touch you," she said.

"Yes," he said, because he didn't know what else to say. He put his left hand on her shoulder, felt her strength and her warmth and the easy smoothness of her skin. His other hand came up to her shoulders, and she kissed him. He hoped that she liked it as much as he did. It was a soft, warm and breathless kiss. When she leaned against him her breasts flattened on his chest and he could feel the hard little knots of nipples focused there. He felt himself hardening against her thigh, her thigh of such strength and grace. She stroked his shoulders, then tightened both arms around his neck and kissed him hard, her small tongue tapping the tip of his own. The boat took a sudden lurch and they both fell in a heap on the deck, laughing.

"How graceful," he said.

"And cold."

She was right. The suns had set as Twisp and Bushka departed. Already there was a stiff chill in the air. It wasn't the hardness of the deck that bothered him, but the sudden shock of cold metal against his sweaty skin. When they sat up he heard the strange unpeeling sound of damp skin. It was the sound that sheets of skin made when a friend had unpeeled his sunburned back as a boy.

Brett wanted to loll with Scudi forever, but Scudi was already trying to get up amid the unsteady rocking of the foil. He took her hand and helped her to her feet. He didn't let go.

"It's nearly dark," he said. "Won't we have trouble finding the base? I mean, it's always a lot darker underwater."

"I know the way," she said. "And you have a night vision that could see for us both. We should go now . . ."

This time he kissed her. She leaned against him for a blink, soft and good-feeling, then pulled back. She still held his hand, but there was an uneasiness in her eyes that Brett translated as fear.

"What?" he asked.

"If we stay here we will, you know . . . we'll do what we want to do."

Brett's throat was dry and he knew he couldn't talk without his voice cracking. He remained quiet, wanting to hear her out. He didn't know much about what it was that they wanted to do, and if she could give him a few clues, he was ready. He did not want her to be disappointed and he did not know what she expected of him. Most important, he did not know how much experience she'd had in these matters and now it was important for him to find out.

She squeezed his hand. "I like you," she said. "I like you very much. If there's anyone I'd like to . . . to get *that* close with, it's you. But there is the matter of a child."

He blushed. But it was not out of embarrassment. It was out of anger at himself for not thinking of the obvious thing, for not considering that the step from child to parent could very well happen all at once and he, too, was not ready.

"My mother was sixteen, too," she went on. "She cared for me, so she was never free. She never knew the free movement that others knew. She made the best of it, and I saw much through her. But I didn't see other children except occasionally."

"So she lost an adulthood and you lost a childhood?"

"Yes. It is not to be regretted. It is the only life I know and it is a good one. It is twice good now that I have met you. But it is not a life to repeat. Not for me."

He nodded, took her by the shoulders and kissed her again. This time their chests did not touch but their hands held tight to each other and Brett at least felt relief.

"You are not angry?" she asked.

"I don't think it's possible for me to be mad at you," he said. "Besides, we're going to know each other for a good long time. I want to be with you when the answer is 'yes.'"

Vata dreamed that something tangled her hair. Something crawled the back of her neck, tickling her in a legless way, and settled over her right ear. The thing was black, slick and shelled like an insect.

She heard the sounds of pain in her dream, as she had in so many dreams past, and projected all of this into Duque, where it took on more the character of consciousness. Now she recognized some of the voices as leftovers from other dreams. She had made many excursions into this void. Someone named Scudi Wang was there and the thing that slithered through Vata's hair snapped cruel jaws at Scudi's voice.

Duque realized that Vata did not like the thing. She twisted and tossed her head to get rid of it. The thing dug in, set its jaws into her hair and pulled up clumps of hair by the roots. Vata groaned a deep-throated groan, half-cough. She snatched the wet little bug out of her hair and crushed it in her palm.

The pieces slipped from her fingers and a few muffled screams faded into the dark. Duque experienced the sudden awareness that the dream-thing might be real. He had sensed other thoughts in it for just an instant—terrified human thoughts. Vata settled herself into a comfortable position and put her mind to changing the dream into something pleasant. As always, she drifted back to those first days in the valley her people had called "the Nest." Within a few blinks she was lost in the lush vegetation of that holy place where she had been born. It was all the best that Pandora's land had to offer, and it was now under many cold meters of

234

unquiet sea. But things could be otherwise in dreams, and dreams were all the geography that Vata retained. She thought how good it felt to walk again, not letting herself know it was only in a dream. But Duque knew—he had *heard* those terrified thoughts in a moment of death and Vata's dreaming was no longer the same for him.

The distresses of choice are our chance to be blessed.
      —W. H. Auden, Shiprecords

In that fading moment before the last of the twilight settled below the horizon, like a dimmed torch quenched in a cold sea, Brett saw the launch tower. Its gray bulk bridged a low cloud layer and the sea. He pointed.

"That's it?"

Scudi leaned forward to peer through the fading light.

"I don't see it," she said, "but by the instruments it's about twenty klicks away."

"We used up some time with Twisp and that Bushka character. What did you think of him?"

"Of your Twisp?"

"No, the other one."

"We have Mermen like that," she hedged.

"You didn't like him, either."

"He's a whiner, maybe a killer," she said. "It's not easy to like someone like that."

"What did you think of his story?" Brett asked.

"I don't know," she said. "What if he did it all on his own and the crew threw him overboard? We can't believe him or disbelieve him on the little we've heard—and all of it from him."

The foil skidded across the edge of a kelp bed, slowing then recovering as its sharp-edged supports cut through the tangled growth.

"I didn't see that kelp," Scudi said. "The light is so bad . . . that was clumsy of me!"

"Will it hurt the foil?" Brett asked.

She shook her head. "No, I have hurt the kelp. We will have to come off the foils."

"Hurt the kelp?" Brett was mystified. "How can you hurt a plant?"

"The kelp is not just a plant," she said. "It's in a sensitive stage of development . . . it's difficult to explain. You'll think me as crazy as Bushka if I tell you all that I know about the kelp."

Scudi reduced the throttle. The hissing roar subsided and the wallowing boat slipped down onto its hull, gently lifting with the heave of the waves. The rams subsided to a low murmur behind them.

"It is more dangerous for us to come in at night," she said. The red instrument lights had come on automatically as the light dimmed outside and she looked at Brett, his face underlighted by the red illumination.

"Should we wait out here for daylight?" he asked.

"We could submerge and sit on the bottom," she said. "It's only about sixty fathoms."

When Brett did not respond, she said, "You don't prefer it down under, do you?"

He shrugged.

"It's too deep to anchor," she said, "but it is safe to drift if we watch. Nothing can harm us in here."

"Dashers?"

"They can't penetrate a foil."

"Then let's shut down and drift. The kelp should keep us stable. I agree with you, I don't think we should go in there at night. We want everybody to see us and know who we are and why we're there."

Scudi shut off the murmuring rams and in the sudden silence they grew aware of the slap of waves against the hull, the faint creaking of the vessel around them.

"How far is it to the base again?" Brett asked. He squinted through the twilight murk toward the tower.

"At least twenty klicks."

Brett, accustomed to judging distance out by the height of Vashon above the horizon, produced a low whistle. "That thing must be pretty high. It's a wonder Islanders haven't spotted it before this."

"I think we control the currents to keep Islands clear of the area."

"Control the currents," he muttered. "Yeah, of course." Then he asked, "Do you think they've seen us?"

Scudi punched a button on the console and a series of familiar clicks and beeps came from an overhead speaker. He'd heard these sounds from time to time as they skipped across the waves.

"Nothing's tracking us," she said. "It would howl if we were targeted. They might know we're here, though. This just means we're not under observation." Brett bent over the button Scudi had punched and read the label: "T-BEAM TEST."

"Automatic," she said. "It tells us if we're targeted by a tracking beam."

The foil lurched suddenly counter to a wave. Brett, used to the uncertain footing of Islands and coracles, was first to catch his balance. Scudi clutched his arm to right herself.

"Kelp," Brett said.

"I think so. We had better—" She broke off with a startled gasp, staring past Brett at the rear hatch.

Brett whirled to see a Merman standing there, dripping sea water, green paint striped across his face and dive suit in a grotesque pattern. The man carried a lasgun at the ready. Another Merman stood in the shadowy passage behind him.

Scudi's voice was a dry whisper in Brett's ear: "Gallow. That's Nakano behind him."

Surprise at the stealth that had allowed the Merman to come this close without detection held Brett speechless. He tried to absorb the import of Scudi's rasping whisper. So this was the Merman that Bushka blamed for sinking Guemes! The man was tall and smoothly muscled, and his dive suit clung to him like a second skin. *Why the green pattern on it?* Brett wondered. His eyes could not help focusing on the business end of the lasgun.

The Merman chuckled. "Little Scudi Wang! Now *that's* what I call luck. We've been having our share of luck lately, eh, Nakano?"

"It wasn't luck saved us when that stupid Islander sank us," Nakano growled.

"Ahhh, yes," Gallow agreed. "Your superior strength broke the bonds that held you. Indeed." He flicked a glance around the cockpit. "Where's the crew? We need your doctor."

Brett, at whom Gallow aimed the question, met Gallow's demanding stare with silence, thinking that the interchange between these two Mermen tended to confirm Bushka's odd story.

"Your doctor!" Gallow insisted.

"We don't have one," Brett said, surprised at the force of his voice.

238

Gallow, noting the accent, flicked a scornful glance at Scudi. "Who's the Mute?"

"A—a friend," Scudi said. "Brett Norton."

Gallow looked Brett over in the dim red light, then turned back to Scudi. "He looks almost normal, but he's still a Mute. Your daddy would haunt you!" He spoke over his shoulder. "Have a look, Nakano."

The *slop-slop* of wet footsteps sounded behind Gallow as Nakano turned back down the passage. He reappeared presently and spoke a single word: "Empty."

"Just the two of them," Gallow said. "Out for a little cruise in one of the big boats. How sweet."

"Why do you need a doctor?" Scudi asked.

"Full of questions, aren't we," Gallow said.

"At least we have the foil," the second man said.

"That we have, Nakano," Gallow said.

Nakano pressed past Gallow into the cockpit and Brett got a full view of the man. He was a hulking figure, his upper arms as thick as some human torsos. The scarred face filled Brett with a sense of foreboding.

Gallow strode forward to one of the command seats. He bent to read the instruments. "We watched you coming in," he said. He turned and sent a baleful glare at Scudi. "You were in one big hurry and then you stopped. That's very interesting for someone in an empty foil. What're you doing?"

Scudi looked at Brett, who blushed.

Nakano guffawed.

"Oh, my," Gallow taunted, "love nests get more elaborate every year. Yes, yes."

"Disgusting." Nakano laughed, and clicked his tongue.

"There's a watch-alert out on this foil, Scudi Wang," Gallow said. His manner sobered too quickly for Brett's comfort. "You stole it. What do you think, Nakano? Looks like the Green Dashers have captured a couple of desperadoes."

Brett looked at the grotesque green dive suits on the two Mermen. Blotches and splashes and lines of green spilled over from their suits into patterns painted on their faces.

"Green Dashers?" Scudi asked.

"We are the Green Dashers," Gallow said. "These suits are the

239

perfect camouflage underwater, particularly around the kelp. And we spend a lot of time in kelp, right Nakano?"

Nakano grunted, then said: "We should've let the kelp finish us. We—"

Gallow silenced him with a flicking gesture. "We secured our outpost with one sub and a handful of men. It'd be a pity to waste such talent in the kelp."

Brett saw that Gallow was one of those types who love to hear themselves talk—more, he was one of those who loved to brag.

"With one little sub and this foil," Gallow said with a sweep of his hand, "we can make sure there's never any more land than we can control. You don't have to be in charge to run the show. Just ruin it for those who do. People will have to come swimming up to me soon enough."

Scudi took a deep, relaxing breath. "Is Kareen one of you?"

Gallow's eyes shifted and almost met Scudi's. "She's . . . insurance . . ."

"Safe deposit box," Nakano blurted, and both men laughed in that loud way men have when they crack a crude or cruel joke.

Brett realized from Scudi's deep sigh that she was relieved at Gallow's bragging. Were her doubts about her father's involvement with Gallow finally laid to rest?

"What about the doctor?" Nakano asked.

Darkness had settled over the ocean and the cockpit was illuminated only by the red telltales and instrument lights on the console. A macabre red glow filled the space around the two Mermen. They stood near the control seats, put their heads close together and whispered while Scudi and Brett fidgeted. Brett kept eyeing the hatchway where the Mermen had entered. Was there a chance to escape down there to the main hatch? But Guemes had been destroyed by a sub. These Mermen had not swum here from the Launch Base. Their sub lay nearby, probably directly beneath the foil's hull. And they needed a doctor.

"I think you need us," Brett said.

"Think?" Gallow asked with a patronizing lift of his eyebrows. "Mutes don't think."

"You have an injury, somebody needs a doctor," Brett said. "How do you intend to get help?"

"He's quick for a Mute," Gallow said.

"And you're not strong enough to go in and take a doctor from Launch Base," Brett said. "But you could trade us for a doctor."

"Ryan Wang's daughter could be traded," Gallow said. "You're fishbait."

"If you hurt Brett, I won't cooperate," Scudi said.

"Cooperate?" Gallow snorted. "Who needs cooperation?"

"You do," Brett said.

"Nakano will break you two into small pieces if I give the order," Gallow said. "*That's* cooperation."

Brett went silent, studying the two men in that blood-red light. Why were they delaying? They said they needed a doctor. Twisp had always said you had to look beyond words when dealing with people who postured and bragged. Gallow certainly fitted that description. Nakano seemed to be something else—a dangerous unknown. Twisp liked to probe such people with outrageous questions or statements.

"You don't need just any doctor," Brett said. "You want a particular doctor."

Both Mermen focused startled glances on Brett.

"What have we here?" Gallow muttered. The smile he flashed across the dark cabin did not disarm Brett in the least.

Nervous, Brett thought. *Keep looking.* He knew the Merman fear that Islanders had mutated into telepathy, and played on it.

Nakano said, "Do you think—"

"No!" Gallow warned.

Brett caught a bare flicker of hesitation in Gallow's face, which did not show in the voice. The man had superb control of his voice. It was his tool for manipulation, along with his ready smile.

"That other foil should be along soon," Nakano said.

A particular foil with a particular doctor and a particular cargo, Brett thought. He glanced at Scudi. Her tired face was clear to him in the dim lights of the cockpit.

"You don't need us as a trade, you need us as a diversion," Brett said. He held his fingertips to his temples, repressing an excited smile.

One of Gallow's eyebrows lifted, a dark ripple in the smeared green of the camouflage.

"I don't like this," Nakano said. There was fear in the big man's voice.

"He's thought something out," Gallow said. "That's all. Look at him. Almost normal. Maybe he has a brain after all."

"But he's hit on—"

241

"Drop it, Nakano!" Gallow kept his attention on Brett. "Why would we need you as a diversion?"

Brett dropped his hands and allowed the smile. "It's pretty simple. You didn't know we were the ones on this boat. It's dark out there and all you saw was a foil. Period."

"Pretty good for a Mute," Gallow said. "Maybe there's hope for you."

"You had to go forward and look at the identification plate on the control console before you realized this was the foil on watch-alert."

Gallow nodded. "Go on."

"You hoped it was another foil, a particular one," Brett said. "The other one will have a Security force aboard. You came in armed and ready for that."

Nakano relaxed, visibly relieved. Obviously, this reasoning had eliminated his fear of telepathy.

"Interesting," Gallow said. "Is there more?"

"So now we're waiting for the other foil," Brett said. "Why else waste time with us? If the Security force jumps aboard to capture Scudi and me, that's your opportunity."

"Opportunity for what?" Gallow's tone said he was enjoying this. Nakano returned to his fidgeting.

"You want someone in particular on that other foil," Brett said. "A doctor. And you want the cargo. Now, you see the opportunity to get not only that but two foils intact. And you would've had to wreck the other foil to stop it because all you have is a sub."

"You know, I might be able to use you," Gallow said. "You want to join up?"

Brett spoke without thinking. "I'd sooner swim in shit."

Gallow's face tightened, his body went rigid. Nakano snickered. Slowly, Gallow's face returned to its political best. But there was a mad light in his eyes, a red reflection that made Brett sorry he'd spoken at all.

Scudi edged away from Brett toward the command seats, moving as though she feared the consequences of his comment.

Nakano moved closer to Gallow and bent to whisper something into the Merman's ear. Even as he whispered, Nakano shot a kick at Scudi's hand, which had moved toward the eject lever between the command seats.

Scudi leaped back with a cry of pain, holding her wrist tight to her chest.

Brett started to step toward Nakano, but the big Merman put up a warning hand. "Easy, kid," he said. "I just stung her. Nothing's broken."

"She was going for the eject lever," Gallow said. There was genuine surprise in his voice. He glared at Scudi. Both men stood on a light seam that divided the forward part of the cabin from the rear.

"It would've cut us to pieces when it blew," Nakano said. "Not nice."

"She's Ryan Wang's daughter, all right," Gallow said.

"Now you see why you need our cooperation," Brett said.

"We need you tied up and gagged," Gallow snarled.

"And what happens when that other foil pulls alongside for a look?" Brett asked. "They'll be very cautious if they don't see us in here. One or two of their Security will come aboard while the others wait in their own boat."

"Are you proposing a deal, Mute?" Gallow asked.

"I am."

"Let's hear it."

"Scudi and I stay inside in plain sight. We act like our foil's disabled. That way, they won't suspect anything."

"And afterward?"

"You deliver us to an outpost where we can get back to our people."

"Sound reasonable, Nakano?" Gallow asked.

Nakano grunted.

"You have a deal, Mute," Gallow said. "You amuse me."

Brett wondered at the insincerity in the man's voice. Didn't he realize his intentions were that transparent? A greased smile couldn't hide a lie forever.

Gallow turned to Nakano. "Go take a look outside. See if everything's secure."

Nakano strode through the rear hatchway and was gone for several minutes while Gallow hummed to himself, nodding. His expression was filled with self-satisfaction. Scudi moved close to Brett, still clutching her wrist.

"Are you all right?" Brett asked.

"Just bruised."

"Nakano's getting soft," Gallow said. "He pulled that kick. He can crush your throat, just like that!" Gallow snapped his fingers to illustrate.

243

Nakano returned, dripping more water. "We're in kelp and it's holding us pretty steady. The sub's stabilized directly under us and the foil's shadow should hide it until it's too late for them to do anything about it."

"Good," Gallow said. "Now, where do we keep these two until it's time for their performance?" He thought for a moment, then: "We turn the cabin lights on and put them in the open hatchway. They'll be seen right away."

"And we wait beside the hatch," Nakano said. "You kids understand?"

When Brett did not respond, Scudi said, "We understand."

"We'll run forward and turn out the lights," Brett said. "That'll make sure the Security people have to come aboard."

"Good!" Gallow said. "Very good."

He sure likes the sound of his own voice, Brett thought. He took Scudi's arm, careful of her wrist. "Let's get those lights on and go back to the main hatch."

"Nakano, escort our guests back and see that they're in plain sight," Gallow said. He moved to the command console and flipped a series of switches. Lights blazed all over the foil.

Brett suddenly hesitated. *Open hatch?* "Dashers," he said.

Scudi tugged him along toward the corridor into the rear of the foil. "Our chances are just as good with the black variety," she muttered.

Survival is staying alive one breath at a time, Brett thought. That was another of Twisp's sayings. And Brett thought if he and Scudi survived this, Twisp would have to learn how his teaching had helped. It was a way of studying things and reacting truly—something that could not be taught, but could be learned.

"Hurry it up, you two!" Nakano ordered.

They followed him down the long passage to the open hatch, its lip washed in a blaze of light. Brett stared out at a dark flow of kelp-littered waves slapping against the hull.

Nakano said, "You two wait right here. And you better be standing in plain sight when I come back." He sped up the passage.

"What's that guy doing up there in the cockpit?" Brett asked.

"Probably disabling the starting system," Scudi said. "They don't intend to let us go."

"Of course not."

She glanced behind her at the storage locker where Brett had found the survival kits. "If it weren't for the sub under us, I'd take off right now."

"There's nobody in the sub," Brett said. "There's just these two . . . and maybe one who needs the doctor. That one won't be able to do anything about us."

"How do you know?"

"It was obvious from what they said and the way they're acting. And remember what Bushka said? Three of them."

"Then what're we waiting for?"

"For them to disable the starting mechanism," he said. "We can't have them dashing around in this thing looking for us." He moved to the storage locker and lifted out two more packs, tossing one to Scudi. "Have they had enough time?"

"I . . . think so."

"I do, too."

Scudi slipped a length of line from an outside pocket on her kit and fixed one end to Brett's belt, the other to her own waist. "We stay together," she said. "Let's go."

Far up the corridor, Gallow's voice suddenly bellowed, "Hey! You two! What're you doing?"

"We're going swimming," Brett shouted. Holding hands, they leaped off into the ocean.

Without the conscious acknowledgment and acceptance of our kinship with those around us there can be no synthesis of personality.

—C. G. Jung, *Shiprecords*

A glut of kelp rasped the coracle's bow in time with the waves. *A touch of reality*, Twisp thought. The otherwise silent blackness yawned before the first hint of dawn. Twisp heard Bushka twisting uncomfortably near the bow cuddy. In the long night since leaving Brett and Scudi, Bushka had not slept well.

Water's very flat tonight, Twisp thought. Only the faintest of breezes cooled his left cheek as the coracles drifted slowly in the encumbering kelp.

Twisp tipped his head to look up at a spattering of cloud-framed stars, picking out the familiar arrowhead shape of the Pointers before the frame shifted to a new section of sky.

Still on course, current favorable.

It was always good to check the compass against the stars. The course angled toward an unmarked place on the sea where they could turn and make a swift run to Vashon. The RDF-RDC announcement of the Island's distant locator-beep had been silenced for the night but a red light blinked near his knee in time with Vashon's signal. His receiver was working.

Dawn would find them still hull-down out of sight of the launch tower but not out of range of the kid and the girl.

Did I do the right thing? Twisp asked himself.

It was a question he had repeated many times, aloud to Bushka and silently to himself. At the moment of decision, it had felt right. But here in the night . . .

Momentous changes gathered force on their world. And who were they, pitted against the evils he could sense in that change? One overage fisherman with arms too long for anything but haul-

246

ing nets. One whining intellectual ashamed of his Islander ancestry, maybe capable of wholesale murder. One kid out to make himself a man, a kid who could see in the dark. And a Merman girl who was heir to the entire food monopoly of Pandora. The consequences of Ryan Wang's death had a bad feel.

The squawks began to stir in their cage near Twisp's feet. Faintly at first, then louder, somewhere off to the right in the thicker kelp, Twisp heard a dasher purring. Putting a finger on the stunshield switch, he waited, straining to see something, anything, in the blackness where that ominous purr stroked the still air.

A purring dasher could mean many things: it might be asleep, or well-fed, or responding to the smell of rich food . . . or just generally contented with its life.

Twisp slipped a leg over the tiller, prepared to start the motor and steer away from that perilous noise. With his free hand he groped for and found the lasgun in its hiding place behind his seat.

Bushka began to snore.

The dasher's purr stopped, then began once more on a lower note. Had it heard?

Bushka snorted, rolled over and resumed his snoring. The dasher continued to purr, but the sound began to fade, moving farther to the right and behind the drifting coracles.

Asleep, Twisp hoped. *Trust my squawks.* The birds had not stirred again.

The dasher's contentment faded away in the distance. Twisp listened for movement there, straining to hear over the sound of Bushka's fatigue. Slowly, Twisp forced himself to relax, realizing that he had been holding his breath. He exhaled, then inhaled a deep breath of the sweet night air. A dry swallow rasped the back of his throat.

Although he could not hear the dasher, tension still rode him. Abruptly, the squawks came full awake and began living up to their name. Twisp flipped the stunshield switch. There came the unmistakable splash of something stiffening in the water close behind, then the frenzied whines and chuckles of dashers feeding.

Filthy cannibals, he thought.

"Whuzzat?" Bushka demanded.

The coracle shifted as Bushka sat up.

247

"Dashers," Twisp said. He aimed the lasgun toward the feeding sounds and fired six quick bursts. The buzzing vibration of the weapon was hard against his sweaty hand. The thin purple beams lanced into the night. At the second shot, the dashers erupted in a frantic cacophony of yelps and screeches. The sounds receded rapidly. Dashers had learned to turn tail at the buzzing, purple shaft of a lasgun.

Twisp turned off the stunshield and reached for his handlight as another sound far off to his left caught his attention: the *hiss-hiss-hiss* of paddles cutting through wet kelp. He aimed the handlight toward the sound but the night sucked it dry without sending anything back but the sea's pulse in dark strands of kelp.

A voice called from the distance: "Coracle! Do you have a load?"

Twisp felt his heart triple-time against his rib cage. That was Brett's voice!

"Riding too high!" he shouted, waving the handlight as a locator. "Careful, there's dashers about!"

"We saw your lasgun."

Twisp could make them out then, an amoebalike blot undulating toward him on the low seas. Two paddles flashed bits of his light back at him.

Bushka leaned against the thwart, tipping it precariously near the water.

"Trim the boat!" Twisp called. "You, Bushka!"

Bushka jerked back but kept his attention on the approaching shape. The paddles struck the water with splashes that burst like blossoms against the black hull of an inflatable raft.

"It's them," Bushka said. "They've blown it, just like I warned you."

"Shut up," Twisp growled. "At least they're alive." He took a deep breath of thanksgiving. The kid had become family and the family was whole again.

"Mother, I'm home!" the kid called, as though reading his thoughts.

So, Brett was sufficiently lighthearted that he could joke. Things could not be too bad, then. Twisp listened for dashers.

Bushka laughed at the quip, a laugh with a dry, cracked edge that set Twisp's anger near the boiling point. The raft was in easy talking distance now. Twisp kept the handlight pointed toward the approaching figures and away from his own face, where tears of fatigue and relief wet his cheeks. At a low word from Brett, both he and Scudi stopped paddling. Brett threw a line to the coracle. Twisp caught it and hauled in the raft like a net of muree, snugging it against the coracle. One long arm snaked out and grabbed Brett. The kid's dive suit was soaked and inflated.

The squawks took that moment to set up a warning commotion, but it subsided immediately. Dashers patrolled just out of sight, wary of the lasgun. *A sizable hunt of them,* Twisp thought. Hunger drove them in and fear kept them away.

Scudi said, "Should we come aboard?"

"Yes," Twisp said, and heaved Brett aboard, then helped Scudi gently over the gunwale and onto the seat-slat in front of him. He secured the line to keep the raft tight against the boat, then stowed the handlight under his seat. Twisp put a hand on Brett's arm, keeping it there, unwilling to break off the reassuring touch.

"They wouldn't listen to you, would they?" Bushka demanded. "You had to run for it again. What happened to your foil?"

"Do we run for Vashon?" Twisp asked.

Brett held both hands up to slow them down. "I think we'd better discuss it," he said. He recounted the story of Gallow and Nakano as briefly as he could. It was a bare-bones account, which Twisp heard with a growing admiration for Brett.

A good head there, he thought.

When Brett had finished, Bushka said, "Let's get away from here! Those are devils, not men. They probably followed you and when they come—"

"Oh, shut up!" Twisp snapped. "If you don't, I'll shut you up." He turned to Brett and asked, in a calmer voice, "What do you think? They have two foils now and could hunt us down with—"

"They're not going to hunt for us, not yet," Brett said. "They have other fish to fry."

"You're a fool!" Bushka blurted.

"Hear him out," Scudi said. Her voice was as flat and solid as plasteel.

"They said they were waiting to capture a doctor," Brett continued, "probably true, from the way they acted. It looked like they tried something and failed. They were shook up and trying to hide it from us. A lot of bragging."

"That's Gallow," Bushka muttered.

"So what were they doing besides waiting to get a doctor?" Twisp asked.

"They were near the Launch Base," Brett said. "With Gallow, I suspect nothing is coincidence. My guess is they want those hyb tanks."

"Of course they do," Bushka said. "I told you that."

"He wants them real bad," Brett said. He nodded to himself. The hyb tanks circling up there in space were the single most speculative subject on Pandora. Guessing the manifests of the hyb tanks ranked right up there with the weather as a conversational staple.

"But what about this threat that he'll prevent the Mermen from reclaiming more open land?" Twisp asked. "Could he do that with one sub and a couple of foils?"

"I think Vashon's in danger," Brett said. "Guemes was much smaller, but still . . . sinking Islands is just too simple a diversion for somebody like Gallow to resist. About the time those tanks come down, he'll try to sink Vashon. I'm sure of it."

"Did he say anything specific?" Twisp asked. "Could he have found a real hyb tank manifest?"

Brett shook his head. "I don't know. Something that big . . . he'd have to brag about it. Bushka, he ever say anything to you about what's up there?"

"Gallow has . . . dreams of grandeur," Bushka said. "Anything that'll feed those dreams is real to him. He never claimed to know what was in the tanks; he just knew the political value of having them."

"Brett's right about Gallow," Scudi said.

Twisp could make out the dark flash of her eyes in the growing light. "Gallow's like a lot of Mermen—they believe the hyb tanks will save the world, destroy the world, make you rich or curse you forever."

"Same with Islanders," Brett said.

"Speculation, but no facts," Twisp said.

Scudi looked from Brett to Twisp and back to Brett. How like Twisp Brett sounded! Laconic, practical—all based on rocklike integrity. She studied Brett more carefully then, seeing the stringy strength in his young body. She sensed the power of the adult he would become. Brett was already a man. Young, but solid inside. It came over her like a quick-dive narcosis that she wanted him for a lifetime.

Twisp turned to the controls, started up the motor and set a course for Vashon. The coracle surged across the kelp into open water.

Scudi glanced around the brightening day. She scratched under the neck seal of her dive suit, and, with an impatient gesture, shucked out of the suit and spread it across the thwarts to dry. She did this after one smiling glance at Brett, who smiled back.

Twisp glanced once at her, noting the vestigial webs between her toes, but otherwise an ideal, Merman-normal body. He hadn't seen that many up close. He forced himself to look away, but noticed that Bushka, too, could not help staring at Scudi. She worked close beside Bushka, turning the dive suit and fluffing it as the wind blew it dry. Twisp watched Bushka's eyes flick up from the water, over Twisp at the stern, up and down Scudi's body, back to the water.

Twisp had long believed that Mermen didn't have the same drives as Islanders, and he related it to the free display of their perfect bodies. Scudi's display bore that out in his mind. Mermen lived so much of their lives either without clothes or in skin-clinging dive suits that they would have to develop different feelings about the body than the bulky-clothed Islanders.

Not much difference between nudity and a dive suit, Twisp thought. He could see that Bushka was bothered by Scudi's proximity and her nudity. Brett was doing what any normal Islander might— giving Scudi the privacy of not looking at her. Scudi, however, was not able to keep her eyes off Brett.

Something going on there, Twisp decided. *Something strong.* He reminded himself that Mermen sometimes married Islanders, and sometimes it worked out.

Bushka shifted his attention from Scudi to Brett and the look on Bushka's face was like a shouted statement to Twisp. It was the kid's eyes.

Not as normal as I am! That was the look on Bushka's face.

Twisp remembered seeing a long-armed Islander once holding hands with a long-armed woman—the first time he'd seen two of them in one place. It had taken Twisp a long time to dig out his personal rejection of that scene and with his digging had come a valuable insight.

Like me. That's how we define human.

He had traced that thought down its dark trail and come up with his own reason for judging that couple.

251

Jealousy.

He had only chosen women who were different from himself. Chances of passing along a specific trait to children got too high when similar mutants paired. Sometimes it was a genetic time-bomb that didn't show for one or two generations.

Most of us aren't willing to pass along anything except hope.

Something similar was going on in Bushka.

He doesn't like Brett, Twisp thought. *He doesn't know it yet. When he figures it out he won't know why. He won't want to admit it's jealousy and it wouldn't do much good to tell him.*

It was obvious to anyone who looked at her when she studied Brett that Scudi had eyes only for the kid.

Brett had found the larder and quick-heated some fish stew. Without looking at Scudi, he said, "Scudi, something to eat?"

Scudi, her dive suit aired out sufficiently, slipped it back over her lithe young body. She finished closing the seals. "Yes, please, Brett," she said. "I'm very hungry."

Brett passed her a filled bowl and looked a question at Twisp, who shook his head. Bushka accepted a bowl from Brett after a slight hesitation that spoke loudly to Twisp.

Doesn't want to owe the kid anything!

Brett had been brought up on Islander courtesy over food and so had Bushka. The early training dominated. Brett completed the usual ritual before filling his own bowl. A dasher couldn't have gobbled it faster. Presently, Brett held his bowl over the side, cleaned it and put it away. He looked up at Twisp.

"Thanks," he said.

"For what?" Twisp asked, surprised. The food belonged to all of them.

"For teaching me how to pay attention, and how to think."

"Did I do that?" Twisp asked. "I thought people were born knowing how to think."

Bushka heard this exchange with an ill-concealed sneer. He sat brooding. The news about Gallow and his crew—*Green Dashers! In striking range!* The proximity of the Gallow-Nakano-Zent trio filled Bushka with terror. They were sure to come looking for the fugitives. Why wouldn't they? Ryan Wang's daughter was here, for Ship's sake! What a hostage! He thought then about Zent, those glossy, unfeeling eyes with their deep-down delight at pain. Bushka wondered how these two young people had outsmarted the likes of them, although Gallow was prone to underestimate his

252

opposition. Bushka looked straight at Scudi. *Ship! What a body!* Whoever owned her owned the world, and he knew that was no exaggeration. There could be little doubt that her father had controlled much of Pandora through his food operations, and now that he was dead it would surely pass to Scudi. Bushka half-closed his eyes and studied the young couple beside him.

Gallow must've thought them a couple of scared kids.

Bushka had learned the danger of assumptions while he'd been boat-bound with Twisp. Scudi obviously had a first-love crush on the kid . . . but that would pass. It always did. Her father's minions were still alive. They would put a stop to it once they found out. Once they took a good look at the kid's mutated eyes.

Twisp stood up at the tiller and peered ahead, shading his eyes against the rising ball of sun. "Foil," he said. "It's heading for Vashon."

"I told you!" Bushka shouted.

"Looked like an orange stripe along the cabin top," Twisp said. "Official."

"They're looking for us," Bushka said. His teeth began to chatter.

"Not changing course," Twisp said. "They're in a real hurry." He reached down and flipped the switch on his emergency-band radio receiver.

The sound of the Vashon announcer came on in midsentence: ". . . who said there was no immediate further threat to Vashon's substructure. We are hanging bottom on a kelp margin of enormous dimensions. There is exposed land and surf immediately to the east of us. Fishermen are advised to approach us through the clear water from the southwest. We repeat: All downcenter areas are being evacuated because of grounding. Vashon itself is in no immediate danger as long as the calm weather holds. Repairs are proceeding and Merman help has been assured. Hourly bulletins will be provided and you are advised to keep tuned to the emergency band."

Scudi shook her head and whispered, "Current Control wasn't supposed to let something like that happen."

"Sabotage," Bushka said. "It's Gallow's doing. I know it."

"Exposed land," Twisp muttered. The big change was happening. He could feel it.

*Down the course of history, people have been the principal
cause of human deaths. It is possible to alter that course
here on Pandora.*

—Kerro Panille, the Histories

Ward Keel's head throbbed in time to his heartbeat. He
opened his eyes a crack but shut them quickly against the painful
stab of white light. A demanding interior whine filled his ears,
blotting out the world around him. He tried to lift his head but
failed. His neck support had been removed. He tried to remember if he had removed it. Nothing came to him. He knew there
should be things to remember but his throbbing head took most
of his attention. Again, he tried to lift his head and gained only a
few millimeters. The back of his head thumped onto a hard, flat
surface. Nausea gripped his throat. Keel gulped quick lungfuls of
air to keep from vomiting. The air tasted thick and humid and did
not help much.

Where in the name of Ship am I?

Bits of memories flickered into his mind. Ale. And someone . . .
that Shadow Panille. He remembered now. There had been an
argument between Ale and someone in Merman Mercantile—the
late Ryan Wang's operation. She had ended it by removing Keel
to . . . to . . . He could not remember. But they had left Ale's
complex. That much he recalled.

Thick air all around him now . . . down-under air. Slowly, he
tried opening his left eye. A dark shape loomed over him, haloed
by a pair of bright ceiling lights.

"He's coming around."

A smooth, unhurried voice, conversational. The piercing whine
in Keel's ears began to wind down. He tried opening both eyes
wider. Slowly, a face came into focus above him: crisscrossed scars
on the cheeks and brow, a twisted mouth. The face turned away

like a receding nightmare and Keel saw streaks of green smeared up to the neck below those awful scars.

"Don't fuss over him, Nakano. He'll keep."

That was a voice edged in ice.

The scarred face regarded Keel once more—two deeply set eyes with something far back in there that refused to emerge. *Nakano?* Keel felt that the name and the scarred face should ignite an important memory. *Blank.*

"He's no good to us dead," Nakano said. "And you hit him pretty hard with that stuff. Hand me some water."

"Get it yourself. I don't tote for Mutes."

Nakano removed himself from Keel's view, returning in a moment to bend closer with a beaker and a straw. A hand striped with green paint put the straw between Keel's lips.

"Drink it," Nakano said. "I think it'll help."

Hit him pretty hard?

Keel remembered someone shouting . . . Kareen Ale screaming at . . . at . . .

"It's just water," Nakano said. He moved the straw against Keel's lips.

Keel sucked in cold water and felt the soothing splash of it into his cramping stomach. He told himself that he should reach for the beaker but his hands refused to cooperate.

Straps!

Keel felt them over his chest and arms. He was being restrained, then. *Why?* He took another deep drink of the water and pushed the straw from his mouth with his tongue.

Nakano removed the beaker and released the restraints.

Keel flexed his fingers and tried to say "thanks," but the word was no more than a dry whistle in his throat.

Nakano placed something on Keel's chest and Keel felt the familiar outlines of his neck appliance.

"Took it off when you puked and damn near choked to death," Nakano said. "Couldn't figure how to get it back on you."

Keel felt weak but his fingers knew this familiar thing. He fumbled over the slips and catches, putting the support into place around his neck. Two raw spots pained him where the braces met his shoulders. Someone had tried to pull it off without unfastening it.

Lucky they didn't break my neck.

With the support in place, Keel's thick shoulder muscles carried the burden of lifting his head upright. The brace slipped into its usual position and he winced at the pain. He saw that he was in a small rectangular room with gray metal walls.

"Do you have a celltape?" he asked. His voice echoed in his ears and sounded much deeper than he remembered. Keel rested his forehead in his hands and listened as someone rummaged through a case. The table that Keel sat on was much lower than he had imagined. It wasn't a gurney, but a low dining table, Merman-style, within a cluster of low padded chairs and a couch. Everything seemed constructed out of old, dead materials.

Nakano handed him a roll of celltape and, as if in answer to an unasked question, said, "We put you on the table because you weren't breathing good. The couch is too soft."

"Thanks."

Nakano grunted and sat back down in a chair behind Keel.

Keel noticed that the room was filled with books and tapes. Some of the bookshelves were packed two deep with well-worn texts of many sizes. Keel turned his head and saw behind Nakano an elaborate comconsole with three viewscreens and racks of tapes. The room felt as though it moved—back and forth, up and down. It was an unsettling sensation, even for one accustomed to riding the waves on an Island.

Keel heard a distant hissing. Nakano stood at his side then and another man, his dive suit smeared with green paint, sat nearby, his back to them. The other man appeared to be eating.

Keel thought about eating. His stomach said, "Forget it."

My medication! he thought. *Where is my case?* He felt his breast pocket. The little case was gone. It came over him then that this rectangular space around him actually was moving—rising and falling on a long sea.

We're still on the foil, he thought. The thick air was a Merman preference. These two Mermen had merely done something to humidify the air.

Still on the foil!

He remembered more now. Kareen Ale had taken him aboard a foil to . . . to go to the Launch Base. Then he remembered the other foil. Memories came rushing at him. It had been after nightfall. He could see daylight now through louvered vents high in the walls of this room: the double yellow-orange of both suns low in the sky. *Morning or evening?* His body could not inform him. He felt the borderline nausea of movement, the constant inner pain

256

of his fatal illness and the headache, now localized in his right temple where, he knew, he had been struck.

Drugged, too, he thought.

The attack had occurred after the foil in which Ale had been taking him to the Launch Base slowed abruptly. A voice had called: "Look there!"

Another foil had bobbed dead in the water with only its anchor lights glowing through the darkness. It drifted slowly in heavy kelp and was not at anchor. A spotlight from Ale's foil illuminated the identification numbers on the bow of the vessel.

"It's them, all right," she said.

"Do you think they're in trouble?"

"You bet they're in trouble!"

"I mean something wrong with—"

"They're waiting out the night on the kelp. It hides them from bottom search and they won't drift far in it."

"But why do you suppose they're here . . . I mean, so close to Launch Base?"

"Let's find out."

Slowly, its jets muted, Ale's foil moved up on the other craft while four Security men readied themselves for boarding from the water.

Keel and Ale on the forward pilot's deck had a commanding view of what happened next. With only a few meters separating the two craft, four dive-suited men slipped into the water, swam the short distance and opened the main hatch on the other foil. One by one, they crept inside and then . . . nothing.

Silence, for what seemed to Keel an interminable time. It ended with a jerky rocking action on Ale's foil followed by shouts from the stern. Abruptly, two green-striped apparitions burst into the pilot's compartment. One of the intruders had been a monstrous Merman with terrible scars on his face. Keel had never seen arms that thickly muscled. Both men carried weapons. There was only time to hear Ale shout: "GeLaar!" Then the blinding pain on his own head.

GeLaar? Keel prolonged his recovery period from the blow, making it appear he was still dazed. His encyclopedic memory pored over names and physical identifications. *GeLaar Gallow, idealized Merman. Former subordinate of Ryan Wang. Suitor to Kareen Ale.* The man at the table pushed a bowl away from him, wiped his mouth and turned.

257

Keel looked at him, shuddering in the cold appraising stare of those dark blue eyes.

Yes, this is the man himself. Keel thought Gallow grotesque in the cover of green paint.

A hatch to Keel's right opened and another green-striped Merman entered. "Bad news," the newcomer said. "Zent just died."

"Damn!" That was Gallow. "She didn't really try to save him, did she!"

"He was badly crushed," the newcomer said. "And she is exhausted."

"If only we knew what caused it," Gallow mumbled.

"Whatever it was," Nakano said, "it was the same thing that damaged the sub. The wonder is he got back to us at all."

"Don't be stupid," Gallow snapped. "The sub's homing system brought him back. He didn't have anything to do with it."

"Except to activate the system," Nakano said.

Gallow ignored him, turning to the newcomer. "Well, how are the repairs going?"

"Very well," the man said. "We got the replacement parts and tools aboard the Launch Base foil marked as rocket supplies. We should be fully operational by this time day after tomorrow."

"Too bad we can't replace Tso as easily," Nakano said. "He's a good man in a fight. Was."

"Yes." Gallow spoke without looking at Nakano, gesturing instead to the newcomer. "Well, get back to your station."

The man hesitated. "What about Zent?" he asked.

"What?"

"His body."

"Green Dashers are kelp food when they die," Gallow said. "You know that. It's imperative if we're to know what happened out there."

"Yes sir." The man left, closing the hatch quietly after him.

Keel brushed at his collar and the front of his jacket. He could smell the sour taint of vomit there, confirming Nakano's account of what had happened.

So, they want me alive. No . . . they need me alive.

As long as he was alive, Keel could probe for weaknesses. Superstition was a weakness. He vowed to pursue this curious burial ritual that Gallow employed. Its very mention had brought a hush over the cabin. They were fanatics. Keel could see it in Gallow's expression. Anything was justified by the sacred nature of their goal. Another matter for probing. Very dangerous. *But . . . I'm dying anyway. Let's see how deep their need for me actually is.*

"A small case was taken from my pocket," he said. "It contains my medication."

"So, the Mute needs medication," Gallow taunted. "Let's see how he does without it."

"You'll see quite soon," Keel said. "You'll have another body to feed to the kelp."

Keel swung his feet casually over the edge of the table and felt for the deck. A startled look passed between Nakano and Gallow. Keel wondered at it. There was shock in that look. Some nerve had been struck.

"You know about the kelp?" Nakano asked.

Keel said, "Of course. A man in my position . . ." He waved off the rest of the bluff as extraneous.

"We need him alive for the time being," Gallow said. "Get the Mute his medication."

Nakano went to a small storage locker in the rear wall and removed a pocket case of cured organics—dark brown and with a tie string closure.

Keel accepted the case thankfully, found a bitter green pill in it and gulped the pill dry. His intestines felt knotted and it would be long minutes before the pill brought relief, but just the knowledge that he had taken it removed some of the discomfort. Another remora, that was what he needed. But what was the use even of that? His rebellious body would only make short work of another remora. Shorter than the last, and the one before that. His first one had lasted thirty-six years. This last one, a month.

"You can always tell," Nakano said. "Someone who isn't bothered by dying, that one knows about the kelp."

With difficulty, Keel kept his face expressionless. *What was the man saying?*

"It wasn't something we could keep secret forever," Gallow said. "They contact the kelp, too."

Nakano looked piercingly at Keel. It was one of those looks that made a big man like Nakano swell even bigger. "How many of you know?" he asked.

Keel managed a noncommittal shrug, which irritated the seating of his brace.

"We'd have heard something before this if it was out," Gallow

259

said. "Probably just a few of the top Mutes like this one know anything."

Keel stared speculatively from one Merman to the other. Something important to know about the kelp. What could that be? It had to do with dying. With contact with the kelp. Feeding their dead to the kelp?

"In a little while we'll go out and try to hear Zent's memories," Gallow said, a new and deeply reflective tone in his voice. "Then we may learn what happened to him."

Nakano, his voice more matter-of-fact, asked Keel: "How do you contact the kelp? Does the kelp answer every time?"

Keel pursed his lips in thought, delaying his response and gaining time. *Talk to the kelp?* He recalled what Ale and Panille had said about the Merman kelp project—teaching the kelp, assisting the spread of it under Pandora's universal sea.

"We have to actually touch the kelp," Nakano prompted.

"Of course," Keel snorted. And he thought, *Hear Zent's memories?* What was going on here? These violent men were suddenly revealing a mystical side that astonished the pragmatic Keel.

Gallow suddenly laughed. "You don't know any more about it than we do, Mute! The kelp takes your memories, even after you're dead. That's all any of us knows, but you Mutes didn't think about what that could mean."

Green Dashers are kelp food when they die, Keel thought. *And somehow their memories can be read by the living—through the kelp.* He recalled the odd stories out of human history on Pandora— dashers talking with human voices, a fully sentient kelp speaking to the minds of those who touched it. So it was true! And the kelp, genetically rebuilt from the genes carried in a few humans, was recovering that old skill. Did Ale know? And where was she?

Gallow glanced around the room and returned his attention to Keel. "Very pleasant, this cabin," he said. "Ryan Wang's gift to Kareen Ale—her personal foil. I think I'll keep it for my command center."

"Where is Kareen?" Keel asked.

"She's busy being a doctor," Gallow said. "Something she should stick to. Politics doesn't suit her. Maybe medicine doesn't, either. She didn't do much for Zent."

"Nobody could've saved Tso," Nakano said. "I want to know what got him. Does Vashon have a new defense weapon?" Nakano glared at Keel. "What about it, Mr. Justice?"

260

"What're you talking about? Defense against what?"

Gallow stepped closer. "Tso and two of our new recruits were given the simple task of sinking Vashon," Gallow said. "Tso returned dying and in a damaged sub. The two recruits were not with him."

Keel was a moment finding his voice, then: "You're monsters. You would scuttle thousands and thousands of lives—"

"What happened to our sub?" Gallow demanded. "The whole forward section—it looked as though it had been crushed by a fist."

"Vashon?" Keel whispered.

"Oh, it's still there," Gallow said. "Do I have to tell Nakano he must be more persuasive? Answer the question."

Keel drew in a deep, trembling breath and exhaled slowly. Here was why they kept him alive! Whatever had happened to the sub, he had no answer, but there was something he could do. *Forward section crushed?*

"So it worked," Keel said.

Both men glared at him. "What worked?" Gallow barked.

"Our cable trap," Keel bluffed.

"I thought so!" Nakano said.

"Tell us about this device," Gallow ordered.

"I'm no technic or engineer," Keel protested. He put a hand up. "I don't know how it's made."

"But you can tell us what you do know," Gallow said. "Or I will direct Nakano to cause you a great deal of pain."

Keel looked at Nakano's massive arms, those bulging muscles, the bull neck. None of that frightened him, and he knew that Nakano knew it. The reference to death earlier, it was a bond between them.

"All I know is it's organic and it works by compression," Keel said.

"Organic? Our sub has cutters and burners!" Gallow clearly did not believe him.

"It's like a net," Keel said, warming to his fiction. "Each surviving part can behave like the whole. And once it's inside your defenses where your cutters and burners can't reach it . . ." Keel shrugged.

"Why would you make such a thing?" Gallow asked.

"Our Security people determined that we were hopelessly vulnerable to attack from below. Something had to be done. And we were right. Look what happened to Guemes. What almost happened to Vashon."

261

"Yes, look what happened to Guemes," Gallow said, smiling.

Monsters, Keel thought.

"Tso must've done some damage," Nakano said. "That's why Vashon's grounded."

Keel tried to speak past a pain in his throat. "Grounded?" His voice was a croak.

"On the bottom and abandoning its downcenter," Gallow said, showing obvious relish in his words. He reached out and tapped Nakano's arm. "Keep our guest company. I will go out and prepare to commune with Tso's kelp-spirit. See if the Mute here can tell us any way to improve our contact with the kelp."

Keel took a deep breath. His improvisation about a Vashon defense weapon had been accepted. It would make these monsters more cautious. It would give Vashon a breathing space—if the Island survived grounding. He took heart from the fact that Vashon had survived groundings in the distant past. There would be damage, though, and economic losses. Ballast pumps would be working frantically to lift and compress the bottom sections of the Island. Heavy equipment would be detached in its own floaters. Mermen would be called in for assistance.

Mermen! Would friends of these vermin be among those summoned for help? It could take days for Vashon to lift its enormous bulk and refloat. If no storm or wavewall came . . .

I have to escape, Keel thought. *My people have to know what I've learned. They need me.*

Gallow had moved to the hatch, looking back thoughtfully at Nakano and the captive. He opened the hatch and stood there a moment, then: "Nakano, he has not given us every detail of their weapon. He has not told us how he communes with the kelp. There are things of value in his head. If he does not reveal them willingly, we will have to feed him to the kelp and hope to recover the information that way."

Nakano nodded, not looking at Gallow.

Gallow let himself out and sealed the hatch behind him.

"I can't protect you from him if he gets angry, Mr. Justice," Nakano said. His voice was casual, even friendly. "You had better sit down and tell me what you know. Would you like some more water? Sorry we don't have any boo, that would make things easier—more civilized."

Keel moved painfully to the table where Gallow had sat and dropped into the chair. It was still warm.

262

What a strange pair, he thought.

Nakano brought him a beaker of water. Keel sipped slowly, savoring the coolness.

It was almost as though these two exchanged personalities. Keel realized then that Nakano and Gallow were playing the old Security game with him—one guard always browbeat a prisoner while the other came on as a friend, sometimes pretending to protect the prisoner from the attacker.

"Tell me about the weapon," Nakano said.

"The ropes are thicker than full-grown kelp," Keel said. And he recalled underwater views of the kelp—strands thicker than a human torso swaying in the currents.

"A burner would still cut them," Nakano said.

"Ah, but the fibers have some way of reattaching to each other when they touch. Cut it apart and put the cut ends together, it's as though there were no cut."

Nakano grimaced. "How? How is it done?"

"I don't know. They talk about fibrous hooks."

"Now you understand," Nakano said, "why Mutes must go."

"What have we done except protect ourselves?" Keel demanded. "If that sub hadn't been out to sink the Island, it wouldn't have been harmed." Even as he spoke he wondered again about the damaged sub, wishing he could see and examine it. What had really done it? Crushed? Truly crushed or damaged by the bottom?

"Tell me how you commune with kelp," Nakano said.

"We . . . just touch it."

"And?"

Keel swallowed. He remembered the old stories, the remnant history, especially the accounts by Shadow Panille's ancestor.

"It's like daydreaming . . . almost," Keel said. "You hear voices."

That much the old accounts had said.

"Specific voices?" Nakano demanded.

"Sometimes," Keel lied.

"How do you contact the specific dead and gain access to what they knew when alive?"

Keel shrugged, thinking hard. His mind had never worked this fast, absorbing, correlating. *Ship! What a discovery!* He thought about the countless Islander dead consigned to the sea by mourning relatives. How many of those had been absorbed by the kelp?

263

"So the kelp doesn't respond to you any better than it does to us," Nakano said.

"I fear not," Keel agreed.

"Kelp has a mind of its own," Nakano said. "I've said that all along."

Keel thought then about the enormous undersea gardens of kelp, forests of gigantic, ropy strands reaching upward toward the suns. He had seen holos of Mermen swimming through those green forests, flashing silvery figures among the fish and fronds. But no Merman had ever before reported kelp responding in the way it had done for the first humans on Pandora. This must mean full sentience was returning. It must be an avalanche of consciousness sweeping through the sea! Mermen thought they controlled the kelp and, through this, controlled the currents.

What if . . .

Keel felt his heartbeat stutter.

A Merman sub had been crushed. He imagined those gigantic strands of kelp wrapped around the sub's hard surface. Cutters and burners flashed in his imagination. And the kelp writhed, sending out its messages of self-protection. What if the kelp had learned to kill?

"Where are we right now?" Keel asked.

"Near the Launch Base. There's no harm in your knowing; you can't escape."

Keel let his body feel the lift and fall of the craft around him. The light through the louvered vents had begun to dim. *Nightfall?* The foil rode on extremely calm seas, for which he was thankful. Vashon needed calm seas just now.

Near the Launch Base, Nakano says. How near? But even a short swim was impossible for this old body with its head supported on a prosthetic brace. He was a cripple in this environment. A Mute. No wonder these monsters sneered at him.

The foil's motion became even steadier and the light dimmer. Nakano flipped a switch, bringing soft yellow illumination into the room from lamps near the ceiling.

"We are going down to commune with the kelp," Nakano said. "We are in old kelp here, the kind that's most apt to respond to us."

Keel thought about this craft sinking into a forest of kelp. Whatever had happened to Tso the kelp now knew. How would the kelp use that knowledge?

I know what I would do with such people in my power, Keel thought. *I'd squash them. They are lethal deviants.*

If the doors of perception were cleansed, everything would appear to man as it is, infinite. For man has closed himself up, till he sees all things through narrow chinks of his cavern.

—William Blake, Shiprecords

Twisp considered abandoning the tow coracle with its supplies. A second foil had passed nearby without slowing down and he was worried.

We could pick up a few more knots that way, he thought. It galled him that the foils, already lost below the horizon, would be at Vashon by nightfall. The first one probably was arriving right now. He had to plod along in this damned creeping coracle!

He laughed at his own frustration. It relaxed him to laugh, even if it was just his usual short bark. Vashon might be aground, but the Island had touched bottom before, and in perilously more dangerous weather. Pandora had subsided into a calmer phase; his fisherman's instincts felt this. It had to do with the looping interrelationship of the two suns, distance from primaries and, just possibly, the kelp. Perhaps the kelp had finally reached an influential population density. Certainly, kelp fronds were more evident on the surface and the kelp's nursery effect showed itself in the recent fish population boom.

Winters on the open sea were easier every year. The familiar drone of the little engine, the balmy warmth under scattered clouds and the coracle's rhythmic wallow toward Vashon reminded Twisp that he would get there in his own good time.

And when I do, I'll straighten out this Bushka's story.

Vashon was not a community to take lightly. There was influence there, power and money.

And Vata, he thought. *Yes, we have Vata.* Twisp began to see the presence of Vata on his home Island in a new light. She was more

265

than a link with humanity's Pandoran past. Living evidence that a myth had substance—that was what Vata and her satellite Duque represented.

"That last foil must've seen us," Bushka said. "Our position is known."

"You really think they'll alert your Green Dashers?" Twisp asked.

"Gallow has friends in high places," Bushka growled. He glanced significantly at Scudi, who was sitting back against a thwart, looking at Brett with a quizzical expression. Brett lay curled up, asleep.

"We don't know what they're saying on the radio," Bushka said. He looked at the device near Twisp's knee. When Twisp didn't respond, Bushka closed his eyes.

Scudi, shifting her attention from one Islander to the other during this exchange, watched a deep listlessness come over Bushka. The man gave up so easily! What a contrast with Brett.

Scudi thought hard about the escape from Gallow, paddling and sailing, homing on the locator beam from the coracle's transmitter. They had inflated only one of the small rafts from the survival kits, holding the other in reserve. Even this they had delayed until they were more than a kilometer from the foil.

It had been heavy going at first in the thick glut of kelp. The two of them, linked by a single belt line, tended to tangle in the surface fronds. Scudi had led the first stage of their flight, holding them hydrostatically balanced with their dive suit controls just under the surface. When they came up for air it was always beneath a cover of kelp and each time they expected to hear sounds of search and pursuit.

Once, they heard the foil start up, but it shut down immediately. Under the protective cover of a kelp frond, Brett whispered to Scudi: "They don't dare chase after us right now. Capturing that other foil is too important to them."

"The doctor?"

"Something more important than that, I think."

"What?"

"I don't know," Brett whispered. "Let's keep going. We have to be out of sight of them by daybreak."

"I keep worrying that we'll run into dashers."

"I'm keeping a grenade handy. They like to sleep in the kelp. We'll have to dive for it if we surprise one."

"I wish I could see better."

Brett took her hand and they moved through the water as silently as possible.

As they brushed through the thick fronds in their maddeningly slow passage, an odd sense of calm came over both of them. They began to feel almost invulnerable to dashers—any variety, green or black. Under the water, touching the kelp, they moved to deep and stately music, something not quite heard but recognized. When they surfaced for air, the world became different, another reality. The air felt clean and satisfying.

Breaking through a profound shyness, they told each other about this feeling. They both imagined telling the other and the telling came out just as they had imagined. They thought they could go on forever this way, that nothing could harm them.

At one break for air, Brett could no longer contain the sense of an alien experience. He put his mouth close to Scudi's ear. "Something's happening down there."

Both of them had grown up on stories of the old kelp days, the mystical detritus of their history, and each suspected what the other was thinking now. Neither of them found it easy to put into words.

Scudi looked back at the foil, which lay in a low outline under its anchor lights. It still seemed much too close. The foil itself appeared so innocent, its hatch a wink against the night.

"You hear me, Scudi?" Brett whispered. "Something's happening to us when we're under water." When she remained silent he said, "They say when you're under water sometimes it's like a narcotic."

Scudi knew what he meant. Cold and the deeps could do things to your body that you did not notice until your mind started to come apart at the dreams. But this was no depth narcosis. And the dive suits kept them warm. This was something else and, here on the surface, knowing they should not delay long, she felt suddenly terrified.

"I'm scared," she whispered, staring at the foil.

"We'll get away from them," Brett said, seeing the direction of her gaze. "See? They're not chasing after us."

"They have a sub."

"The sub couldn't go fast in kelp. They'd have to cut their way through." He pulled himself closer to her along their belt line. "But that's not what's scaring you."

Scudi didn't say anything, she floated on her back under a swatch of kelp, conscious of a heavy iodine smell from the leaves. The weight of the kelp frond on her head was like an old, kindly hand. She knew they should be going. Daylight must not find them in sight of the foil. Her hand on the concealing kelp, she turned and a bit of the kelp came away in her grip. Immediately, she was thrust into the euphoria she had felt underwater. There was wind all around. A sea bird she had never seen shrieked somewhere in perfect time with the waves. The hypnotic effect unfocused her eyes, then centered them on a human being—prone and very old. An old woman. The old woman existed in a glowing space without any sense of world around her. The vision moved closer and Scudi tried to relax an intense pressure in her stomach. Monotony of waves and the shrieking bird helped, but the vision would not fade.

The old, old woman lay on her back in the blur of light. Alone . . . breathing. Scudi noticed a clump of white hair jutting from a mole near the old woman's left ear. The eyes were closed. The old woman did not appear to be a mutant. Her skin was dark and heavily wrinkled. It gave off a greenish cast like the beginning patina on a piece of old brass.

Abruptly, the woman sat up. Her eyes remained closed but she opened her mouth to say something. The old lips moved slow as cold oil. Scudi watched the play of wrinkles released across the face by movement. The woman spoke, but there was no sound. Scudi strained to hear, pressing close to the wrinkled lips.

The vision dissolved and Scudi found herself coughing, retching, held across her floating survival kit by strong hands.

"Scudi!" It was Brett's voice in a loud whisper close to her ear. "Scudi! What's happening? You started to drown. You just sank under the water and . . ."

She coughed up warm water and took in a choking breath.

"You just started sinking," Brett said. He was struggling to balance her on the kit. She pushed herself across its rasping surface and slipped back into the water, holding the kit by one hand. She saw immediately what Brett had done—set the kit's hydrostatic controls for surface and used it as a platform to support her.

"It was like you just went to sleep," Brett said. The worry in his voice seemed amusing to her, but she restrained a laugh. Didn't he know yet?

Brett glanced back at the foil about a kilometer away. Had they heard?

"Kelp," Scudi choked. Her throat hurt when she spoke.

"What about it? Did you get tangled?"

"The kelp . . . in my mind," she said. And she remembered that old face, the open mouth like a black tunnel into a strange mind.

Slowly, hesitantly, she described her experience.

"We've got to get out of here," Brett said. "It can take over your mind."

"It wasn't trying to hurt me," she said. "It was trying to tell me something."

"What?"

"I don't know. Maybe it didn't have the right words."

"How do you know it wasn't trying to hurt you? You almost drowned."

"You panicked," she said.

"I was afraid you were drowning!"

"It let go of me when you panicked."

"How do you know?"

"I . . . just . . . know." Without waiting for more argument, she reset her survival kit's controls, pulled it under and began swimming away from the foil.

Brett, attached to Scudi by the belt line, was forced to follow, towing his own kit and sputtering.

Much later, on the coracle with Twisp and Bushka, Scudi debated recounting the kelp experience. It was late morning now. Still no sign of Vashon on the horizon. Brett and Bushka had fallen asleep. Before they had reached the coracle, Brett had warned her to say nothing of the kelp experience to Twisp, but she felt that this time Brett could be wrong.

"Twisp will think we're crazy as shit pumpers!" Brett had insisted. "Kelp trying to talk to you!"

It really happened, Scudi told herself. She looked from the sleeping figure of Brett to Twisp at the coracle's tiller. *The kelp tried to talk to me . . . and it did talk!*

Brett came abruptly awake as Scudi shifted her position. She leaned back now with her elbows over the thwart. He looked up and met her eyes, realizing immediately what she had been thinking.

About the kelp!

He sat up and looked around at an empty horizon. The wind had picked up and there was spray in the air, scudding off the wavetops. Twisp swayed with a rhythm that marked both the pitch of the waves and the throb of the engine. The long-armed fisherman stared off across the water ahead of him the way he always did when they were chugging along in the fish runs. Bushka remained asleep near the bow cuddy.

Scudi met Brett's gaze.

"I wonder if they got their doctor," Brett said.

Scudi nodded. "I wonder why they needed one. Nearly everyone down under is trained as a med-tech."

"It was something pretty bad," Brett said. "Had to be."

Twisp shifted his position. He did not look at any of them and said, "You got doctors to spare down under."

Brett knew what the older man meant. Twisp had spoken of it bitterly many times, as had many Islanders. Topside technology, predominantly organic, meant that most topside biologists who might otherwise go into medicine were lured by higher-status maintenance positions in the cash business of the Islands' bio-engineering labs. It was an ironic twist that had them keeping an Island itself fit while the Islanders made do with a handful of med-techs and a family shaman.

Bushka sat up, awakened by their voices, and immediately returned to his insistent fear. "Gallow will have that sub after us!"

"We'll be at Vashon by tomorrow," Twisp said.

"You think you can get away from Gallow?" Bushka snorted.

"You sound like you want him to catch us," Twisp said. He pointed ahead. "We'll be in kelp pretty soon. A sub would think twice about going in there."

"They're not Islander subs," Bushka reminded him. "These have burners and cutters." He sat back with a sullen expression.

Brett stood, one hand steadying him against a thwart. He stared ahead where Twisp had pointed. Still no sign of Vashon, but the water about a kilometer ahead gave off the dark, oily slickness of a heavy kelp bed. He sank back onto his haunches, still steadying himself against the top roll of the boat.

Kelp.

He and Scudi had inflated one of the rafts while still in the kelp bed and perilously close to the foil. Brett had been surprised how easily a raft glided over the big fronds. The kelp did not drag at the raft the way it did on a coracle's hull. The raft slid across the

270

fronds with only the barest whisper of a hiss. But the stubby paddles, fitted into sleeve pockets of their dive suits, splashed water into the raft. And the paddles tended to pick up torn pieces of kelp.

Remembering, Brett thought: *It happened. No one will believe us but it happened.*

Even in memory, the experience remained frightening. He had touched a piece torn from the kelp. Immediately, he had heard people talking. Voices in many pitches and dialects had blended into the hiss of the raft's passage. He had known at once that this was not a dream or hallucination. He was hearing snatches of real conversation.

As he touched the torn bits of kelp in the night, Brett had felt it trying to reach up to him, seeking his hands on the paddles.

Scudi Scudi Scudi Brett Brett Brett

The names echoed in his mind with a feeling of music, a strange inflection but the clearest tones he had ever heard—undistorted by air or wind or the music-devouring dampers of an Island's organic walls.

A wind had come up then and they had raised the raft's crude sail. Scudding across the kelp's surface, huddled close in the stern, they had held a paddle between them as a rudder. Scudi had watched the little receiver that aimed them toward Twisp's transmitter.

Once, Scudi had looked up at a bright star low on the horizon. She pointed at it. "See?"

Brett looked up to a star that he had known from his first awareness, out onto a Vashon terrace with his parents on a clear warm night. He had thought of it as "the fat star."

"Little Double," Scudi said. "It's very close to our sunrise point."

"When it's that low on the horizon, you can see the hyb tanks make a pass *there*." He pointed to the horizon directly opposite the position of the fat star. "Twisp taught me that."

Scudi chuckled, snuggling close to him for warmth. "My mother said Little Double was far off across the horizon to the north when she was young. It's another binary system, you know. From Little Double we could see both of our suns clearly."

"To them, we're probably the fat star," he said.

Scudi was quiet for a time, then: "Why won't you talk about the kelp?"

"What's to talk about?" Brett heard his own voice, brittle and unnatural.

"It called our names," Scudi said. She gently pulled a bit of leaf from the back of her left hand.

Brett swallowed hard. His tongue felt dry and thick.

"It did," she said. "I have trailed my hand through it many times. I get images—pictures like holos or dreams. They are symbols and if I think on them I learn something."

"You mean you still wanted to touch it, even after it almost drowned you?"

"You're wrong about the kelp," Scudi said. "I'm speaking of the times before, when I worked at sea. I have learned from the kelp . . ."

"I thought you said you taught the kelp."

"But the kelp helps me, too. That is why I have such good luck when I mathematic the waves. But now the kelp is learning words."

"What does it say to you?"

"My name and your name." She dipped a hand over the side and dragged it across a huge vine. "It says you love me, Brett."

"That's crazy."

"That you love me?"

"No . . . that it knows. You know what I mean."

"Then it's true."

"Scudi . . ." He swallowed. "It's obvious, huh?"

She nodded. "Don't worry. I love you, too."

He felt a hot flush of exuberance plunge out of his cheeks.

"And the kelp knows that, too," she said.

Later, as Brett squatted in the coracle watching the distance to another kelp bed grow shorter and shorter, he heard Scudi's words over and over in his memory: "The kelp knows . . . the kelp knows . . ." The memory was like the gentle rise and fall of the seas beneath the wallowing boat.

It called our names, he thought. Admitting this did not help. *It could be calling us to be its dinner.*

He turned his thoughts to something else Scudi had said in the raft: "I like it that our bodies find comfort with each other."

A very practical woman. No giving in to the demands of sex, because that could complicate their lives. She did not hesitate to admit that she wanted him, though, and anticipation counted for something. Brett sensed the strength in her as he looked across the coracle to where she rested with both elbows hooked over a thwart.

"We're in the kelp," she said. She dropped her left hand over the side. Brett wished they could explain what she was doing, but he felt sure the others would think the explanation proof of insanity.

"Would you look at that!" Twisp said. He nodded toward something ahead of them.

Brett stood up and looked. A wide lane had opened through the kelp, the fronds spreading wide, then completely aside, still spreading farther ahead. He felt the water boil under them and the two coracles surged forward.

"It's a current going our way," Twisp said, astonishment in his voice.

"Merman Current Control," Bushka said. "See! They know where we are. They're delivering us someplace."

"That's right," Twisp said. "Directly toward Vashon."

Scudi straightened and brought her dripping hand out of the water. She bent forward and moved across the coracle, tipping it.

"Trim ship!" Twisp snapped.

She hesitated. "The kelp," she said. "It's helping us. This isn't Current Control at all."

"How do you know?" Twisp asked.

"It . . . the kelp talks to me."

Now she's done it, Brett thought.

Bushka let out a loud snort of laughter.

Twisp, however, stared at her silently for a moment, then: "Tell me more."

"I have shared images with the kelp for a long time," she said. "At least three years since I first noticed. Now it speaks words in my head. To Brett, too. The kelp called his name."

Twisp looked at Brett, who cleared his throat and said, "Well, that's how it seemed."

"Our ancestors claimed the kelp was sentient," Twisp said. "Even Jesus Lewis said it. 'The kelp is a community mind.' You're a historian, Bushka, you should know all this."

"Our ancestors said a lot of crazy things!"

"There's always a reason," Twisp said. He nodded at the lane through the kelp. "Explain that."

"Current Control. The girl's wrong."

273

"Put your hand over the side," Scudi said. "Touch the kelp as we pass."

"Sure," Bushka said. "Use your hand for bait. Who knows what you might catch?"

Twisp merely leveled a cold stare at Bushka, then steered the coracle close to the right side of the open lane and dipped his long right arm over the side. Presently, a look of amazement came over his face. The expression hardened.

"Ship save us," he muttered, but he did not withdraw his hand.

"What is it?" Brett asked. He swallowed and thought about the sensation of kelp contact. Could he put his hand over the side and renew that connection? The idea both attracted and repelled him. He no longer doubted a central reality to the night's experience, but the intent of the kelp could not be accepted without question.

Scudi almost drowned. That is a fact.

"There's a sub coming behind us," Twisp said.

All of them peered back along their course but the surface gave no sign of what might be under it.

"They have us on their locator," Twisp said, "and they mean to sink us."

Scudi turned around and dipped both hands into the passing kelp.

"Help us," she whispered. "If you know what help is."

Bushka sat silent, pale-faced and shuddering at the entrance to the tiny cuddy in the bow. "It's Gallow," he said. "I told you."

With a slow stateliness the channel ahead of them began to close. A passage opened to the left. Current surged into it, swinging the coracles wide. The towed supply boat pulled far to the right. Twisp fought the tiller to center his craft in the new channel.

"The channel's closing behind us," Brett said.

"The kelp is helping us," Scudi said. "It *is*."

Bushka opened his mouth and closed it without speaking. All of them turned to stare where he pointed. A black conning tower broke surface, tipped and sank from sight. Kelp curled over the scene. Giant bubbles began breaking the surface, thick rainbows of air and oil. Small waves surged under the boats, forcing the four people in the coracle to hold on to the rimlines.

As quickly as it had started, the turbulence subsided. The coracles continued their agitated rocking. Water splashed across the gunwales. This, too, quieted.

274

"It was the kelp," Scudi said. "The sub cut into the kelp trying to follow us."

Twisp nodded to where the kelp still curled among a few small bubbles. He gripped the tiller with both hands, guiding them through a channel that curved open ahead of them, once more aiming toward Vashon. "The kelp did that?"

"It clogged the sub's intakes," Scudi said. "When the crew tried to blow ballast and surface, the kelp jammed vines into the ballast ports. When the crew tried to get out, the kelp tore them apart and crushed the sub." She jerked her hands out of the water, breaking contact with the kelp.

"I warned you it was dangerous," Brett said.

A stricken look on her face, Scudi nodded. "It's finally learned to kill."

Hasn't the water of sleep dissolved our being?
—Gaston Bachelard, "The Poetics of Reverie,"
from *The Handbook of the Chaplain/Psychiatrist*

Duque woke to a nudge, a deliberate jostling intended to do the waking. He had been prodded, pricked, rubbed, shocked, bled and rocked in his liquid cradle with the great Vata, but this was the first time since childhood that he had been nudged. What surprised him was that it was Vata who did it.

You're awake! he thought, but there was no answer. He felt a focus, a channeling of her presence such as he had never felt before. For this he roused himself, twisted an arm up to his face and fisted his good eye open.

That brought the watchers to the Vata Pool on the double. What he saw with his one eye was worth calling those fools poolside. One of Vata's huge brown eyes, her left one, was pressed nearly to his own. It was open. Duque swallowed hard. He was sure she could see him.

Vata? He tried it aloud: "Vata?"

The growing crowd gasped, and Duque knew that the C/P would push her way to them soon.

He felt something breeze through his consciousness like a heavy sigh. It was a wind with hidden thoughts in it. But he felt them. Something big, waiting.

Duque was shocked. He had long been used to the mind-rocking power Vata could hurl between his eyes. This was the way she threw tantrums, by jamming whatever frustrated her right into his head. Now, she sent him a vision of the C/P, naked, dancing in front of a mirror. For some time now Vata had kept the naked female thoughts out of his head. Anger! Vata contained anger. He blocked out the anger and riveted his inner eye on the supple, firm-breasted Chaplain/Psychiatrist who thrust her pale hips again and again at the mirror. The tank was unbearably warm.

Simone Rocksack's favorite robe lay in a trampled blue heap at her feet. Everything in Duque strained to touch this vision, this body of raw beauty that the C/P locked away from the world.

That was when he saw the hands. A pair of large, pale hands snaked around her from behind and he watched in the mirror as they cupped her swaying breasts while she moved in a rhythmic step-slide, step-slide. It was a man, a large man, and he continued his intense caress of her body until she slowed her dance and stopped, quivering, while his lips brushed her shoulders and breasts, her abdomen, those glistening thighs. The man's shock of blonde hair was magnet to her fingers. Her hands pulled him close, closer, and they began to make love with him standing behind her, facing the mirror.

The vision ended with an angry white flash and the name *Gallow* blared across his consciousness. What he saw when he refocused on Vata's eye was danger.

"Danger," he muttered. "Gallow danger. Simone, Simone."

Vata's great brown eye closed and Duque felt relieved of a massive, clawlike grip that had held his guts tight. He lay back, breathing deeply, and listened as the knot of watchers grew and the babble of their speculations lulled him back to sleep.

When the C/P came to poolside there was nothing visible of the strange thing the watchers reported.

To survive Pandora's time of madness, we were forced to go mad.

— Iz Bushka, *The Physics of Political Expression*

Brett woke at dawn, feeling the coracle riding gently under him. Scudi lay curled against his side. Twisp sat at his usual place by the tiller but the boat chugged along on autopilot. Brett could see the little red traveler lights blinking across the face of the receiver, keeping them on course to Vashon.

Scudi sniffed in her sleep. A light tarp kept the damp night air from both of them. Brett inhaled a deep breath through his nose and faced the fact that he would never again accept the stench that surrounded every place Islanders lived. He had experienced the Mermen's filtered air. Now, the fish odors, the thick miasma from Twisp's body, all of it forced Brett to think even more deeply about how his life had been changed.

I smelled like that, he thought. *It's a good thing Scudi met me in the water.*

Mermen joked about Islander stink, he knew. And Islanders returning topside spoke longingly of the sweet air down under.

Scudi had said nothing on meeting Twisp, nor on boarding the coracle. But the distaste on her face had been evident. She had tried to hide it for his sake, he knew, but the reaction was unmistakable.

Brett felt guilty about his sudden embarrassment.

You shouldn't be embarrassed by your friends.

The first long shaft of dawn washed across the coracle, a lazy pink.

Brett sat up.

Twisp, his voice low and muffled at the stern, said, "Take the watch, kid. I'll need a few winks."

"Right."

278

Brett whispered to keep from waking Scudi. She lay curled up close, her back and hips fitting into the socket of his body as if they were built together. One hand lay flung backward around Brett's waist. He gently disengaged her light grip.

Looking up at the clear sky, Brett thought, *It's going to be a hot one.* He slid out from beneath the tarp and felt the damp bow spray wet his hair and face.

Brett brushed a thick lock of hair from his eyes and crept aft to take the tiller.

"Gonna be a hot one," Twisp said. Brett smiled at the coincidence. They thought alike now, no question about it. He scanned the horizon. The boats still glided down a narrow avenue of current between the hedging kelp.

"Aren't we going kinda slow?" Brett asked.

"Eelcells are getting low," Twisp said. He gestured with a foot at the telltale pink of discharge on the cellpack set into the deck. "Gonna have to stop and charge them or raise sail."

Brett wet a finger in his mouth and raised it to the air. There was only the coolness of their own passage—flat calm everywhere he looked, and gently undulating kelp fronds as far as the eye could see.

"We should be raising Vashon pretty soon," Twisp said. "I caught the Seabird program while you were asleep. Everything's going well, so they say."

"I thought you wanted some shut-eye," Brett said.

"Changed my mind. I wanta see Vashon first. 'Sides, I miss all the times we'd just sit up and shoot the shit. I've just been dozing and thinking here since I relieved you at midnight."

"And listening to the radio," Brett said. He indicated the half-earphone jacked into the receiver.

"Real interesting, what they had to say," Twisp said. He kept his voice low, his attention on the mound that was the sleeping figure of Bushka.

"Things are going well," Brett prompted.

"Seabird says Vashon is in sight of land that is well out of the water. He describes black cliffs. *High* cliffs and waves foaming white at the base. People could live there, he says."

Brett tried to visualize this.

Cliff was a word Brett had heard rarely. "How could we get people and supplies up the cliff?" Brett asked. "And what happens if the sea rises again?"

279

"Way I see it, you'd have to be part bird to live there," Twisp agreed. "If you needed the sea. And fresh water might be scarce."

"LTA's might help."

"Maybe catch basins for the rain," Twisp mused. "But the big problem they're worried about is nerve runners."

In the bow, Bushka lifted himself out of his tarp and stared aft at Brett and Twisp.

Brett ignored the man. *Nerve runners!* He knew them only from the scant early holos and the histories from before the dark times of the rising sea and the death of the kelp.

"Once there's open land, there'll be nerve runners," Twisp said. "That's what the experts are saying."

"You pay for everything," Bushka said. He patted the back of his open hand against his mouth, yawning widely.

Something had changed in Bushka, Brett realized. When he accepted that his story about Guemes was believed, Bushka had become a tragicomic figure instead of a villain.

Did he change or is it just that we're seeing him different? Brett wondered.

Scudi lifted herself from beneath her tarp and said, "Did I hear somebody say something about nerve runners?"

Brett explained.

"But Vashon can see land?" Scudi asked. "Real land?"

Twisp nodded. "So they say." He reached down and tugged at a pair of lines trailing over the side of the coracle.

Immediately, their squawks set up a flapping commotion beside the boat, spattering cold water all around. Bushka caught most of the splashing.

"Ship's teeth!" he gasped. "That's cold!"

Twisp chuckled. "Wakes you up good," he said. "Just imagine what—" He broke off and bent his head in a listening attitude.

The others heard it, too. All turned toward the horizon on their port where the distant pulse of a hydrogen ram could be heard. They saw it then—a white line far off across the kelp.

"Foil," Bushka said. "They're turning toward us."

"Their instruments have locked onto us," Twisp said.

"They're not going to Vashon . . . they're coming to us!" Bushka said.

"He may be right," Brett said.

Twisp jerked his chin down and up. "Brett, you and Scudi take your dive suits and those kits. You hit the water. Hide in the kelp.

Bushka, there's an old green duffle bag under the deck forward. Haul it out."

Brett, struggling into his suit, remembered what was in that bag. "What're you going to do with your spare net?" he asked.

"We'll lay it here."

"I don't have a dive suit," Bushka moaned.

"You'll hide under the tarp there in the cuddy," Twisp said. "Over the side, you two. Hurry it up, Scudi! String that net along the kelp."

Presently, after hurried preparations, Bushka burrowed his way beneath the tarp and crawled under the forward deck. Brett and Scudi rolled backward over the side of the boat, pulling the net with them. The sound of the approaching foil was growing louder.

Twisp stared toward the sound. The foil was still eight or ten kilometers to port but closing faster than he had thought possible. He hauled in his squawks and caged them, then found two hand-lines. He baited them with dried muree and slung them over the side.

The raft!

It bobbed against the side of the supply coracle like a beacon. Twisp shot out a long arm, grabbed the line and pulled it to him. He slit it open, rolled the air out of it as fast as he could and stowed it under his seat. Brett and Scudi, he saw, were getting something out of the supply coracle. Harpoon? Damn! They had better hurry.

He glanced around his coracle then. Bushka lay concealed under the bow cuddy. The net trailed aft. Scudi and Brett had gone under water into the kelp. Why did Brett want a harpoon? Twisp wondered. They were safely under the kelp, though, taking their surface air from beneath huge leaves.

Twisp cut his motor and slipped the lasgun out of its hiding place behind him. He put it under a towel beside him on the seat and kept his hand on it.

"Bushka," he called. "Stay as quiet as a dead fish. If it's them . . . well, we don't know. I'll give you the all-clear if it's not." He wiped the back of his free hand across his mouth. "Here they are."

He raised a hand in greeting as the foil circled in over the kelp, scattering torn green fronds in its wake. It avoided the net and the side of the channel where Brett and Scudi had taken to the water.

No response came to his greeting, just intense stares from two dark figures in the high cockpit. Twisp saw streaks of green on the figures up there. He breathed deeply to slow his heartbeat and steady the trembling in his legs.

Be ready, he warned himself, *but don't be jumpy.*

The foil swung wide astern and sank into the channel through the kelp. The jet subsided to a faint hiss. A heavy wave rolled out from the foil's bow and rocked the coracles. The squawks set up a loud complaint.

Once more, Twisp raised a hand in greeting and waved the approaching foil to the left, indicating the long line of his net with its bobbing floats. When no more than twenty meters separated the craft, Twisp shouted, "Good weather and a good catch!"

He tightened his grip on the lasgun. The choppy cross-waves set up by the foil broke over the coracle's thwarts and soaked him.

Still no response from the foil, which now loomed high over him and no more than ten meters away. Its side hatch slid open and a Merman appeared there in a camouflaged dive suit—green blobs and stripes. The foil slid alongside and came to a stop.

The Merman standing above Twisp said, "I thought Mutes never fished alone."

"You thought wrong."

"I thought no Mute fished out of sight of his Island."

"This one does."

The Merman's quick eyes flitted over both coracles, followed the line of floats astern, then fixed on Twisp.

"Your net's strung along a kelp bed," he said. "You could lose it that way."

"Kelp means fish," Twisp said. He kept his voice level, calm. He even flashed a smile. "Fishermen go where the catch is."

Under the foil's bow, too low to be visible to the Merman, Twisp saw Scudi slip up for air, then drift down.

"Where's your catch?"

"What's it to you?"

The Merman squatted on the deck above Twisp and looked down at him. "Listen, shit-bug, you can disappear out here. Now I've got some questions and I want answers. If I like the answers, you keep your net, your boat, your catch and maybe you keep alive. Do you understand?"

Twisp remained silent. Out of the corner of one eye he caught a glimpse of Brett's head surfacing under the other side of the foil's bow. Brett's hand came up gripping the harpoon from the supply coracle.

What's he doing with that thing? Twisp wondered. *And he's in too close for me to use the stunshield if the chance comes.*

"Aye," Twisp said. "No catch yet. Just got set up." Brett and Scudi disappeared from his sight around the other side of the foil.

"Have you seen anyone else on the water?" the Merman asked.

"Not since the wavewall."

The Merman looked at Twisp's grizzled, weather-beaten face and said, "You've been out ever since the wavewall?" There was awe in his voice.

"Yeah."

He dropped the awe. "And no catch?" he snapped. "You're not much of a fisherman. Not much of a liar, either. You sit still, I'm coming aboard." He signaled his intentions to someone out of view in the foil, then flipped a stubby ladder over the side.

The Merman's movements were deft and controlled. He used no more than the minimal energy required for each action. Twisp noted this and felt a deep sense of caution.

This man knows his body, Twisp thought. *And it's a weapon.* It would be difficult to take this man by surprise. But Twisp knew his own strengths. He had leverage and a net-puller's power. He also had a lasgun under his towel.

The Merman began lowering himself into the coracle. One foot probed backward for the thwart and, as the Merman put his weight onto that foot, Twisp moved backward as though compensating for the weight shift. The Merman smiled and released both hands from the ladder. He turned to make the last step down into the coracle. Twisp reached his long left arm out to steady the man and, as he moved, shifted his weight. Twisp allowed the man to feel a firm grip in the clasp of the hand, steadying him against the roll of the boat until the last possible blink. Then, in one smooth move, Twisp shifted farther toward the Merman, shortened his long-armed grip and tipped that side of the boat completely under water. The Merman lurched forward. Twisp twisted his grip, jerking the man toward him. The long left arm released its grip and snaked around the Merman's neck while the other hand came up with the lasgun pressed against the back of his head.

"Don't move or you could disappear out here," Twisp said.

283

"Go ahead and kill me, Mute!" The Merman thrashed against Twisp.

Twisp tightened his grip. Muscles that single-handedly pulled loaded nets over a coracle's rim stood out in sinewy ropes.

"Tell your mates to step out on deck!" Twisp growled.

"He won't come out and he's going to kill you," the Merman choked. He twisted again in the powerful grip. One foot braced against a thwart and he tried to push Twisp backward.

Twisp lifted the lasgun and brought it down sharply against the man's head. The Merman grunted and went limp. Twisp lifted the lasgun's barrel toward the open hatch and started to rise. He didn't like the idea of going up that ladder fully exposed.

Brett appeared in the hatchway, saw the lasgun directed at him and ducked, shouting: "We've got the foil! Don't shoot!"

Twisp noted blood down Brett's left side, then, and felt his stomach tighten. "You hurt?"

"No. It's not me. But I think we killed this guy in here. Scudi's trying to help him." Brett shuddered. "He wouldn't stop. He came right at the harpoon!"

"Only one in there?"

"Right. Just the two of them. This is the foil Scudi and I stole."

"Bushka," Twisp called, "practice your knots on this one." He heaved the unconscious Merman across the coracle's motor box.

Bushka crept aft, trailing a length of line from the bow. He looked fearful, and kept well back of the Merman.

"Know him?" Twisp asked.

"Cypher. Works for Gallow."

Scudi appeared in the hatchway behind Brett. She looked pale, her dark eyes wide.

"He's dead," she said. "He kept telling me I had to feed his body to the kelp." Her hands didn't know what to do with their smears of blood.

"This one wouldn't give up, either." Twisp looked to where Bushka was tying the limp Merman's hands behind his back and then to his feet. "They're crazy." Twisp returned his attention to Scudi. She slipped a black-handled survival knife back into its sheath at her thigh.

"How'd you get inside?" Twisp asked.

"There's a diver's hatch on the other side," Brett said. "Scudi knows how to work it. We waited until that one stepped off into the boat before boarding. The pilot didn't suspect a thing until we

284

were right behind him." Brett was talking fast, almost breathless. "Why'd he keep coming for me, Queets? He could see I had the harpoon."

"He was stupid," Twisp said. "You weren't." He glanced at Scudi above him, then at her knife.

She followed the direction of his gaze and said, "I didn't know if he was faking."

That one can take care of herself, Twisp thought.

Bushka stood up from tying the Merman. He looked the foil over approvingly. "We've got ourselves a machine."

The Merman on the deck beneath him stirred and muttered.

"Kid!" Twisp used the command tone that Brett remembered so well from their days at sea. He responded without thinking: "Sir?"

"You think we should move aboard the foil?"

Brett flashed a wide grin. "Yes, sir. It's bigger, faster, more mobile and more seaworthy. I certainly do think we should move aboard, sir."

"Scudi, can we get my coracles aboard of her?"

"The cargo hatch is plenty wide enough," she said, "and there's a winch."

"Brett," Twisp said, "you and Scudi start moving our gear aboard. Iz and I will just ask a few questions of this chunk of eelshit."

"If you want to help the kids," Bushka said, "I can handle this one alone." He nudged the Merman at his feet with a toe.

Twisp studied Bushka for a couple of blinks, noting the new tone of assurance in the man's voice. Anger crawled across Bushka's face now and it was directed at the captive.

"Find out what he was looking for," Twisp said. "What was he doing out here?"

Bushka nodded.

Twisp took his boat's bow line and tied it to a foil strut below the boarding ladder. They began shifting gear, moving presently to the tow coracle.

When both coracles were emptied, Twisp paused. He heard Brett and Scudi shifting gear aboard the foil. In the dozens of trips they'd made packing supplies, the two youngsters had touched, bumped against each other or brushed together as often as appeared discreetly possible. Twisp felt good just watching them. Nothing in the world ever felt as good as love, Twisp thought.

Below Twisp, Bushka sat back on his heels, glaring at the captive Merman.

"You getting anything from him?" Twisp asked.

"They've taken the Chief Justice."

"Shit," Twisp snapped. "Let's haul that tow coracle aboard. Keep at him."

Even with the winch, it was sweaty work getting the first coracle aboard. Scudi opened a cargo compartment aft of the loading hatch and the three of them wrestled the boat inside. They lashed it against cleats in the walls.

Scudi stepped out onto the loading deck, glanced behind her and stiffened. "You better come out and look," she said. She was pale as a sun-washed cloud.

Twisp hurried outside, followed by Brett.

Bushka stood over the bound Merman. The man was no longer lashed to the coracle's bow. The naked Merman had been pulled to a hanging position, hung by the wrists, bound up behind his shoulder blades. His dive suit lay in ragged pieces about the deck and his knees barely touched the floors. Bushka held a fish-knife in his right hand, its slender tip directed at the Merman's belly.

The muscles of the captive's arms stood out red but his thin-drawn lips were white. His shoulders strained at their sockets. His penis was a shrunken stump of fear tucked against his pelvis.

"All right," Twisp demanded, "what's going on?"

"You wanted information," Bushka said. "I'm getting information. Trying out a few tricks Zent bragged about."

Twisp squatted in the opening, suppressing feelings of revulsion. "That so?" He kept his voice level.

When Bushka turned, Twisp realized that this was not the whining castaway he had jerked out of the sea. This one talked slow and even. He did not take his eyes off the target.

"He claims the kelp makes them immortal," Bushka said. "They have to be fed to the kelp when they die. I told him we'd burn him and keep the ashes."

"Take him off the cleat, Iz," Twisp said. "You shouldn't treat a man that way. Haul him aboard here."

A sullen expression flitted across Bushka's face and was gone. He turned and cut the captive down. The Merman flexed his arms behind his back, restoring circulation.

"He says the kelp keeps your identity, all your memories, everything," Bushka said.

Scudi pulled Brett close and whispered: "That may be possible."

Brett merely nodded, looking down at where Bushka had been torturing the captive. He found the thought of what Bushka had done revolting.

Sensing Brett's reaction, Scudi said: "Do you think Iz would really have killed and burned him?"

Brett swallowed in a dry throat. Honesty forced him to say: "I harpooned the guy in the foil."

"That was different! That one would've killed you. This one was tied and helpless."

"I don't know," Brett said.

"He scares me," Scudi said.

The foil lurched slightly, and again. Something uncoiled into the sea behind them.

"Net," Brett whispered. "Twisp cut it loose." *And it broke his heart,* he thought. *Fish dying for nothing always breaks his heart.*

A chill wind passed over them and they both looked up. Thin clouds had begun a drift in from the north and there was a light chop to the water where the kelp opened that strange lane. The lane still pointed them directly toward Vashon.

"I thought it was going to stay hot," Brett said.

"Wind's changed," Twisp said. "Let's get this boat aboard. Vashon might be in for a bad time after all."

They secured the boat, sealed the hatch and joined Scudi and Bushka in the pilot house. Scudi took the command chair, with Bushka standing to one side, flexing his fingers. Rage still seethed in Bushka's eyes.

"Iz," Twisp said, his voice low. "Would you really have cooked that Merman alive?"

"Every time I close my eyes, I see Guemes and Gallow." Bushka glanced aft where they had left the Merman secured. "I'd be awful sorry, I know, but . . ." He shrugged.

"Not much of an answer."

"I think I'd burn him," Bushka said.

"That wouldn't help you sleep any better," Twisp said. He nodded at Scudi. "Let's get this thing to Vashon."

Scudi fired up the ram and gently lifted the foil up onto its step.

In a minute they were scudding along the kelp channel with a slight bouncing motion against the chop.

Twisp directed Bushka to a couch at the rear of the pilot house. Sitting beside Bushka, Twisp asked, "Did he say how they captured Keel?"

"Off another foil. They had two foils then."

"Where's Gallow?"

"He's gone to Outpost Twenty-two on the other foil," Bushka said. "That's the rocket pickup station. He thinks there's an army in the hyb tanks. Whoever opens them owns them. He wants control of both launch and recovery and obviously he thinks he can get it."

"Is it possible?"

"An army in the hyb tanks?" Bushka snorted. "Anything's possible. They could come out shooting for all we know."

"What does he want with Keel?"

"Trade. For Vata. He wants Vata."

"Gallow's crazy!" Brett blurted. "I've been downcenter and seen the Vata support system. It's *big*. They couldn't possibly . . ."

"Cut out the whole support complex with a sub," Bushka said. "Seal it off, tow it out. They could do it."

"They'd need doctors—"

"They have their doctor," Bushka said. "When they snatched Keel they picked up Kareen Ale. Gallow's covering all angles."

Silence came over the pilot cabin while the ram pulsed around them. The foils slapped the seas in a well-absorbed rhythm.

Twisp looked forward to Scudi in the pilot's seat. "Scudi, can we make radio contact with Vashon?"

"Anyone could hear," she spoke without looking back.

Twisp shook his head once in frustrated indecision.

Without warning, Bushka yanked the lasgun from Twisp's pocket and jammed it against his ribs.

"Up!" Bushka snapped.

Stunned, Twisp obeyed.

"Very careful how you move," Bushka said. "I know how strong you are."

Brett saw the lasgun in Bushka's hand. "What's—"

"Sit!" Bushka ordered.

Brett sank back into the seat beside Scudi. She glanced aft, eyed the scene and jerked her attention back to her course.

"Whether we radio or take the message to Vashon in person, it's

288

all the same," Bushka said. "Gallow learns that his secret is out. But right now, we have the advantage of surprise. He thinks this is his foil."

"What do you mean?" Twisp asked.

"Turn this foil around, Scudi," Bushka ordered. "We're going after Gallow. I should've killed him when I had the chance."

Don't call me her father. I was nothing more than an in-
strument of Vata's conception. "Father" and "daughter"
don't apply. Vata was born more than the sum of our parts.
I caution the sons and the daughters after us: Remember
that Vata is more mother to us than sister to you.
                              —Kerro Panille, Family Papers

Shadow Panille stood in the gloom of Current Control thinking that at last he had found the woman of his life. With Kareen Ale, he had the faith that only Merman-normal offspring could evidence.

Current Control was aswarm with work, the usual routines pre-empted by the impending launch and the code yellow grounding of Vashon.

"Too many people working too hard for too long," he muttered to himself. Impulses moved out into the kelp from Current Control, signals of drift sensors flashed in their cobalt-blue numerals. LTA reports were rolling on the number six screen.

Wouldn't get me up in one of those things, he thought. Lighter-Than-Air craft challenged a medium where unstable currents and the unforeseen were standard issue. Air was much more dangerous than water.

Safest down under, he thought. Safety had taken on a new attraction to him. He wanted to live to spend more time with this woman.

Where is Kareen right now? He found himself facing this question constantly since their separation. By now she would be at Launch Base. Panille didn't like to think of the distance separating them . . . distance was time, and after that last night he didn't want to spend any time without her.

His head had ached and he had been dizzy with fatigue but still sleep had not come. Every time his eyelids slipped his head filled

290

with visions of Guemes survivors littering the triage floor. Torn flesh, blood, moans and whimpers still ghosted around him in the dim bustle of Current Control.

Kareen, too, had been drained of energy. They had gone to her quarters with little discussion, each aware only of the need to be together, alive after wading through all that death. They had walked from the tube station, holding hands. Panille had held himself under tight control, sure that a white-tipped anger might explode if he once relaxed. Something hot and twisting clenched his guts.

Where plaz lined the corridors, the ripple effect of surface light combined with the cadence of their steps to mesmerize Panille into a dreamy detachment. He felt that he floated above himself, watching their swaying progress. There was tenderness in the arms, the bone-weary arms, and in Kareen's cheek as it brushed his shoulder. Her muscles worked their smooth magic and he no longer suspected that she might try to rule him with her body.

At her quarters, Panille had stared out at a different kind of undersea, a garden lush with ferns waving and butterfly fish grooming the leaves. A thick column of kelp spiraled upward out there, twisting and untwisting with some distant surge.

No death here. No signs of the Guemes disaster.

Just at the edge of visibility lay the Blue Reef with corridors of pale blue vine-tulips that opened and closed like small mouths beyond the plaz. Bright orange flashes of minuscule shrimp darted in and out, feeding on the vine-tulip stamens. Kareen led him to her bedroom.

They did not hesitate. Kareen stood tiptoe and pressed her mouth against his. Her open eyes watched his eyes and he saw himself reflected in her black pupils. Her hands pressed at first against his chest, then slipped around his neck and unfastened his braid. Her fingers felt strong and sure. *Surgeon's fingers,* he thought. His black hair spread over his shoulders. Panille brought his hands down from her shoulders to her tunic, releasing it clasp by clasp.

They undressed each other slowly, wordlessly. When she stepped out of her underwear, the light caught and danced in the flaming red triangle of her hair. Her nipples pressed like children's noses against his ribs.

We have decided to live, he thought.

The vision of Kareen Ale was a mantra that shut out all doubts about his world. Nothing existed in memory except the two of them and their perfectly complementary bodies.

As they had started slipping into sleep, Kareen startled them both with a sudden cry. She clung to him then like a child.

"Bad dreams," she whispered.

"Bad reality is worse."

"Dreams are real while you're in them," she said. "You know, every time I think of us, the bad goes away. We heal each other."

Her words and the pressure of her against him stirred Panille fully awake. Kareen sighed, rolled astride him in one smooth movement and gripped him deep inside her. Her breasts brushed his chest as they swayed back and forth. His breath was her breath then, and she called out his name as she collapsed, gasping, against him.

Panille held her gently, stroking her back.

"Kareen," he said.

"Mm?"

"I like to say your name."

He remembered this as he stood watch in Current Control and murmured her name under his breath. It helped.

The main entry hatch to Current Control behind Panille swung open with a sharp hiss, indicating quick entry without waiting for the outer lock to seal. Surprised, Panille started to turn and felt hard metal pressed against his back. A downward glance showed him a lasgun against his flesh. Panille recognized the man holding it—Gulf Nakano, Gallow's man. Nakano's bulky form stepped clear of the entryway, pushing Panille ahead of him. Nakano was followed by three other Mermen, all dive-suited, all armed and all thin-lipped serious.

"What is this?" Panille demanded.

"Shhhh," Nakano hissed. He motioned the others around him, then: "All right! Everybody stand up!"

Panille watched the other intruders move swiftly, methodically to equidistant positions near the center of the room. One operator protested and was clubbed to the deck. Panille started to speak but Nakano thrust a huge palm against his mouth, saying, "Stay alive, Panille. It's better."

The three attackers set their lasguns on short-flame and began demolishing Current Control. Plaz melted and popped, control boards sizzled. Small black snakes of vinyl precipitated out of the air. Everything was done with a chilling deliberation. In less than a minute, it was all over and Panille knew they would be at least a year replacing this . . . *brain.*

He was outraged but the destruction daunted him. His assistants leaned against one wall, shock and fear in their eyes.

One woman knelt over the downed operator, dabbing at the side of his face with a corner of her blouse.

"We have Kareen Ale," Nakano said. "I'm told that would interest you."

Panille felt his chest tighten.

"Your cooperation insures her safety," Nakano said. "You are to come with us, on a litter as a casualty we're transporting for the medics."

"Where are we going?"

"That's not your concern. Just tell me whether you will come quietly."

Panille swallowed, then nodded.

"We're welding the inner hatch closed as we leave," Nakano said. "Everyone here will be safe. When the next shift tries to get in, you'll get out."

One of the Mermen stepped forward. "Nakano," he whispered past Panille, "Gallow said we should—"

"Shut up!" Nakano said. "I'm here and he's not. The next shift doesn't come in for at least four hours."

At Nakano's nod two of his men brought an emergency litter from the space between the hatches. Panille lay on the litter and was strapped to it. A blanket was tucked around him.

"This is a medical emergency," Nakano said. "We hurry but we don't run. Carry him through all hatchways headfirst. Panille, you close your eyes. You're unconscious and I want you to stay that way or I'll make it real."

"I understand."

"We don't want anything nasty happening to the lady."

This thought haunted Panille as they maneuvered through the hatchways and corridor.

Why me? Panille couldn't imagine being that important to Gallow.

They stopped at a transport tube and Nakano tapped out the Emergency code. The next car stopped and a half-dozen curious faces peered out at Panille's form on the litter.

"Quarantine!" Nakano said, his voice curt. "Everybody out. Don't get too close."

"What's he got?" one woman asked. She skirted the litter widely.

"Something new picked up from the Mutes," Nakano said. "We're getting him out of Core. This car will be sterilized."

The car emptied quickly and Panille's bearers hustled him inside. The doors snicked closed and Nakano chuckled. "Every sniffle, every ache and pain will have sickbay crowded for days."

"Why all this rush?" Panille asked. "And why cook Current Control?"

"Launch countdown has been resumed now that the Guemes matter is over. Medical emergency guarantees us a fast, nonstop trip. The rest . . . trade secrets."

"What does the launch have to do with us?"

"Everything," Nakano said. "We're headed for Outpost Twenty-two, the recovery station for the hyb tanks."

Panille felt the hot surge of adrenaline. *The hyb tanks!*

"Why take me there?" he asked.

"We've set up a new current control. You're going to direct it."

"I thought you were too smart to get caught up in Gallow's wake," Panille said.

A slow smile touched Nakano's heavy face. "We're going to free hundreds, maybe thousands, of humans in hyb. We're going to liberate the prison they've endured for thousands of years."

Panille, strapped on the litter, could only look from Nakano to the three henchmen. All three wore the same bliss-ninny grins.

"People from the hyb tanks?" Panille asked, his voice low.

Nakano nodded. "Genetically clean—pure humans."

"You don't know what's up there," Panille said. "Nobody knows."

"Gallow knows," Nakano said. There was hard belief in his voice, the kind of tone that indicates the necessity to believe.

The transport capsule's overhead panel came to life and a recorded male voice droned: "Lighter-Than-Air, Base Bravo loading facility."

The hatches hissed open. Panille's litter was picked up and carried out onto the loading platform with near-surface light trickling through heavy plaz panels overhead.

Panille watched as much as he could through slitted eyelids.

An LTA facility? he wondered. *But they said we were . . .* The truth dawned—they were going to fly him to the outpost!

He almost opened his eyes but restrained himself. Blowing it now would not bring him closer to Kareen.

The litter moved with swift lurches and Panille heard Nakano's voice behind him: "Medical emergency, clear the way."

Panille's slitted eyes showed him the LTA gondola interior—a squashed sphere about ten meters in diameter. It was nearly all plaz, with a canopy of gray above the orange hydrogen bag. He found himself both excited and fearful, filled with confusion at this fierce activity. He heard the hatch seal behind him and Nakano's unruffled voice.

"We made it. You can relax, Panille. Everybody in here is secure."

Panille's straps were loosed and he sat up.

"Tether release in two minutes," the pilot reported.

Panille looked up at the orange canopy—the bag was a taper of pleats, its long folds hung down against the cabin's plaz. Once they were up and clear of the tube, more hydrogen would flow into the bag and fill it out. He glanced right and left, saw the two hydrogen jets that would propel them once they were topside.

The whine of a cable winch filled the gondola then. The pilot said, "Strap down, everyone. A bit rough up there today."

Panille found himself dragged backward into a seat beside Nakano. A strap was fitted around his waist. He kept his attention on the pilot. No one spoke. Switches clicked like the hard-shelled chatter of molluscs.

"Topside hatch open," the pilot said, speaking into a microphone at his throat.

A halo of white light filtered around the bag above them.

The cabin lurched and Panille glanced out to his left, momentarily dizzy with the sensation that the gondola had stayed stationary and the launch tube was moving downward past him at increasing speed.

The winch sound silenced abruptly and he heard the hiss of the bag against the tube's walls. The bag cleared the tube then and light washed the cabin. Panille heard a gasp behind him, then they were clear of the water, into a cloudy gray day, swaying beneath the expanding hydrogen bag. The jets swung out with a low whine and were ignited. The swaying motion of the gondola steadied. Almost immediately, they entered a rain squall.

"Sorry, we won't be able to see the rocket launch because of this weather," the pilot said. He flicked a switch beside him and a small screen on the panel in front of him came alight. "We can watch the official coverage, though."

Panille couldn't see from where he sat and the pilot had the sound turned down. The gondola emerged from the rainstorm, still pelted by the runoff from the bag overhead. They began swaying wildly and the pilot fought to control the motion. His flurried movement had little effect. Panille noted with some satisfaction that the Merman guards had green expressions that had nothing to do with their camouflage.

"What's going on?" This was a woman's voice from behind Panille. A voice he could not mistake. He froze, then slowly turned and stared past his captors. *Kareen.* She sat beside the entry hatch where she had been hidden from him as he entered. Her face was very pale, her eyes dark shadows above her cheeks, and she did not meet his gaze.

Panille felt a hard emptiness in his stomach.

"Kareen," he said.

She did not respond.

The gondola continued to lurch and sway.

Nakano looked worried. "What's going on, pilot?"

The pilot pointed to a display on the board to his right. Panille tore his gaze away from Kareen Ale's ashen face. He could not see all that was indicated on the control panel, only the last two numbers of a digital display and those were changing so rapidly they were a blur.

"Our homing frequency," the pilot explained. "It won't stay on target."

"We can't find the outpost without locking on the right frequency," Nakano said. There was fear in his voice.

The pilot withdrew his hand and this revealed once more the display for the launch broadcast. The picture was gone, replaced by wavelike lines and pulsing colored ribbons.

"Try your radio," Nakano ordered. "Maybe they can talk us in."

"I *am* trying it!" the pilot said. He flipped a switch and cranked up the volume control. A keening, rhythmic sound filled the gondola.

"That's all I'm getting!" the pilot said. "Some kind of interference. Weird music."

"Tones," Panille murmured. "Sounds like computer music."

"What's that?"

Panille repeated it. He glanced back at Kareen. Why wouldn't she meet his eyes? She was very pale. Had they drugged her?

"Our altimeter just went out," the pilot called. "We're adrift. I'm taking us up above this weather."

He punched buttons and moved his controls. There was no apparent response from the LTA.

"Damn!" the pilot swore.

Panille stared once more at the screen on the pilot's board. The pattern was familiar, though he wouldn't tell Nakano. It was a pattern Panille knew he had seen on his own screens in Current Control—a kelp response. It was what they saw when the kelp complied with an instruction to shift the great currents in Pandora's sea.

The repressed share the psychoses and neuroses of the caged. As the caged run when released, the repressed explode when confronted with their condition.

—Raja Thomas, the Journals

17 Alki, 468. In captivity at Outpost 22.

Jealousy is a great teacher if you allow it. Even the Chief Justice can learn much from his jealousy of Mermen. Compared to Mermen, we Islanders live squalid lives. We are poor. There are no secrets among the poor. The squalor and close sweat of our lives oozes information and rumor. Even the most clandestine arrangements become public. But Mermen thrive on secrecy. It is one of their many luxuries.

Secrecy begins with privacy.

As Chief Justice of the Committee on Vital Forms I enjoy private quarters. No more stacked cubbies pressed head to foot along some rimside bulkhead. No more feet stepping on hands in the night or grunting lovers bumping against your back.

Privilege and privacy, two words that share the same root. But down under, privacy is the norm.

My imprisonment represents a special kind of privacy. These Green Dashers do not understand that. My captors appear exhausted and a little bored. Boredom opens paths into secrecy, thus I anticipate learning something of their lives because their lives are now my life. How little they understand of true secrecy. They do not suspect the chanting in my head that records these things that I may share with others if I wish . . . and if I survive that long. These fanatics give no quarter. Guemes is proof that they can commit murder skillfully and easily . . . perhaps even cheerfully. I have few illusions about my chances here.

Little can survive me except my record on the Committee. I admit to a little pride about that record. And some regrets about

my other choices. The child that Carolyn and I should have had
. . . she would have been a daughter, I think. By now there would
be grandchildren. Did I have the right to prevent that generation
out of fear? They would have been beautiful! And wise, yes, like
Carolyn.

Gallow wonders why I sit here with my eyelids opened only to
slits. Sometimes, he laughs at what he sees. Gallow dreams of
dominating our world. In that, he is no different from Scudi's
father. Ryan Wang fed people to control them. GeLaar Gallow
kills. Their other differences are just as profound. I suppose
death is a form of absolute control. There are many kinds of
death. I see this because I have no grandchildren. I have only
those whose lives have passed through my hands, those who have
survived because of my word.

I wonder where Gallow sent that big assistant, Nakano? What a
monster . . . on the outside. The very vision of a terrorist. But
Nakano's goals are not on the surface. No one could call him
transparent. His hands are gentle when there is no need for his
great strength.

They have suspended this foil beneath the surface. More secrecy. More privacy. Such stillness can be frightening. I am beginning to find it captivating—I see that my mind jokes with me in its
choice of words. Privacy, too, is captivating. Islanders do not know
this reality of life down under. They imagine only the privacy.
They envy the privacy. They do not imagine the stillness. Will my
people ever encounter this immense quiet? I find it difficult to
believe that the C/P will order all Islanders to move down under.
How could she do this? Where could the Mermen put us and not
lose their precious privacy? But even more than fear of Ship, our
envy would cause us to obey. I cannot believe that Ship enters into
such a scheme except by innuendo. And the innuendo of Ship
suffers a sea of change in human interpretation. A moment's
reflection back through the histories, especially upon the writings
of that maverick C/P, Raja Thomas, makes this as clear as plaz.
Ah, Thomas, what a brilliant survivor you were! I thank Ship that
your thoughts have come down to me. For I, too, know what it is
to be caged. I know what it is to be repressed. And I know myself
better because of Thomas. Like him, I can turn to my memory for
company, and he is there, too. Now, with kelp to record us, no
lock seals the hatchway to memory . . . ever.

If you don't know about numbers you can't appreciate coincidence.

—Scudi Wang

Brett marveled at Scudi's control. All during the ordeal in the control cabin her attention remained on the operation of the foil. She kept them skimming along the edge of the kelp in the bright light of morning, avoiding stray tangles of leaves that might catch the struts. There were moments when Brett thought the kelp opened special channels for the foil. *Directing them?* Why would it do that? Scudi's eyes widened from time to time. What did she see in the kelp channels to cause that reaction? Her tan face paled at what she heard behind her where Twisp and Bushka argued, but she kept the foil cruising smoothly toward its rendezvous with Gallow.

Her reaction was not natural, Brett thought. Bushka was crazy to think they could surprise Gallow and overcome him—just the four of them here. Vashon had to learn what was happening. Scudi must realize this!

Within an hour they came out of the heaviest kelp infestation onto open water where the seas were steeper and the motions of the foil more abrupt.

Bushka sat alone on the command couch at the rear of the cabin, forcing Twisp to sit on the floor well away from him. Between them, trussed like a kelp-tangled dasher, their captive Merman lay quiet. Occasionally he opened his eyes to study his surroundings.

Twisp bided his time. Brett understood the big fisherman's silent waiting. There was a limited future arguing with a man holding a lasgun.

Brett studied Scudi's profile, the way she kept her attention on

300

the water ahead of them, the way she tensed when she corrected course. A muscle in her cheek trembled.

"Are you all right?" Brett asked.

Her knuckles whitened on the wheel and the tremble disappeared. She looked childlike in that big seat with the spread of instruments around her. Scudi still wore her dive suit and he could see a red irritation where it rubbed against her neck. This made him acutely conscious of the constrictions in his own suit.

"Scudi?"

She barely whispered: "I'm OK."

She took a deep breath and relaxed against the padded seat. He saw the whiteness retreat from her knuckles. The foil lurched and shuddered along the wavetops and Brett wondered how long it could take such punishment. Twisp and Bushka began a conversation too low for Brett to make out more than the occasional word. He glanced back at them and focused on the lasgun still held firmly in Bushka's hands. Its muzzle pointed in the general direction of Twisp and the Merman.

What was Bushka really doing? Was it only rage? Surely Bushka could never escape memories of his part in the Guemes massacre. Killing Gallow wouldn't erase those memories, it would only add more.

Scudi leaned toward Brett then and whispered, "It's going to be a bad storm."

Brett jerked his attention around and looked out the sweep of plaz, aware for the first time that the weather was changing dramatically. A gusting wind from port had begun to blast the tops off the waves, whipping scuds of foam along the surface. A gray curtain of rain slanted into the sea ahead, closing the tenuous gap between black clouds and gray water. The day suddenly had the feel of cold metal. He glanced up at the position vector on the overhead screen and tried to estimate their time to Gallow and his hunt of Green Dashers.

"Two hours?" he asked.

"That's going to slow us." Scudi nodded toward the storm line ahead. "Fasten your safety harness."

Brett swung the shoulder strap across his chest and locked it in place.

They were into the rain then. Visibility dropped to less than a hundred meters. Great pelting drops roared on the foil's metal fabric and overcame the airblast wipers on the cabin plaz. Scudi

301

backed off the throttle and the foil began to pitch even more with the steepening waves.

"What's going on?" Bushka demanded.

"Storm," Scudi said. "Look at it."

"How soon will we get there?" Bushka asked.

His voice had taken on a new note, Brett realized. Not exactly fear . . . *Anxiety? Uncertainty?* Bushka had the Islander's dream-like admiration for foils but really did not understand them. How would the foil survive a storm? Would they have to stop and submerge?

"I don't know how long," Scudi said. "All I know is we're going to have to slow down more, and soon."

"Don't waste any time!" Bushka ordered.

It had grown darker in the cabin and the wave action outside looked mean—long, rolling combers with their tips curling white. They were still in kelp, though, with a broken channel through it.

Scudi switched on the cabin lights and began paying more attention to the screens overhead and in front of her.

Brett saw his own reflection in the plaz and it startled him. His thick blonde hair fanned his head in a wild halo. His eyes were two dark holes staring back at him. The gray of the storm had become the gray of his eyes, almost dasher-black. For the first time, he realized how close to Merman-normal he appeared.

I could pass, he thought.

He wondered then how much this fact figured in his attraction for Scudi. It was an abrupt and startling thought, which made him feel both closer and more removed from her. They were Islander and Merman and they always would be. Was it dangerous to think that they might pair?

Scudi saw him staring toward the plaz in front of them.

"Can you see anything?" she asked.

He knew immediately she was asking whether his mutant eyesight could help them now.

"Rain's just as bad for my eyes as it is for yours," he told her. "Trust your instruments."

"We've got to slow down," she said. "And if it gets much worse we'll have to submerge. I've never—"

She broke off as a violent, creaking shudder engulfed the foil, rattling the hardware until Brett thought the boat might split. Scudi immediately backed the throttle. The foil dropped off the step with an abrupt plowing motion that sent it sliding down a wave face and pitched it up the next one. Brett was hurled against his safety harness hard enough to take his breath away.

Curses and scrambling noises came from behind him. He whirled and saw Bushka picking himself up off the deck, clutching the grabs beside the couch he had occupied. His right hand still gripped the lasgun. Twisp had been dumped into a corner with the captive Merman atop him. One long arm came out of the tangle, pushing the captive aside, finding a handhold and lifting himself to a standing position at the side of the cabin.

"What's happening?" Bushka shouted. He shifted his grip to a handhold behind his couch and eased himself onto the cushions.

"We're into kelp," Scudi said. "It's fouled the struts. I've had to retract them, but they're not coming fully back."

Brett kept his attention on Bushka. The foil was riding easier, its jet only a low murmur far back in the stern. It was in Scudi's hands now and he half suspected she had exaggerated the nature of their predicament. Bushka, too, looked undecided. His large head bobbed in the constant motion of the foil as he tried to peer past Scudi at the storm. Brett was suddenly struck by how Mermanlike Bushka appeared—powerful shoulders tapering to sinewy, almost delicate hands.

The assault of the wind and waves against the hull increased.

"There's a heavy kelp bed in our path," Scudi said. "It shouldn't be here. I think it may have broken loose in the storm. We don't dare go up on the step again."

"What can we do?" Bushka demanded.

"First, we'll have to clear the struts so I can retract them," she said. "Hull integrity is vital for control. Especially if we have to submerge."

"Why can't we just clear the struts and go back up on the foils?" Bushka asked. "We have to get to the outpost before Gallow suspects!"

"Lose a strut at high speed, very bad," Scudi said. She gestured at the captive Merman. "Ask him."

Bushka looked at the man on the deck.

"What does it matter?" The Merman shrugged. "If we die in kelp we are immortal."

"I think he just agreed with you," Twisp said. "So, how do we clear the struts?"

"We go out and do it by hand," Scudi said.

"In *this?*" Twisp looked out at the long, white-capped rollers, the gray bleakness of the storm. The foil rode the waves like a chip, quartering into them and twisting at every crest when the wind hit it with full force.

"We will use safety lines," Scudi said. "I have done it before." She hit the crossover switch to activate Brett's controls. "You take it, Brett. Watch out at the crests. The wind wants to take it and the struts being half-out that way makes it hard to control."

Brett gripped the wheel, feeling perspiration slippery against his palms.

Scudi released her safety harness and stood, holding fast to her seatback against the roll and pitch of the foil. "Who's going to help me?"

"I will," Twisp said. "You'll have to tell me what to do."

"Just a minute!" Bushka snapped. He studied Twisp and Scudi for a long blink. "You know what happens to the kid if you cause me any trouble?"

"You learned very fast from this man Gallow," Twisp said. "Are you sure he's your enemy?"

Bushka paled with anger but remained silent.

Twisp shrugged and made his way along overhead grabs to the rear hatch. "Scudi?"

"All right." She turned to Brett. "Hold it steady as you can. It's going to be rough out there."

"Maybe I'm the one should go with you."

"No . . . Twisp has no experience handling a foil."

"Then he and I could—"

"Neither of you knows how to clear the struts. This is the only way. We will be careful." Abruptly, she leaned down and kissed his cheek, whispering, "It is all right."

Brett was left with a warm sense of completeness. He felt he knew exactly what to do at the foil's controls.

Bushka checked the Merman's restraints, then joined Brett at the controls. He took Scudi's seat. Brett only spared the slightest glance for him, noting the lasgun still at the ready. Heavy seas swept them steadily sideways at every crest and the foil barely had enough headway to recover. Brett listened to voices out on the deck, Scudi shouting to Twisp. A steep swell broke over the cabin, then another. Two long rollers swept under them, then one more breaking crest curled over the plaz. The foil stood almost vertical on its stern, slapped back into the trough and the crest crashed onto the cabin-top. The boat shuddered and wallowed in a side-slip while Brett fought to bring its nose back into the weather.

Twisp shouted something. Abruptly, his voice came crying up the passage: "Brett! Circle port! Scudi's lost her safety line!"

Without any thought for whether the foil could take it, Brett cranked the wheel hard left and held it. The boat turned on a crest, slipped sideways down a wave, lifted at the stern and water washed down the long passage into the cabin. It swirled around their feet, lifting the captive and sending him against Bushka's thigh. The foil almost rolled over on the next wave. It came up broadside to the weather as it continued its mad circle. Brett felt the sea slosh through the cabin and realized that Twisp had opened the rear hatch to be heard.

Get her, Brett prayed. He wanted to abandon the wheel and run back to help but knew he had to keep the foil tight in this pattern. Twisp was experienced—he would know what to do.

A wave in the cabin broke almost up to his waist and Bushka cursed. Brett saw that Bushka was struggling to keep the Merman in one place.

Brett's mind kept repeating: *Scudi Scudi Scudi . . .*

The storm's roar in the cabin diminished slightly and Bushka shouted, "He's closed the hatch!"

"Help them, Bushka!" Brett hollered. *"Do* something for once!"

The foil lifted once more over a crest, rolled heavily with the weight of the water they'd taken on.

"No need!" Bushka shouted. "He has her."

"Get back on course." It was Twisp's voice behind Brett, but Brett dared not turn. "I have her and she's all right."

Brett swung the foil's bow back into the seas, quartering into a high comber that rolled over them at the crest. Water sloshed through the cabin as the foil pitched down into the next trough. The sound of pumps chuffing below decks came clearly to Brett's ears. He risked a glance back and saw Twisp backing into the cabin, Scudi's limp form over his shoulder. He dogged the hatch behind him and dumped Scudi on the couch where Bushka had been.

"She's breathing," Twisp said. He bent over Scudi, a hand on her neck. "Pulse is strong. She hit her head on the hull as we tipped."

"Did you clear the struts?" Bushka demanded.

"Eelshit!" Twisp spat.

"Did you?"

305

"Yes, we cleared the damn struts!"

Brett looked at the overhead screen and brought the foil around ten degrees, putting down a surge of rage against Bushka. But Bushka was suddenly busy with the keyboard at his position.

"Finding how to retract these foils. That was the whole idea, wasn't it?" Bushka's fingers flurried over the keys and a schematic appeared on the screen in front of him. He studied it a moment and manipulated controls at his side of the board. Within blinks, Brett heard the *hiss* and *clunk* of struts retracting.

"You're not on course," Bushka said.

"As close as I can be," Brett said. "We have to quarter these seas or we'll pound ourselves to pieces."

"If you're lying, you're dead," Bushka said.

"You take it if you know better than I do," Brett said. He lifted his hands from the wheel.

Bushka brought the lasgun up and pointed it at Brett's head. "Steer us the way you have to but don't give me any shit!"

Brett dropped his hands onto the wheel in time to catch the next crest. They were riding easier now. A green light showed at the "Foils Retracted" marker.

Bushka swiveled his seat and hunched down, positioning himself to watch both Brett and Twisp. The captive Merman lay beside Bushka, his face pale but he was breathing.

"We're still going after Gallow," Bushka said. There was a note of hysteria in his voice.

Twisp strapped Scudi into the couch and sat beside her. He held a grab near her head for balance. Twisp looked forward past Bushka, then up at the overhead display. "What's that?" he asked, nodding at the screen.

Bushka did not turn.

Brett glanced up at the screen. A green diamond-shaped marker flashed near the course line and off to the right.

"What is it?" Twisp repeated.

Brett leaned forward and punched the identity key under the screen.

"Outpost 22" flashed on the screen beside the diamond.

"That's the pickup station for the hyb tanks," Brett said. "That's where Gallow's supposed to be. Scudi's brought us out right on target."

"Get us in there!" Bushka ordered.

Brett turned onto the new heading while he tried to recall everything Scudi had told him about the hyb-tank recovery project. There wasn't much.

"Why's it flashing?" Twisp asked.

"I think it does that when you get within range," Brett said. "I think it's a warning that we're getting close to the shallows around the outpost."

"You *think?*" Bushka snarled.

"I don't know this equipment any better than you do," Brett countered. "Take over any time you want."

"Throw some water on that woman, get her awake," Bushka ordered. Again, that note of hysteria in his voice. He brought the lasgun around until it pointed at Brett. "You stay put back there, Twisp!" Bushka ordered. "Or the kid gets burned."

With his free hand, Bushka began working the keyboard in front of him. "Incompetents," he muttered. "Everything's right here if you just ask for it." Chart-reading instructions scrolled upward on his screen. Bushka bent to read them.

"Ship's balls!" Twisp shouted. "What's *that?*"

Through the spray-drenched plaz ahead and to his left, Brett saw a great splash of bright orange, something floating a wave out there. He bent forward to peer through the salted plaz. It was a long orange something that stretched into the anonymous gray of the storm. Kelp lay tangled all around it.

The foil was coming up on the orange thing fast, bringing it close to their port side.

"It's an LTA bag," Bushka said. "Somebody's gone down."

"Can you see the gondola?" Twisp asked. "Brett! Stay downwind from it. The bag will act like a sea anchor. Don't get fouled in it."

Brett swung the foil to the left and it wallowed in a trough, rocking dangerously at the crest, then into the next trough. At the following crest, he saw the gondola, a dark shape awash in the long seas. The orange bag trailed out behind it with kelp laced across it. The gondola was coming up on their right. The seas were smoother there, flattened by the great spread of the bag. Another crest and Brett saw faces pressed against the gondola's plaz.

"There are people in there!" Twisp shouted. "I saw faces!"

"Damn!" Bushka said. "Damn, damn, damn!"

"We have to take them off," Brett said. "We can't leave them there."

307

"I know that!" Bushka snarled.

Scudi took this moment to begin muttering . . . words Brett couldn't understand.

"She's all right," Twisp said. "She's coming out of it. Bushka, you come back here and look after her while I get a line aboard that gondola."

"How're you going to do that?" Bushka asked.

"I'm going to swim it over! What else? Brett, hold us steady as you can right here."

"They're Mermen," Bushka said. "Why can't they bring a line to us?"

"The minute they open their hatch, that gondola is going down," Twisp said. "It'll fill like a punctured float."

Scudi's voice came clearly then: "What's . . . what's happening?"

Bushka released his safety harness and made his way back to her. Brett heard the hatch open and close. Bushka's voice, quite low, gave Scudi her answer.

"An LTA?" she asked. "Where are we?"

"Near Outpost Twenty-two." There was a scuffling sound and Bushka's voice: "Stay down there!"

"I have to get to the controls! It's shallow here. Very shallow! In these seas—"

"All right!" Bushka said. "Do what you have to do."

Scuffing footsteps on the deck, then water sloshing from a wet dive suit. Scudi's hand gripped Brett's shoulder. "Dammit, but my head hurts," she said. Her hand touched his neck and he felt a flash of pain on the side of his temple. It was a throbbing pain, as though something had struck him there.

Scudi leaned across him, her hand over his shoulder to steady herself. Their cheeks touched.

Brett felt something flow between them, creating a moment of panic followed by a sudden inrush of awareness. His neck hair prickled as he realized what had happened. He felt that he was two people become one but aware of the separation—one person standing beside the other.

I'm seeing with Scudi's eyes!

Brett's hands moved automatically on the wheel, a new expertise he had not known he possessed. The foil gentled its way close to the gondola and hung there with just enough headway to counteract the wind.

What's happening to us?

308

The words formed silently in their minds, a simultaneous question, shared in an instant and answered in an instant.

The kelp has changed us! We share our senses when we touch!

With this odd double vision, Brett saw Twisp swimming now, moving through a channel in the kelp and very close to the gondola. Faces peered out through the plaz. Brett thought he recognized one of those faces and, with that recognition, came a bursting daydream, instantaneous—a sense of people talking inside the gondola. The sensation vanished and he was left staring at white-whipped waves breaking across the LTA, Twisp clinging there while he fastened his line to a handgrab beside the plaz lock.

Scudi whispered to Brett: "Did you hear them talking?"

"I couldn't make out the words."

"I could. Gallow's people are in there and they have prisoners. The prisoners are being taken to Gallow."

"Where is Gallow? Here?"

"I think so, but I recognized a prisoner—it's Dark Panille, Shadow. I've worked with him."

"The man who treated me in the passageway!"

"Yes, and one of the captors is that Gulf Nakano. I'm going to warn Bushka. He has the weapon. We will have to lock them into one of the cargo bays."

Scudi turned away and worked her way back to Bushka, steadying herself along the overhead grabs. Brett heard her explain the situation to Bushka, saying she had recognized Nakano through the gondola's plaz.

"They've opened their hatch," Brett said. "People are coming out. I see Shadow . . . there's Nakano. Waves are slopping into the hatch. Everybody's coming out."

Scudi slipped into the command seat beside Brett. "I'll take it. You help Bushka at the entry hatch."

"No tricks!" Bushka yelled as he followed Brett down the passageway.

"We've got to get Twisp out of there!" Brett said.

"He's staying at the gondola to unfasten the line when it goes under."

They were at the hatchway then, wind whipping around them and spray in their eyes. Brett was thankful for his dive suit. In spite of the chill, sweat poured from his body. The muscles of his arms and legs were tightly humming bands. A wave broke against the hull below them. Brett sighted along the line—a long row of bobbing heads worked their way toward the foil. He recognized Nakano in the lead, staying close to Panille. The line snaked up and down the waves.

"We'll bring them aboard one at a time, right into the cargo bay behind me," Bushka said.

"We'll have to disarm them."

Nakano was first through the hatch. His face had the single-minded aggressiveness of a bull dasher. Bushka leveled the lasgun from the far side of the hatchway, slipped a similar weapon from the thigh pocket of Nakano's dive suit, grabbed a knife from Nakano's waist sheath and motioned with his head for the Merman to enter the open hatch to the cargo bay.

For a blink, Brett thought Nakano would attack Bushka despite the lasgun, but the man shrugged and ducked through into the bay.

Panille stayed down below to help others and the next person through was a woman, red-haired, beautiful.

"Kareen Ale," Bushka said. "Well, well." He sent his gaze licking over her body, saw no weapon and nodded toward the cargo hatch. "In there, please."

She stared at the lasgun in Bushka's grip.

"Do it!"

A shout from below the hatch brought Brett whirling around to face the sea.

"What is it?" Bushka demanded. He was trying to divide his attention between the open cargo hatch and the outer hatch where survivors still waited to be brought aboard.

Brett peered out across Panille, who hung below the hatch with an arm wrapped through a loop in his safety line. The gondola beyond him had begun to sink, slowly dragging the orange LTA bag under the waves. The safety line lay across the waves with Twisp pulling himself along it. Something was happening about midway along the line, though, and Brett tried to make out what had caused the shout.

"What's happening?" Bushka asked.

"I don't know. There's a length of kelp across the line. Twisp released the line from the gondola and it's already under. But something's . . ."

A human hand came out of the water near the kelp and one, two kelp strands whipped across the hand and the hand vanished. Twisp reached the kelp barrier and hesitated there. A questing strand of kelp touched his head, paused there and withdrew. Twisp continued his way along the line, stopping finally beside Panille, exhausted. Panille put an arm under Twisp's shoulder and helped support him. Waves lifted both men and lowered them beside the foil.

"Shall I help bring him up?" Brett called.

Twisp waved a hand to stop him. "I'll be all right." One of his long arms snaked up the line and took a firm grip.

"Two people," Twisp said. "The kelp took them. It just *took* them, wrapped around them and took them."

He hauled himself up the line, quivering every muscle on the way. He slumped through the hatch, then turned to help Panille. Bushka waved Panille toward the cargo bay.

"No," Brett said. He stepped between Bushka and Panille. "Shadow was a prisoner. He helped me. He's not one of them."

"Who says?"

"The kelp says," Twisp said.

Control the religion and the food and we own the world.
                                              —GeLaar Gallow

Vata's growing restlessness sloshed nutrient over the rim of her tank. At times she arched her back as if in pain, and the pink knobs of her nipples broke the surface like the bright peaks of two blue-green mountains. A relief attendant, an Islander high on boo, reached out to tweak one of the gnarled, vein-swollen things and was discovered catatonic, his blasphemous thumb and forefinger still held in position over the vat.

This event redoubled C/P Simone Rocksack's efforts to effect the Islander move down under. Stories of "The Wrath of Vata" circulated freely and no one on the C/P's staff made any effort to sort fact from fantasy. Rocksack silenced one underling who objected to the rumors by saying, "A lie is not a lie if it serves a higher moral purpose. Then it is a gift."

Vata herself, locked inside her tank and her skull while generation after generation of her people evolved around her, explored her world with the tender new frond-tips of the kelp.

Kelp was fingertip and ear to her, nose and eye and tongue. Where massive stalks lazed on the sea's bright surface she witnessed pastel sunrises, the passage of boats and Islands, the occasional ravages of a hunt of dashers. Scrubberfish that cleaned the kelp's broadest leaves whiskered the deep crevasses of her opulent flesh.

Like herself, the kelp was single, incomplete, unable to reproduce. Mermen took cuttings, rooted them in rock and mud. Storms ripped whole vines loose from the mother plant and some of the wounded stragglers wedged safely into rock and grew there. For two and a half centuries, at least, the kelp had not bloomed. No hylighter broke the surface of the sea to rise on its hydrogen bag and scatter its fresh spores to the winds.

Sometimes in her sleep Vata's loins pulsed with an ancient rhythm and a sweet emptiness ached in her abdomen. These were the times she curled close to Duque, her massive body engulfing him in a frustrating approximation of an embrace.

Now her frustration focused on GeLaar Gallow. A jungle of kelp strained each strand to reach the walls and hatchways of Outpost 22, with no success. The perimeter was too wide, the stalks too short.

New pairs of eyes joined the kelp to reveal Gallow's treachery. The clearest of these eyes belonged to Scudi Wang. Vata enjoyed the company of Scudi Wang, and it became more difficult to let her go each time they met.

Vata met Scudi in the kelp. A few bright glimpses of a fresh young mind, and she searched for Scudi daily. When Vata dreamed the terrors of kelp, storm-ripped from its ballast-rock and dying, the touch of Scudi's skin on vine or frond smoothed those churning dreams to a warm calm. Those times Vata, in turn, dreamed back to Scudi. She dreamed small histories, images and visions, to keep the fear of kelp-madness out of Scudi's head. Vata had dreamed to others who had never come out of the dream. She knew now that Scudi's mother was one of those lost dreamers. Stunned by the hot dream sparking into her from the kelp, the woman had floated wide-eyed and helpless into a passing net. The tender airfish at her neck was crushed and she drowned. And the Merman crew supporting her had made no move to rescue her. Deliberate!

Vata watched the strange odyssey that worked its way back toward Outpost 22. She flexed her kelp when the gondola went down and acquainted herself with Bushka and Shadow Panille. This Panille, he was blood to her.

Brother, she thought, and marveled over the word. She trusted Bushka and Panille to Scudi's presence. The message she sent Scudi was simple and clear: *Find Gallow, drive him out. Kelp will do the rest.*

Life is not an option, it is a gift. Death is the option.

—Ward Keel, Journal

It was late evening, but Ward Keel had lost all inclination to sleep. He accepted the buzz of fatigue as a logical consequence of captivity. His eyes refused to stay closed. They blinked slowly and he glimpsed the brush of his long lashes in the plaz beside him. His brown eye faced itself in the plaz. It was a small dark blur. Beyond it lay the perimeter of kelp, almost gray at this depth. His prison cubby was warm, warmer even than his quarters on Vashon, but the gray of down under washed his psyche cold.

Keel had been watching the kelp for hours as Gallow's men streamed into the outpost. At first the kelp pulsed as usual with the current. Fronds waved at full extension downcurrent like a woman's long hair in an evening breeze. Now there was a different rhythm. And the larger kelp fronds downcurrent of the outpost stretched directly toward Keel. The currents were no longer consistent. The outpost was being battered by sudden changes of current that had the kelp outside flickering in a fire-light dance.

Gallow's morning crew had never arrived. His medical team was lost. Keel could hear Gallow's rantings from the next room. The syrupy voice was cracking.

Something strange about that kelp, Keel thought. *Stranger than moving against the current.*

Keel never even considered that Brett and Scudi might be dead. In the reverie generated by the gentle undulations of the kelp, Keel thought often about his young friends.

Had they reached Vashon? He worried about that. But he heard no echoes of this in Gallow's angry words. Surely Gallow would be reacting if that message had reached Vashon.

314

GeLaar Gallow is attempting to take over Merman Mercantile and the recovery of the hyb tanks. Merman rockets are being sent into space for the tanks. Mermen are changing our planet in ways Islands cannot survive. If Gallow succeeds, Islanders are doomed.

How would the C/P react? Keel wondered. He might never know.

Keel held out little hope for himself. His gut had begun to burn again, precisely as it had four years ago. He knew that all traces of the remora were gone. Without it, the food he ate would pass undigested and his intestines would gnaw at themselves until he either bled to death or starved. There was no reason to doubt the word of his personal physician, and the evidence was too painfully immediate to disguise, even to himself.

It used to make me tired all the time, he thought. *Why won't it let me sleep now?* Because last time he'd almost bled to death in his sleep, and now sleep was impossible.

It wasn't the constant burning that kept him awake. Pain he had learned to bear over the years of ill-fitting support devices for his long neck. This was the crisp wakefulness of the condemned.

Wakefulness had brought Keel's attention to the kelp. Sometime in midmorning the kelp stalks began defying the currents and reaching toward the outpost. The perimeter of growth began about two hundred meters from the outpost walls. The outpost itself lay in the center of this massive kelp project like a jewel in a fat ring. The fish were gone, too. Keel's few earlier glimpses of the outer compound had shown a richness of fishes that rivaled the gardens at Core—fanlike butterfly fish with iridescent tails, the ever-present scrubberfish grazing leaves and plaz, mud-devils raising and lowering the tall sails of their dorsal fins with every disturbance. None was visible now and the gray filter of evening quickly washed itself black. Just the kelp remained, sole proprietor of the world beyond the outpost's perimeter. This day Keel felt that he had watched the kelp go from graceful to stately to full alert.

That's my translation, he reminded himself. *Don't attribute humanity to other creatures. It limits study.* A quick shudder iced his spine when he realized that this kelp had been grown from cells carried by mutant humans.

The kelp had an infinite memory. The histories said that, but so did GeLaar Gallow. *Conclusion?* he asked himself.

315

It's waking up, he answered. *And it absorbs the memories of the living and the newly dead.* Therein lay great temptation for Ward Keel.

I could leave more than scratchings in these journals, he thought. *I could leave everything. Everything! Think of that!* He entered these thoughts into his journal, and wished that he had his journals and his life's collection of notes around him now. It was possible, he knew for fact, that no Islander had given more direct thought to life and life forms than Justice Keel. Some of these observations he knew to be unique—sometimes illogical, but vital every one. These data he hated to see lost when a struggling humanity needed them so very much.

Someone else will think those thoughts, in time. If there is more time.

His attention was caught by the arrival of another sub overhead. The sub gave the kelp a wide berth. Gallow's orders. As the sub disappeared on its way to the interior docking bay, Keel marveled at the movement of the kelp. Huge stalks tracked the sub's path even though it came in against the current. Like a blossom following the slow arc of sunlight across the sky, the kelp followed all of the incoming Mermen. An occasional blur of gray moved amongst the tendrils as one snapped out suddenly toward an intruder, but all Mermen kept well out of reach.

If the kelp is waking, he thought, *the future of all the humans left may be at stake.*

Perhaps after contacting enough humans the kelp would find some way of saying, "Like me. If you're human, you're like me." There was a biological kinship, after all. Keel swallowed, and hoped silently that it was true that Vata was the key to the kelp. He hoped, too, that mercy was a part of Vata's personality.

Keel thought he detected a change in the perimeter. It was hard to tell, with night coming on and visibility so poor anyway, but he was sure that the two-hundred-meter perimeter had closed. Not much, but enough to notice.

Keel cast about in his memory for all the information that he'd ever stored on the kelp. Sentient, capable of nonverbal communication by touch, firmly anchored to ballast-rocks and mobile in its bloom state—except the bloom state had been extinct for hundreds of years. That was the kelp the first humans on Pandora destroyed. What surprises lay in store with this new kelp? This creature had been regrown from gene-prints present in human carriers. *Could it be that the kelp has learned how to move?* It didn't feel

316

like a trick of the imagination. The dark outside was now nearly total, only a thin barrier of light escaped from the outpost itself.

Morning will tell, he thought. *If there is a morning.* He chuckled to himself. With most of his world dark, Keel was left staring at himself in the port, haloed by the glare of the one bare light. He moved away from the plaz after a passing glance at his nose. It spread over his face like a mashed fruit, the tip touched his upper lip whenever he pursed his mouth in thought.

The hatch door behind him slammed into the wall and startled him. His stomach took a bad turn, then turned again when he saw Gallow, alone, carrying two liters of Islander wine.

"Mr. Justice," Gallow said, "I thought I'd liberate these from the men. I present them to you as a gesture of hospitality."

Keel noted that the label showed that the wine was from Vashon, not Guemes, and breathed easier. "Thank you, Mr. Gallow," he said. He allowed his head to drop in a slight bow. "I seldom have the pleasure of a good wine anymore—sour stomach comes with age, they say." Keel sat heavily and indicated the other chair next to his bunk. "Have a seat. Cups are on the sideboard."

"Good!" Gallow flashed the wide, white smile that Keel was sure opened many a reluctant hatch.

And many a lady, he thought. He shook it off, suddenly embarrassed by himself. Gallow took two stoneware cups from a shelf and set them on the desk. The handles, Keel noted, were thick to accommodate the calloused fingers of outpost riders.

Gallow poured but did not sit.

"I have ordered supper for us," Gallow said. "One of my men is a passable cook. The outpost is crowded, so I took the liberty of ordering the meal delivered here. I hope that meets your approval?"

How very polite, Keel thought. *What does he want?* He took a cup of the amber wine. Both lifted cups, but Keel only sipped.

"Pleasant," Keel said. His stomach churned with bitter wine and the thought of lumps of hot food. It churned at the prospect of listening to more of Gallow's egocentric prattle.

"Cheers," Gallow said, "and to the health of your children." It was a traditional Islander toast that Keel acknowledged with a raised eyebrow. Several acid replies teased the tip of his tongue, but he bit them back.

317

"You Islanders have mastered the grape," Gallow said. "Everything we have down under tastes like formaldehyde."

"The grape needs weather," Keel said, "not racks of lamps. That's why each season has its own distinct flavor—you taste the story of the grape. Formaldehyde is an accurate summation of conditions down under, from the grape's point of view."

Gallow's expression darkened for a blink, the barest hint of a frown. Again, the wide, winning grin. "But your people are anxious to leave all this behind. They prepare to move down under en masse. It seems they have developed a taste for formaldehyde."

So it would be that kind of a meeting. Keel had heard these conversations before—the justifications of men and women in power for their abuse of that power. He imagined that many a condemned man had to listen to the guilty prattle of his jailer.

"Right is self-evident," Keel said. "It needs no defense, just good witness. What is it that you come here for?"

"I come here for conversation, Mr. Justice," Gallow said. He brushed a stray shock of blonde hair back from his forehead. "Conversation, dialogue, whatever you might call it—it's not readily available among my men."

"You must have leaders, officers of some sort. Why not them?"

"You find this curious? Perhaps a bit frightening that the one privacy of your imprisonment is breached here? At your ease, Mr. Justice, conversation is all I'm after. My men grunt, my officers plan, my enemies plot. My prisoner thinks, or he wouldn't keep a journal, and I admire anyone who thinks. The rational mind is a rare creature, one to be respected and nurtured."

Now Keel was positive that Gallow wanted something—something particular.

Watch yourself, Keel cautioned, *he's a charmer.* The sip of wine found the hot spot deep in Keel's belly and started its slow burn into his intestines. He was tempted to end this conversation. *How much respect did you have for the minds on Guemes?* But he couldn't afford to end the conversation, not when there was a source of hard information that the Islanders might desperately need.

As long as I'm alive I'll do what I can for them, Keel thought.

"I'll tell you the truth," Keel said.

"The truth is most welcome," Gallow answered. A deferential

318

nod graced the comment, and Gallow drained his wine. Keel poured him another.

"The truth is that I have no one to talk with, either," Keel said. "I am old, I have no children and I don't want to leave the world emptier when I go. My journals"—Keel gestured at the plaz-jacketed notebook on his bunk—"are my children. I want to leave them in the best possible shape."

"I've read your notes," Gallow said. "Most poetic. It would please me to hear you read from them aloud. You have more interesting musings than most men."

"Because I dare to muse when your men dare not."

"I am not a monster, Mr. Justice."

"I am not a Justice, Mr. Gallow. You have the wrong person. Simone Rocksack is Justice now, as well as C/P. My influence is minimal."

Gallow toasted him again with the wine. "Most perceptive," he said. "Your information is correct—Simone is Chief Justice and C/P. A first. But because of the memory of one corrupt C/P, others have always been under scrutiny. You, as Justice, have satisfied the people that there is a balance of power. They wait to hear from you. It is you who can relieve their worries, not Simone. And for good reason."

"What is the reason?"

Gallow's easy smile uncurled and his eyes leveled their cold blue power at Keel.

"They have good reason to worry, because Simone works for me. She always has."

"That doesn't surprise me," Keel said, though it did. He tried to keep his voice even, conversational.

Get everything out of him, he thought, *that's the only skill I have left.*

"I think it did surprise you," Gallow said. "Your body betrays you in subtle ways. You and the C/P aren't the only ones trained in observation."

"Yes, well . . . I find it hard to believe that she'd go along with the Guemes massacre."

"She didn't know," Gallow said, "but she'll adjust. She's a very depressing woman when you get to know her. Very bitter. Did you know that there's a mirror on every wall in her quarters?"

"I've never been to her quarters."

319

"I have." Gallow's chest swelled with the statement. "No other man has. She raves about her ugliness, tears at her skin, contorts her face in the mirror until she can bear its natural form. Only then will she leave her room. Such a sad creature." Gallow shook his head and freshened his cup of wine.

"Such a sad *human,* you mean?" Keel asked.

"She doesn't consider herself human."

"Has she told you this?"

"Yes."

"Then she needs help. Friends around her. Someone to—"

"They only remind her of her ugliness," Gallow interrupted. "That's been tried. Pity, she has a succulent body under all those wraps. I am her friend because she considers me attractive, a model of what humanity *could* be. She wants no child to grow up ugly in an ugly world."

"She told you this?"

"Yes," Gallow said, "and more. I listen to her, Mr. Justice. You and your Committee, you *tolerate* her. And you lost her."

"It sounds like she was lost before I ever knew her."

Gallow's white smile returned. "You're right, of course," he said. "But there was a time when she could have been won. And I did it. You did not. That may shape the whole course of history."

"It may."

"You think *your* people will continue to revel in their deformities forever? Oh, no. They send their good children to us. You take in our rejects, our criminals and cripples. What kind of life can they build that way? Misery. Despair . . ." Gallow shrugged as though the matter were unarguable.

Keel didn't remember Islander life that way at all. It was crowded beyond Merman belief, true. Islands stank, also true. But there was incomparable color and music everywhere, always a good word. And who could explain to someone under the sea the incredible pleasure of sunrise, warm spring rain on face and hands, the constant small touchings of person to person that proved you were cared for merely by being alive.

"Mr. Justice," Gallow said, "you're not drinking your wine. Is the quality not to your liking?"

It's not the wine, Keel thought, *but the company.* Aloud, he said, "I have a stomach problem. I have to take my wine slow. I generally prefer boo."

320

"Boo?" Gallow's eyebrows lifted in genuine surprise. "That nerve-runner concoction? I thought it—"

"That only degenerates drank it? Perhaps. It's soothing, and to my taste even if it is dangerous to collect the eggs. I don't do the collecting." *That's one he can relate to.*

Gallow nodded, then his lips pressed into a firm, white line. "I heard that boo causes chromosome damage," he said. "Aren't you Islanders pushing your luck with that stuff?"

"Chromosome damage?" Keel snorted. He didn't even try to suppress a laugh. "Isn't that a little like roulette with a broken wheel?"

Keel sipped his wine and sat back to see Gallow fully. The look of disgust that shadowed the Merman's face told Keel that Gallow had been reached.

Anyone who can be reached can be probed, Keel thought. *And anyone who can be probed can be had.* His position on the Committee had taught him this.

"You can laugh at that?" Gallow's blue eyes blazed. "As long as you people breed, you endanger the whole species. What if . . . ?"

Keel raised his hand and his voice. "The Committee concerns itself with matters of 'what if,' Mr. Gallow. Any infant that carries an endangering trait is terminated. For a people trained in life-support, this is a most painful event. But it guarantees life to all the others. Tell me, Mr. Gallow, how can you be so sure that there are only harmful, ugly or useless mutations?"

"Look at yourself," Gallow said. "Your neck can't support your head without that . . . *thing*. Your eyes are on the sides of your head—"

"They're different colors, too," Keel said. "Did you know that there are more brown-eyed Mermen than blue-eyed by four to one? Doesn't that strike you as a mutation? You're blue-eyed. Should you, then, be sterilized or destroyed? We draw the line at mutations that actually endanger life. You prefer cosmetic genocide, it seems. Can you justify that to me? Can you be sure that we haven't 'bred' some secret weapons to meet the contingency you've presented us?"

Find his worst fears, Keel thought, *and turn them on himself.*

The clatter of loose dishes sounded from the hatchway and a small cart bounced over the threshold. The young man who pushed it stood in obvious awe of Gallow. His eyes took in every

321

move his boss made and his hands shook as they distributed the dishes on a small folding table. He served the steaming food into bowls and Keel smelled the delicious tang of fish stew. When the steward finished laying out the bread and a small cake dessert he picked up a small dish of his own and spooned a taste of everything.

So, Keel thought, *Gallow's afraid he's going to be poisoned.* He was glad to see the orderly delicately taste Keel's portions, as well. *Things are not going quite as Gallow would like us to believe.* Keel couldn't let the moment pass.

"Do you taste to educate your palate?" he asked.

The orderly shot a quizzical look at Gallow and Gallow smiled back. "All men in power have enemies," he said. "Even youself, I'm told. I choose to encourage protective habits."

"Protection from whom?"

Gallow was silent. The orderly's face paled.

"Very astute," Gallow said.

"By this you imply that murder is the current mode of political expression," Keel said. "Is this the new leadership you offer our world?"

Gallow's palm slapped the tabletop and the orderly dropped his bowl. It shattered. One shard of it skidded up to Keel's foot and spun there like an eccentric top winding down. Gallow dismissed the orderly with a sharp chop of his hand. The hatch closed quietly behind him.

Gallow threw down his spoon. It caught the edge of his bowl and splattered Keel with stew. Gallow dabbed at Keel's tunic with his cloth, leaning across the rickety table.

"My apologies, Mr. Justice," he said. "I'm generally not so boorish. You . . . excite me. Please, relax."

Keel nursed the ache in his knees and folded them under the short table.

Gallow tore a piece of bread from the loaf and handed Keel the rest.

"You have Scudi Wang prisoner?" Keel asked.

"Of course."

"And the young Islander, Norton?"

"He's with her. They are unharmed."

"It won't work," Keel said. "If you hinge your leadership on stealth and prisoners and murder then you set yourself up for a

322

long reign of the same thing. No one wants to deal with a desperate man. Kings are made of better stuff."

Gallow's ears pricked at the word "king." Keel could see him trying it on his tongue.

"You're not eating, Mr. Justice."

"As I said before, I have a stomach problem."

"But you have to eat. How will you live?"

Keel smiled. "I won't."

Gallow set his spoon down carefully and dabbed at his lips with his cloth. He knit his smooth brow in an expression of concern.

"If you choose not to eat, you will be fed," Gallow warned. "Spare yourself that unpleasantry. You won't starve yourself out of my care."

"Choice has nothing to do with it," Keel said. "You snatched inferior merchandise. Eating causes pain, and the food merely passes undigested."

Gallow pushed himself back from the squat table.

"It's not catching, Mr. Gallow."

"What is it?"

"A defect," Keel said. "Our bioengineers helped me up to this point, but now the Greater Committee takes matters out of our hands."

"The Greater Committee?" Gallow asked. "You mean that there is a group topside more powerful than yours? A secret clan?"

Keel laughed, and the laugh added frustration and confusion to Gallow's otherwise perfect face.

"The Greater Committee goes by many names," Keel said. "They are a subversive bunch, indeed. Some call them Ship, some call them Jesus—not the Jesus Lewis of your school-day histories. This is a difficult committee to confront, as you can see. It makes the threat of death at your hands not much of a threat at all."

"You're . . . *dying?*"

Keel nodded. "No matter what you do," he said, smiling, "the world will believe that you killed me."

Gallow stared at Keel for a long blink, then blotted his lips with the napkin. He extricated himself from the table.

"In that case," Gallow announced, "if you want to save those kids, you'll do exactly as I say."

. . . *it comes to pass that the same evils and inconveniences*
take place in all ages of history.
　　　—Niccolo Machiavelli, *Discourses,* Shiprecords

From his position at the foil's controls, Brett watched the
late afternoon sun kindle a glow in the cloud bank ahead of him.
The foil drove easily across deep storm swells, picking up speed
on each downslope, losing a bit on each advancing wave. It was a
rhythm that Brett had come to understand without conscious attention. His body and senses adjusted.

A gray wall of rain skulked a couple of hundred meters above
the wavetops to the right. A line storm, it appeared to be rolling
away from them.

Brett, his attention divided between the course monitor above
him and the seas ahead, abruptly throttled back. The foil dropped
off its step and moved with minimal headway beside a kelp bed
that stretched away into the storm track.

The change in motion aroused the others, who, except for
Bushka and the captive Merman, whom Bushka had locked in the
cargo bay with the survivors of the LTA, were sprawled around
the cabin catching what rest they could. Bushka sat in regal isolation on the couch at the rear of the cabin, his eyes oddly indrawn,
his face a mask of concentration as he stroked a fragment of kelp
that lay across his lap. The bit of kelp had come up from the sea
on Twisp's rescue line and had attracted little attention until
Bushka plucked it off and kept it.

Panille spoke from the copilot's seat as he came abruptly alert.
"Something wrong?"

Brett indicated the green glow of their position on the course
monitor. "We're only a couple of klicks out." He pointed at the
line squall. "The outpost is in there."

Twisp spoke from behind them: "Bushka, you still going through with this?"

"I have no choice." Bushka's voice carried a distant tone. He stroked the fragment of kelp, which had begun to dry and crisp. It rasped under his hand.

Twisp nodded at the net of weapons Bushka had taken from the LTA survivors. "Then maybe we all better be armed."

"I'm thinking on it," Bushka said. Again, his hand rasped across the drying kelp.

"Panille," Twisp said, "how are outposts defended?"

Scudi, seated on the deck across from Twisp, answered for him. "Outposts aren't expected to need defenses."

"They have the usual sonar, perimeter alarms against dashers, that sort of thing," Panille said. "Each outpost has at least one LTA for weather observation."

"But what weapons?" Twisp asked.

"Tools, mostly," Scudi said.

Bushka nudged the netful of captured weapons at his feet. "They will have lasguns. Gallow arms his people."

"But they'd be effective only inside the outpost compound," Panille said. "We're safe in the water."

"Which is why I stopped here," Brett said. "Do you think they know we're here?"

"They know," Bushka said. "They just don't know who we are." He peeled the dried kelp from his dive suit and dropped it to the deck.

Scudi stood and moved to Brett's side, resting an arm on the back of his seat. "They will have welders, plasteel cutters, some stunshields, knives, pry-bars. Tools are very effective weapons." She looked at Bushka. "As Guemes should have taught us."

Panille swiveled and looked at the passage that led back to the cargo compartment. "Some of those people back there might know some details about what we can expect down there—"

"This is stupid!" Brett said. "What can we do against Gallow and all his men?"

"We will wait for nightfall," Bushka said. "Darkness is a great equalizer." He looked at Scudi. "You say you've worked at this outpost. You can draw up a plan of the access hatches, the power station, tool storage, vehicle bays . . . that sort of thing."

Scudi looked at Brett, who shrugged.

Twisp glanced once at the lasgun in Bushka's hand, then at his face. "You really mean for us to attack them, don't you?"

"Of course."

"Unarmed?"

"We will have the inestimable arm of surprise."

Twisp let out a barking laugh.

"Let me talk to Kareen," Panille said. "She can't be one of them. She may have learned—"

"She's not to be trusted," Bushka said. "She belonged to Ryan Wang when he was alive, and now she belongs to Gallow."

"No, she doesn't!"

"Men are so easily manipulated by sex," Bushka sneered.

Panille's dark face darkened further with anger, but he held his silence for a blink. Then: "The kelp! The kelp can tell us what we need to know!"

"Do not trust the kelp, either," Bushka said. "Every sentient thing in this universe thinks of itself first. We don't know what the kelp fears or desires."

Panille glanced at the bit of dried kelp on the deck. "Scudi, what do you say about the kelp? You've worked in and around it more than any of us."

"She is Ryan Wang's daughter!" Bushka blared. "You ask the enemy for advice?"

"I ask where I might get an answer," Panille said. "And if you're not going to use that lasgun, quit waving it around." He turned from a flabbergasted Bushka to Scudi. "What's the kelp's range, from your experience?"

"Worldwide," she said, "and almost instantaneous."

"*That* fast?"

Scudi shrugged. "And what it learns, it never forgets." She noted the look of surprise on Panille's face and went on. "We've made reports. Most supervisors don't go out there, so they write this off to narcosis and keep us out of deep water for a week."

"What else might help us?"

"There are weak spots," Scudi said. "Immature kelp is strictly a conductor. Mature kelp carries a presence all its own."

"What do you mean?" Twisp asked.

"If I touch a young patch of kelp and you touch a mature one, we sense each other. But now . . . it is doing something more. Bushka's right that it may do things on its own."

"It has learned to kill," Bushka said.

Scudi said, "I always thought it could trans*mit*, but not trans-*late*."

Bushka asked, "How many people can the outpost support?"

Scudi juggled the question a moment. "They have accommodations, food and other supplies for about three hundred. But they have open land at the center. They could shelter a lot more people."

Brett turned to Bushka. "Does Gallow have three hundred people?"

Bushka nodded. "More."

"Then we can't confront them," Twisp said. "This is crazy."

"I'm going to kill Gallow," Bushka said.

"That's it?" Twisp demanded. "That's all? Then they'll quit and go home?"

Bushka would not meet Twisp's gaze. "All right," he said with a flick of the weapon, "let's see what Kareen Ale has to say. Put the foil on autopilot, Brett."

"Autopilot?" Brett asked. "Why?"

"We're all going back to see Kareen," Bushka said. "Everybody move easily, no sudden surprises."

No one argued with those jumpy, glittering eyes. Brett and Scudi led the way through the hatch and down the passageway. At the cargo hatch Bushka motioned Twisp to the lock.

"Open the exterior hatch first," he ordered. "We might want to throw something overboard."

Slowly, reluctantly, Twisp obeyed. A fresh breeze tasting of iodine and salt ricocheted through the hatchway. Wave-slaps against the hull were loud in the passage.

"Open the cargo hatch and stand aside," Bushka said.

Twisp lifted the security bar, released the latch and slid the hatch to one side.

Without warning, Brett was knocked down by something wet and ropy coming from behind him. A large strand of kelp snaked past him, swerved left and slammed the LTA's survivors against the bulkhead. It held them there. The thumpings of the kelp turned the passageway into a great drum. Brett snatched a grab, caught his balance and saw the rapt features of Iz Bushka, who was held in loops of kelp.

Bushka stood with both arms upraised, the lasgun still clutched in his right fist. Strands of kelp caressed his body, their leaves particularly drawn to his face and hands. More strands lay like ropes on the deck, fanned out on both sides. Scudi and the others were not in sight.

A branch of kelp detached itself from the captives and undulated toward Brett. The fronded tip lifted and enclosed Brett's face.

Brett heard whistling—the wind against the foil, but enhanced, every tonal component identifiable. He felt his senses amplified—the touch of the deck, other people around him . . . many others . . . thousands. He sensed Scudi then, as though the kelp gave her to him with her thoughts clear. Bushka was there, an enraptured Bushka drinking from the kelp's reservoir of memories. A historian's paradise: firsthand history.

Scudi spoke in Brett's head: "The rocket is up. They're on their way to get the hyb tanks."

Brett saw it then, a fiery ascent that flamed through the cloud cover and became an orange glow on the gray until it vanished and only the clouds remained. With the vision went a questioning thought, a profound wonder that was not human. The rocket was a wondrous thing of anticipation in this thought. It was a seeking after great surprises.

The thought and the vision vanished. Brett found himself sitting on the deck in the foil's passage and looking into the cargo bay. Bushka sat there sobbing. The bay behind him was empty. The kelp was gone.

Brett heard others then and Scudi's voice came overloud. "Brett! Are you all right?"

He scrambled to his feet, turning. Scudi stood there with movements of others behind her, but Brett could focus only on Scudi. "As long as you're here, I'm all right," he said.

328

Symbols are worth a damn.

—Duque Kurz

19(?) Alki, 468. Outpost 22.

When they call me "Mr. Justice" I feel the scales of law and life freeze in my palm. I am not Ward Keel to them, the big-headed man with the long neck and stiff shuffle, but some god who will see the right thing and do it. And good *will come.* God and good, evil and devil—words are the symbols that flesh out our world. We expect that. We act on it.

Resentment, that's expectation gone bad. I must admit, our crises are legion, but we live to confront our crises and that's something no god ever promised.

Simone Rocksack thinks she knows what Ship has promised. That's her job, she says. She tells the faithful what Ship meant and they believe her. The Histories are there for the reading. I come to my own conclusions: We are neither rewarded nor punished. We *are.* My job as Chief Justice has been to keep as many of us *being* as possible.

The Committee's foundations were in science and fear. Original questions were quite simple: kill it or care for it. Terminate if dangerous. That power over life and death in a time of much death lent an aura to the Committee that it should never have accepted. In lieu of law, there is the Committee.

It is true that the C/P asserts the law of Ship and it is also true that her people enforce it. They give unto Ship that which is Ship's . . . together we keep the human world flowing.

"Flow" is the right word. We Islanders understand current and flow. We understand that conditions and times change. To change, then, is normal. The Committee reflects that flexibility. Most law is simply a matter of personal contracts, agreements. Courts deal with squabbles.

329

The Committee deals with life and life alone. Somehow that has extended to politics, a matter of group survival. We are autonomous, elect our own replacements, and our word is as close to absolute law as Islanders get. They trust nothing fixed. Rigidity in law apalls them as much as cold statuary.

Part of our enjoyment of art derives from its transitory nature. It is made constantly new and if it is to survive over time it does so in the theater of memory. We Islanders have great respect for the mind. It is a most interesting place, a tool at the base of all tools, torture chamber, haven of rest and repository of symbols. All that we have relies on symbol. With symbols we create more world than we were given, we become more than the sum of our parts.

Anyone who threatens the mind or its symbolizing endangers the matrix of humanity itself. I have tried to explain as much to Gallow. He has the ears for it; he simply doesn't care.

When power shifts, men shift with it.
                    —George Orwell, Shiprecords

The argument was over whether to arm Nakano. Bushka favored it and Twisp did not. Ale and Panille remained aloof, listening but not watching. They stood, each with an arm around the other's waist, looking out on the lowering gray sky visible through the open hatchway. The foil circled on autopilot in a wide pool of open water surrounded by kelp. The outpost lifted from the sea about ten klicks away—a foam-collared pillar of rock set in a ring of kelp. A kelp-free area surrounded the outpost. The rock appeared to be at least one klick away from this vantage.

Brett found himself alarmed by the change in Bushka. What had the kelp done to Bushka there in the cargo bay? And where were the other captive Mermen? Only Ale, Panille and Nakano remained of those rescued from the LTA.

Twisp voiced it for all of them: "What did the kelp do to you, Iz?"

Bushka looked down at the net of weapons by his right foot. His gaze passed over the lasguns he had already distributed to the others—to everyone except Nakano. A look of childlike bewilderment swept over Bushka's face. "It told me . . . it told me . . ." He brightened. "It told me we must kill Gallow and it showed me how." He turned and stared past Ale and Panille at the kelp drifting on the surging waves. A rapt expression came over his face.

"And you agreed, Nakano?" Twisp demanded.

"It makes little difference," Nakano said, his voice gruff. "The kelp wants him dead but he will not be dead."

Twisp shuddered and looked at Scudi and Brett. "That's not what it said to me. How about you, kid?"

331

"It showed me the launching of the rocket."

Brett closed his eyes. Scudi pressed herself against him, leaning her head into his shoulder. He knew the experience they had shared: thousands of people alive now only in the kelp's memories. The last agony of the Guemes Islanders was there and everything the dead had ever thought or dreamed. He had heard Scudi exclaiming in his mind: *"Now, I know what it feels like to be a Mute!"*

Scudi pushed herself a bit away from Brett's embrace and looked at Twisp. "The kelp said it's my friend because I'm one of its teachers."

"What did it say to you, Twisp?" Brett asked. Brett opened his eyes wide and stared hard at the long-armed fisherman.

Twisp inhaled a deep, quick breath and spoke in a sharp voice: "It just told me about myself."

"It told him he's a man who thinks for himself and likes to keep his thoughts private," Nakano said. "It told me we're alike in this. Isn't that it, Twisp?"

"More or less." Twisp sounded embarrassed.

"It said our kind's dangerous to leaders who demand blind obedience," Nakano said. "The kelp respects this."

"There! You see?" Bushka smiled at them, lifting a lasgun out of the pile of weapons he had taken from the people off the LTA. He balanced the lasgun on his open palm, staring at it.

Panille turned from the hatchway and looked at Bushka. "You all accept this?" His voice was flat. He glared at Nakano. "Only you and Kareen and I are left!" He jerked his chin toward the hatchway. "Where are the others?"

Silence settled over the group.

Panille turned toward the perimeter of kelp visible in the darkening light. He remembered hurdling the glut of kelp and reaching for Kareen as a giant vine released her. She had grabbed him close and they had clung to each other while cries of fear lifted all around them.

In that instant of kelp-awareness, he had been inundated by Kareen: Gallow's captive—sent with Nakano to be used as bait in the capture of Dark Panille. She had her loyalty problems, too. Her family, with all its power, wanted a hold on Gallow in case he was victorious. But Kareen loathed Gallow.

Kareen's fingers had held a painful grip on Panille's water-frizzed hair while she cried against his neck. Then the kelp had returned . . . and touched them once more. They had both felt the kelp's selective fury, sensed the leaves and vines writhing seaward . . . bottomward. Presently, the hatchway had framed a churning gray sea, not a sign there to betray the fact that humans had been removed from the foil . . . and drowned.

But that was the past. Bushka cleared his throat, breaking Panille's reverie. "They were Gallow's people," Bushka said. "What does it matter?"

"Nakano was one of Gallow's people," Twisp said.

"It's not an easy choice," Nakano said. "Gallow saved my life once. But so did you, Twisp."

"So you go with whoever saved you most recently," Twisp said, scorn in his voice.

Nakano spoke in a curious lilting tone: "I go with the kelp. There is my immortality."

Brett's throat went dry. He had heard that tone in Guemes fanatics, the hardest of the hard-core WorShipers.

Twisp, obviously having a similar reaction, shook his head from side to side. *Nakano did not care who he killed! The kelp justified everything!*

"Gallow wants Vata," Bushka said. "We can't allow that." He passed the lasgun to Nakano, who slipped it into its holster at his thigh.

At Bushka's movement, Twisp put his hand on his own weapon. He did not relax even when Nakano displayed empty hands and smiled at him.

"Seven of us," Twisp said. "And we're supposed to attack a place that could have more than three hundred armed people in it!"

Bushka closed the hatchway before looking at Twisp. "The kelp told me how to kill Gallow," he said. "Do you doubt the kelp?"

"You're damned right I do!"

"But we are going to do it," Bushka said. He pushed past Twisp and went up the passageway toward the pilot cabin. Brett took Scudi's hand and followed. He could hear the others coming after them, Twisp muttering: "Stupid, stupid, stupid . . ."

For Brett, Twisp's voice lay immersed in what the kelp had insisted, a chant imprinted on the vocal centers. Certainly this was what the kelp had told Bushka.

Drive Gallow out. Avata will do the rest.

333

The chant surged there, background to a persistent image of Ward Keel imprisoned in plaz, beckoning to him. Brett felt sure that Keel was Gallow's prisoner at this outpost.

Panille went to the left-hand pilot's seat and checked the instruments. The foil was making minimal headway in the wide circle of open water enclosed by kelp fronds.

Brett stopped near the pilot station. Feeling Scudi's hand tremble in his, he squeezed her hand firmly. She leaned against him. He looked out the plaz to his right. Framed there was a churning gray sea. Rain slanted with a stiff breeze. Kelp fronds lifted and danced on the wavetops, smoothing them and dampening the chop. Even as he looked, darkness settled over the sea. Automatic lighting came on to rim the edges of the cabin ceiling. Course vector lights winked on the screens in front of Panille.

Twisp had stopped at the entrance to the cabin, his hand on the lasgun, his attention on Nakano.

Noting this, Nakano smiled. He moved across in front of Brett and went to the pilot station beside Panille, activating the exterior lights. A spotlight fanned brilliant illumination across the open water and the edge of kelp. Abruptly, swift motion entered the illuminated area.

"Dashers!" Panille said.

"Look at that big bull!" Nakano said.

Brett and Scudi stared out at the scene, the blanket of kelp, the hunt of dashers.

"I've never seen such a big one," Ale said.

The hunt swept along in an undulating glide behind the monster bull. Nakano tracked them with the spotlight. They circled the dark perimeter of kelp, then worked into the leaves.

Nakano turned from the control station and opened the plaz hatch beside him, letting in a damp rush of wind and rain. Lifting his lasgun, he sent a burning arc at the hunt, tumbling the lead bull and two followers. Their dark green blood washed over the kelp fronds, foaming in the waves.

The rest of the hunt turned on its own dead, spreading blood and torn flesh across the fan of light. Abruptly, kelp stalks as thick as a man's waist lifted from the sea, whipped the gore to a foam and drove the dashers from their feed.

Nakano drew back and secured the hatch. "You see that?" he asked.

334

No one answered. They had all seen it.

"We will submerge," Bushka said. "We will go in with the foil underwater. Nakano will be visible. The rest of us will appear to be captives until the last blink."

Brett released Scudi's hand and crossed to confront Bushka. "I'll not have Scudi used as bait!"

Bushka made a grab for his lasgun but Brett caught the man's wrist. Young muscles, made powerful by months of hauling nets, flexed once, twisted Bushka's wrist and the lasgun dropped to the deck. Brett kicked it toward Twisp, who picked it up and hefted it.

Bushka eyed the weapons he had left near the passage entrance.

"You'd never make it," Twisp said. "So relax." He held the lasgun casually, muzzle pointed downward, but his manner suggested poised readiness.

"So what do we do now?" Ale asked.

"We could run for the Launch Base and alert everyone to what's happening," Panille said.

"You'd start a civil war among Mermen and the Islanders would be drawn into it," Bushka protested. He rubbed at his wrist where Brett had twisted it.

"There's something else," Scudi said. She glanced at Brett, then at Twisp. "Chief Justice Keel is being held prisoner here by Gallow."

"In Ship's name, how do you know that?" Twisp demanded.

"The kelp says it," Scudi said.

"It showed me a vision of Keel in captivity," Brett said.

"Vision!" Twisp said.

"The only important thing is to kill Gallow," Bushka muttered.

Twisp looked at Kareen Ale. "The only reason we went back to the cargo bay was to ask you for advice," he said. "What does the ambassador suggest?"

"Use the kelp," she said. "Take the foil down to the inner edge of the kelp in sight of the outpost . . . and we wait. Let them see Scudi and me. That should tempt Gallow to come out. And yes, Justice Keel is there. I've seen him."

"I say we run for Vashon," Brett said.

"Let me remind you," Ale said, "that the hyb tanks will be brought down here. The pickup team is at this outpost."

335

"And they're either Gallow's people or Gallow's captives," Twisp sneered. "Any way you look at it, the hyb tanks are his."

Ale glanced at the chrono beside the control panel. "If all goes well, the tanks could be here in a little more than eight hours."

"With seven of us aboard, we couldn't stay down eight hours," Panille said.

Bushka began to giggle, startling them. "Empty argument," he said. "Empty words. The kelp won't permit us to leave until we do its bidding. It's kill Gallow or nothing."

Nakano was the first to break the subsequent silence. "Then we'd better get busy," he said. "Personally, I like the ambassador's plan but I think we also should send in a scout party."

"And you're volunteering?" Twisp asked.

"If you have a better idea, let's hear it," Nakano said. He returned to the cabin's rear bulkhead and opened a supply locker, exposing fins, air tanks, breathers and dive suits.

"You saw the kelp crush that sub," Brett reminded Twisp. "And you saw what happened with the dashers."

"Then I'm the one who goes in," Twisp said. "They don't know me. I'll carry our message so they get it real clear."

"Twisp, no!" Brett protested.

"Yes!" Twisp glanced at the others, focusing on each face for a blink, then: "With the exception of the ambassador there, who can't go in for obvious reasons—they want her, for Ship's sake! But except for her, I'm the obvious one. I'll take Nakano with me." Twisp sent a dasher grin at Nakano, who looked both surprised and pleased.

"Why you?" Brett asked. "I could—"

"You could get yourself in eelshit for no good reason. You've never dealt with people who want to get the best of you, kid. You've never had to drive the best bargain you could for your fish. I know how to deal with such people."

"Gallow is no fish dealer," Bushka said.

"It's still bargaining for your life and everything you want," Twisp said. "The kid stays here with Panille. They keep an eye on you, Bushka, to see you don't do something crazy. Me, I'm going to tell this Gallow just what he gets—so much and no more!"

Do that which is good and no evil shall touch you.
—Raphael, Apocrypha,
The Christian Book of the Dead

Within the first minute of the dive, Twisp tumbled along, flailing his long arms, his fins thrusting inefficiently. He watched helplessly as the gap between himself and Nakano widened. Why was Nakano speeding off that way?

Like most Islanders, Twisp had trained with Merman-style breathers for emergency use; he had even considered at one time that he might permit himself to become one of the rare Islanders fitted for an airfish. But airfish were a cash crop and the operation was outrageously costly. And his arms, superb for net pulling, were not suited to swimming.

Twisp struggled to keep Nakano in sight. He skimmed the bottom, his fins puffing sand along a blue-black canyon illuminated by Merman lights set into the rock. The sea above him remained a black remoteness hidden in the short-night.

When Panille had locked the foil against a rocky outcrop within the outpost's kelp perimeter, he had warned them: "The current's ranging between two and four knots. I don't know where the current came from, but it'll help you get to the outpost."

"Kelp is making that current," Bushka had said.

"Whatever is causing it, be careful," Panille had said. "You'll be moving too fast for mistakes."

Brett, still protesting the assignment of duties, had demanded: "How will they get back to us?"

"Steal a vehicle," Nakano had said.

As he had sealed the dive hatch behind them and prepared to flood the foil's lock, Nakano had said: "Stay close, Twisp. We'll be about ten minutes getting to the outpost hatch. I'll tow you the last few meters. Make it look like you're my prisoner."

337

But now Nakano was far ahead in the chill, green-washed distance. The floppy bubbles of his exhalations raced upward behind him, creating strange prism effects in the artificial light. The Merman obviously was in his element here and Twisp was the muree-out-of-water.

I should've anticipated that! Twisp thought.

Abruptly, Nakano rolled to one side in a powerful turn, clutched one of the light mountings anchored in the canyon's wall and held himself against the current, waiting for Twisp's arrival. Nakano's air tank glistened yellow-green along his back and his masked face was a grotesque shadow beside the rock.

Twisp, somewhat reassured by the Merman's action, tried to change course but would have missed Nakano had not the latter pushed off smoothly and grabbed the breather valve at Twisp's left shoulder. They rode along together then, swimming gently as the current slackened near the underwater cliff into which the outpost had been planted.

Twisp saw a wall of black rock ahead, some of it looking as though it were part of the sea's natural basement complex, some appearing man-changed—great dark shapes piled one atop another. A wide plaz dive lock outlined in light had been set into this construction. Nakano operated controls at the side of the plaz with one hand. A circular hatch opened before them. They swam into the lock, Nakano still holding Twisp's breather valve.

It was an oval space illuminated by brilliant blue lights set into the walls. A plaz hatch on the inner curve revealed an empty passage beyond.

The outer hatch sealed automatically behind them and water began swirling out of the lock through a floor vent. Nakano released his grip on Twisp when their heads emerged from the water.

Removing his mouthpiece, Nakano said: "You're being very intelligent for a Mute. I could've shut off your air at any time. You'd have been eelbait."

Twisp removed his own mouthpiece but remained silent. Nothing was important except getting to Gallow.

"Don't try anything," Nakano warned. "I could break you into small pieces with only one hand."

Hoping Nakano was playing a part for any would-be listeners, Twisp looked at the Merman's heavily muscled body. Nakano's threat could be real, Twisp thought, but the Merman might be surprised at the strength in a net-puller's arms . . . even if those arms did appear to be mutated monstrosities.

Nakano took off his tank and harness and held the equipment in his left hand. Twisp waited for the last of the water to swirl through the floor vent, then shucked off his own tank. He held it loosely cradled in one long arm, feeling the weight of it and thinking how potent a weapon this would be if hurled suddenly.

The inner hatch swung aside and Twisp tasted hot, moist air. Nakano pushed Twisp ahead of him through the hatchway and they emerged into a rectangular space with no other visible exit.

Abruptly, a voice barked at them from an overhead vent: "Nakano! Send the Mute topside. You get off at level nine and come to me. I want to know why you didn't bring the foil straight in."

"Gallow," Nakano explained, looking at Twisp. "After I get off, you go straight on up."

Twisp's gut felt suddenly empty. How many people did Gallow have here? Was Gallow so confident of his Security that he could release an Islander prisoner to wander around without a guard? Or was this a ploy to disarm the *stupid Islander?*

Nakano looked up at the vent. Twisp, peering at the ceiling construction, saw the glittering oval of a Merman remote-eye.

"This man's my prisoner," Nakano said. "I presume there are guards topside."

"The Mute can't run away anywhere up there," Gallow's voice snapped. "But he had better wait near the lift exit. We don't want to hunt all over for him."

Twisp felt himself get heavier then and realized that the entire rectangular room was rising. Presently, it stopped, and a thin seam in the back wall opened to reveal a hatch and a well-lighted passage with many armed Mermen in it.

Gallow grasped Twisp's dive tanks by the harness. "I'll take them," he said. "Wouldn't want you using these as a weapon."

Twisp released his hold on the equipment.

Gallow went out and the hatch sealed.

Again, the room lifted. After what seemed to Twisp an interminable wait, the room again came to a stop. The hatch opening was haloed in dim light. Hesitantly, Twisp stepped out into hot, dry air. He looked up and around at high, black cliffs and open sky—dawn light, still some stars visible. Even as he looked, Big Sun lifted over the cliffs, illuminating a great rock-girdled bowl with much square-edged Merman construction in it and an LTA base in the middle distance.

Open land!

Twisp heard someone nearby using a saw. The sound was reassuring, a thing heard often in an Island's shop areas—metal and plastics being cut by carpenters for assemblage into necessary nonorganic utensils.

The rocks were sharp under Twisp's bare feet and Big Sun blinded him.

"Abimael, simple one! Come here out of the sun!"

It was a man's voice and it came from a building ahead of Twisp. He saw someone moving in the shadows. The sound of sawing continued.

The air in his lungs felt hot and dry, not the cool metallic dampness of the dive tanks nor the warm moisture that blew so often across Vashon. The surface underfoot did not move, either. Twisp felt this as a dangerous, alien thing. *Decks should lift and move!*

All the edges are hard, he thought.

He stepped gingerly forward into the building's shade. The sawing stopped and now Twisp discerned a figure in the deeper shadows—a dark-skinned man in a diaperlike garment. Long black hair frizzed out from the man's head and he had a gray-streaked beard. It was one of the few beards Twisp had ever seen, reaching nearly to the man's navel. Twisp had heard that some Mermen grew beards and the beard-gene cropped up occasionally among Islanders, but this luxurious growth was something new.

As the man moved in the shadows, Twisp saw the evidence of great physical strength, particularly in the shoulders and upper body. This Merman would make a good net-puller, Twisp thought. The Merman's midsection displayed the preliminary settlings of middle age, however. Twisp guessed the man at a hard-driven forty or forty-five . . . very dark-skinned for a Merman. His skin glowed with a layer of red within the leathery tones.

"Abimael, come now," the man said. "Your feet will burn. Come have a cake till your mama finds you."

Why does he call me Abimael? Twisp glanced around at the basin

340

enclosed by the high black cliffs. A squad of Mermen worked in the middle distance, sweeping the ground with flamethrowers.

It was a dreamlike scene in the hot light of swiftly rising Big Sun. Twisp feared suddenly that he had been narced. Panille had warned him about it: "Don't swim off into a deep area and you be sure to breathe slow and deep. Otherwise you could be narced."

Narc, Twisp knew, was the Merman term for nitrogen narcosis, intoxication they sometimes encountered in the depths when using pressurized air tanks. There were stories—narced divers releasing their tanks at depth and swimming away to drown, or offering their air to passing fish, or going off into a euphoric water-dance.

"I hear the flamethrowers," the old carpenter said.

The matter-of-fact confirmation of what Twisp saw eased his fears. *No . . . this is real land . . . open to the sky. I am here and I am not narced.*

"They think they'll sterilize this land and they'll never have nerve runners here," the carpenter said. "The fools are wrong! Nerve-runner eggs are in the sea everywhere. Flamethrowers will be needed for as long as people live here."

The carpenter moved across his shadowed area toward a brown cloth folded on a bench. He sat on the end of the bench and opened the cloth, revealing a paper-wrapped package of cakes, dark brown and glossy. Twisp smelled the sweet stickiness rising from the cakes. The carpenter lifted a cake in thick knuckle-swollen fingers and held it toward Twisp.

In that instant, Twisp saw that the man was blind. The eyes were cloud-gray and empty of recognition. Hesitantly, Twisp accepted the cake and sampled it. Rich brown fruit in the cake sweetened his tongue.

Again, Twisp looked at the scene in the bowl of open land. He had seen pictures and holos from the histories but nothing had prepared him for this experience. He felt both attracted and repelled by what he saw. This land would not drift willy-nilly on an uncertain sea. There was a sense of absolute assurance in the firmness underfoot. But there was a loss of freedom in it, too. It was locked down and enclosed . . . limited. Too much of this could narrow a man's vision.

"One more cake, Abimael, and then you go home," the carpenter said.

Twisp stepped back from the carpenter, hoping to escape silently, but his heel encountered a stone and he tumbled backward, sitting sharply on another stone. An involuntary cry of pain escaped him.

"Now, don't you cry, Abimael!" the carpenter said.

Twisp heaved himself to his feet. "I'm not Abimael," he said.

The carpenter aimed his sightless eyes toward Twisp and sat silent for a moment, then: "I hear that now. Hope you liked the cake. You see Abimael anywhere around?"

"No one in sight but the men with the flamethrowers."

"Damned fools!" The carpenter swallowed a cake whole and licked the syrupy coating off his fingers. "They're bringing Islanders onto the land already?"

"I . . . I think I'm the first."

"They call me Noah," the carpenter said. "You can take it as a joke. Say I was the first out here. Are you badly deformed, Islander?"

Twisp swallowed a sudden rise of anger at the man's bluntness.

"My arms are rather long but they're perfect for pulling nets."

"Don't mind the useful variations," Noah said. "What's your name?"

"Twisp . . . Queets Twisp."

"Twisp," Noah said. "I like that name. It has a good sound. Want another cake?"

"No, thank you. It was good, though. I just can't take too much sweetness. What're you making here?"

"I'm working with a bit of wood," Noah said. "Think of that! Wood grown on Pandora! I'm fashioning some pieces that will be made into furniture for the new director of this place. You met him yet? Name's Gallow."

"I haven't had that . . . pleasure," Twisp said.

"You will. He sees everybody. Doesn't like Mutes, though, I'm afraid."

"How were you . . . I mean, your eyes?"

"I wasn't born this way. It was caused by staring at a sun too long. Bet you didn't know that, did you? If you stand on solid ground so you don't move around, you can stare right at the sun . . . but it can blind you."

"Oh." Twisp didn't know what else to say. Noah seemed resigned to his fate, though.

"Abimael!" Noah raised his voice into a loud call.

There was no answer.

"He'll come," Noah said. "Saved a cake for him. He knows it."

Twisp nodded, then felt the foolishness of the gesture. He stared across the enclosed basin. The land glared at him from all sides, everything highlighted by the brightness of Big Sun. The buildings were stark white, shot through with streaks of brown. Water or the illusion of water shimmered in a flat area near the far cliffs. The flamethrowers had been silenced and the Merman workers had gone into a building toward the center of the basin. Noah returned to his woodworking. There was no wind, no sound of seabirds, no sound of Abimael, who was supposed to be coming to his father's call. Nothing. Twisp had never before heard such silence . . . not even underwater.

"They call me Noah," Noah said. "Go to the records and look up the histories. I call my first-born Abimael. Do you dream strange things, Twisp? I used to dream about a big boat, called an ark, in the time when the original Terrahome was flooded. The ark saved lots of humans and animals from the flood . . . kinda like the hyb tanks in that, you know?"

Twisp found himself fascinated by the carpenter's voice. The man was a storyteller and knew the trick of flexing his voice to hold a listener's attention.

"The ones who didn't get on the ark, they all died," Noah said. "When the sea went down, they found the stinking carcasses for months. The ark was built so animals and people couldn't climb aboard unless they were invited and the ramp was lowered."

Noah mopped sweat from his brow with a purple cloth. "Stinking carcasses everywhere," he muttered.

A slight breeze came over the cliff walls and wafted the heavy stink of burned things across Twisp. He could almost smell the rotting flesh Noah described.

The carpenter hefted two joined pieces of wood and hung them on a peg in the wall behind him.

"Ship made a promise that Noah would live," Noah said. "But watching that much death was very bad. When so many die and so few live, think how dead the survivors must feel! They needed the miracle of Lazarus and it was denied them."

Noah turned away from the wall and his blind eyes glittered in reflected light. Twisp saw that tears rolled unchecked down the man's cheeks and onto his dark, bare chest.

"I don't know whether you'll believe it," Noah said, "but Ship has talked to me."

Twisp stared at the tear-stained face, fascinated. For the first time in his life, Twisp felt himself to be in the presence of an authentic mystery.

"Ship spoke to me," Noah said. "I smelled the stink of death and saw bones on the land still clotted with rotting flesh. Ship said: 'I will not again curse the ground for mankind's sake.'"

Twisp shuddered. Noah's words came with a compelling force that could not be rejected.

Noah paused, then went on: "And Ship said, 'The imagination of man's heart is evil from his youth.' What do you think of that?"

For mankind's sake, Twisp thought.

Noah frightened him then by speaking it once more aloud: "For mankind's sake! As though we begged for it! As though we couldn't work out something better than all that death!"

Twisp began to feel a deep sympathy for the carpenter. This Noah was a philosopher and a profound thinker. For the first time, Twisp began to feel that Islander and Merman might achieve a common understanding. All Mermen were not Gallows or Nakanos.

"You know what, Twisp?" Noah asked. "I expected better of Ship than slaughter. And to say He does it for mankind's sake!"

Noah came across the shadowed work area, skirting the bench as though he could see it, and stopped directly in front of Twisp.

"I hear you breathing there," Noah said. "Ship spoke to me, Twisp. I don't care whether you believe that. It happened." Noah reached out and grasped Twisp's shoulder, moved the hand downward and explored the length of Twisp's left arm, then returned to trace a finger over Twisp's face.

"Your arm *is* long," Noah said. "Don't see anything wrong in that if it's useful. You got a good face. Lots of wrinkles. You live outside a lot. You see any sign of my Abimael yet?"

Twisp swallowed. "No."

"Don't you be frightened of me just because I talk to Ship," Noah said. "This new ark of ours is out on dry land once and for all. We're going to leave the sea."

Noah pulled away from Twisp and returned to the workbench.

A hand touched Twisp's right arm. Startled, he whirled and confronted Nakano. The big Merman had approached without a sound.

"Gallow wants to see you now," Nakano said.

"Where is that Abimael?" Noah asked.

And the dove came in to him in the evening; and, lo, in her mouth was an olive leaf pluckt off.
    —Genesis 8:11, The Christian Book of the Dead

Duque ignored the gasps of the watchers ringed around the constant gloom of the Vata Pool. His ears did not register the strangled moan that came clearly from the wide, flaccid throat of the C/P. The heavy fist that Vata clamped to his genitals captured Duque's attention completely. Her fervor hurled him painfully out of pseudosleep, but her touch softened with every blink. The poolside gasps were replaced by sporadic mutterings and a few hushed giggles. When Duque's hand began its complementary stroking of Vata's huge body the room stilled. Vata moaned. The poolside watchers were soaked by the wave set up under the rhythmic strokes of her mighty hips.

"They're going to pair!"

"Her eyes are open," one said, "and look, they move!"

Vata licked her lips, pinned Duque to the bottom of the pool and straddled him there. Her head and the tops of her shoulders broke the surface and she gasped great, long breaths with her head thrown back.

"Yes!" Vata said, and the C/P's mind registered, *Her first word in almost three hundred years.* How could the circumstances of that first word be explained to the faithful?

It's to punish me! The thought flooded Simone Rocksack's mind. *She saw it all.* The C/P wondered, then, what sort of punishment Vata might have in mind for Gallow.

It was then the C/P noted that the sloshing from the Vata Pool was not all resulting from the activity inside. The decks themselves heaved in the same slow rhythm.

"What's happening?" The C/P caught herself muttering the

346

question and glanced around to see that she had not been over-heard.

A series of tight-throated moans from Vata, then another explosive, breathless "Yes!" Duque was nearly undetectable under her rippling flanks and hamlike hands.

The C/P's eyes widened in horror and humiliation as she realized that Vata's performance with Duque was a grotesque parody of her last hours with Gallow. Her position wouldn't even allow her to leave the room, to escape the heat that crept outward from the collar of her blue robe to burn her cheeks and her breasts. A trace of sweat graced her upper lip and temples.

Someone burst into the room and shouted, "The kelp!" The voice strained to reach over the babblings of a crowd that was well into a serious hysteria. "The kelp's rocking the Island. It's rocking the whole fucking sea!"

The little stump-legged messenger clapped a fingerless hand over his mouth when he caught sight of the C/P.

There were three sudden cries that brought a chill to the C/P's spine; Vata's thighs shuddered in their grip on Duque and Vata fell back into the pool, wide-eyed and smiling, still anchored to him by their short but stout tether.

The heavy rocking of the decks slackened. The crowd at poolside had stilled with the outburst from Vata. The C/P knew better than to lose this moment. She swallowed hard, lifted her robe to clear her ankles and knelt at the rim of the quieting pool.

"Let us pray," she said, and bowed her head. *Think,* she thought to herself, *think!* Her eyes squinted shut against fear, reality and those difficult traitors, tears.

*Physically, we are created by our reverie—created and lim-
ited by our reverie—for it is the reverie which delineates the
furthest limits of our minds.*
   —Gaston Bachelard, *"The Poetics of Reverie,"*
   from *The Handbook of the Chaplain/Psychiatrist*

On the way down to confront Gallow, Twisp ignored the
spying devices in the ceiling and spoke openly to Nakano. Twisp
no longer doubted that Nakano was playing a devious double
game. What did it matter? Meeting the carpenter, Noah, had
heartened Twisp. Gallow would have to accept the new realities of
Pandora. The kelp wanted him dead and would have him dead.
The open land belonged to everyone. Gallow could only delay the
inevitable; he could not prevent it. He was a prisoner here. All of
his people were prisoners here.

   Nakano only laughed when Twisp spoke of this. "He knows he's
a prisoner. He knows Kareen and Scudi are out there, one step
out of reach."

   "He'll never get them!" Twisp said.

   "Maybe not. But he has the Chief Justice. A bargain may be
possible."

   "It's strange," Twisp said. "Before I met that carpenter up
there, I didn't really know what I was bargaining for."

   "What carpenter?" Nakano asked.

   "The man I was talking to topside. Noah. Didn't you hear him
talking about the ark and Ship speaking to him?"

   "There was no man up there! You were alone."

   "He was right there! How could you have missed him? Long
beard down to here." Twisp passed a hand across his belt line.
"He was calling for a child—Abimael."

   "You must've been hallucinating," Nakano said, his voice mild.
"You were probably narced by the dive."

348

"He gave me a cake," Twisp whispered.

Remembering the fruity flavor of the cake, the sticky feeling of it on his fingers, Twisp lifted his right hand to the level of his eyes and rubbed his fingers together. There was no stickiness. He smelled the fingers. No smell of the cake. He touched his tongue to his fingers. No taste of the cake.

Twisp began to tremble.

"Hey! Take it easy," Nakano soothed. "Anyone can be narced."

"I saw him," Twisp whispered. "We spoke together. Ship made him a promise: 'I will not again curse the ground for mankind's sake.'"

Nakano took a backward step away from Twisp. "You're crazy! You were standing out in the sun all alone."

"No workshop?" Twisp asked, his voice plaintive. "No bearded man in the shadows?"

"There were no shadows. You probably had a touch of the sun. No hat. Big Sun beating down on you. Forget it."

"I can't forget it. I felt him touch me, his finger on my face. He was blind."

"Well, put it behind you. We're about to see GeLaar Gallow and if you're going to bargain with him you'll need your wits about you."

The moving cubicle came to a stop and the hatch opened onto a passage. Nakano and Twisp emerged and were flanked immediately by six armed Mermen.

"This way," Nakano said. "Gallow is waiting for you."

Twisp took a deep, trembling breath and allowed himself to be escorted along the Merman corridor with its sharp corners and hard sides, its unmoving, solid deck.

That Noah was really there, Twisp told himself. The experience had contained too much sense of reality. *The kelp!* He tingled out to the tips of his fingers with realization. Somehow, the kelp had insinuated itself into his mind, taken dominion over his senses!

The realization terrified him and his step faltered.

"Here! Keep up, Mute!" one of the escort barked.

"Easy does it," Nakano cautioned the guard. "He's not used to a deck that doesn't move."

Twisp was surprised by the friendliness in Nakano's voice, his sharpness with the escort. *Does Nakano really sympathize with me?*

They stopped at a wide, rectangular hatchway open to the pas-

349

sage. The room exposed beyond it was large by Islander standards—at least six meters deep and about ten or eleven meters
wide. Gallow sat before a bank of display screens near the back
wall. He turned as Twisp and Nakano entered, leaving the escort
in the passage.

Twisp was immediately struck by the even regularity of Gallow's
features, the silkiness of that long golden mane, which reached
almost to the Merman's shoulders. The cold blue eyes studied
Twisp carefully, pausing only briefly on Twisp's long arms. Gallow came to his feet easily as Nakano and Twisp stopped about
two paces from him.

"Welcome," Gallow said. "Please do not consider yourself our
prisoner. I look upon you as a negotiator for the Islanders."

Twisp scowled. So Nakano had revealed everything!

"Not you alone, of course," Gallow added. "We will be joined
presently by Chief Justice Keel." Gallow's voice was softly persuasive. He smiled warmly.

A charmer, Twisp thought. *Doubly dangerous!*

Gallow studied Twisp's face a blink, those cold blue eyes peeling
the Islander. "I'm told"—he glanced at Nakano standing near
Twisp's left shoulder, then back to Twisp—"that you do not trust
the kelp."

Nakano pursed his lips when Twisp glanced at him. "It's true,
isn't it?" Nakano asked.

"It's true." The admission was wrenched from Twisp.

"I think we have created a monster in bringing the kelp to
consciousness," Gallow said. "Let me tell you that I have never
believed in that part of the kelp project. It was demeaning . . .
immoral . . . treachery against everything human."

Gallow waved his hand, the gesture saying clearly that he had
explained himself sufficiently. He turned to Nakano. "Will you
ask the guard out there if the Chief Justice has recovered enough
to be brought in here?"

Nakano turned on one heel and went out into the passage
where a low-voiced conversation could be heard. Gallow smiled at
Twisp. Presently, Nakano returned.

"What's wrong with Keel?" Twisp demanded. "Recovered from
what?" And he wondered: *Torture?* Twisp did not like Gallow's
smile.

"The Chief Justice, as I prefer to call him, has a digestion problem," Gallow said.

A scuffling sound at the entrance to the room brought Twisp's attention around. He stared hard as two of the escort brought Chief Justice Ward Keel into the room, supporting him as he shuffled stiffly along.

Twisp was shocked. Keel looked near death. Where his skin was visible it was pale and moist. There was a glazed look in his eyes and they did not track together—one peering back toward the passage, the other looking down where he placed each painful step. Keel's neck, supported by that familiar prosthetic framework, still appeared unable to support the man's large head.

Nakano brought a low chair from the side and placed it carefully behind Keel. The escort eased Keel gently into the chair, where he sat a moment, panting. The escort departed.

"I'm sorry, Justice Keel," Gallow said, his voice full of practiced commiseration. "But we really must use what time we have. There are things that I require."

Keel raised his attention slowly, painfully to look up at Gallow. "And what Gallow wants, Gallow gets," Keel said. His voice came out faint and trembling.

"They say you have a digestion problem," Twisp said, looking down at the familiar figure of the Islander who had served so long as a center of topside life.

One of Keel's oddly placed eyes moved to take in Twisp, noting the long arms, the Islander stigmata. Twisp's Islander accent could not be denied.

"You are?" Keel asked, his voice a bit stronger.

"I'm from Vashon, sir. My name's Twisp, Queets Twisp."

"Oh, yes. Fisherman. Why're you here?"

Twisp swallowed. Keel's skin looked like pale sausage casing. The man obviously needed help, not this demanding confrontation with Gallow. Twisp ignored Keel's question and turned on Gallow.

"He should be in a hospital!"

A faint smile tugged at Gallow's mouth. "The Chief Justice has refused medical help."

"Too late for that," Keel said. "What's the purpose of this meeting, Gallow?"

351

"As you know," Gallow said, "Vashon is grounded near one of our barriers. They have survived a storm, but took severe damage. For us, they are now a sitting target."

"But you're trapped here!" Twisp said.

"Indeed," Gallow agreed. "But then, not all of my people are with me. Others are placed strategically throughout Merman and Islander society. They still do my bidding."

"Islanders work for you?" Twisp demanded.

"The C/P among them." Again, that faint smile touched Gallow's mouth.

"That's remarkable after what he did to Guemes," Keel said. He spoke almost normally, but the effort of sitting upright and carrying it off was apparent. Perspiration dotted his wide forehead.

Gallow pointed a finger at Twisp, eyes glittering. "You have Kareen Ale, fisherman Twisp! Vashon has Vata. I will have both!"

"Interesting," Keel said. He looked at Twisp. "You really have Kareen?"

"She's out there in our foil, just within the kelp line where Gallow and his people can't go."

"I think Nakano could go there," Gallow said. "Nakano?"

"Perhaps," Nakano said.

"The kelp passed him unmolested coming in here," Gallow said, smiling at Twisp. "Doesn't it appear likely that Nakano has immunity from the kelp?"

Twisp looked at Nakano, who once more stood passively at one side, obviously listening but not focusing his eyes on any of the speakers.

It came to Twisp then that Nakano did, indeed, belong to the kelp. The big Merman had made some kind of pact with the monster presence in the sea! To Twisp, Nakano appeared the embodiment of Merman killer-viciousness, all of it concealed within a warmly reasonable mask. Was that Nakano's value to the kelp? There could be no missing the fanatic's tone when Nakano spoke of the kelp.

The kelp is my immortality. That was what Nakano had said.

"Really, there should be no need for violence and killing," Gallow said. "We are all reasonable men. You have things you want; I have things I want. Surely there must be some common ground where we can meet."

Twisp's thoughts darted back to that odd topside encounter

with the carpenter, Noah. *If that was really the kelp projecting halluci-nation into his mind, what was the purpose? What was the message?*

Slaughter was wrong. Even if Ship commanded it, slaughter was wrong. Twisp had felt this strongly in Noah's manner and words.

The ark has grounded and the land no longer will be cursed by Ship. Twisp knew vaguely of the ark legend . . . was there a message from Ship here, sent through the kelp?

Gallow, on the other hand, represented treachery, a man who would do anything to gain his ends. Did the C/P really work for him? If so, an evil pact had been forged.

And what if Noah was just hallucination? Nakano could be right: I might have been narced.

Nakano focused abruptly on Twisp and asked: "Why aren't you nauseated?"

It was such a startling question, suggesting Nakano had read Twisp's mind, that Twisp was a moment focusing on the possible implications.

"Are you also sick?" Keel asked, peering up at Twisp.

"I am quite well," Twisp said. He tore his gaze away from Nakano and looked more closely at Gallow, seeing the marks of self-indulgence in the man's face, the sly twist of the smile, the frown lines in the forehead, the downturned creases at the corners of the mouth.

Twisp returned then to the knowledge of what he had to do. Speaking slowly and distinctly, directing his words at Gallow, Twisp said: "The imagination of your heart has been evil from your youth."

Ship's words as reported by Noah came easily from Twisp's mouth and once he had said them, he felt their rightness.

Gallow scowled, then: "You're not much of a diplomat!"

"I'm a simple fisherman," Twisp said.

"Fisherman, but not simple," Keel said. A chuckle turned into a weak, dry cough.

"You think Nakano has immunity from the kelp," Twisp said. "I was his passport. Without me, he would have joined the others. He has told you about the others that the kelp drowned, hasn't he?"

"I tell you the kelp is out of control!" Gallow said. "We have loosed a monster on Pandora. Our ancestors were right to kill it off!"

"Perhaps they were," Twisp agreed. "But we'll not be able to do it again."

"Poisons and burners!" Gallow said.

"No!" The word was torn from Nakano. He glared at Gallow.

"We will only prune it back to manageable size," Gallow said, his voice soothing. "Too small a number to be conscious but large enough to preserve our dead forever."

Nakano nodded curtly but did not relax.

"Tell him, Nakano," Twisp ordered. "Could you really return to the foil without me?"

"Even if the kelp passed me, the crew probably wouldn't let me aboard," Nakano said.

"I don't see how you're going to sink Vashon when it's already aground," Keel said. A painful smile curved the edges of Keel's mouth.

"So you think I'm helpless," Gallow said.

Twisp glanced back at the open hatchway into the passage, the guards clustered there trying to make it appear that they were not listening.

"Don't your people know how you've trapped them?" Twisp demanded, his voice loud and carrying. "As long as *you* live, *they're* prisoners here!"

Blood suffused Gallow's face. "But Vashon—"

"Vashon is in a perimeter of kelp that you can't penetrate!" Twisp said. "Nobody you send against Vashon can get through!" He looked at Keel. "Mr. Justice, isn't that—"

"No, no," Keel husked. "Go on. You're doing fine."

Gallow made a visible attempt to control his anger, taking several deep breaths, squaring his shoulders. He said: "LTAs can—"

"LTAs are limited in what they can do," Nakano interrupted. "You know what happened to the one I was on. They are vulnerable."

Gallow looked at Nakano as though seeing the man for the first time. "Do I hear my faithful Nakano correctly?"

"Don't you understand?" Nakano asked, his voice softly penetrating. "It doesn't matter what happens to us. Come, I will go into the kelp with you. Let it take us."

Gallow backed two steps away from Nakano.

354

"Come," Nakano insisted. "The Chief Justice obviously is dying. The three of us will go together. We will not die. We will live forever in the kelp."

"You fool!" Gallow snapped. "The kelp can die! It was killed once and that could happen again!"

"The kelp does not agree," Nakano said. "Avata lives forever!" His voice lifted on the last sentence and a wild light came into his eyes.

"Nakano, Nakano, my most trusted companion," Gallow said, his voice pitched to its most persuasive tone. "Let us not permit the heat of the moment to sway us." Gallow sent an apprehensive glance toward the listening guards at the hatchway. "Of course the kelp can live forever . . . but not in such numbers that it threatens our existence."

Nakano's expression did not change.

Keel, watching the scene through pain-glazed eyes, thought: *Nakano knows him! Nakano does not trust him!*

Twisp entertained a similar thought and knew he had found the ultimate leverage to use against Gallow. *Nakano can be turned against his chief.*

Gallow constructed a rueful smile, which he turned toward Keel. "Mr. Justice Keel, let us not forget that the C/P is still mine! And *I* will have the hyb tanks."

That's his best shot! Keel thought.

"I'll bet the C/P doesn't know it was you who sank Guemes," Keel managed.

"Can anyone carry such an accusation to her?" Gallow asked. He looked blandly around him.

Is that our death warrant? Twisp wondered. *Will we be silenced permanently?* He decided on a bold attack.

"If we do not return to the foil, they will broadcast that accusation and Bushka's statement confirming it."

"Bushka?" Gallow's eyes showed both shock and glee. "Do you mean Bushka, the Islander who stole our sub?" Gallow smiled at Nakano. "Do you hear that? They know where to find the sub thief."

Nakano did not change expression.

Gallow glanced at the chrono beside his communications terminal. "Well, well! It's almost time for the midday meal. Fisherman Twisp, why don't you stay here with the Chief Justice? I'll have

355

food sent in. Nakano and I will dine together and consult on possible compromises. You and the Chief Justice can do the same."

Gallow moved to Nakano's side. "Come, old friend," Gallow said. "I didn't save your life to provide myself with an opponent."

Nakano glanced at Twisp, the thought plain on the big face. *Why did you save my life?*

Twisp chose to answer the unspoken question. "You know why." And he thought: *I saved you simply because you were in danger.* Nakano already knew this.

Nakano resisted the pressure on his arm.

"Do not quarrel with me, old friend," Gallow said. "Both of us will go to the kelp in time, but it's too soon. There's much yet for us to do."

Slowly, Nakano allowed himself to be guided from the room.

His muscles trembling so hard that his great head shook with visible tremors, Keel lifted his attention to Twisp. "We do not have much time," Keel said. "Clear that table at the end of the room and help me to stretch out on it."

Moving quickly, Twisp swept the objects off the table, then returned to Keel. Slipping his long arms under the Chairman, Twisp lifted the old body, shocked at how light the man was. Keel was nothing but thin bones in a loose sack of skin. Gently, Twisp carried the Chairman across the room and eased him onto the table.

Weakly, Keel fumbled with the harness of his prosthesis. "Help me get this damned thing off," he gasped.

Twisp unbuckled the harness and slipped the prosthesis away from Keel's back and shoulders, letting it drop to the floor.

Keel sighed with relief. "I prefer to leave this world more or less as I came into it," he grated, every word draining him. "No, don't object. Both of us know I'm dying."

"Sir, isn't there anything I can do to help you?"

"You've already done it. I was afraid I'd have to die in the midst of strangers."

"Surely, we can do something to . . ."

"Really, there's nothing. The best doctors on Vashon have conveyed to me the verdict of that higher Committee on Vital Forms. No . . . you are the perfect person for this moment . . . not so close to me that you'll become maudlin, yet close enough that I know you care."

"Sir . . . anything I can do . . . anything . . ."

"Use your own superb good sense in dealing with Gallow. You've already seen that Nakano can be turned against him."

"Yes, I saw that."

"There is one thing."

"Anything."

"Don't let them give me to the kelp. I don't want that. Life should have a body of its own, even such a poor body as this one I'm about to leave."

"I'll—" Twisp broke off. Honesty forced him to remain silent. What could he do?

Keel sensed this confusion. "You will do what you can," he said. "I know that. And if you fail, I am not your judge."

Tears filled Twisp's eyes. "Anything I can do . . . I'll do."

"Don't be too hard on the C/P," Keel whispered.

"What?" Twisp bent close to the Chairman's lips.

Keel repeated it, adding: "Simone is a sensitive and bitter woman and—and you've seen Gallow. Imagine how attractive he would seem to her."

"I understand," Twisp said.

"I'm filled with joy that the Islands can produce such good men," Keel said. "I am ready to be judged."

Twisp wiped at his eyes, still bending close to hear the Chairman's last words. When Keel did not continue, Twisp became aware that there was no sound of breathing from the supine figure. Twisp put a hand to the artery at Keel's neck. No pulse. He straightened.

What can I do?

Was there anything combustible here to burn the old body and prevent the Mermen from consigning Keel to the sea? He looked all around the room. Nothing. Twisp stared helplessly at the body on the table.

"Is he dead?" It was Nakano speaking from the hatchway.

Twisp turned to find the big Merman standing just inside the room.

The tears on Twisp's face were sufficient answer. "He's not to be given to the kelp," Twisp said.

"Friend Twisp, he died but he need not be dead," Nakano said. "You can meet him again in Avata."

Twisp clenched his fists, his long arms trembling. "No! He asked me to prevent that!"

"But it's not up to us," Nakano said. "If he was a deserving man, Avata will wish to accept him."

Twisp jumped to the side of the table and stood with his back to it.

"Let me take him to Avata," Nakano said. He moved toward Twisp.

As Nakano came within range of those long arms, Twisp shot out a net-calloused fist, leaning his shoulder behind it. The blow struck with blinding speed on the side of Nakano's jaw. Nakano's heavily muscled neck absorbed most of the shock but his eyes glazed. Before he could recover, Twisp leaped forward and wrenched one of Nakano's arms backward, intending to throw the man to the deck.

Nakano recovered enough to tense his muscles and prevent this. He turned slowly against Twisp's pressure, moving like a great pillar of kelp.

Abruptly, the guards swarmed into the room. Other hands grabbed Twisp and jerked him aside, pinning him to the deck.

"Don't hurt him!" Nakano shouted.

The pressures on Twisp eased but did not leave.

Nakano stood over Twisp, a sad look on the big face, a touch of blood at the corner of his mouth.

"Please, friend Twisp, I mean you no harm. I mean only to honor the Chief Justice and Chairman of the Committee on Vital Forms, a man who has served us so well for so long."

One of the guards pinning Twisp down snickered.

Immediately, Nakano grasped the man by a shoulder and lifted him like a sack of fishmeal, hurling him aside.

"These Islanders you sneer at are as dear to Avata as any of us!" Nakano bellowed. "Any among you who forgets this will answer to me!"

The abused guard stood with his back to a bulkhead, his face contorted with fear.

Indicating Twisp with one thick finger, Nakano said: "Hold

358

him but let him up." Nakano went to the table and lifted Keel's body gently in his arms. He turned and strode past the guards, pausing at the hatchway. "When I have gone, take the fisherman to our leader. GeLaar Gallow is topside and has things to say." Nakano looked thoughtfully at Twisp. "He needs your help to get the hyb tanks—they're on their way down."

Hybernation is to hibernation as death is to sleep. Closer to death than it is to life, hybernation can be lifted only by the grace of Ship.

—the Histories

While Brett held Bushka down, Ale tied off the stump of Bushka's left arm with a length of dive harness. Bushka lay just inside the main hatch, the sea surface visible through the plaz port behind him. Big Sun, just entering its afternoon quadrant, painted oily coils across the kelp fronds out there, now bright and now dulled as clouds scudded overhead.

A moan escaped Bushka.

The foil rolled gently in a low sea. Ale braced herself against a bulkhead while she worked.

"There," she said as she tied off the dive harness. Blood smeared the deck around them and their dive suits were red with it.

Ale turned and shouted up the passage behind Brett. "Shadow! Do you have that cot ready?"

"I'm bringing it!"

Brett took a deep breath and looked out the plaz at the quiescent kelp—so harmless-looking, so tranquil. The horizon was an absurd pinkish gray where Little Sun would soon lift into view, joining its giant companion.

It had been a hellish half hour.

Bushka, meandering aimlessly around the pilot cabin, had lulled them into a sense of security by his casual movements. Abruptly, he had dashed down the passageway and hit the manual override on the main hatch. Water had come blasting in at the high pressure of their depth—almost thirty-five meters down. Bushka had been prepared. Standing to one side of the blasting

360

water, he had grabbed an emergency tank-breather outfit stored beside the hatch, slipping swiftly into the harness.

Brett and Panille, running after him, had been spilled and tumbled in the wash of water boiling down the passage. Only Scudi's alertness in sealing off a section between them and the open hatch had saved the foil and its occupants.

Bushka had kicked easily out into the kelp jungle where the foil lay on bottom.

Scudi, faced with tons of water in the foil, had blown tanks and started the pumps, shouting for Kareen to help Brett and Shadow. The foil had lifted slowly, floating upward through the massed kelp.

Brett and Panille, splashing their way back into the cabin, had accepted a hand from Kareen. Scudi, seated at the controls, spared a glance for Brett to reassure herself that he was safe, then returned her attention to the watery world visible through the plaz.

"It's tearing him apart!" Scudi gasped.

The others sloshed to a position behind Scudi and looked outside. The foil slithered upward against giant kelp fronds, giving those inside the pilot cabin a dimly lighted view of Bushka close beside them. One large kelp tentacle, wrapped around his body, held Bushka fast while another tentacle gripped his left arm. A cloud of dark liquid flooded the water around Bushka's arm.

Kareen gasped.

Brett understood then—the cloud: *blood!* The arm had been torn from Bushka's body.

As though it wanted to spit him out, the kelp tentacles whipped away from Bushka and shunted him swiftly upward.

Scudi tipped the foil's nose up and drove for the surface. They found Bushka there, half-conscious and bleeding dangerously. A hunt of dashers, coming to the smell of blood, was whipped back by kelp fronds.

Later, after Kareen had treated Bushka, Brett and Panille lashed him to the cot and carried him forward. Ale walked alongside. "He's lost a lot of blood," she said. "The brachial artery was wide open."

Scudi remained at the helm, sparing only a brief glance at Bushka's pale face as the cot was lowered to the deck behind her. She held the foil in a tight circle within a kelp-free area. Choppy waves drummed a dulled *tunk-tunk* against the hull. The last of the unwanted water had gone overboard but the decks were still damp with it.

Scudi, the image of Bushka's injuries fresh in her mind, thought: *Ship save us! The kelp has turned vicious!*

Panille stood above Bushka. A wash of agony grayed Bushka's face but he appeared conscious. Seeing this, Panille demanded, "What were you trying to do?"

"Shhhh," Ale cautioned.

"'S'all right," Bushka managed. "Was gonna kill Gallow."

Panille could not suppress his outrage. "You almost killed us all!"

Kareen pulled Panille away.

Brett slid into the seat beside Scudi and looked out at the dark pile of the outpost with its foam-laced base. Little Sun had risen and the water was bright with the double light.

"Kelp," Bushka said.

"Hush," Ale said. "Save your strength."

"Gotta talk. Kelp has all the Guemes dead . . . in it. All there. Said I tore off arm of humanity . . . punished me in kind. Damn! Damn!" He tried to look at the place where his arm had been but the lashings on the cot restrained him.

Scudi stared wide-eyed at Brett. Was it possible the kelp took on the personality of all the dead it had absorbed? Would all the old scores be settled? Given consciousness finally and words in which to express itself, the kelp spoke in violent action. She shuddered as she looked out at the green fronds surrounding the foil.

"There are dashers all over the place," Scudi said.

"Where . . . where's my arm?" Bushka moaned.

His eyes were closed and his large head looked even larger against the pale fabric of the cot.

"Packed in ice in the cooler," Ale said. "We'll interfere as little as possible with the wound tissue. Better chance for reattachment."

"Kelp knew I was just a fool that Gallow . . . took advantage of," Bushka groaned. He twisted his head from side to side. "Why'd it hurt *me?*"

A heavy gust of wind popped the foil hard and thrust it sideways against the kelp. A loud thump sounded amidships and the foil heeled, righting itself with a rasping hiss.

"What is it? What's that?" Ale demanded.

Brett pointed to the sky above the outpost. "I think we've just had our attention called to something. Look! Have you ever seen that many LTAs?"

"LTAs hell!" Panille said. "Ship's guts! Those are hylighters! Thousands of them."

Brett stared open-mouthed. Like all Pandoran children, he had watched holos of the kelp's spore carriers, a phenomenon unseen on Pandora for generations. *Panille was right! Hylighters!*

"They're so beautiful," Scudi murmured.

Brett had to agree. The hylighters, giant organic hydrogen bags, danced with rainbow colors in the doubled sunlight. They drifted high across the outpost, moving southwest on a steady wind.

"It's out of our hands now," Panille said. "The kelp will do its own propagating."

"They're coming down," Brett said. "Look. Some of them are trailing tentacles in the water."

The flight of hylighters, well past the outpost now, moved in a gentle slope of wind toward the sea.

"It's almost as though they were being directed," Scudi said. "See how they move together."

Once more, something hard banged against the foil's hull. A channel opened beside them, spreading outward toward the place where the hylighters were coming down close above the water. Slowly at first, a current moved the foil into the new channel.

"Better go along with it," Panille said.

"But Twisp is still there at the outpost!" Brett objected.

"Kelp's directing this show," Panille said. "Your friend will have to take his own chances."

"I think Shadow's right," Scudi ventured. She pointed toward the outpost. "See? There are more hylighters. They're almost touching the rock."

"But what if Twisp comes back and we aren't . . . ."

"I'll bring us back as soon as the kelp lets us," Scudi said. She fired up the ramjets.

"No! I'll take breather tanks and go out to—"

"Brett!" Scudi put a hand on his arm. "You saw what it did to Bushka."

"But I haven't hurt it . . . or anyone. That Merman would have killed me."

363

"We don't know what it'll do," Scudi said.

"She's right," Panille said. "What good would you be to your friend without arms?"

Brett sank back into the seat.

Scudi pushed the throttles ahead and lowered the foils. The boat gathered speed, lifted and swept down the channel toward the descending hylighters.

Brett sat in silence. He felt suddenly that his Mermen companions had turned against him, even Scudi. How could they know what the kelp wanted? So it opened a channel through its heavy growth! So it directed a current through that channel! Twisp might need him back there where they were supposed to be waiting.

Abruptly, Brett shook his head. He thought how Twisp would react to such protests. *Don't be a fool!* The kelp had spoken without misunderstanding. Bushka . . . the channel . . . the current— words could say no clearer what had to be done now. Scudi and the others had merely understood and accepted it more quickly.

With a quick chopping motion, Scudi cut the power and the foil settled in a heaving surge that sent waves curling outward on both sides.

"We're blocked," she said.

They looked ahead. Not only had kelp closed the channel through which the foil had come, but fronds and stalks lifted out of the water ahead of them. A low, thick forest of green blocked their passage.

Brett glanced left. The outpost loomed high there, no more than three klicks away. Hylighters continued to descend about a klick ahead of them, massed flocks of them.

Panille spoke from directly behind Brett. "I don't remember them as being that colorful in the holos."

"A new breed, no doubt of it," Kareen said.

"What do we do now?" Brett asked.

"We sit here until we find out why the kelp directed us to this place," Scudi said.

Brett looked up at the descending flocks of hylighters. Dark tentacles reached down toward the water. Sunlight flashed rainbow iridescence off the great bags.

"The histories say the kelp makes its own hydrogen the way you Islanders do," Panille said. "The bags are extruded deep underwater, filled and sent flying to spread the spores. One of my ancestors rode a hylighter." He spoke in a breathless whisper. "They've always fascinated me. I've dreamed of this day."

"What are they doing?" Scudi asked. "Why would they bring spores here? There's kelp all around us."

"You're assuming they're intelligently directed," Kareen said. "They're probably going wherever the wind takes them."

Panille shook his head sharply. "No. Who controls the currents controls the temperature of the surface water. Who controls that directs the winds."

"Then what are they doing?" Scudi repeated. "They're not drifting very fast anymore. It's as though they were assembling here."

"The hyb tanks?" Kareen asked.

"How could the kelp—" Scudi began. She broke off, then: "Is this where they're supposed to come down?"

"Near enough," Kareen said. "Shadow?"

"The correct quadrant," he said. He glanced at a chrono. "By the original schedule, splashdown's already overdue."

"There's a strange hylighter," Brett said. "Or is that really an LTA?" He pointed upward, his finger almost touching the overhead plaz.

"Parachute!" Panille said. "Ship's guts! There comes the first hyb tank!"

"Look at the hylighters!" Scudi said.

The colorful bags had begun a swirling motion, opening a space in their center. The open space drifted somewhat south and a bit west, presenting a net of sea to catch the descending parachute.

Something could be seen dangling from the parachute now—a silvery cylinder that reflected bright flashes from the suns.

"Ship! That thing is big!" Panille said.

"I wonder what's in it," Kareen whispered.

"We're about to discover that," Brett said. "Look! Above the parachute—there comes another one . . . and another."

"Ohhhh, if I could only get my hands on one of them . . . just one," Panille said.

The first hyb tank was now little more than a hundred meters above the water. It descended swiftly, the actual splashdown concealed within the ring of hylighters. A second hyb tank fell into the open circle, a third . . . fourth . . . The watchers counted twenty of them, some larger than the foil.

The circle of hylighters closed in as the last tank hit the water. Immediately, a lane through the kelp began to spread from the foil's blocked position to where the hylighters had collected.

"We're being asked to join them," Scudi said. She fired up the rams and eased the foil ahead at hull speed, keeping it just off the step. A bow wave spread on both sides. The hylighters parted as the foil drew near them, opening a passage into a kelp-free circle where the great tanks bobbed.

The occupants of the foil stared in wonder at the vista opened to them. Hylighter tentacles could be seen working over the closure mechanisms of the tanks, opening them and snaking inside. Wide curved hatches swung aside to the probing tentacles. Abruptly, one of the opened tanks tipped, admitting a surge of water. White-bellied sea mammals emerged and immediately dove into the water.

"Orcas," Panille breathed. "Look!" He pointed across Brett's shoulder. "Humpback whales! Just the way they looked in the holos."

"My whales," Scudi whispered.

The channel that had been opened for the foil curved left now, directing them to a cluster of six tanks being held side by side in a nest of kelp. Hylighter tentacles could be seen writhing and twisting into the tanks.

As the foil neared this cluster, a dark tentacle emerged with a struggling human form—pale-skinned and naked. Another tentacle came up with another human . . . another . . . another . . . A spectrum of skin shades came out of the tanks—from darker than Scudi to paler than Kareen Ale.

"What are they doing with those poor people?" Kareen demanded.

The faces of the people being taken from the tanks betrayed obvious terror, but the terror began to subside even as the foil's occupants watched. Slowly, hylighters carrying humans began to drift toward the foil.

"There's why we were brought in," Brett said. "Come on, Shadow. Let's open the hatch."

Scudi silenced the foil's jets. "We can't handle that many people," she said. She pointed at the massed hylighters removing

366

other humans from the adjacent tanks. More than a hundred human figures could be seen grasped in hylighter tentacles and more humans were being removed from the tanks every second. "That many will sink us!" Scudi said.

Brett, hesitating in the passageway to follow the direction of Scudi's pointing finger, said: "We'll have to tow them to the outpost. We'll see if we can get a line to them." He whirled and dashed down the passage toward the main hatch. Panille could be heard running behind him.

Hylighters already were clustering around the hatchway when Brett opened it. A tentacle snaked in the opening and grasped Brett. He froze. Words filled his mind, clear and perfect, without any secondary sounds to distort them.

"Gentle human who is loved by Avata's beloved Scudi, do not fear. We bring you Shipclones to live in peace beside all of you who share Pandora with Avata."

Brett gasped and sensed Panille beside him: muddy thoughts— nowhere near as clear as those bell-like words entering his senses through the hylighter tentacles. Panille projected awe, schoolboy memories of holoviews displaying hylighters, family stories of that first Pandoran Panille . . . then fear that the mass of humans being delivered by the hylighters would sink the foil.

"Hylighters will buoy you," the tentacles transmitted. "Do not fear. What a splendid day this is! What marvelous surprises have come to us, the gift of blessed Ship."

Slowly, Brett regained the use of his own senses. He found himself braced against loops of hylighter tentacles. Naked humans were being slipped through the hatchway one after another. How tall the newcomers were! Some of them had to duck in the passageway.

Panille looked dazed in a similar tentacle grasp. He waved the newcomers up the passage toward the control cabin.

"Some of you can go into the cargo bays along this passage," Brett called.

They went where Brett and Panille directed them . . . no questions, no arguments. They appeared to be in shock from awakening into the tentacles of hylighters.

"We're being moved toward the outpost," Panille said. He nodded toward the edge of black rock visible out the hatchway. The

367

sound of the surf against the base of the outpost was clearly audible.

"Gallow!" Brett said.

As Brett spoke, the hylighter tentacles unwound from his body. Panille, too, was released. The space around them remained crowded with silent newcomers. More could be seen held in hylighter tentacles, other tentacles clutching the lip of the hatchway. Slowly, he began squeezing his way forward, apologizing, feeling the pressure of naked skin that made way for him.

The pilot cabin was not quite as crowded as the passage. Space had been left around the unconscious form of Bushka on the cot. More space insulated the command seats where Scudi and Kareen sat. A lacework of hylighter tentacles covered most of the plaz, leaving only small framed bits of the forward view. The outpost loomed high there, the surf sound loud.

"Kelp is right up against the outpost now," Kareen said. "Look at it! There's almost no open space left."

One of the newcomers, a man so tall that his head almost touched the top of the cabin, came forward and bent to peer through a small opening in the lacework of hylighter tentacles. He straightened presently and looked down at the webs between Scudi's toes, then to the similar growth on Kareen's feet. He brought his attention at last to Brett's large eyes.

"God save us!" he said. "If we breed on this planet will our offspring all be deformed?"

Brett was caught first by the man's accent, an odd lilting in the way he spoke, then by the words. The man looked at Mermen and Islanders with the same obviously revolted expression.

Kareen, shocked, shot a glance at Brett and then at the cabin full of giant humans, the looks of dazed withdrawal slowly vanishing from all of those faces—those strangely similar faces. Kareen wondered how these people could identify each other . . . except for the variations in skin tone. They all looked so much alike!

It dawned on her then that she was seeing Ship-normals . . . human-normals. She, with her small stature and partly webbed toes, she was the freak.

Ship! How would these newcomers take to people like the Chief Justice or even Queets Twisp with his ungainly arms? What would they say on encountering the C/P?

368

The foil grated against rock then . . . again . . . again. It lifted slightly and was set down hard on a solid surface.

"We've arrived," Scudi said.

"And we're going to have to deal with GeLaar Gallow somehow," Panille said.

"If the kelp hasn't already done it for us," Kareen said.

"There's no telling what it'll do," Panille said. "I'm afraid Twisp was right. It's not to be trusted."

"It can be damned convincing, though," Brett said, recalling the touch of hylighters at the hatchway.

"That's its real danger," Panille said.

Fools! who slaughtered the cattle sacred to the sun-king;
behold, the god deprived them of their day of homecoming.
                                        —Homer, Shiprecords

Twisp could hear Gallow's people talking down in the basin, a nervousness in their chatter that told him the strength of his own position. Gallow had brought him up a narrow trail cut in the rock and out onto a flat promontory that jutted seaward on the southeastern edge of the outpost. A breeze blew against Twisp's face.

"One day, I will have my administrative building here," he said, gesturing expansively.

Twisp glanced around him at the black rock sparkling with mineral fragments in the light of both suns. He had seen many days such as this one—both suns up, the sea rolling easily under a blanket of kelp—but never from such a vantage. Not even the highest point on Vashon commanded such a view—high, solid and unmoving.

Gallow would build here?

Twisp tried to catch snatches of the conversations from below them, but mostly it was words of nervousness that permeated this place. Gallow was not immune to it.

"The hyb tanks will be coming down soon," he said, "and I'll have them!"

Twisp looked out at all that kelp, remembering Nakano's words. *"He needs your help."*

"How will you recover the tanks?" Twisp asked, his tone reasonable. He felt no need to mention the ring of kelp around this rocky outcrop lifting from the sea. From this vantage, it appeared to Twisp that the kelp was even closer than it had been when he and Nakano had swum away from the foil.

370

"LTAs," Gallow said, pointing at the partly filled bags of three LTAs waiting on their pad. The Mermen working around the LTAs appeared to be the only purposeful figures in the basin.

"It would help, of course, if we had your foil," Gallow said. "I'm prepared to offer a great deal in return for that."

"You have a foil," Twisp said. "I saw it anchored next to the lee side of this place." He kept his tone casual, thinking how like so many other times this was—bargaining for the best price on his catch.

"We both know the kelp won't give passage to our foil," Gallow said. "But if you were to return to your foil with Nakano . . ."

Twisp took a deep breath. Yes, this was like bargaining for his catch, but there was a profound difference. You could respect the fish-buyers even while you opposed them. Gallow revolted him. Twisp fought to keep this emotion out of his voice.

"I don't know that you have anything to offer me," he said.

"Power! A share in the new Pandora!"

"Is that all?"

"All?" Gallow appeared truly surprised.

"Seems to me the new Pandora's going to happen anyway. I don't see where you're going to have much influence in it, the kelp wanting your hide and all."

"You don't understand," Gallow said. "Merman Mercantile controls most of the food sources, the processing. Kareen Ale can be bent to our needs and her shares will—"

"You don't have Kareen Ale."

"With your foil . . . and the people in it . . ."

"From what I could see, Shadow Panille has Kareen Ale. And as far as Scudi Wang is concerned—"

"She's a child who—"

"I think maybe she's a very wealthy child."

"Exactly! Your foil and the people in it are the key!"

"But *you* don't have that key. *I* have it."

"And I have you," Gallow said, his voice hard.

"And the kelp has Chairman Keel," Twisp said.

"But it does not have me and I still have the means of recovering the hyb tanks. The LTAs will be clumsier and slower, but they can do it."

"You're offering me a subordinate position in·your organization," Twisp said. "What's to prevent me from grabbing it all once I'm back on the foil?"

"Nakano."

Twisp chewed his lip to keep from laughing. Gallow had very little buying power. None at all, really, with the kelp against him and the foil in the hands of someone who wanted to beat him to the tanks. Twisp looked up at the sky. The tanks would be coming down within sight of this place, Gallow said. His people at the Launch Base had alerted Gallow. And that was another consideration: Gallow had followers in many places . . . Islanders as well.

But the hyb tanks!

Twisp could not prevent a deep sense of excitement at the thought of them. He had grown up on stories speculating about the tanks' contents. They were a bag of prizes meant to humanize Pandora.

Could the kelp prevent that?

Twisp turned and looked at the LTAs. No doubt those things could move above the kelp's reach. But would the kelp let airborne humans pluck the prize from the sea? It all depended on where the tanks came down. There was kelp-free sea surface visible from this high point. A very uncertain lottery, though.

Gallow moved up beside Twisp to share his view of the outpost's interior basin and its waiting LTAs.

"There's my fallback position," Gallow said. He nodded toward the LTAs.

Twisp knew what he would do now if this were bargaining for his catch. Threaten to go to another buyer. Get caustic and let this buyer know he had no status in the larger game.

"I think you're nothing but eelshit," Twisp said. "Concentrate on the facts. If the tanks land in kelp, you're finished. Without hostages, you're just a pitiful handful of people on one little bit of land. You may have followers elsewhere but I'm betting they'll desert you the second they recognize how powerless you really are."

"I still have you," Gallow grated. "And don't make any mistakes about what I can do to you!"

"What can you do?" Twisp asked, his voice at its most reasonable. "We're alone up here. All I have to do is grab you and dive off this place into the sea. The kelp will get us both."

Gallow smiled and slipped a lasgun from the pouch pocket at his waist.

"I thought you'd have one of those," Twisp said.

"I would take great pleasure in cutting you into pieces slowly," Gallow said.

"Except that you need me," Twisp said. "You're no gambler, Gallow. You like sure things."

Gallow scowled.

Twisp inclined his head toward the LTAs. The bags were beginning to swell. Someone was pumping hydrogen into them.

"Those are not a sure thing," Twisp said.

Gallow forced his features into a semblance of a smile. He looked down at the weapon in his hand. "Why are we arguing?"

"Is that what we're doing?" Twisp asked.

"You are stalling," Gallow said. "You want to see where the tanks come down."

Twisp smiled.

"For an Islander, you're pretty smart," Gallow said. "You know what I'm offering. You could have anything you want—money, women . . ."

"How do you know what I want?" Twisp asked.

"You're no different from anyone else in that," Gallow said. He sent his glance along Twisp's long arms. "There might even be a few Mermen women who wouldn't find you objectionable."

Gallow pocketed his lasgun and displayed his empty hand. "See? I know what'll work with you. I know what I can give you."

Twisp shook his head slowly from side to side. Again, he looked at the LTAs. *Objectionable?* One step and he would have his long arms on the most objectionable human he had ever met. Two more steps and they would be over the side into the sea.

But then I might never know how it came out.

He thought about finding himself conscious in the kelp's vast reservoir of awareness. He shared Keel's revulsion to that end. *Damn! And I couldn't help the old man! Gallow owes us for that!*

A shadow passed across Twisp, bringing an immediate coolness from the breeze that tugged at him. He thought it just another cloud but Gallow gasped and something touched Twisp's shoulder, his cheek—a long and ropy something.

Twisp looked up into the base of a hylighter then, seeing the

373

long, dark tentacles all around, feeling them grab him. Somewhere, he could hear screaming.

Gallow?

A flawless voice filled Twisp's senses, seeming to come at him along every nerve channel—hearing, touch, sight . . . all of him was caught up in that voice.

"Welcome to Avata, fisherman Twisp," the voice said. "What is your wish?"

"Put me down," Twisp gasped.

"Ahhh, you wish to retain the flesh. Then Avata cannot put you down here. The flesh would be damaged, very likely destroyed. Be patient and have no fear. Avata will put you down with your friends."

"Gallow?" Twisp managed.

"He is not your friend!"

"I know that!"

"And so does Avata. Gallow will be put down, as you so quaintly phrase it, but from a great height. Gallow is no longer anything but a curiosity, no more than an aberration. Better to consider him a disease, infectious and sometimes deadly. Avata is curing the infected body."

Twisp grew aware then that he dangled high in the air, wind blowing past him. A great expanse of kelp spread out far below him. A sudden feeling of vertigo tightened his chest and throat, filled him with dizziness.

"Do not fear," the flawless voice said. "Avata cherishes the friends and companions of beloved Scudi Wang."

Twisp slowly twisted his head upward, feeling the ropy tentacles holding him tight around the waist and legs, seeing the dark underside of the bag that suspended this twining mass.

Avata?

"You see what you call hylighter," the voice told him. "Once more Avata spawns in the mother-sea. Once more there is rock. That which humans destroyed, humans have restored. Thereby, you learn from your mistakes."

A great feeling of bitterness welled up in Twisp. "So you're going to fix everything! No more mistakes. Everything perfect in the most perfect of worlds."

A sense of laughter without sound permeated Twisp then. The

374

flawless voice came light and cajoling: "Do not project your fears upon Avata. Here is only the mirror that reveals yourself." The voice changed, becoming almost strident. "Now! Here below you have your friends. Treat them well and share your joys with them. Have not Islanders learned this lesson well from the human errors of the past?"

*If war does come, the best thing to do will be to just stay
alive and thus add to the numbers of sane people.*
—George Orwell, Shiprecords

The forward bulk of Vashon was close enough in the darkness that Brett could pick out the lights of the more prominent
structures. He sat beside Scudi in the control seats of the foil,
hearing the low-voiced conversations behind him. Most of the
Shipclones had been deposited on the outpost amidst the fearful
and chastened Green Dashers. The task of feeding all those newcomers had become a primary problem. Only a representative few
of the people from the hyb tanks remained in the foil. The Clone
called Bickel stood close behind Brett, watching the same night
view of their approach to Vashon.

That Bickel would be one to watch, Brett thought. A demanding, powerful man. And large. All of these Shipclones were big!
This amplified the food problem in a daunting way.

Someone came up from the rear of the cabin and stopped near
the big Shipclone.

"There will be a lot of debriefing once we get there." The voice
was Kareen Ale's.

Brett heard Twisp cough at the rear of the cabin. *Debriefing?
Probably. Some of the old routines still had value.* Twisp's experience in
the grip of the hylighter must be added to all of the other new
knowledge.

. . . *beloved Scudi Wang.*

Brett glanced at Scudi's profile outlined in the dim lights from
the instruments ahead of her. Something filled his breast at the
very thought of Scudi. *Beloved, beloved,* he thought.

The twin lane of blue lights that marked Vashon's main harbor
entrance loomed dead ahead. Scudi dropped the foil down onto
its hull.

376

"They'll have medical people waiting for Bushka," Scudi said. "Better get him back to the hatch."

"Right." Ale could be heard leaving.

"Is that land just beyond the Island?" Bickel asked.

Brett shuddered. The newcomers always sounded so loud!

"It's land," Scudi said.

"It must be at least two hundred meters high," Brett said. He had to remind himself that neither this newcomer nor Scudi could see the land mass as clearly as he could.

The foil was into the enclosing arms of Vashon's harbor then. Brett popped the cabin emergency hatch beside him and leaned out into the wind, seeing the familiar outline of this haven he had known so intimately. That other time of intimacy with this place seemed to him now eons in the past. His position in the foil's control cabin gave him a commanding view of the approach—the rimlights, Islanders racing to grab the foil's lines as Scudi backed the jets. The hissing of the jets went silent. The foil rocked and then was snugged against the bubbly at the dockside. Scudi turned on the cabin lights.

Familiar faces looked up at Brett—Islander faces he had noticed in passing many times. And with them came the old familiar stench of Vashon.

"Whew!" Bickel said. "That place stinks!"

Brett felt Scudi's arm go around his neck and her head bent close to his. "I don't mind the smell, love," she whispered.

"We'll clean it up when we get on land," Brett said. He looked up at the great mass of starlighted rock that dominated the sky behind Vashon. Was that where he and Scudi would go? Or would they return down under and work to reclaim other places like this one?

A voice called up to them from dockside. "That you, Brett Norton?"

"Here I am!"

"Your folks are waiting at the Hall of Art. Say they're anxious to see you."

"Would you tell them we'll meet them at the Ace of Cups?" Brett called. "I've got some friends I want them to meet."

"Jesus Christ!" Bickel's voice was a sharp exhalation behind Brett. "Look at the deformities! How the hell can those people live?"

377

"Happily," Brett said. "Get used to it, Shipclone. To us, they're beautiful." Gently, he pressed back against Scudi, indicating that he wanted to get out of the control seats.

Together, they slid out of the seats and looked up at the towering figure of Bickel.

"What'd you call me?" Bickel demanded.

"Shipclone," Brett said. "Every living human being Ship brought to Pandora was a Clone."

"Yeah . . . yeah." Bickel rubbed at his chin and glanced out at the throng on dockside. The newcomers emerging there towered over the Islanders.

"Jesus help us," Bickel whispered. "When we created Ship . . . we never suspected . . ." He shook his head.

"I would be careful who you tell your story of Ship's origin," Brett cautioned. "Certain WorShipers might not like it."

"Like it or lump it," Bickel growled. "Ship was created by men like me. Our goal was a mechanical consciousness."

"And when you achieved this . . . this consciousness," Scudi said, "it . . ."

"It took over," Bickel said. "It said it was our god and we were to determine how we would worship it."

"How strange," Scudi murmured.

"You better believe it," Bickel said. "Does anyone here have any idea how long we were in hybernation?"

"What difference does it make?" Brett asked. "You're alive here and now and that's what you'll have to deal with."

"Hey, kid!" It was Twisp calling from the passageway. "Come on! I've been waiting for you dockside. Lots of things happening. We've got Merman Patrols underwater all around that land mass—burning dashers. Dashers want back on the land, too."

"We're coming." Brett took Scudi's hand and headed toward the passage.

"Vata and Duque are gone," Twisp said. "Someone broke open the Vata Pool and they're just gone."

Brett hesitated, feeling the sweat start in his hand against Scudi's. *Gallow?* No . . . Gallow was dead. Then some of Gallow's people? He quickened his pace.

A raucous sound came from the dockside, echoing up the passage.

"What was that?" Scudi asked.

"Haven't you ever heard a rooster crow?" Bickel demanded from close behind them.

"A hylighter brought them," Twisp called ahead of them. "Chickens, they're called. They're something like a squawk."

In the world you shall have tribulation: but be of good
cheer. I have overcome the world.
                    —The Christian Book of the Dead

Vata lolled on a buoyant bed of kelp fronds, her head held high to give her a view across Duque nestled sleeping in the curve of her great left arm. The dawnlight of Little Sun cast a sharp horizontal illumination across the scene. The sea lifted and fell in gentle waves, their crests damped by the giant leaves.

When either of them hungered, minuscule cilia from the kelp wormed into a vein and nutrients flowed—kelp to Vata . . . kelp to Duque. And back from Vata flowed the genetic information stored in its purest form within her cells: Vata to Avata.

What a wonderful awakening, Vata thought.

Probing kelp tendrils had crept through the walls of her pool in the depths of Vashon, admitting a great wash of sea water that swept away the watchers and the Chaplain/Psychiatrist. The swiftly darting tendrils had encased Duque and herself, pulling them out into the sea and up to the nighttime surface. There, a swift current had hurried them away from Vashon's injured bulk.

At some distance from the Island, hylighter tendrils had plucked the two of them from the sea and brought them to this place where only the sea prevailed.

In the grasp of the hylighter tendrils, Vata had found her true awakening.

How marvelous . . . all of the stored human lives . . . the voices . . . what a wonderful thing. Strange that some of the voices objected to their preservation in the kelp. She had heard the exchange between Avata and one called Keel.

"You're editing me!" That was what Keel had said. "My voice had flaws and I could always hear them. They were part of me!"

"You live in Avata now." How all-encompassing, how calming that beautiful voice.

"You've given me an unflawed voice! Stop it!"

And true enough, when next she heard Keel's voice it had a different tone, something of hoarseness in it, throat clearings and coughs.

"You think you speak the language of my people," Keel accused. "What nonsense!"

"Avata speaks all languages."

That was telling him, Vata thought. But Duque, sharing her awareness of this internalized conversation, had grinned agreement with Keel.

"Every planet has its own language," Keel said. "It has its own secret ways of communication."

"Do you not understand Avata?"

"Oh, you have the words down well enough. And you know the language of actions. But you've not penetrated my heart or you wouldn't have tried to edit me and improve me."

"Then what would you have of Avata?"

"Keep your hands off me!"

"You do not wish to be preserved?"

"Oh, I have enough curiosity to accept that. You've showed us your Lazarus trick and I'm thankful I no longer have that old body's pains."

"Is that not an improvement, then?"

"You can't improve me! I can only improve myself. You and Ship can stuff your miracles! That's one of the real secrets of my language."

"A bit uncouth but understandable."

"That language was born on the planet where Lazarus lived and died and lived. My kind first learned to speak there! The original Lazarus knew my meaning. By all the gods, he knew!"

When Vata awakened Duque and expressed her puzzlement to him, Duque laughed. "You see?" he shouted. "We care who forces our dreams onto us!"